Daughter of Fortune— Sons of Destiny...

"Don't touch him, Maria," Cristobal shouted as Maria darted forward. "If he gets up again, I will kill him."

She stopped where she was, her eyes on Cristobal.

He did not see her. "He is like all the rest, my own brother! He will not take the word of an Indian. Not even an Indian he calls brother."

Maria stood watching him. Cristobal took her arm, his touch gentle. She raised her face to his face.

"Come with me, Maria. It will not be safe here soon. And do not ask me how I know. Just come with me. Perhaps—perhaps I can protect you." He was holding her with both hands now, his fingers warm on her arm.

Maria looked down at Diego, who was beginning to stir, then back to Cristobal. "I cannot," she said. ...

"A fascinating novel ... Readers ... will be thrilled with *DAUGHTER OF FORTUNE*."
—*Romantic Times*

CARLA KELLY
DAUGHTER OF FORTUNE

PUBLISHED BY POCKET BOOKS NEW YORK

POCKET BOOKS, a division of Simon & Schuster, Inc.
1230 Avenue of the Americas, New York, N.Y. 10020

Copyright © 1985 by Carla Kelly
Cover artwork copyright © 1986 Sharon Spiak

Published by arrangement with Donald I. Fine, Inc.
Library of Congress Catalog Card Number: 84-073448

ISBN: 0-671-60754-5

First Pocket Books printing July, 1986

10 9 8 7 6 5 4 3 2 1

POCKET and colophon are registered trademarks
of Simon & Schuster, Inc.

Printed in the U.S.A.

THIS BOOK IS DEDICATED TO THOSE WHO DIED,
AND THOSE WHO LIVED. AND AS DIEGO
MASFERRER WOULD SAY, "IS THAT NOT ALL OF US?"

Author's Note

I can make no apology for the events or the people depicted in this novel. These things happened, no matter how we in this century view the 1680 Pueblo uprising. Seen in historical perspective, these Spanish New Mexicans lived and died in the belief that what they did was right and just. If we see their actions differently, it is because we live in a more enlightened, if not less cruel, age.

—Carla Kelly
Springfield, Missouri

DAUGHTER OF FORTUNE

To Santa Fe

M aria, we pray for those who despitefully use us."

Until Father Efrain spoke, Maria hadn't realized she was crying. Hands clenched tight by her sides, she watched Carmen de Sosa's wagon lurch out of the rut. She sobbed, exhausted by the effort to push the cart. She heard the embarrassed whispers of the teamsters, but she could not stop the tears.

Like all men, eager to be away from tears they could not understand, the muleteers and freighters hurried to catch up with the wagons. Carmen de Sosa did not even look around at the sound of Maria's distress. With a kid-gloved hand, she patted her hair and pulled her silk shawl higher on her shoulders, as if to ward off such vulgar display.

Only Father Efrain remained with Maria. He was too wise to say anything, or too weary, but after a small hesitation, he rested his arm on her shoulder.

"See there, you tore your dress," he said finally, when her sobs turned to hiccups. "But as it appears to be a seam," he continued smoothly when Maria began to cry again, "you can mend it."

1

Maria wiped her nose on her sleeve and felt the rip in the fabric. It had given way when she was pushing the wagon, struggling to free it from the rut. Six months ago she would have been mortified if strangers had seen her with even an ankle showing. Now when the seam gave way, she felt only a helpless fury that such a woman as Carmen de Sosa had the power to command, and she only to follow.

"Father," she said, "do you realize that we could have pushed all day and she never would have considered getting out to lighten the load?"

Her anger was bringing tears again. "I could have fallen under the wheel and she would only have clucked her tongue!"

As Father Efrain opened his mouth to speak, she turned on him. "And don't tell me to turn the other cheek! I have turned so many times in the last six months that I am dizzy!"

He let her cry then, drawing her close to him as she sobbed. *"Pobrecita,"* he murmured, "and when was the last time you cried?"

Her voice was muffled against his habit. "When I closed Papa's eyes. When the lawyers came. When I closed Mama's. I cannot recall." She wiped her eyes on the hem of her skirt. "Oh, *mira,* Father, soon the wagons will be out of sight over that rise."

He laughed. "Maria, Maria, are you still such a city girl? *De veras,* do you think we cannot follow this wretched trail and catch up with them?"

She could not share his levity. "Oh, Father," she whispered, "I am weary with this journey."

They started after the wagons, picking their way carefully around the rocks and holes of El Camino Real—the King's Highway—that they had followed for half a year from Mexico City. They had set out in August of 1679. It was now February of 1680.

"You, Padre," Maria commanded, mimicking Carmen de Sosa in an attempt to match the priest's levity, "I cannot decide whether to beat my servant or snub Maria some more. Which should it be?"

Father Efrain did not join in her mockery. "Maria Espinosa de la Garza," he said softly, "pray for her."

Maria was silent. She hadn't the heart to tell this priest that if there was a God, He had no use for those fallen from grace,

2

as they surely must be. She shaded her eyes with her hand, looking about her for some sign of grace in this barren land they traveled through. There was none that she could see, no evidence that God had ever given New Mexico a second thought after the Creation. She didn't know why she looked anymore. God had withdrawn His grace from her as surely as He had withdrawn it from the land around. But still she searched for it, thinking such rejection scarcely fair.

Father Efrain seemed to know what she was thinking. "God loves you, my child, and He does know where we are."

They were in sight of the last wagon by then, or at least the dust of it. Unconsciously, Maria slowed her pace, sick of the sight of the lumbering freight wagons.

Father Efrain did not try to hurry her. "And soon we will be in Santa Fe, and you will be with your sister again. All will be well."

"Will it?" she asked out loud, thinking of Carmen de Sosa. "Or will my sister, like Senora de Sosa, decide that because I am poor now, I have no worth?"

But the fear went deeper than that. Maria did not belong anywhere. She thought again of Carmen de Sosa and wiped the tears from her eyes. Her own father had called Carmen's family pretentious mushrooms. Before the Espinosa fortune had fallen with a crash that was heard from the silver mines of Mexico to the Spanish Main, Maria never would have given Carmen and her family the merest nod. And now Maria had nothing but the dress she stood in, while Carmen had the power to order her to help push a wagon out of a rut.

She is just the bride of a toadying government official, thought Maria, someone my Papa would have ignored only a year ago.

But if Maria did not belong in the world of wealth and position any longer, neither did she belong with the teamsters and muleteers, rough men who could not read or write but only look down on those poorer still. Nor did she belong with Father Efrain, who walked with a light step toward a future of exhausting labor with the Indians. Religious fervor no longer burned in Maria. It had been extinguished by the shattering changes in her life.

But Father Efrain was speaking to her. "And Maria, you still have the jewels."

Yes, she had the jewels, trinkets really, mere baubles that she had rescued from the little cask by Mama's bed as her mother lay dead, killed by cholera and the shame of misfortune. Even as the creditors and clerks had scavenged the rooms below, pinging the crystal and counting forks, Maria had calmly poured the contents of the little jewel box down the front of her dress and later hidden the shining pile under her pillow.

She had parted with a brooch here and a ring there, seeing to Papa and Mama's funerals—small affairs, really. By then the town had been emptied of the wealthy who had fled the cholera. Another pin had earned her a month's lodging at the convent where she had been educated as a child. A gold button had been sufficient to send a letter on its interminable way north with a courier heading to Santa Fe, a letter much agonized over to a sister she scarcely remembered. And then a handful of silver chain links had bought her minor membership on the next mission supply caravan leaving for the colony of New Mexico. Only a little jewelry remained, but surely it would sweeten her reunion with the sister she had not seen in fourteen years, since Maria herself had been only a year in age and the sister a bride setting out on a new life.

"I am sure," said the priest, steering her around a chuckhole, "your sister will see that the jewels become a dowry for you."

She looked at the priest then, her heart opening to him. Dear Father Efrain. How sure he was that all would turn out well. He had not known how it was after Papa's ruin, when the young man who dealt with matchmakers withdrew their offers, one by one.

The priest went on looking at her with the belief that his own goodness was the goodness of others, and she could not bear to disappoint him. "Father, I am sure you are right," she lied, hating herself for deceiving a priest.

She looked closer at Father Efrain, and her smile was one of genuine affection. He had made himself her protector on the journey and she was grateful. He strode with enthusiasm among the rocks and pitfalls of the King's Highway, nimbly avoiding the cactus and animal refuse. His hair, neatly shaped into a priestly tonsure at the start of the journey, was long now and as ragged as the hem of his blue robe, his face tanned by the sun's slanting rays of fall and winter. But he still hummed to himself as he walked the path of empire, cheerful no matter what condition of disrepair the empire currently enjoyed.

He belongs here, she thought, and how strange it is, considering that he is new to this place, too. But he belongs here and I do not.

She smiled at him. "You know, Father, I have not plagued you in recent months, but tell me now, when will this journey end?"

"Soon, my child, soon."

And he was right, terribly so.

They joined the wagons when the teamsters stopped the ox-drawn carts for the nooning. Before the wagons had ceased rolling, Carmen's cook leaped down, ready to begin the preparation of beans and tortillas. While Maria and the teamsters ate their dried beef and hardtack—*carne seca* and *biscoche*—Carmen de Sosa dined on cornmeal tortillas and sipped wine from a silver cup.

The teamsters passed around their own wine, drinking from a jug handed from muletenders, drivers, and priests to Maria. By the time the jug reached her the rim was greasy, but she closed her eyes and drank. She remembered Mama's words: a lady drinks only from a cup.

After the midday meal, they proceeded into that unforgettable afternoon, Maria sitting next to the teamster in the wagon assigned to her. He was a young man, a year or two older than she. In six months' travel, she had learned only that he was the son of the caravan head, and on his first journey, too. His name was Miguel. It wasn't much information, but Maria had overcome agonies of maidenly shyness to learn even that little about him. She had never spoken to a man, other than her father and priests. Only her loneliness had compelled her to go as far as she had in awkward conversation with Miguel.

Before she drifted off into the half-sleep that filled most of her long afternoons in the wagon, the teamster handed her something.

"For you, Senorita," he said.

She took the metal object he held out to her, careful not to touch his hand, and turned it over. It was a mirror.

"Where did you find this?" she asked, amazed at the boldness of her question. Praise God that the journey was nearly over. If it went on much longer, she would not recognize herself. As it was, Mama was probably tossing in her grave over the forwardness of her youngest child.

The man showed no surprise at her address. He pointed with his whip to the oxcart ahead.

"I believe it fell out of her wagon."

It was a joke of sorts between them. The freighter appropriated items from the de Sosa wagon and squirreled them away for future use. Maria caught him at it once, and they had laughed. It was sport that would have mortified her in Mexico City, but here it was only a small way to alleviate the boredom of their oxcart journey.

Maria had never accepted anything he'd tried to give her, though she enjoyed looking over the spoils of his agile fingers, wondering if Carmen de Sosa in her plenitude ever missed anything. But this time, instead of just looking and handing it back, she tucked the mirror in her pocket.

"Are you not going to look at yourself?" Miguel asked, lazily tickling his whip around the ear of the front right oxen.

She shook her head. "Not now. After we stop. Then I'll give it back."

She wanted to be alone when she looked at her face. In the half-year's journey, she had not looked into a mirror, and she had to be by herself when she surveyed the ruin of her complexion and the state of her hair. Maria had never been vain, but she remembered how Mama used to utter little cries of delight as she brushed Maria's hair each night before bed, exclaiming over the copper-gold highlights of the thick auburn hair. It was her one glory. She had no height to recommend her, an ordinary figure, freckles sprinkled liberally over her nose, but in the soft light of evening's candleglow, her hair used to shimmer around her face like a nimbus.

Maria sighed, thinking of her mother's great silver-backed hairbrush that was probably resting now on a dressing table belonging to Papa's lawyers. Her eyes narrowed for a moment as she remembered the solicitors with their red tape and sealing wax, then she sighed again and patted the mirror in her pocket. It was going to take more than six months to become accustomed to poverty and charity from teamsters.

In late afternoon they paused at the edge of the meandering Rio del Norte. The freighter cleared his throat and pointed with his whip.

"Santa Fe," he said.

Maria shaded her eyes with her hand. She could see nothing except a series of mountains rising before them to the north and east. The mission supply caravan had been climbing steadily for weeks now, from desert to plain to gentle slope, and she had watched those mountains growing slowly closer each day. She looked at the freighter, a question in her eyes.

"It is in the foothills below the Sangre de Cristos. Tomorrow. The next day, perhaps. You will see."

Sangre de Cristo. The name frightened her. "Why are they called after the blood of Our Lord?"

"The afternoon sun will turn them red. Watch for it."

She nodded, suddenly shy again, remaining silent as the wagons circled near the riverbank. She jumped down then, not waiting for the freighter to give her a hand, touched her pocket and felt the smooth edge of the mirror.

Maria looked around, then turned away quickly. The men had gathered in a small circle by the river to relieve themselves. Carmen de Sosa sat with her back to the men. She glanced at Maria, then flicked her eyes away.

A distance away from the river there was a circle of bushes and a small stand of cottonwoods, testimony to an earlier path of the river. Maria walked toward it, rubbing the small of her back. She could relieve herself in the bushes, then rest in the shade of the trees. Maybe if she gathered the courage, she would look in the glass and determine if she still bore any resemblance to the young lady who had begun a journey on the King's Highway six months before.

The leader of the caravan had admonished her never to stray from it, but she was heartily weary of all of them—the unwashed freighters, the uncomplaining missionaries, the uncommunicative Carmen de Sosa—tired of their food, their coarse conversation, the endless journey, but most of all tired to her very soul of her worry over what awaited her in Santa Fe.

The small grove was shady and cool, a change from the gathering warmth of the late winter sun. After taking care of private matters, Maria sat down under one of the cottonwoods and leaned against the trunk, lifting her heavy woolen skirt, removing her shoes, and stretching her legs out in front of her. She took the mirror out of her pocket and gazed into it.

A stranger looked back. Maria blinked. Gone was the smooth,

7

light pink complexion she had nurtured with buttermilk and flour paste in Mexico City. She was as brown as an Indian. And dirty. So dirty. She rubbed her face, appalled at the layers of dirt. She had tried to wash regularly, but the journey of the last few weeks through the Jornada del Muerto had given her no opportunity to bathe. On the route of the Dead Man's March, there was scarcely water to drink, let alone bathe in. And even if she could have found water, there were the men, always the men.

The dirt would wash off, but her skin was so brown. Maria patted her face. It used to feel soft, but now the skin was stretched tight over high cheekbones. Her deep blue eyes held a hungry look. There was nothing even remotely appealing about her.

"Why, I look eighteen or nineteen," she said out loud, then burst into tears. In helpless misery, she threw the mirror outside the grove, rested her head on her arms and cried until she fell asleep.

Later, she could not have said what woke her, what nerve was touched to compel her into instant wakefulness. Evening had come and brought with it something strange and terrible. Then she saw the flickering lights against the blackness. Every wagon was blazing with fire. Maria dropped down behind the tree she had slept against and peered out through the underbrush. A scream started deep in her throat but never reached her lips.

Some of the freighters were already dead, the bodies piled here and there, appearing, then vanishing in the flickering light of the burning wagons. Indians swarmed around the remaining men of the wagon train, herding them close to the water's edge. Their weapons had been left at the wagons. They were helpless as the Indians hacked and tore at them. And they were silent, except for Father Efrain who prayed, his voice as calm and matter-of-fact as if he were offering morning prayers. Maria listened to him as his voice droned on and on, only changing pitch as he was pushed from Indian to Indian. He stopped suddenly before the end of his supplication and Maria pushed her fist into her mouth to keep from crying out.

When Father Efrain was silenced, Carmen de Sosa began to scream, a thin, whining cry that made Maria hunker down lower in the bushes, take her hand out of her mouth and cover her ears. But still she could hear Senora de Sosa. Maria's heart beat like a drum. Carmen was calling for her. "Maria! Maria!" she screamed over and over, seeking after six months of silence for a deadly friendship.

Maria sucked in her breath. "Father in heaven," she whispered, "please do not let the Indians understand what she is saying." If the Indians had any idea that there was another woman on that supply caravan, they would search for her until they found her.

Maria gasped aloud at the sudden sound of tearing cloth, then was silent as Carmen's screams filled the enormous night. Finally, they fell away to a moaning sob that Maria could barely hear above the laughter of the Indians. The end was near, but the end was more terrible than what had gone before. Maria watched an Indian peel Carmen de Sosa's scalp away from her skull, cutting off the ears expertly, then holding them up in the light to catch the firelight glinting on the dripping earrings.

To keep from crying out, Maria stuffed the hem of her dress in her mouth and burrowed into the ground she was lying on. Wildly her mind raced through an entire catalog of saints to pray to, but another part of her brain told her that prayer was useless. As the Indians hacked and scalped their way through the growing pile of bodies, Maria knew that the heavens were closed, that God slept on this February night.

She must have fainted then, because when she opened her eyes, it was morning. She was lying on her back looking up at the sky. The air was cool and clouds like lamb's wool scudded overhead. A bird sang in the tree nearby. She almost closed her eyes again, then, in a flood of terror that left her weak, as she remembered. She crept cautiously to her knees, then sat back quickly. The Indians were still there.

Dressed in the clothes of the dead, they squatted close together against the chill of the early dawn. One of the savages wore Father Efrain's robe, stiff with the blood of the padre. Another Indian had draped Carmen de Sosa's skirts around his shoulders. As Maria watched, he clapped Carmen's bloody blond scalp on his head and pranced around while the other men laughed.

Dead men lay everywhere, some of them hacked to pieces, their body parts flung along the riverbank. The heads stared with sightless eyes and open mouths at the same blue sky Maria had awakened to. Other freighters had been scalped but left in one piece, their bodies scattered at random. They lay in grotesque poses like overgrown dolls, tossed by a child in a rage.

Maria tried to look away from the fly-covered, bloated corpses, but she could not. With dreadful obsession, she stared at the hunks of skin and bones that only hours before had been fathers, husbands and brothers, looking forward to the completion of a tedious journey.

When she finally forced herself to avert her gaze, she looked around to get her bearings. She was lying under the trees in a small gully, the merest incline. By sitting up slightly, she could see the Indians through a skimpy cover of bush and tall grass. Anyone approaching the grove from behind would spot her immediately. She must move farther into the bushes.

Maria slowly pulled her legs up under her dress, grateful for once that her poverty had allowed only dull brown wool, instead of the brightness of Carmen de Sosa's sea-green silks that were now warming the Indian by the fire. The color of the wool blended with the dry winter grass around her. She pulled herself into a compact ball and started inching toward the bushes.

A flash of light caught her eye as she began to move. It was the mirror. With a sudden stab at her insides, she remembered how she had tossed the mirror outside the circle of trees. As it glittered at her in the morning light, she knew that sooner or later one of the Indians would notice the gleam and come closer to investigate. She would be discovered.

She had to get the mirror. Slowly she turned and crawled to the edge of the bushes. The Indians were not looking in her direction, but if she leaned out far enough to snatch the mirror, they would notice.

For the first time, she cried, laying her face down in the dirt until the soil under her cheek turned to mud. She dug her fingers into the ground, running the loose dirt through her fingers. Then it came to her. By tossing the dirt beyond the bushes, a pinch at a time, she could cover the mirror until its betraying reflection was buried.

The first handful only camouflaged the tiniest corner of the mirror. Cursing her vanity of yesterday, Maria grabbed another fistful of dirt. She scraped the dirt off the surface of the ground, fearing that the darker earth underneath would attract attention.

When she had a dry handful, she tossed it gently toward the mirror.

For an hour Maria threw dirt on the small mirror. Whenever one of the Indians glanced her way, she would freeze, her face in the earth, her arm outstretched and still. As she lay there she imagined footsteps behind her and waited silently, almost gratefully, for the arrow biting deep into her back, the hands on her waist, the knife on her hair.

By the time the sun was high over the rim of the Sangre de Cristo Mountains, the mirror's sparkling eye was covered. Maria's arm ached from the slow and steady motion of hundreds of tiny particles of dirt thrown. Her muscles throbbed with a life of their own as she lay in the shade of the bushes and rubbed her arm, watching the Indians.

They showed no disposition to leave their kingdom of burned wagons, dead animals and men. They crouched by their fire silent and watchful.

Her eyes never leaving them, Maria slowly pulled her legs up under her dress and inched toward the tall underbrush. She eased her way among the sheltering foliage and curled up in a tight ball. The chill of the late February morning penetrated her body and she shook until she feared her teeth would rattle and reveal her hiding place. Or was it simply the chill of fear? Yesterday on the wagon she had not been cold.

Her mind was curiously devoid of any thought at all. For the first time in her life, there was nothing. All she could do was huddle in the grass, her teeth chattering, and watch the Indians less than 100 yards away. Her mind took in every detail of their dress and attitude, but it did nothing with the information. So intent was she on survival that every breath she drew, every blink of her eyes, was concentrated on the effort of getting through the day. For the moment she had no energy to waste on memory or speculation, pain or sorrow. For Maria Espinosa de la Garza, lying by the clump of trees, there was nothing but those Indians. She would have thought of other things if she could have—her parents, the silver necklace her father had given her on her fourteenth birthday, the Rosary, the Stations of the Cross—but she could not think beyond the enormity of the Indians before her. Her mind refused to go forward or backward. And so she sat there watching them until her eyes closed and her head fell forward on her chest.

She was yanked out of sleep by the sound of a horse grazing. It was the horse of one of the caravan guards, cropping grass only inches from her legs. The animal showed no alarm at her presence. She had petted, fed and cried against him at odd moments on the six-month journey. Often she had given him small scraps of her food when she couldn't stomach the taste of one more lump of hardtack. And here he was now, nuzzling her leg as she tried to draw deeper into her miserable refuge. The animal snorted when she moved, so she stayed where she was, more alert than she had ever been in her life.

If only he would move off. She forced herself to lie where she was, sweating despite the chill that still lingered in the air. Perspiration rolled down her face and made her nose itch, but she did not dare raise a hand to scratch.

And then what she feared most happened. One of the Indians by the dying fire looked up and called to the horse, which continued to graze, practically nibbling her leg. When the animal did not move, the Indian rose and started toward the grove.

Maria stared at him, in terrified fascination. His hair was long and black, his legs bowed, his eyes half-closed in the perpetual squint of one who has spent a lifetime resisting the sun's glare on the desert he roamed. His high moccasins came up to his long loincloth, which hung to his knees and was dark brown with the blood of his slaughter. He did not look like the Pueblo Indians whose adobe villages the supply caravan had passed through in recent weeks.

And still he came closer. Maria could only stare at him, mouthing the words, "Saint Francis, Saint Francis," over and over. Her lifetime of familiarity with the saints had evaporated and she could remember only the name of the saint of Santa Fe. She had no way of knowing if he enjoyed any power over Indians, but she said his name and made it her prayer.

She wanted to run, but she knew that her only hope, growing slimmer with each footstep, was to lie still. She tasted blood on her mouth, saw it drip onto the front of her dress, and realized that she was gnawing on her lip. Her hands were cold and wet, her feet numb. She no longer had the power to move.

When he was less than ten yards from the grove, the Indian squatted suddenly and scooped up a handful of small rocks. He stood and lazily pitched stones at the animal. The horse shied, but would not stop eating. The Indian said something to himself and walked closer. He threw another rock that hit Maria squarely in the middle of her forehead. She let out a gasp. The animal's ears pricked up, but then his head dropped again to the tall grass he was cropping. The Indian gave no sign of hearing.

The blood trickled down Maria's forehead. She watched it drop onto her dress. She had to do something to stop the Indian from coming closer. When she saw the man draw his arm back to throw another stone, she kicked the horse in the nose.

The animal's head jerked up and he snorted and backed away, shaking his mane. The Indian, apparently satisfied that his stone had done its work, stood there until the horse ambled back to the other horses grazing by the river. Then he turned back to his fellows. They were rising and stretching. While one of them kicked the embers apart and brushed dirt over the coals, the rest walked toward the caravan horses.

As Maria watched, she realized there were no native ponies. The Indians must have made a surprise attack on foot. They possessed no horses of their own—until now.

With the greatest leisure and two fights among themselves, the Indians loaded the horses with their booty. The Indian wearing Father Efrain's habit passed a cord between his legs and tied up the long fabric so he could mount. When the last of the horses was bridled, the Indians mounted and rode off slowly, laden with spoils, leaving behind destruction. The ground, littered with great mounds of rotting human and animal flesh, was white with flour from ripped bags. Above the smell of smoke and death, Maria sniffed the sharp fragrance of cinnamon and cloves. The Indians vanished as suddenly as they had come, into the vastness of the empty land to the west of the river.

Maria raised her hand and felt her forehead. The cut from the rock was not deep. She packed a pinch of dirt in the wound and the bleeding stopped.

She would not leave the shelter of the tall grass and trees, though she could see no sign of the Indians. What if one of them rode back for another look? What if all of them rode back? She would wait where she was.

The sky filled with the flap and squawk of countless buzzards. The black birds circled and swooped, coasting along on the wind currents above the desert floor, then dropping like

13

stones onto the carcasses cooking in the midday sun. Awkward on land, they waddled among the bodies of oxen and men, fighting with each other over the most tempting morsels, reminding Maria of old women in Mexico City's great bazaars, squabbling over ribbons and lace. Here it was not ribbons but intestines, deep purple now and puffy with death, and not lace but lung tissue, filigreed and black from exposure.

All day the buzzards flocked to the massacre until the whole ground around the burned wagons was a moving mass of black feathers. The earlier arrivals attempted to fly off but they were so gorged with the flesh of dead men that they could not rise in the air. They lurched along the ground, croaking and flapping their useless wings.

As the hours dragged by in her sheltering grove, Maria's thirst grew. The last moisture that had passed her lips was the wine in the goatskin bag that Miguel the freighter had offered her yesterday afternoon. She wanted to run down to the river, fling herself into the water, and drink the Rio del Norte dry, but still she feared to move. She spent the long, dreadful afternoon leaning against a tree watching the buzzards, her mind neither moving forward nor back. She had nowhere to go and her thoughts took no flight.

Finally after the sun reflected its blood red rays on the flanks of the distant Sangre de Cristos and sank below the western horizon, she slept. The air was colder than the night before. Her teeth chattered and she hugged her knees to herself, burrowing farther down in the slight sheltering ridge of the bank of dirt. The earth was still warm from the afternoon sun and she pressed her cheek against it and closed her eyes.

She dreamed then, restless dreams filled with groans and shrieks and deadly silences. Carmen de Sosa crawled on her hands and knees among the weeds and grass, calling "Maria! Maria!" over and over in a thin, whining whisper and patting the ground before her, searching for her scalp. And there was Father Efrain, smiling at her, then taking off his head and tossing it in her lap.

Maria sat up and screamed. The buzzards roosting in trees and on the flat ground rose in a turgid cloud, then slowly settled back, quarreling among themselves.

Maria sobbed. She forced herself to look down in her lap, but there was no grinning head. She drew her legs up tight against her body and leaned against the ridge, pressing herself close to the earth, which by now was cold.

She slept again for several hours, and Carmen de Sosa reappeared, patting the ground with bloody fingers and whispering Maria's name. She came closer and closer, searching for her hair. She patted Maria's leg.

Maria leaped up, screaming. She stepped backward and fell over the ridge of earth. All around her were buzzards. The ones which could not fly had crept into her grove, seeking warmth from the night's chill. They had been crowding close to her as she slept, their feathers tickling her legs.

The smell of them made Maria gag. They stank of death and putrefaction, nameless diseases and all the horrors of the centuries. They were legion and she could not escape them.

Maria stood on the flood plain by the Rio del Norte, unutterably alone and surrounded by death in unimaginable forms. She stood there clenching her fists against her breasts, crying. She took a few steps toward the river and the buzzards waddled out of her way, muttering as they scuttled off, still too gorged to fly.

She took another tentative step, then drew back quickly. She had trod on someone's hand, the fingers curling around her bare foot as though still alive. She shrieked and raced to the river, scattering buzzards as she pounded toward the water that glimmered in the starlight. All the ghosts of the dead men pursued her. She screamed "Saint Francis!" and leaped into the water.

The shock of the freezing river woke her completely. She sank to the sandy bottom up to her knees. The water was frigid and fast-moving, but it was clean. She took her hands away from her face and spread them over the surface of the water in a benediction of her own. She leaned forward and drank.

She drank until her stomach gurgled, then she washed her face, scrubbing at the dirt and dried blood. With numb legs she forced herself to leave the water and struggle up the riverbank.

There were no buzzards at the water's edge, but no sheltering protection of the trees either. Instinct told her to go back to the trees and tall grass, but she knew nothing could ever force her to enter that grove again. If the Indians returned, then they would find her.

Maria slid back down the riverbank and crouched by the water again. The bank offered some shelter and she leaned back and stared at the stars. Sleep was far from her, but even if her eyes did grow heavy, she would keep them open. The terror of her dreams was too real to chance again in this lonely spot.

She willed the sun to come up and hours later it did, slowly topping the hulk of the mountains. She reminded herself that somewhere over there in the shelter of the Sangre de Cristos, her sister and other citizens were now rising, lighting kitchen fires, preparing for morning prayers.

How far away were they? Could she walk there? Would people begin to suspect the supply caravan was overdue? Or did this community function like all the other small villages in King Carlos' domain that they had plodded through on their tedious journey, the villagers moving slowly through the pace of ordinary days and nights, not suspecting that caravans ever came in any fashion except late.

Diego

*S*he must have slept then, *hugging* the side of the riverbank, shivering in the cold that rose off the water.
The sound of a fish leaping woke her hours later and she sat
up with a start, nearly sliding into the river. She dug her feet
into the sandy soil and crouched, watching the water. Another
fish jumped and fell back with cascading sparkles that reminded
Maria of jewels.

Jewels. In her fright, she had not thought once about her
little wooden cask hidden in the bottom of the oxcart underneath
her clothing.

Maria stood slowly and climbed the riverbank. Her dress
clung to her in wet, muddy folds and the glorious hair that
Mama had so prized was stringy on her back. She had left her
shoes behind in that tainted grove, but she was not going back
for them.

The buzzards still roosted in the floodplain, huddled together
like the Indians of yesterday, waiting for the sun to warm them.
The trees of the grove were so full of the scavengers that the
branches bent close to the ground.

She looked around her. The bodies which might have been

recognizable yesterday had been picked over by the buzzards. They bore no resemblance to human beings anymore, but were only so much rotting meat now, bloated and stinking.

Maria retched, spitting up water and bile. She wiped her mouth with the back of her hand and then covered her nose and breathed through her mouth. She approached the burned wagons slowly, watching where she stepped, determined this time not to tread on anything that might once have been human.

Most of the wagons had been destroyed by flames. She approached the few that remained. There was the smallest chance that the jewelry had gone undetected, she told herself, scrupulously keeping her mind on the wagons and not on the death around her.

She walked carefully among the wagons and came upon her own. Young Miguel was slumped forward over the wagon box. An arrow driven completely through his back had pinned him to the wood beneath. He had been scalped and his head picked clean by the buzzards.

As Maria stepped over the body to get into the wagon, her foot accidentally struck the corpse. Evil-smelling gas wheezed out of the arrow wound and a cloud of flies rose and then settled again. Maria leaned over the edge of the cart and retched until she felt that her stomach would turn inside out.

She trembled as she knelt in the wagon. The fire had gone out before it consumed everything. She found her bundle of clothing, ripped and shredded by knives. She burrowed deeper in the pile. Nothing. The cask was gone.

Maria sagged against the wagon bed, blinking back tears. She had been foolish beyond all reason to hope that the Indian raiders would not find her prize. That pitiful handful of baubles represented her only chance, her entire future. They were gone now, and she was left with the muddy dress she sat in.

She remained in the wagon until the stench of death forced her out, then she clambered over the side of the high cart and shinnied down the partially burned wheel, unwilling to pass Miguel again.

She was thirsty again, hungry and dirty—but not alone. When the sun was higher in the sky, the buzzards drove her out from among the wagons. They flew back to yesterday's banquet and continued feasting where they had left off, ripping and tearing at the corpses. Maria ran back to the river. By now, the smell was no better there, but at least she would not have to watch the scavengers, or hear the dreadful noises they made as they fought over the scraps remaining.

Her stomach rumbled and ached. Earlier Maria had told herself that she could never eat again, not after witnessing the buzzards, but here she was now, holding her middle and rocking back and forth. The jerked meat and hardtack that she had only tolerated for six months would have tasted like the best food her mother had ever prepared.

She unbuttoned her dress and took it off, shimmying out of her petticoat and chemise. Perhaps she could wash her clothing and rid it of the smell of death. It could dry on the bank of the river. Then, in clean clothes, she could start walking toward the Sangre de Cristos. She had no idea what waited for her beyond the circle of death, but it could not be any worse.

Teeth chattering, her skin dimpled with cold, she scrubbed with river sand until her fingers ached. Then she spread the garments out on the bank and sat down to wait.

The cold defeated her. When she couldn't stand another minute of the breeze on her body, she pulled on her chemise. Damp as it was, the skimpy covering reached to her knees and afforded some protection. She waited another hour, then tied on her petticoat. She was walking toward her dress when she heard the horses.

At first she wasn't sure. She stood still and listened, her fists clutching her petticoat in tight bunches. She still couldn't be sure, so she crawled up the side of the bank and looked. The buzzards were beginning to move around restlessly. Some flew off, and those that could not fly flapped and waddled back and forth, squawking.

Then she saw them, a small group of horses and riders coming from the north and west where the Indians had disappeared.

Maria whirled around, looking for shelter. She knew she had to make a run for the grove again, but she hesitated at the horror. By the time her instincts cancelled out her fear, the horsemen were crossing the river. Without stopping to see if they were Indians, she hiked up her petticoat, turned and ran east.

Her bare feet flew over the ground and for one crazy moment she remembered Mama's tales of the giants in seven-league boots who could cover ground in enormous strides. She became that giant, her legs moving in swift motion across the plain. But the real giants were behind her and pounding closer. "Saint Francis," she gasped, "Saint Francis!" Spittle dribbled down her chin as she stumbled over rocks and thorns. She ran and ran, her breath coming in noisy croaks.

She heard someone shouting to her but kept running, not daring to look back. Perhaps death would not hurt as much if she did not see it coming. She soon heard only one horse following her. The others must have dropped back, content in their curious Indian way to let one go alone. She thought of Carmen de Sosa and the ripping cloth and whimpered in terror.

The horse pounded closer behind her. Again she heard a man yelling at her, but what he said did not sound like the language the Indians had spoken.

As the horse closed the gap between them, she shrieked and changed courses, darting like a rabbit, now toward the river, now toward the plain. Her feet were bloody from gashes, but she refused to stop running. She could not. The rider would have to kill her first.

The horse was almost breathing in her ear when a hand reached down and grabbed the back of her chemise, jerking her off the ground. She cried and struck out with her hands, struggling to get away. Her eyes closed, she fought and scratched until the man flopped her over his legs and clamped his hand on her windpipe. She choked and gagged and finally lay still, draped over his lap like a sack of meal.

"By all the saints, *chiquita*—young one—will you be still?" The rider's voice was soft and low, but she could hear him clearly above the pounding of his horse, which was only beginning to slow down after its race across the plain.

The man loosened his grip on her throat, and Maria lay across his lap coughing, her eyes shut tight. She opened them slowly. All she could see was his leg, booted and leather-covered.

The man reined in his horse, his hand resting on her back. "Here, let me help you," he said, pulling Maria into a sitting position in front of him. "Why did you not stop running when I called to you?" he asked in the same quiet voice.

Maria could only shake her head, not trusting to words. If

he did not know already, she could not tell him. He didn't sound like a man who knew anything of fear.

When she said nothing, the rider gathered up the reins around her. *"Pues, no le aflige,"* he said in her ear. "Never mind."

They rode slowly back to the other men who were grouped together on horseback a distance away from the wreckage of bodies and wagons. Exhausted from her race, Maria wanted to lean back against the horseman but would not. She still had not seen his face, but he did not sound like an old man. She could almost hear her mother's voice: "Daughter, there has been no introduction."

They joined the little troop between the river and the grove of trees. The men, some of them soldiers, dismounted and came close. The rider tossed the reins over his horse's head and dismounted. He held up his arms for Maria and lifted her down.

He was a short man, not much taller than she. His hair was curly and black and stuck out from under the red silk scarf he wore stretched tight over his head under his flat black hat. His face was deeply tanned, his eyes like pools of chocolate. His beard, cut close to his skin, could not hide the tiny weather wrinkles around his eyes and lips. He was a young man, perhaps twenty, but the country had already made him old.

She looked around her, relieved, yet disquieted to see the living again. All the men had the same young-old look. She shivered in spite of the afternoon's heat. This was a hard country. She could see it in the faces around her and confirm it in her soul. The nightmare of the past day had made her old, too.

Once begun, she could not stop shivering. Her rescuer took off his short cloak, leather like everything else he wore except his shirt, and swung it around her shoulders. She continued to shiver, the cold coming from deep within her.

"I have . . ." she began, then stopped in confusion. She had not spoken in more than a day, and her voice was strange to her ears. "I have a dress . . . down by the river."

The man tied the cords of his cloak around her neck and gestured with his head toward the river. One of the soldiers walked to the water, making a detour around the wagons.

"What is your name?"

"I am called . . ." She hesitated again, and panic pushed the cold deeper into her bones. *Dios, Dios,* who was she? Was she a person anymore, or did she wander now in some curious fashion between the quick and the dead, who lay in a thousand pieces around them.

The man shook her by the shoulders. The movement snapped her head up. She looked at him, staring into his eyes, and he gazed back.

"I am Maria Luisa Espinosa de la Garza," she said clearly, wondering why she wasn't paralyzed with the embarrassment of staring at a man, a stranger. "I have come north to live with my sister, Margarita Espinosa de Guzman."

The horseman dropped his gaze, and the other men exchanged glances with each other.

"Is that how it is? Well, I am Diego Masferrer, a landowner from north of the *villa* of Santa Fe."

The soldier returned from the river with her dress. She took it from him, suddenly aware of the glances of the other men as she stood there in her chemise and petticoat.

"Perhaps you would go over to that grove of trees to put on your dress?" Diego took her by the elbow.

"No!" she shouted at him, shaking off his hand. He stepped back in surprise. "No," he said again, this time her voice low and pleading. "Don't make me go in there again."

Maria clutched her dress to her and started to cry, deep sobs that shook her whole body. Shaking her head, she picked her way through the ruined bodies to the only other shelter on the plain. Standing behind one of the charred wagons, she let the cloak fall to the ground and pulled her dress over her head.

She tried to fasten the wooden buttons, but her fingers shook. Her arms dropped to her sides and she stood there in the shelter of the oxcart, her head bowed, tears falling.

"You will be well."

It was Diego Masferrer. He had followed her to the wagon. He stood in front of her and buttoned her dress. He smiled at her.

"I have sisters," he said, "plenty of them."

When her dress was fastened, he took out his handkerchief and made her blow her nose. "That's better," he said. "Now come away from here. Anywhere you say."

She walked to the river and sat down on the bank. The rest of the riders joined them there and sat watching her.

"Can you tell us what happened?"

Could she tell them what happened? Maria was silent, look-ing at Diego. He sat close to her and she wanted to reach out and touch his face. After living with phantoms for two days, she was deeply conscious of the life around her.

"First," she said, clearing her throat, "do you have any food?"

Several of the men got up and went through their saddles, bringing back hardtack and jerky—*biscoche* and *carne seca*. Maria smiled as she took the food from them. Was there nothing in this difficult land but hardtack and jerked meat?

Between bites, she told the little party of men what had happened, as far as she knew. Once during the recounting she started to breathe rapidly, her voice sounding high and tight to her ears. Diego took her hands and held them in his own until her breathing returned to normal. When she finished, several of the men crossed themselves. They were silent then, all of them, turned inward to their own thoughts.

"These things are always with us," Diego said at last, then shook his head. "I do not mean that to sound hard. Still," he paused, looking across the river to the west, "they have never struck so hard before."

"Who?"

"Apache," he answered, spitting out the word like a foul taste. "They are our scourge, our special plague. We have good reason to fear them."

The other men nodded, speaking among themselves in low tones. Although she could not hear their words, she could tell from the seriousness of their expressions that each man had witnessed the handiwork of the Apache before.

"You were the lucky one. *La Afortunada,*" commented Diego Masferrer. "From now on, that's what we shall call you. Daugh-ter of Fortune."

She smiled faintly at him, then shivered involuntarily. He got to his feet. "Stay where you are, chiquita," he said. "We have work to do."

Silently the men followed Diego toward the wagons. He stopped suddenly and turned to Maria again, his hands on his hips.

"Tell me. Were the Indians on horseback?"

She considered. "Not at first. When they left, they were riding the caravan's horses and mules."

The men exchanged glances. "Now it has come to that," one of the soldiers said, clapping his hands together in a frustrated gesture that made Maria jump. "They will never attack on foot again."

The men went to the wagons. Maria sat with her back to them so she could not see. But she heard them dragging what remained of the bodies together into a heap. The stench was dreadful, and she closed her eyes and covered her ears as the men gagged and retched. As afternoon yielded to early evening, she grew chilled sitting by the water, but she refused to move until the work behind her was done. She could not bear to gaze on all that death again.

She listened as the men ripped the boards off the unburned wagons and soon she heard the crackle of fire. The sound startled her and she leaped up. For one terrible moment she was back in the grove, hearing the caravan fire for the first time, waking to a nightmare of torture and death. Then she remembered where she was and stood in silence, her head bowed. She could think of no words or prayers to offer for the wretched ones. Their troubles were over. Hers had only begun.

"It is done now."

Diego was speaking to her. She turned to him, then glanced quickly away. His face was lined and drawn, even as she knew hers was. He walked past her to the river where he squatted to wash his hands and face. He was joined by the other men who also sought to remove from hands and clothing stains that could only dissolve slowly, if at all, through the years.

I can tell you it will not wash off, thought Maria.

She was seized then by a fierce desire to be away from that place of carnage and death. She could not sleep there again and risk a visit from Father Efrain or Carmen de Sosa, crawling around in search of her scalp.

Already the sky was dark. She looked toward the grove for a glimpse of those two specters peering at her through the tall grass, waiting for her to sleep so they could claim her again. She sobbed, covering her face with her hands in mortification. Her fingers were ice cold, as though death were already on them. "If you please, Senor, can we not leave this place? Now?"

Diego spoke to her out of the shadows. "We are going. After lighting such a fire, we dare not stay. Come."

They walked to the horses, Maria hurrying ahead in her

anxiety to be away from the bloody ground and the nightmares biding their time in the grove. The horses were restless, milling around with nervous whinnies, tossing their manes, stepping here and there in impatience.

Maria saw the looks the men exchanged with each other. Several of them checked their heavy firing pieces before swinging into the saddle. Diego loosened the strap holding his sword.

"We may have work this night," he murmured to no one in particular. He looked at her frightened face. "And yet, they might not attack. But they are here."

She nodded. She too could sense the presence of the Indians. The Apaches were never far away. She watched Diego as he mounted his horse. And he had called her *La Afortunada*, the Lucky One. How strange.

The others mounted. Diego held out his arms, and Maria put her foot in his stirrup. He pulled her up into the saddle with him. "Hang on," he directed. She grasped the high saddle horn.

They left the blazing funeral pyre at a gallop, traveling two abreast and moving fast over the darkened land. The moon was only a slice in the sky, and Maria could not see the path they followed, but she did not question the abilities of the men she rode with. They knew where they were headed. They knew this road as they knew their own wives and children.

After nearly a league of rapid, silent travel, the pace slowed to a walk. Maria dozed in the saddle, trying not to lean back. She struggled to stay awake. She had never been this close to a man before, not even her father. When she felt herself falling against him, she pulled herself awake. Once when she relaxed against Diego Masferrer, she yanked her head up, cracking him under the chin. Without a word, he transferred the reins to his left hand and with the other, firmly pushed her against his chest. Her eyes closed and she slept.

In her dream, Carmen de Sosa ran alongside Diego's horse, tugging at Maria's dress with her bloody hands. Maria whimpered. *"Por Dios,* they follow me," she whispered, pulling her legs up out of Carmen's dripping grasp. She cried out and tried to scramble from the saddle, but Diego held her down, his arms clamped firmly around her body.

Diego was silent, as if trying to understand what she feared. "Maria," he said finally, "go back to sleep. I shall keep them away." She shut her eyes. "Sleep, sleep," he said over and over, until sleep overtook her and closed out the soothing sound of his voice.

They halted for the night several hours later in the shelter of an abandoned building. The adobe had crumbled away from the tops of the walls, and the roof was missing, but it was shelter of sorts, protection.

The men quartered their horses inside the small enclosure, leaving the saddles on and lying down beside their animals, the reins wrapped around one wrist. Diego helped Maria into the most protected corner of the ruin and lay down without a word. He was asleep at once. After looking around at the other men, Maria sank to the ground and closed her eyes, knowing that she could never sleep in such a circumstance.

She woke with the sunrise, and discovered to her acute embarrassment that at some point during the night she had curled up against Diego Masferrer. He had covered them both with his cloak and his arm was thrown over her waist, drawing her up tight against his body. She feared to move and wake him so she lay still, looking at his hand close to her face. His fingers were slender but strong-looking, and he wore a heavy gold ring on his index finger. The reins of his horse were still wrapped around his wrist. Maria closed her eyes again and sighed.

The movement of her ribcage woke her protector. He untangled the rein and sat up, rubbing the back of his neck.

"*Válgame*, it is late," he said under his breath. "We are old women."

Maria sat up. All the men were asleep except the guard, who was seated in the empty window, looking out at the morning. Diego waved to him and then went from man to man, shaking them awake. Maria got to her knees. Her whole body ached from sleeping on the gravel and bits of adobe littering the ground, but she was warm. The attitude of the guard at the window told her they had nothing to fear at the moment. She sat back cross-legged on the ground and leaned against the wall, feeling a contentment wholly out of proportion to her circumstances, feeling safety in the presence of these hard men from Santa Fe.

But I will have to say goodbye to him—to them—in Santa Fe, she reminded herself silently. I owe them so much.

Maria performed her ablutions in a puddle of standing water behind the adobe building, wondering as she splashed muddy water on her face if she would ever be really clean again. She thought of the tin hip bath that used to hang in her dressing room in Mexico City. Surely her sister Dona Margarita had a bathtub, perhaps even some clothing besides the everlasting brown serge—*jerga*—she had been wearing for six months.

She dried her face on the hem of her dress and joined the men for more hardtack and jerky. One of the soldiers gave her a handful of dried apple. The linty bits of fruit tasted better than anything she had eaten in months. She smiled at the soldier, who blushed and turned away, a grin on his face.

Diego lifted Maria onto his horse and then mounted behind her again. It was still a tight fit, but after sleeping next to him in the adobe shelter, Maria did not feel the constraints of yesterday. What was it her mother used to say? "Necessity is the sop that helps the food down," she said out loud, as if reciting from a primer.

"Qué es, chiquita?" Diego asked.

She repeated the proverb and Diego laughed. "Yes, Maria chiquita, and let me tell you another *dicho*—'One must cut the cloak to fit the cloth.' This is our motto, as you will discover." He felt rather than heard her sigh. "As perhaps you have already discovered."

She said nothing more, closing her eyes against the brightness of the morning sun. She did not even have cloth to cut, only the dress she sat in and the shoes one of the men had retrieved from the grove of trees. Her only hope was that at the end of this dreadful journey her sister was waiting. Her sister and her sister's husband who would become her protector.

She sat up straighter, narrowly missing Diego's chin again. "What do you know of Dona Margarita Espinosa de Guzman?" she asked.

He was silent for a moment, and when he finally spoke it seemed to Maria that he chose his words with particular care. "You do not remember her?"

"Not well. I was so young when she married and moved here." She laughed softly to herself, and Diego leaned toward her, his hat brushing her hair.

"Qué es, chiquita?" he asked.

"During Margarita's wedding I threw up all over the chapel, and she boxed my ears after the ceremony."

He laughed. "You cannot be her favorite sister!"

"Al contrario, Senor," she said, "I am her only sister, she my only living relative. Why else would I have come to this sinkhole?" She paused, embarrassed. "Senor, I did not mean to insult your colony."

Diego nudged her with his shoulder. "A sinkhole it may be to you, Maria. However, some of us like it. But tell me of your sister."

"You probably know her better than I do. She was almost nineteen when she married Felix de Guzman, and glad enough to find a man, I think."

She felt him chuckle, his good humor restored. "Chiquita, there are those who would say that Felix de Guzman was a poor substitute for a man."

Again doubts assailed her. "And pray, Senor, what do you know of him?"

"He was a *cabrón*," he said quickly without thinking.

Maria gasped.

"Forgive me, Maria, that was a dreadful thing to say." He thought for a moment. "But I do not know how I can improve on it."

Her doubts growing, Maria pushed the insult aside. "You say 'was,' Senor."

"Your sister is fortunately a widow, praise be to God," he said, no apology in his voice.

"What are you saying?"

"Did you not know? Ah, of course you did not know. Don Felix was killed three months ago."

The familiar chill was settling in her bones again. Even Diego's warmth could not take it away. "How did it happen?"

"His own Indians slit his throat from ear to ear. The general feeling in Santa Fe is that he richly deserved to suffer more than he did."

"How can you say that, Senor?" she burst out.

"Don Felix was a wretched man who beat his wife and daughters and abused his Indians. He was also the town moneylender. I think all of us owed him money." He sighed. "Still owe it. The wonder of it is that he did not die sooner, but indeed, the Lord's ways are mysterious."

28

"Why were you all in such debt to him?"

"Times have been rough here, chiquita. The drought has burdened us for four years." His tone hardened. "And do not imagine that de Guzman's death cancelled our debts. La Viuda Guzman, your sister, sees to it that we are reminded quarterly."

Maria could not think of anything to say, but Diego's good humor took over. "But never fear, Maria. Two years ago, even before Felix went to his reward, Margarita told me how I could wipe out my debt."

The lightness of his tone should have warned her. "And how was that, Senor?" she asked.

"I had only to wed and bed her eldest daughter, your cousin Isabella." He laughed out loud and spurred his horse forward. "I chose not to take her advice."

She could not help but laugh. "And this would be so dreadful?"

He leaned forward, his brown eyes twinkling into her blue ones. "La Dona Isabella de Guzman has buck teeth and one eye that wanders. I cannot believe you are related to her."

She was again acutely aware of her dishevelment and Diego's nearness. She brushed at the dried mud on her arm and tried to straighten her skirts. Diego's arms tightened around her as he slowed his horse to a walk again.

"I truly did not mean to embarrass you, Maria," he said, "and do not fret over your appearance. My Erlinda would say that miracles are performed in bathtubs!"

She laughed because she knew he was trying to cheer her, but then she was silent. Margarita was a widow. For the next few miles she mulled over this new misfortune and concluded finally that her sister would be more delighted than ever to see her. She would turn to a relative for consolation. Surely it could be no other way.

The horsemen rode steadily toward the Sangre de Cristo Mountains. As they passed a hacienda, two of the riders waved to Diego and turned off. Maria watched them until they disappeared within the brown adobe walls of the estancia.

"What do they grow here?" she asked, looking at the barren landscape.

"Cattle. Sheep. Children. We are not precisely covered with the wealth of the conquistadors here, chiquita."

They did not pause for the nooning, but ate their hardtack

and jerky in the saddle, riding on into the afternoon. Maria would have welcomed the opportunity to climb down from Diego's saddle and walk around, but the men were intent on reaching Santa Fe with word of the Apache massacre.

She leaned forward and shaded her eyes with her hand. She could see nothing that resembled civilization. No majestic cathedral, seat of a bishop. No *zócalo*, its impressive space covered with the shops and stalls of merchants and Indios engaged in the big and little commerce of Mexico. No elegant homes fronting the streets with stark walls, opening into cool interiors. No floating gardens as she remembered from Lake Texcoco. There was nothing familiar, nothing of home here.

The horses and riders continued their gradual climb over an empty land, dotted here and there with distant *estancias* that she did not see until Diego tapped her shoulder and pointed to them. The ground was dry and barren, but the air was cooler and the land covered with piñon pines and scraggly juniper. Maria sniffed the air. How sharp and pleasant was the smell of the trees, how unlike the recent odors of death.

The steady climb continued, and then after hours of seeking, she saw fields of corn and beans, newly planted and tended by Indians, who looked up when the horsemen rode by, then turned back, silent, to their stooping work. Maria noticed the veins of irrigation ditches outlining each field. Then in the distance she saw a church's stubby spire made of wood, then another. She pointed toward the nearer church.

"You have found San Miguel," Diego replied. "In the middle of Analco. It is the Indian parish, the church of the Indians brought originally from Mexico by our grandfathers." He pointed toward the other spire. "And that is San Francisco, named after our worthy patron saint. Our town is named *la villa real de la Santa Fe de San Francisco*. A lot of name for something so small, eh, chiquita?"

She did not answer. They rode slowly through Analco, a collection of mud huts on narrow streets surrounding the church of San Miguel. Maria craned her neck for a glimpse of something better.

There was nothing better. The closer they rode to Santa Fe, the lower her heart sank. Santa Fe, *la villa real de la Santa Fe de San Francisco*, was a jumble of adobe houses, all the color of the red earth around them. The streets were narrow and dirty, the penetrating smell of piñon wood smoke everywhere. It was so small.

Diego sensed her disappointment. "And what did you expect?" he asked.

"I . . . I . . . don't know, really," she faltered. "Something more."

"I have never seen your Mexico City," he said. "We are an outpost, nothing more. A fort on the frontier. All the grandness here is in the name. I suppose we have little to recommend us." He paused and chuckled. "Could you not have found relatives somewhere else?"

The riders slowed their horses to a walk as they passed the church of San Francisco and entered a plaza straggly with weeds and empty of people.

"It is the dinner hour."

Dinner. People sitting down at tables. Napkins. Tablecloths. Food in plates and bowls, food that did not have to be broken in small chunks and soaked to softness. Conversation. "It has been so long," Maria murmured. Her eyes filled with unexpected tears. How long had it been since she had sat down to a meal with family and friends?

Diego shifted in his saddle as he said his farewells to the accompanying riders. "We will have to rouse the governor from his table, Maria chiquita," he said as he dismounted. "Let us enter the courtyard of the palace."

A palace? Maria scrubbed the tears from her eyes and looked around. Surely there could be no palace in this place. With an ache of homesickness, she remembered the tall buildings of Mexico City, and the mighty Aztec temples, most of them torn down, others jungle-claimed. Mexico City was a town of plazas that welcomed with trees and cooling fountains.

Diego laughed at the bewildered expression on her face and pointed to the north. "Our palace," he said.

Maria stared at the long, low building with stunted towers on either end. The *zaguan*—vestibule—was open, brass cannons pointing out on both sides of the massive gates. She shook her head and Diego laughed again.

"What is that? You are not impressed?"

But Diego was wrong. She was impressed, not by the beauty of this building but by its solidity. There was none of the grace of height and form she remembered from the city of her birth.

The walls here were thick and squat and solely functional, but they had been whitewashed with gypsum—*yeso*—and the particles sparkled in the afternoon sun. This primitive frontier outpost had been built to last and she was impressed in spite of herself.

As Diego led his horse through the gates of the palace, his long spurs clunked on the hard-packed earth, sending up clouds of dirt. Maria looked at him and smiled. He was covered with the white dust of the trail, even as she was.

When Diego lifted Maria down, she looked around her. The courtyard of the governor's palace was a spacious plaza, surrounded on all sides by government buildings. A small man-made stream emptied itself into a tile-rimmed pool. Grass grew with more success here than in the plaza outside and paths had been laid out with gravel and rimmed with early spring flowers in orderly beds. She could hear the tinkle of a wind chime.

Maria ached from her hours in the saddle. She wanted to dip her dusty fingers in the tiled pool but was too sore to move beyond the nearby bench. She hobbled to the low wooden seat and sat, rising again quickly. *"Dios mio!"* she exclaimed.

Diego laughed again, taking off his black hat white with gypsum dust and slapping it against his leg.

"It is well for you, caballero," she snapped, and then was instantly sorry for her bad humor. It would not do to offend this man who had rescued her. Indeed, she did not want to, but her backside was on fire.

"Oh, chiquita," he said, ignoring her outbursts. "Oh, Maria chiquita! Things will get better soon. Let me rouse the governor from his table." He smoothed the red silk scarf pulled tight over his hair, brushed off his leather doublet and entered the palace.

He returned in scarcely a minute with a look of genuine frustration on his face. "I can't even get in to see him. I gave the message to his clerk, who tells me he will pass it on!" He sat down heavily on the bench next to Maria. "Is it any wonder that we flounder here?" Maria looked at him, and after a moment he smiled. "I am sorry. I just wish . . . well, I do not know what I wish. I do know that Antonio de Otermin is not overly fond of us rancheros."

They sat for a moment in silence. "I have sent a man to your sister, La Viuda Dona Margarita."

La Viuda. The widow. Maria thought of the missing cask of jewels, then of the glances the horsemen had exchanged when she mentioned her sister's name. But she refused to worry. She had reached Santa Fe. Surely she was safe now.

She sighed and tried to run her fingers through her tangled hair, but it was matted with dirt. All her hairpins were gone and the auburn tresses hung dull and stringy around her face. She was painfully aware that her dress was ripped in several places, that she wore no stockings, that her petticoat was in tatters. She brushed futilely at the brown serge of her skirt and blinked back tears.

"Never mind, Maria chiquita," said Diego, watching her. "At least you are alive," he added quietly. They sat together, shoulders touching.

"Diego!" said a voice behind them. Maria turned to see a man hurrying through the door of the palace, tugging off his napkin as he approached. He was dressed in dark red velvet, the doublet glittering with gold buttons and the sleeves slashed with cloth of gold showing through. His high boots were of soft, crushed leather and shone to a high polish. The man was altogether grand. As Maria got to her feet, she was terribly conscious of her disheveled state.

"My clerks have trouble sorting out what is news from what is not news. Excuse my seeming reluctance. It was not intentional. Now tell us of this which has come to pass."

He spoke to Diego, but his eyes were on Maria. They were kind eyes, worried eyes. Maria's uneasiness increased. The governor walked to her and took her hand in both of his, looking deep into her troubled eyes. "You are..."

"Maria Espinosa de la Garza," she replied in a whisper.

He patted her hand. "What can we say?"

Diego came closer. "Maria, this is His Excellency, Don Antonio de Otermin, governor of our province of New Mexico." He turned to the governor. "And did your clerk tell you of the massacre?"

"He told me, but not until the first course of my dinner was finished," said the governor dryly. "We will begin an immediate inquiry."

"There is no need, Governor. All are dead except Maria. Why waste reams and reams of paper and send a report to the viceroy in Mexico who will probably not bother to read it anyway?" Diego turned away and gazed out toward the open gates.

The governor looked at Diego's back. "The paperwork would choke you, Masferrer. But the viceroy sends me no troops and the garrison's horses are plugs. And so I have to commandeer you reluctant rancheros to double as militia." His voice rose. "But I will do the paperwork, too, Masferrer, because it is the law . . . something you New Mexicans prefer to avoid."

Diego turned around quickly, his face brick red. He started to speak, glanced at Maria's white face, and was silent. The men regarded each other until the governor finally turned back to Maria. He spread his hands expressively. "There are no words to express my distress, Senorita."

There was silence again, except for the sound of the water dribbling into the tile pool. Maria closed her eyes in exhaustion. All she wanted to do was go to her sister's home, have a bath and sleep. Diego cleared his throat and she opened her eyes.

"I must go now, Maria. I have to ride another three leagues to Tesuque or Erlinda will worry." He paused, reluctant to leave. "Your sister will be here soon."

Maria held out her hand and Diego took it. Her hand was trembling, but he held it firmly.

"I . . . do not . . . words are not sufficient," she began. How could she ever express to Diego Masferrer what she really felt? He had saved her life. She knew that she was in his debt, but she also knew that to state such a fact would only embarrass them both. She looked at the ground, then started in surprise when he put a finger under her chin and raised her head.

"I know, chiquita," he said, "I know. But had our places been reversed, you would have done the same, Maria La Afortunada."

It was a compliment of vast proportions, difficult for a man to say. Maria smiled faintly, then turned when she heard a rustle of silk behind her.

It could be no one but Margarita, her sister.

Margarita stopped suddenly and stared at her sister. Once again Maria became conscious of the tatters she wore. She brushed nervously at her rags, unable to interpret the expression on her sister's composed face. Maria turned to Diego for reassurance, but he and the governor, bristling at each other only moments ago, were now exchanging glances.

So there they were again, those looks. Maria moved closer to Diego, a motion that was not lost on the widow. She looked from Diego to Maria, not a flicker of feeling showing on her face.

"Well, Masferrer, have I you to thank for this unexpected blessing?"

Her words were not at all kind. Diego opened his mouth to speak, but the governor interrupted. "Come, Diego," he began, his voice jarringly loud in the quiet courtyard. "You must reach your holdings before nightfall, and I am facing an unpleasant task with Hidalgo de Sosa. Perhaps Senora Guzman would appreciate a moment alone with her sister."

Diego's glance flickered back to Maria, the same disquiet in his eyes that had been in his voice when he spoke of Margarita's dead husband. Maria fought the urge to grab his arm and plead with him to stay. What would Margarita think? Her own sister stood before her, but as Diego tipped his hat to her, turned back to his horse and swung into the saddle, Maria felt her strength leaving with him.

The governor patted her arm, then hurried toward his palace, calling for his clerk. She was alone with her sister, La Viuda Guzman.

Margarita took a step closer, then stopped. "So you are here," she said.

"I had no place to stay, and could not wait for a reply before setting out. The journey, as you know, is interminable."

This interview was not going as Maria had hoped. There was no welcome in her sister's eyes, no soft expression of sisterhood. Maria was acutely aware of her own dirt and rags. If the situation were reversed, she knew that she would have flung out her arms and held Margarita close, but her sister made no move. She stood there fingering the rosary that dangled from her belt, her eyes raking Maria, appraising what stood before her like the disappointed assayer of precious metal.

"You have not grown tall," she commented.

"No, Senora," Maria replied.

"Well, where is it?"

Maria frowned and shook her head. What did she mean? "Where is what, *hermana mia*—my sister?" she asked, twining her fingers together.

"The cask of jewels. Your letter mentioned some jewels of

our mother's. As older sister, they are rightfully mine," she said impatiently, her fingers clicking the beads in her hand.

Maria slowly sank down on the bench. "They are lost," she whispered. And so am I, she thought.

"Come now, Maria, do not mumble," her sister demanded, coming a step closer.

Maria looked up, her eyes bright with tears. "The jewels are gone," she repeated. "The Indians took them."

"So you come to me with nothing?" her sister murmured. "And now I am to provide for you and my five daughters besides? Five daughters, Maria, bless the Lord. And now you."

Maria said nothing. There was no refuge for her in this miserable mud town on which she had pinned all her hopes. She had made a terrible mistake, one she had no power to rectify.

Again there was that cool appraisal from Margarita Espinosa de Guzman, the bloodless assessment of the auctioneer, the slave master. Maria clasped her hands tighter and raised her head. She would not give Margarita the satisfaction of knowing how terrified her little sister was.

Finally Margarita spoke. "As the situation stands now, Maria, I cannot help you," she said evenly. "My husband, rest his soul, left me in debt. Great debt."

"But Diego said you . . . he said . . ." Maria interrupted, then stopped.

"Lies! You can no more trust a ranchero than fly! I am a poor widow. When I received your letter, I had hopes that our mother's jewels would clear the books."

Maria interrupted again, a cold column of fear running the length of her back. "But, sister, I told you in the letter that it was not much!"

"Don't interrupt," the widow snapped. "I have five daughters who must be provided for. It will take all my resources to keep them fed and clothed. You will have to look elsewhere for help." She paused and again scrutinized Maria as she would a melon in the marketplace. "A pity you are not married."

Maria wrenched her eyes from her sister's unwavering gaze. "After Papa died, my dowry money went to help pay off his debts. There was nothing left."

Margarita continued her scrutiny. "But then, I am not sure

that the fortune of Cortez himself could have secured you a husband. Men have some taste."

Maria raised her eyes again to her sister. "I look more pleasing when I am clean!" she shot back, biting off each word. She felt a great anger growing in her.

This time La Viuda looked away. "Well, as I have said, you must look elsewhere for help. I can offer you none."

Maria rose slowly. She had thought that she would be relegated to some menial position in her sister's household, but not this, never this. She understood Diego's uneasiness now, and panic rose in her. "But Dona Margarita," she whispered, fighting to control her voice, "I have nowhere to go. I know no one. I have no clothes, no money."

"Then you must become a ward of the town," said Margarita decisively. She reached into the reticule that hung from her waist and pulled out a lace handkerchief. Dabbing at her dry eyes, she continued, "I am a poor widow now, Maria. Surely I cannot be expected to nurture every stray and waif that it is my misfortune to know."

"But I am your sister," Maria said simply.

"So you say, but I have no proof of that. You were a small child the last time I saw you. Who can say that you are not an imposter, seeking to work into my good graces? Why should you survive cholera in Mexico City and an Indian raid here?"

Maria shook her head. "No, no," she whispered.

Margarita turned to go, then looked back. "I have lived in this miserable place for ten years now. I learned early that survival is the only consideration. A ward of the town you will be, Maria. Good day."

Maria followed her to the palace gates, but the widow would not look back. Squaring her shoulders as if to shake off the demeaning experience she had been subjected to, the widow pushed her dry handkerchief back into her reticule and walked rapidly away, her black skirts sweeping the ground behind her.

Maria leaned against the gate and closed her eyes. A ward of the town! With pain she remembered the wards of Mexico City—the homeless, the unwanted, the confused. She remembered as a child following the ragged shadows as they swept offal from the streets, taunting them, teasing them. She remembered the handful of coins her father used to give her to put in the church's poor box, money for the minimal upkeep of Los Olvidados, the Forgotten Ones.

"And now I am La Olvidada," Maria said out loud. What was it Diego had called her only yesterday? La Afortunada, the lucky girl.

Diego. Maria looked around quickly, then glanced out into the plaza. He had gone, riding away to his own holdings as soon as La Viuda appeared. Numb, she sat on the bench again, oblivious to the pain in her back and legs, still as a statue. Her mind was as blank as it had been during the Indian raid. She could think of nothing except that there was nothing. She was hungry, dirty, and above all, afraid, but no one cared. La Viuda had told her to become a ward of the town, but Maria knew that she could not seek refuge from the splendid Governor Otermin. She would be too humiliated ever to do that.

I am not the daughter of my father for nothing, she thought then, jarring her mind back into action. Even after his fortunes were gone, Papa had swept his cloak about him with the same swirling bravado, faced his friends with the same pride of presence. He had gone uncomplaining and courageous to his death.

Maria looked down at her hands. They were scratched and brown, her fingernails broken and dirty. She smoothed her tattered remnant of a dress. Eight months ago, she had been somebody, a beloved, pampered daughter. Now she was nobody. As a ward of the town, she would be less than nobody. She belonged nowhere, not in Mexico City anymore, and not even here in this depressing backwater mud fortress. For one terrible moment, she trembled with a great, overpowering hatred for her parents. How could they have left her, Maria Espinosa de la Garza, in such a situation? La Afortunada, indeed.

The moment passed, as she had known it would. She sat in silence on the bench, her back straight, her ankles properly together, her hands folded in her lap. "I was supposed to have died twice over, but I did not," she said out loud to the water splashing in the tile pool. She stood up, arranging the tatters of her dress around her with the same delicacy of movement her mother had taught her to use when walking in velvet and silk. She folded her hands in front of her again and looked back at the governor's palace. She would not give anyone the satisfaction of her defeat. Margarita had said something about survival. She, Maria Espinosa, would survive, and in a style that would bring a smile to her dead father's face, a nod of recognition.

She glanced through the window into the offices. She could see the governor bending over a man seated with his head bowed. Surely the husband of Carmen de Sosa, she thought. Poor man. She straightened her shoulders and walked out of the courtyard and into the plaza. Diego had mentioned that he lived three leagues north, a place called Tesuque. She would find him. Perhaps he would take her into his household as a servant. She had no skills, but she could learn household tasks.

If I cannot gratify my relatives and die, well, then, I must live. There is revenge of sorts in that, she told herself as she started north on the road out of Santa Fe.

Emiliano el Santero

$\mathcal{T}$he streets of Santa Fe were deserted. The calm stillness
of the late afternoon rested on the town, the same stillness to be found in any township or city in any part of the
Spanish New World. Maria was long familiar with it and the
very silence around her offered comfort in its familiarity. The
citizens were eating dinner behind the strong, cool adobe walls
of their homes.

Her stomach rumbled. She had eaten nothing since the hasty
meal of hardtack and jerky, taken in the saddle. She found a
rain barrel leaning against someone's wall, wiped away the
green film, and scooped up a drink.

The road north was the same rough oxcart path she had
followed with increasing weariness for the last six months. She
stood in the middle of it, looking north. Camino Real, indeed.
This King's Highway held no promise, but she could almost
hear Diego's words in her ear, reminding her to cut the cloak
to fit the cloth. She started walking north.

The road continued the steady climb from lower plain to
mountain plateau winding now around conical hills and green
juniper, fragrant with early spring.

She had gone less than a league when the strap on her shoe broke. She took it off and kept walking, her damaged shoe in one hand, her eyes looking north. The sun was low in the west, and she looked east toward the Sangre de Cristo Mountains. They were red, the red of dried blood. When the sun left them they would be dark and mysterious again. And with night would come the dreams. Maria shuddered and hugged herself. She knew she had not left Father Efrain and Carmen de Sosa behind, and now there was no Diego with his sword to send them loping into the bushes. Well, then, she would not sleep. She would walk until she dropped.

She knew she ought to be rehearsing in her mind what to say to Diego Masferrer when she found him. He would be surprised, of course, and shocked, perhaps even angry. No, she decided, he would not be angry. Then she shook her head. How could she know? Only an hour or two ago she would never have guessed that her own sister would spurn her; how could she say that she knew anyone's heart anymore? But she would throw herself on his mercy. She could do nothing else. She would offer to wait on his wife and children, serve as their maid. He had mentioned someone called Erlinda. Maria could offer to dress his wife's hair. She had some talent in those directions. Mama had always liked her to arrange her hair on special occasions, even though Mama had had a servant girl whose sole duty it was to wash and display her mistress's hair.

Maria fingered her own tangled hair. Diego would never believe her. The only other possible talent she possessed was a certain cleverness with paint and likenesses. She smiled to herself, remembering the small portrait she had done for her mother, presenting it with a mixture of shyness and pride on Mama's last birthday. Her smile faded and she stumbled on the road. Two weeks after her birthday, Mama was in the arms of death. Where was the miniature now? Probably sneered at by the *fiscales*, tossed out by the solicitors and long since burned. Her talent for painting would do her no good, not in this hard place.

The sun hung for a long, tantalizing moment on the rim of the western edge of the world, then sank suddenly out of sight. Maria stopped in the middle of the trail, whimpered, then looked around to make sure that no one had heard such weakness from an Espinosa, a descendant of *conquistadores*. She

41

began to walk faster. She must come to this Tesuque before all light left the western sky.

When she thought she heard someone following her, she started to run, but surely it was only the sound of her own feet. Maria looked over her shoulder and gasped. There was an Indian behind her. She caught her foot in her dress, fell and cut her knee. The blood ran down her leg and she dabbed at it with her skirt, her fingers cold and stiff. She was too tired to run, too weary to care anymore. Her mind was blank again of everything except the approaching Indian.

He did not hurry his pace, but walked steadily on, burdened by the load on his back. He was not dressed like the Apaches who had massacred the mission supply caravan. His hair hung long and free, and he was dressed in the shirt and loincloth common to the Indians of the pueblos she had seen in her months of travel in the province of New Mexico. He came toward her slowly, bent almost double by the weight on his back. Maria closed her eyes in relief. He was an old man. He approached with slow steps, then stopped in front of her and smiled, a wide, almost toothless smile.

Maria raised her hand slightly in tentative greeting and began, *"Buenos noches, viejo. Habla espanol?"*

He nodded. "Of course I speak Spanish. Would you tell me to my face that I have learned nothing in fifty years?"

"Oh, no, not I, Old One."

He was a tiny man, even shorter than she, looking smaller still bent over as he was by the load he carried. His hair was white and his face wrinkled, but his hands were shapely and his fingers long. They were the hands of an artist, but that could not be. Not in this hard place. He shifted his feet and dropped part of the load, muttering under his breath. Maria smiled. She stooped to retrieve what had fallen to the ground. It was a bundle of deerhides, scraped clean and softened.

"Let me carry it for you, Old One," she said, holding the hides to her.

Without a word, he set off again, moving faster than before, now that his load was lighter. She hurried to keep up with him.

As they walked, he watched her out of darting eyes. "Where are you traveling, Senorita?" he finally asked.

"I really don't know," she replied. "To Tesuque, to the

hacienda of Diego Masferrer. Do you know him? Am I going in the right direction?"

He grunted, and she tagged along beside him, hard pressed to keep up. The hides were heavier than lead in her arms, and she wondered that he could carry his own pack. The Old One said nothing more. After his initial long, sideways glance, he did not even look at her again.

They climbed steadily for another hour, then two. The moon rose over the mountains and the stars came out. Still they plodded on. Maria's arms were numb and her mind blank again, this time from weariness. She was beyond hunger, maybe even beyond sleep, so all-consuming was her exhaustion. All she desired was to lean against a wall somewhere and remain motionless, not thinking about the future. Or the past.

While she was convinced that her next step would be her last, the old pueblo Indian stopped so suddenly that she nearly fell over him. He threw down his pack and took the hides from her arms, placing them at her feet.

"We are in Tesuque."

"We are?" She looked around, squinting in the dark.

Then she could see the pueblo looming before her, dark and silent. There were no people about, but she could see dogs roaming and sniffing. She stared at the silent creatures. "Why do they not bark?" Her slow journey up the Camino Real had acquainted her with the habits of the snarling, scarcely domesticated dogs that inhabited each Indian pueblo.

The old man shrugged. "Senorita, they do not bark at me." He bent down by the pile of hides and gestured with his head. "Come with me."

She drew back. "I dare not," she whispered. The sleeping pueblo was full of Indians. But the Old One picked up his pack by the ties and dragged it behind him, and she had no choice but to follow him. She snatched up her deerhides and tagged close to his heels as the dogs began to growl at her. She could only trust him.

The old Indian climbed a ladder, tugging his hides after him. Maria pushed her pack in front of her up the ladder, hurrying so she would not lose sight of him. He entered a low doorway and Maria followed. She stopped in the doorway and dropped the hides, her hand to her mouth.

The room was alive with moving figures. She leaned against

the wall, her heart pounding so fast she feared it would leap from her breast. She forced herself to peer closer to the bobbing and swaying dancers. They were paintings on deerhide. The dancing candlelight and the breeze from the cool night made them appear to be in motion. She rubbed her eyes and brushed her hair from her face.

She recognized Miguel el Arcángel, with his wings and sword. Over by the interior doorway stood San José, carrying lilies that looked more like yucca blossoms. And there was Esteban el Martir, pincushioned with arrows and looking heavenward. Several Marias swayed in the evening breeze, each gently rocking a small Indian baby with a halo. The figures were crude, so unlike the magnificence of Mexico City's religious paintings, but they had a powerful presence.

The old man watched her. The smile on his face was almost hidden by his wrinkles, but his eyes were appreciative. "Do you like my saints?"

"Oh, yes," she replied, tearing her eyes away from a sweat-soaked Christ, his body red and drooping from his moving cross, the agony of centuries reaching out to her in this New Mexican pueblo.

The old man brushed off the front of his homespun shirt. "I am Emiliano, *santero* to Diego Masferrer."

Saintmaker. She looked at him and smiled, extending her hand. When he stared down at her hand, she wondered about the propriety of offering her hand to an Indian, but there was something about Emiliano that measured him as equal. Perhaps it was his paintings.

After a long pause, he took her hand, giving it one brief shake.

"I am Maria Espinosa de la Garza," she said. "Thank you for helping me."

He snorted. "You have helped me. If my old woman were alive, she would have called that a lazy man's load that I carried. But it was too much." He peered at her face in the dim light. "Do you think I am too old?"

It was a curious question. She looked around her at the figures dancing in slow motion. There was San Antonio, he who finds lost things. Her eyes filled with tears, and she struggled against them. San Antonio, dear San Antonio. He would never retrieve her losses. "No. You will never be really old, not so long as you can make the saints dance."

He smiled. "Only another artist would say such a thing. Are you an artist?"

She shook her head. "Oh, no. I cannot pretend such a thing. But I like to paint."

He turned toward the door. "We shall see. But now, let us go. You spoke of Diego Masferrer. Let me take you to Las Invernadas."

"Where?"

"Las Invernadas. It is what he calls his hacienda and lands. I will take you to him."

They descended the ladder. "Is everyone asleep?" she asked in a whisper.

"Yes. It is late. Besides, no one bothers me. I come and go as I please."

The dogs still roamed silently. Maria stayed close to Emiliano. Without his burden he walked even faster. She struggled to keep up with him. When he saw how she hurried and noticed her limp, he slowed his pace.

"It is yet another league," Emiliano said, and she sighed. He peered at her. "Well, Senorita Espinosa de la Garza, you have come this far. Keep walking!"

Her head felt two sizes too large and her vision seemed to sparkle around the edges. Her feet were a mass of scratches, and she had left her broken shoe behind in the *santero*'s workshop, but she followed the old Indian doggedly.

After an hour of silent struggle, Maria saw Las Invernadas. The hacienda was reddish adobe like the pueblo, but of only one story, long and low in the moonlight. She saw men walking slowly back and forth on the roof, ghostly visions in the waning moon.

"Guards," said Emiliano. "They are there every night. I will speak to them."

Maria's old uneasiness returned. What right had she to lay her troubles at Diego Masferrer's feet? She should have done as Margarita insisted and thrown herself on the governor's mercy. Perhaps Margarita would have changed her mind in the morning light. Mama had said she had been changeable as a young girl. Maria stopped in the road, reluctant to move closer.

"Come, come," said Emiliano impatiently.

She trailed after him to the gate. He called up to the guards now standing still and watchful on the hacienda's roof. One of them waved Emiliano on and the men resumed their slow walk. Emiliano jangled the bell by the front gate, the noise loud in the midnight stillness. The crickets in the trees stopped singing, but the dogs standing by the massive front door began to bay.

They were enormous dogs, probably descendants of the first mighty dogs that Cortez had brought in armor from Spain. One of them bounded to the gate and stuck his jaws through the grillwork, growling and showing his teeth. Maria drew back, but the old saintmaker stood there, his hand on the bell.

"Who is there?" called a voice. Maria straightened, clutching her dress in tight bunches. It was Diego, and he sounded angry. She should never have come.

"It is Emiliano, my lord," called the Indian.

Maria could hear several bolts thrown on the other side of the door.

"And what do you want, old man?" Diego called, his voice kinder.

"I have something for you, Senor, that will not keep until morning. Something you must have carelessly left behind in Santa Fe." For an Indian, Emiliano spoke with great familiarity. Maria wondered at the relationship between the old man she stood by and the lord of the hacienda.

Before Diego opened the door, he called to his dogs. They bounded to him and crouched by his bare feet, watchful.

The ranchero had thrown on a robe and was still tying the sash around his waist. He ran a hand over his curly hair as he walked toward the gate. Maria shrank into the shadows.

"What have you for me, old man, that could not wait until Christians are abroad in the land again?"

The *santero* smiled and pulled Maria toward the open gate. "This one, my lord."

Diego stared at her. *"Dios mio,"* was all he said.

It was enough. Maria flung herself into his arms, sobbing. Diego put his arms around her, his hand heavy on her hair. "Thank you, Emiliano."

The *santero* turned to go. "I will return later."

Diego and Maria walked slowly toward the hacienda. Maria tried to speak, tried to explain, but her face was muffled against Diego's robe and she was crying too hard to be understood.

They crossed the *galería* slowly and went into the house. Diego released her and shut the bolts.

He turned to her then, his face in shadow. Maria wiped her nose on her sleeve. She dropped slowly to her knees and held her hands in front of her, palms up. "I throw myself on your mercy, my lord," she said.

Quickly he put his hands under her elbows and jerked her to her feet. His face was still puffy with sleep, but his eyes were alive, his color livid. She tried to draw back, but he held her by the elbows.

"La Viuda?" was all he could get out.

Terrified, Maria nodded. "She would not have me," she managed to say. She had never seen anyone so angry before. Maria started to cry again as Diego held her by the elbows.

Then it was over. He let her go and ran his fingers through his tousled hair. "Maria chiquita, I am not angry with you. I am angry at myself."

She stopped crying, bending down to dry her face on her skirt. He continued, his voice weary. "I should never have left you there. I should have known better. *Dios mio,* I did know better!"

Maria shook her head. His words were not making sense to her anymore. She needed to sit down, but the room was dark and she could not see any benches. "Please, Senor, is there a place to sit?" Diego appeared to be growing and shrinking, moving from side to side, and again there was that sparkle around her eyes.

"Oh. Of course. My pardon, chiquita. I was not thinking." He picked up the candle from the table by the door and led her to the low outcropping that lined the wall. She sank down gratefully and leaned against the cool adobe wall.

Diego lit a branch of candles on another table nearby and walked to an inside door. "Erlinda! Erlinda!" he called. "Come, my dear!" He turned back to Maria, who sat with her eyes closed. "And what did Dona Margarita say, or can I guess?"

Maria opened her eyes. Diego was standing close to her, hands on his hips, looking down at her. She straightened her tattered, filthy dress and patted it carefully around her legs, a ladylike gesture that was not lost on the landowner. Her feet were bare—she had lost her other shoe—and bleeding, her hair a mess, and her dress in ruins, but she sat there, back straight, ankles together, as fine a lady as had ever graced his hacienda. The contrast of her present life to her former expectations brought the hard light glittering into his eyes again.

She looked away. "She said there was no room for me. She has five daughters." She paused, the humiliation making her voice scarcely audible. "She was so disappointed when I arrived with no jewels and. . . ."

"I'll wager she was," interrupted Diego bitterly. He sat beside Maria, put the candle next to him on the bench and looked across the dim hall to the deerhide painting hanging there, moving slowly in the cool breeze. "I was born here. I have lived here all my life. I do not claim to be very observant, or nearly as smart as my brother Cristobal, but I have noticed one thing. This country changes those who come into it, Maria chiquita. Sometimes for the better, sometimes for the worse. In Margarita Espinosa de Guzman's instance, it has made her harder than obsidian."

"But why?" she asked, her voice soft.

"Indeed, I cannot say." She shifted and their shoulders touched. "She was not married to a good man. Whatever kindness there may have been in her is gone."

They sat in silence until Maria saw a woman standing in the doorway. She was taller than Diego and fairer, with blond hair and pale skin. Maria sighed with the same pleasure that an artist feels when seeing a lovely portrait. This must be Diego's wife. She was beautiful. Maria could scarcely bear to think of her own dishevelment in the same room with such a pretty one as this. The woman held her candle high and peered at them. "Diego?" she asked uncertainly.

"Over here, Erlinda. I want you to meet someone."

He stood, tucking his robe closer around him. Maria got to her feet slowly, wishing that the room would stop moving. She wanted to sit down again, but Diego was holding her hand.

"Erlinda, this is Maria Espinosa de la Garza from Mexico City, she of whom I told you last evening. Maria, this is my sister Erlinda Castellano."

"Your sister?" asked Maria, as the other woman stepped forward and held out her hand.

"Yes. You see, my sister got all the height and looks in the family."

"Oh, Diego!" said Erlinda gently, taking Maria's other hand.

He laughed. "It is not a matter of great concern to me."

Erlinda smiled. Maria tried to smile, but suddenly her knees buckled under her. Diego grabbed her and picked her up in one motion.

"Diego," said Erlinda in her gentle voice. "What kind of host are you? Our company is worn with fatigue and you stand there talking. Follow me."

She picked up the larger branch of candles and led the way down the hall. Maria tried to speak, to tell Diego to put her down, but the words were not there. I will tell him to put me down, she thought, after I close my eyes for just a few seconds.

The Masferrers

The sun was high, and the light fell across Maria's pillow. She tried to sit up, but she ached all over. She propped herself up on one elbow and looked around her.

It was a small, plain room, with white walls and no ornamentation save for a deerskin painting of Santa Ana on the wall. Maria leaned back against her pillow and regarded the painting. It was the work of Emiliano the saintmaker. The figure was tall and blond, and reminded her of Erlinda. Beside the painting was a small altar. Compared to her bedroom at the family estate in Mexico City, the room was bare. And yet somehow it was as friendly as the people who inhabited the hacienda. Las Invernadas, Emiliano had called it. Maria remembered little of last night, except that Diego had set her down on the bed and covered her. She had awakened once before morning and saw him sitting in the window alcove, the moonlight outlining his curly hair. She had gone back to sleep then, comforted, peaceful.

She took a deep breath and stirred. The whole house smelled of piñon wood and the faint aroma of chocolate and cinnamon.

Her mouth watered. When had she last eaten? She could not remember.

She was lying in her chemise and tattered petticoat. Her dress was nowhere in sight, but there was a muslin robe at the foot of the bed. She sat up and put it on. The sleeves hung over her wrists. It must belong to Erlinda.

And then, as if the thought had summoned her, there was a soft tapping on the door. Erlinda opened it and peered in. "I was hoping you would be awake. God's blessings on you and good morning," she said. Erlinda carried a tray of food, which she set down on Maria's lap. There was chocolate, frothy and hot in an earthenware mug, several eggs and a small plate of tortillas, the steam still rising from them. "I would have given you more food," said Erlinda in apology, "but Diego said that too much at once would not be wise."

Maria ate every bite, savoring the eggs and wiping the plate clean with the last bit of tortilla. She drank the chocolate slowly, relishing the smooth liquid as it traveled down her throat. If Erlinda had not been standing there, her hands folded in front of her, Maria would have run her finger around the inside of the cup.

Erlinda took the tray when Maria finished. "I am glad to see you smiling. Diego said you were restless last night, calling out for Carmen. I thought your sister was Margarita."

She could not remember the nightmare, but she thought again of Diego sitting in the window. "No. No. Carmen was just someone . . . I knew," she said, starting to get out of bed.

Erlinda paused at the door. "I will send servants in with Mama's tub. My sisters and I generally bathe in the *acequia*— the irrigation stream—but you will not be accustomed to that yet, and besides, it is morning."

"Your mother? Your sisters?" asked Maria.

Erlinda opened the door. "Oh, yes. You have not met all of us yet. There are others." Her voice trailed off and she looked away, occupied for a moment with private thoughts. Then she brightened again. "After you are bathed and dressed, I will take you to Mama."

Maria spoke up. "My dress is gone."

Erlinda put her hand to her mouth to hide a smile. "For that, you must forgive my brother. When he left your room early this morning, he had your dress. I think he tossed it on the fire pit in the back. My sisters and I will find you something to wear."

Erlinda left then, closing the door quietly behind her. Maria sat cross-legged on the bed until two Indian servants brought in a large tin tub and filled it with steaming water from copper kettles. They left a container of soft soap that Maria picked up and sniffed. It smelled of yucca blossoms.

She stripped off her chemise and petticoat and stepped into the water, standing on one foot, then the other, until she was accustomed to the warmth. Her last real bath had been more than a month ago in a small stream late at night by the side of the wagons, long after everyone was sleeping. She sat in the tub finally and leaned back, closing her eyes. As she sat there, soaking in the heat and comfort, she concluded that this was as close as she would ever get to heaven in this life. Then she picked up a bar of rough brown soap and scrubbed herself until her skin was raw. She washed her hair three times with the soft soap, rinsing it with the pitcher of cool water next to the tub.

Erlinda knocked and came back into the room as Maria was drying herself. "I have found you some clothing, but I cannot find you any shoes that fit. Diego said he would do something about it."

Maria took the clean chemise and petticoat from Erlinda and dressed quickly. The morning air was cool and she shivered in the breeze from the window facing the interior courtyard. Her new dress was simple homespun, much worn and washed to a whiteness that contrasted with the brown of her skin. She was grateful that the room had no mirror. She did not want to look at her ruined complexion. Not even the lead-white powder that her mother used to put on her face would lighten her brownness.

But there was no point in pining over what could not be changed. She finished buttoning her dress, then sat with Erlinda on the bed, taking the comb the woman offered her. They began to untangle Maria's long auburn hair.

"Such glorious color," murmured Erlinda. "Wait, Maria. Do not pull so hard."

"But there are so many tangles!"

"And are you expecting a visit from the viceroy? What is your hurry? Do it a strand at a time, like so."

An hour later Maria's hair hung down to her waist, free of tangles and shining copper and gold in the morning sun.

Someone knocked on the door. Erlinda glanced up from her contemplation of Maria's hair. *"Pasa, hermano,"* she said, recognizing the knock.

Diego walked in, holding a piece of paper and a pointed lump of charcoal. He set the paper on the floor and motioned to Maria to stand on it while he traced the outline of her feet, his hand on her ankle. "My sister is tall," he said as he worked. "She has a beautiful face, it is true, but her feet are large. Like boats, almost."

Erlinda pushed him, and he nearly fell. He laughed, finishing the outline. "The truth hurts, Erlinda," he said, stepping out of her way before she could push him again.

Maria laughed. How different Diego was this morning from the angry man of last night.

Diego stood with the piece of paper in his hand. "Such small feet!" he marveled. "Erlinda, when Pablo gets through with Maria's slippers, he might have enough leather left to make you one shoe."

Erlinda rolled her eyes. "Do you see what we have to bear here, Maria? Are you sure that you would wish to join our household?"

Maria was silent, thinking of her own sister. Erlinda put her hand on her arm. "I am sorry. It was thoughtless of me to remind you of your situation."

Maria shook her head. "I am grateful to be in this household." She paused, then glanced shyly at Diego. "That is, if it is agreeable to everyone."

Diego smiled but made no reply. His eyes were on her hair. He lifted a handful of it and let it fall, cascading to her shoulders. "See the different colors in it, Erlinda," he said, then left the room with his drawing of Maria's feet.

"Pablo, our cobbler, will make you slippers," said Erlinda "He is not as proficient as the cobblers who come up from Santa Fe in the winter, but it will do for now. Here, let me braid your hair, then I will take you to my mother."

Maria sat quietly while Erlinda plaited her hair and talked of her family. "There are five of us. No, there are six," she amended. "Diego would say six. Diego, me, Francisco, who is studying in a seminary in Mexico City, and our two younger sisters." She finished one braid, tied the end with a rawhide strip, and rested it on Maria's breast. As she began the second, Maria ran the tally in her head. Erlinda had said there were six in the family but had only named five. "I am Erlinda Masferrer de Castellano. My husband Marco died two years ago and I have returned home. I am seventeen years old."

"I am sorry for your misfortune," said Maria, holding her head still while Erlinda braided.

"He was a fine man, my husband," said Erlinda. "You are not the only one to have suffered because of the Apaches. We have all suffered here in this kingdom, one way or another." She finished Maria's hair in silence, then made a visible effort to smile. "And now, let me take you to Mama. And my sisters, if we can find them."

She led the way down the hall, Maria following. The hall was cool, even chilly in the morning air. Portions of it opened onto a patio bright with early flowers and a small fountain. Two young girls were seated close together on a bench by the fountain, their heads bent over the samplers they held in their laps.

Erlinda whispered to Maria. "And here they are. In truth, I did not expect to see them thus engaged. Old Martin is harvesting honeycomb and I was sure they would be bothering him."

Maria nodded. She remembered all the samplers she had labored and cried over when she was their age. The slightest distraction was always sufficient excuse to leave tangled threads behind. But Mama had insisted. "I tell you, daughter," she had scolded, "no man will ever approach your father for your hand if you cannot even sew." And so Maria had learned, little good would it do her these days without a dowry. Maria sighed, watching the girls at their work.

Erlinda clapped her hands. "Sisters," she began, and both girls looked up quickly, their eyes eager for diversion, even of the smallest sort. "Come forward and make yourselves known to Maria Espinosa."

The girls put down their embroidery and came to the edge of the patio. They were dressed alike in sober green gowns, embroidered around the hem and sleeves with floral designs. The sisters were as different as Diego and Erlinda, the older

54

child blond and bidding to be tall like Maria's companion, and the other short and dark like Diego, with curly black hair.

Erlinda placed a hand on each head and smiled when the girls put their arms around her. "This is Luz and this is Catarina," she said, her voice vibrant with affection. "Luz has five years, and Catarina six."

Luz was silent, staring at Maria, but Catarina dropped a small curtsy and then darted behind Erlinda, who laughed and drew her out in front of her own full skirts again. "Maria is from Mexico City," she said, and both little girls regarded Maria with the same kind of awe that she remembered reserving for the viceroy himself. She smiled as the little girls looked at each other and giggled.

Catarina took a step forward. "You have come all the way from Mexico City to stay with us?" she asked, and then turned to her sister. "Imagine such a thing, Luz!"

Luz only nodded and drew closer to Erlinda, who absently straightened the collar on the child's dress and patted her head.

"I suppose I have come all that way to stay with you," Maria said. "It would seem that way."

Catarina looked at her older sister. "Was this Diego's idea?" she asked.

Erlinda smiled, her face lit with an inner repose that Maria was already coming to recognize. "I suppose it was," she replied gently, her hand still on Luz's head but her eyes on Maria.

Catarina advanced again. "Diego brings things home," she confided, then retreated in earnest behind Erlinda's skirts when Maria laughed and clapped her hands.

"He probably surprised even you this time," Maria said.

"Maria, you will come to know my brother better," exclaimed Erlinda, torn between embarrassment at Catarina's words and amusement over her brother. "I suppose the other rancheros laugh at him, but he is the son of his father, and we would wish nothing different."

Luz looked at her older sister and tugged at her sleeve. Erlinda leaned down and listened to her little sister whispering in her ear. She straightened and patted both girls. "By all means, you may go. I imagine Martin el viejo is wondering how he can possibly get the honey from the hives without the two of you to tell him how to go on."

The girls scampered away, samplers forgotten. Maria watched

them. "They are charming," she said to Erlinda, who had walked over to the bench and was examining the morning's work. She held up Catarina's effort and made a face.

"Do you remember your first sampler?" Erlinda asked, holding up the grubby cloth with thumb and forefinger.

"Indeed," answered Maria. "Mama kept it in her . . ." She stopped. The sampler must have been discarded with all the other useless rubbish by the solicitors. Everything she owned was gone, all treasures large and small. She stood in someone else's dress now on someone else's patio, her feet bare. She tugged at one of her braids, unable to meet Erlinda's eyes.

Erlinda put down the embroidery, her voice smooth as she gently glided over the awkward moment. "Sometimes I think of my sisters as my own children. Luz was born after Papa's death. It seems they have always been in my charge."

Maria made an effort to carry her thoughts away from Mexico City. "But what of your mother?"

"I will take you to her, and you will understand us better."

They left the patio and continued down the hall together. Erlinda paused at a bright blue door, knocked and entered. Maria followed.

The room was dark. Erlinda crossed to the window that opened onto the hallway by the patio and pulled back the heavy curtain. "Mother, I have a guest for you to greet."

Even with the curtain open the room was deep in morning shadows. A woman sat in a straight-backed chair by the altar, a little woman with curly black hair drawn back in a chignon low on her neck, the shorter hair curling around her face. As she turned, Maria saw that she was blind.

Erlinda led Maria closer, took her hand and put it on her mother's. The woman grasped Maria's hand with a firm grip.

"Mama," said Erlinda, bending close to the small woman. "This is Maria, she of whom Diego spoke."

Maria leaned closer to the woman. Diego resembled her, with the same black hair and brown eyes. But while his eyes seemed to be a window on his soul, La Senora Masferrer's eyes were without depth, mirroring no emotion.

She reached up and patted Maria's face gently. Lightly she ran her hand over the contours of the young woman's face, pausing on the chin and jawline. "Ah, I feel considerable force of will."

"You can tell that from my face?" asked Maria, kneeling by the woman's chair.

The blind woman smiled, her smile reaching everywhere on her delicate face except her dead eyes. "And I am seldom wrong, child. But now, are you sitting by me? Good. Diego told me about you this morning. How pleased we are that you have chosen to honor our hacienda with your presence."

Maria eased herself onto the stool by the blind woman's knees. She felt tears rising in her eyes again. She could not trust her voice.

"You need have no fear in the household of Diego Masferrer. Our kindness extends to all who pass by. And those who have need of it."

Maria could only be silent in the presence of such giving hearts. She was ashamed for her own sister, who could not extend even half so generous a heart to her own relative.

As if sensing what Maria was thinking, the woman patted her hand again. "Your wounds will heal here," she said softly, so softly that even Erlinda could not hear. "We mean only to help. Perhaps there are circumstances with your sister that you and I know nothing about."

"It may be so," Maria managed to say.

La Senora patted her hand again, her fingers warm and strong. "Of course it is, Maria," she answered. "All of us do the best we can."

Erlinda's voice was a whisper in the cozy room. "We do not wish to tire you, Mama. I will bring Maria back another day. Perhaps she will read to you some afternoon."

"Oh, yes," said Maria, "I would like that."

"Then you are welcome any time," said La Senora, releasing the young woman's hands. "Erlinda always has a thousand tasks, and Diego is seldom indoors."

Erlinda sensed what Maria was thinking and spoke as soon as she had closed the door behind her. "Mama has always been blind, so please do not feel sorry for her. We would wish that she could get around more, but her heart is not strong." She smiled at Maria. "And do not look so troubled! If Diego could see your face he would say, 'Do not pine over what you cannot remedy.' And he would be right, of course."

"But Erlinda, such a burden on all of you, and I only add to it!"

"No, not a burden. And not on me. Diego, perhaps, but not on me." She shook her head decisively then. "No, not even on Diego." She turned to look at the bright blue door. "Papa had Mama's door painted blue, as if he could make her see it somehow. I remember him standing over Emiliano—and how our *santero* hates that kind of scrutiny—as he mixed the paint. Papa gladly shouldered Mama's burdens and did what he could to make things brighter for all of us. He taught us to read. I remember how he used to sit at the table and read to us for hours, teaching us in turn. He did it for Mama, so we could read to her when he was busy. Papa died when Diego was fifteen."

"Indians?"

Erlinda shook her head. "We do not know what it was. He grew thinner and thinner. He had our Indians build him a special bed so he could be carried from room to room. I still remember the hours he spent in the corral with Diego, instructing his riding, making him rope fenceposts over and over until they were both exhausted and in tears. Such urgency! Papa continued to oversee our lives right up to his final breath."

"And now the burden is Diego's?" Maria asked.

"Diego has had to learn so much so fast. But although he never speaks of it, he does not see his duties as a burden. He rules us with his love, like Papa. He is generous of heart. Diego does not ride his Indians like horses. Some say he is too lenient with his people, that he allows them privileges not within his power to grant. But we are happy here, no matter what our neighbors think of us."

They continued down the hall into the kitchen that jutted out from the rear of the hacienda, breaking the symmetry of the square adobe building. Maria looked about her in delight. The colors leaped out at her from all sides. As in the other rooms, the walls were whitewashed with gypsum, but here the powerful white was met halfway up from the floor by blue tiles with windmills and flowers. The walls were lined with copper pots that winked in the morning light and rows of knives arranged from the biggest to the smallest. Although the floor was earthen as in other parts of the hacienda, it was immaculate.

The fireplace at one end of the room was big enough to stand in, and hung with hooks for pots and spits for roasting. An Indian woman squatted before it. Covering the opposite wall was a cabinet that rose from the floor to the ceiling, with real panes of glass showing off the silver and porcelain behind. A long table, half the length of the room, was covered with a homespun cloth of Indian design.

"Such a room!" Maria exclaimed, "with colors so vivid! How did you get tiles from the Low Countries?"

"That was Papa's doing, to create brightness that Mama could feel, if not see. He went all the way to Mexico City for those tiles, and for the glass in the windows. Our neighbors still accuse us of putting on airs, but he did it for Mama." Erlinda put her hands on her hips and mimicked, "'Those Masferrers with their blue doors and Dutch tiles!' But it pleases us."

The kitchen opened onto a garden where Maria saw Indian children weeding the young plants. Beyond the garden were other outbuildings. In the distance she could see Catarina and Luz bobbing around the beehives, staying just ahead of the old Indian with them.

"Beyond them is the *acequia* for irrigation," said Erlinda, following Maria's gaze. "Part of it runs under the wall, so we always have water, even in times of siege."

Maria continued gazing out the window. A tall man on horseback opened the heavy gate and came into the hacienda's enclosure. He closed the gate behind him and sat there on his horse, leaning forward in the saddle, his arms crossed on the saddle horn. He seemed to be watching the girls and the bees, then his glance shifted suddenly to the kitchen window where Maria stood looking out. He was far enough away so that she could not discern his features, but she drew back, unaccustomed to such scrutiny.

"Who is that man?" Maria asked Erlinda, who had crossed to the fireplace and was stirring the contents of a pot hanging on a firehook.

Erlinda put the spoon back in the pot and walked to Maria, looking out. "Oh," she remarked and turned back to the fireplace with a studied coolness, "that is Cristobal."

When she said no more, Maria looked out the window again. The horse and rider were gone.

"Who is he?" she asked.

"Diego will tell you about Cristobal," Erlinda said coolly.

"He is the other one of us that I mentioned, the sixth. He, too, is a child of my father."

She said no more, and Maria did not press her. She looked out the window again, wondering where he had gone, wondering why he would bring out such unexpected sharpness in Erlinda.

"Let us go outside, Maria," said Erlinda, swinging the firehook back over the hot coals and admonishing the Indian cook squatting on her heels by the fireplace to tend it well.

They went into the garden. After a quick look around at the Indian children weeding and a nod to them, Erlinda led Maria to the great beehive-shaped ovens behind the tomato plants. Indian servant women were removing the round loaves of bread, steam rising from the sign of the cross on each loaf. Maria closed her eyes and breathed deeply. The smell of baked bread was overpowering.

"Maria chiquita," said Diego behind her, "you like our bread?"

She turned around. Diego was standing there, and with him was Cristobal. The man looked at her, a smile crossing his face, then leaving it as quickly as it had come.

Maria spoke to Diego. "I think I will always be hungry. After my six-months' diet of *carne seca* and *biscoche,* I had forgotten that anyone still made bread."

Cristobal stepped forward and drew his sword. Maria watched as he speared a loaf from the cooling shelf. He set the loaf down on the stone ledge by Maria and with two rapid cuts, sliced the bread in quarters. He called in an unfamiliar language to old Martin by the beehives, who brought over a hunk of comb honey, dripping and sweet. Cristobal whacked off a corner of the honey, put it on one section of bread and handed it to Maria, who stood with her hands behind her.

"Go ahead," he said. "Take it and eat."

She took the bread from him, and he licked the honey off his fingers as he stood watching her. Maria ate the bread, her eyes on Cristobal. Diego accepted the bread Cristobal offered him and sat with Maria on the stone ledge. He nodded his head in Cristobal's direction.

"Maria, this is my brother, Cristobal Masferrer."

Cristobal nodded back at Maria and joined them on the

ledge. So this is the sixth Masferrer, thought Maria to herself, and she understood Erlinda's hesitation. He was a magnificent man, a head and shoulder taller than Diego. He was obviously part Indian, although Diego's skin was tanned to the same mahogany as his brother's. But his features were Indian, although he had the look of Erlinda about his eyes and mouth and in the graceful way he held himself. His hair was longer than Diego's and drawn back with a rawhide thong. He was dressed like Diego, in leather vest and knee-length breeches, with homespun shirt and high boots, but he was Indian.

"Cristobal is part Tewa, Maria," said Diego, watching her reaction. "We had the same father." He paused and glanced at his sister, who was looking at the three of them. "This is his house and his land, too." When he said this, Erlinda turned away.

Maria looked from one brother to the other. Cristobal smiled at her again, his curious, fleeting smile. He appeared oblivious to the angry glances exchanged by his brother and sister. When he finished the bread, he wiped his hands on his breeches and stood. "And now I must work," he said. His voice was deep, and his accent gave the words a pleasant musical lilt. He turned to Maria. "You are welcome in our house," he said. He spoke to her but his eyes were on Erlinda, who stiffened as he spoke. "Some would say I have no right to speak thus," he continued, his voice low.

With a slight wave in Diego's direction, he was gone. Erlinda turned to Diego, her eyes stormy. "You should not encourage him!"

"I should throw him out like every other half-breed of every other ranchero in these parts? You would ask me to treat a son of my father that way, Erlinda? Would you?" he flashed back, the veins in his neck standing out.

Erlinda looked down at her hands. "I do not know. Papa insisted on raising him with the rest of us, and I suppose it was the Christian thing to do," she said. Her voice fell to a whisper that made Maria shiver, despite the warming sun on her back. "But Diego, I fear for you! For all of us! Someday . . ." She stopped, looking at Maria in distress.

Diego turned away with a short laugh that had no humor in it. "Maria chiquita, you will think that we are at each other like this all the time. Indeed, we are not." He started toward the acequia and the women followed. He did not look back at his sister, but his words were for her. "I like to listen to my sister, but on this I must be firm, Erlinda." He stopped, his back still to Erlinda. "He will be treated as my brother, if not yours."

"Very well, Diego, as you will," said Erlinda. "I will be in the kitchen, Maria."

Maria and Diego continued on to the *acequia*. A sloping path led to the water's edge. Diego stopped at the top of the low bank, his mind still occupied with Cristobal. "Do not be afraid of him, Maria," he said. "Though Erlinda's biggest objection to Cristobal is not that he is the bastard son, but that he is Indian." He spread his hands expressively. "As for me, I like Cristobal. I hope you will, too."

Maria stood looking at the water. She noticed a flash of petticoat against the bank further downstream. *"Mira.* Look there," she said, pointing.

Diego looked where she pointed. "My sisters," he said. "They have dug a small tunnel in the side of the bank. The water is so low this year. I suppose their tunnel will drop dirt on them someday, but until it does, they play dolls in there." He waved at his sisters and blew them a kiss.

"Do you ride, Maria?" Diego asked. "Well, certainly you do. Did we not already share a horse?"

"I do ride," she answered, "but not well."

"Someday I will take you with me around my land." He pointed to the tilled and newly planted fields beyond the *acequia* and the wall. "That is Masferrer land. And that. And that. Look in all directions. We have taken a substantial entitlement of Indians to work the place, but there is never enough water. Which is why much of my land is for grazing."

He stood by her, looking out over his land and his Indians working in the fields. A gentle smile played around his lips and the sun wrinkles around his eyes were deep with squinting into the noonday sky. Maria touched his arm and he looked at her. "Yes, Maria?"

"My lord," she began, and stopped when he waved her to silence.

"There will be none of that, Maria," he said quietly.

"But it must be," she interrupted. "I did not walk all the way from Santa Fe to become a parasite in your household. I expect to work here, and I want to know what is expected of me. I need to know."

He held his hands out to her, palms up. "I cannot put you to work like one of my *Indios*, Maria. You are of gentle birth, carefully raised."

"And now I stand here before you, my feet bare, clothed by the goodness of others. I will not be a hanger-on here, and if that is what you would make me, then I will walk back to Santa Fe and become a ward of the town after all." He was silent, looking at her. "I have no dowry. No one will marry me. My own sister has cast me off. I possess nothing. But I will work. I can learn."

"I do not like it," he said finally.

"I do not ask you to like it," she replied quickly. "But it must be this way."

"Why do I have the feeling that in spite of what I say, you will follow your own mind?" he murmured, half to himself.

"Because I must," she declared, feeling an unexpected stubbornness rising in her.

He stared down at the waters of the *acequia*, unmindful of his little sisters calling him downstream. Then he sighed and threw up his hands. "What choice do you give me, Maria chiquita? We will put you to work, but I do insist that you live in the family quarters. This must be."

"Very well." She put out her hand. After a moment's hesitation, Diego shook it.

"I have never shaken on a bargain with a woman," he said.

"It will do you good, Senor," she replied.

"I doubt it," he said, smiling a little. He turned his head toward her in sudden seriousness. "There is something you can do for me, if you will."

"Anything," she replied.

He chuckled. "Come now, Maria, we do not know each other well, but I know you have too much of a mind of your own to make such a rash statement."

"Anything within reason," she amended.

"That is better. It is a simple thing. Be a friend to my sister Erlinda." He stuck his hands in his pockets. "She came back to us four months ago, a widow. She has never spoken about the events of Marco's death." He paused and brushed a hand across his eyes. "Dear Marco. How I loved him." With a visible

63

effort, Diego continued. "I confess to you that I know little of the human heart, but I do know one thing—pain goes away faster when it is spoken of, when tears are shed. Help her, if you can."

He held out his hand to her this time and she shook it. "This could become a habit." He gestured toward the house. "Come then, Maria. If you will become a citizen of the river kingdom, then I suppose you must work like the rest of us."

Diego was as good as his word. He put Maria to work in his household, instructing Erlinda, who argued with him in her gentle fashion, to teach her the daily tasks of the hacienda, the labor of his Mexican servants.

"These Indians are descendants of the Christian Mexicanos my grandfather brought with him when he made the *entrada* with Onate in 1598," Diego explained. "Their work is the labor of the house, and tasks requiring some skills."

"What of the Indians in the field?" she asked.

"They are my Indians from Tesuque."

"Your Indians?"

"Yes, my Indians," he replied firmly. "They were given by *encomienda* to my father's father, and now their work is mine."

She should have been warned by the deepening lines around his mouth and eyes that this was a touchy subject, but she couldn't stop herself. "Can you own them now? I thought that was forbidden by the Council of the Indies."

"They gave me their work." His answer was short, the lines more pronounced.

"But the Viceroy says you cannot do that anymore, that the days of Indian allotment are long over." Some demon was driving her on. A year ago she would not have cared about anyone's Indians, but now, with her own status so radically altered, she had new vision. "My own father got in tro . . ."

"Maria!" Diego was past the point of toleration. "I had no idea women were so interested in such matters. Here we own Indians. Don't think there hasn't been trouble from the Church and the governor."

"I would think so," she murmured.

He banged his hand on the table. "That is the way it is here. You tell me how else to get Indians to work except to force them, Maria Formidable, and I will try it!"

She dropped the subject, and Diego made an obvious effort

to control his temper. He folded his hands in front of him and sat silent for a moment.

"You will find it different here, Maria, of this I have no doubt. Do not judge us until you know us." He grinned then, his anger gone as quickly as it had come. "And still you must not judge us! Is it not against the teaching of the Gospels?"

"So it is, Senor," she replied quietly.

He rose. "And now, if I do not mistake, we will find Erlinda in the shed by the smokehouse, wringing her hands. Today she will give you the baptism by fire that Our Lord spoke of."

Mystified, she followed him outdoors, hurrying to keep up. Diego laughed as he came to the shed, where Erlinda was standing just as he had said.

"Oh, I cannot bear it, Diego mio," she said, wrinkling her nose.

He put a hand on her shoulder. "How grateful I am to be a man! But plunge ahead, *mi capitana,* for I have brought reinforcements."

Erlinda glanced back at Maria. "I almost hate to do this to you, so newly arrived in our kingdom, but candles must be made."

"Then you must show me, Erlinda," Maria replied.

"It is a simple task, merely smelly. You would be amazed how many tasks my servants can find to do when I need them here!"

"Then you two will manage?" Diego asked.

"Of course," said Erlinda, "and I am sure that you also have urgent business that will take you far from this smell."

Diego put his arm around his sister and kissed her. "How did you guess?" he asked, backing away quickly before she could grab him.

Cristobal passed through the yard on his way to the fields to join his brother. *"Dios bendiga a ustedes,"* he called to Erlinda and Maria.

"Y a Veustra Merced," Maria replied.

He came closer. "Oh, no, you must reserve that title for the lord of the hacienda," he said. "I see that *Vuestra Merced* has put you to work."

Something in his tone made Maria look at him. "It was my idea, Cristobal," she said. "I must learn to work."

He laughed. "Then you have come to the right place, for

you will work here. Diego has a genius for attracting free labor."

"Cristobal!" Erlinda said. "Haven't you duties of your own?" He bowed to her, a sweeping bow that made Erlinda redden and turn away. "It is enough, Cristobal," she said quietly.

He left without another word. Erlinda turned to watch him go. "Something is wrong there, Maria," she said, "and I do not know what it is." She turned back to the vats of tallow and wooden frames of candle wicks. "But let us work."

They made candles all day. Even though Maria wrapped her long hair in one of Diego's old scarves and rolled up her sleeves to the shoulder, she knew the smell would linger for days.

When they had made the common household candles until they did not think they could bear to dip another one, Old Martin lugged in his beeswax and the process began all over again, but with a difference. These candles were destined for the family chapel and *sala*. Erlinda and Maria made the sign of the cross over each candle and recited Psalms from memory as they dipped, then cooled, the cylinders of creamy beeswax.

"I wish that the Bishop of Mexico could bless these for the chapel," said Erlinda, twisting one wick to make it stand straighter. She looked at Maria. "Have you ever seen His Excellency?"

Maria tucked her hair tighter under Diego's scarf. "I have. Indeed, on my last birthday, my fifteenth, he gave me a special blessing."

"Imagine!" said Erlinda, her eyes wide with surprise.

"Yes, it was quite a birthday," Maria said. She could not hide the bitterness in her voice. "Indian runners brought snow down from the mountains for ices, Papa arranged a fireworks display and all my friends came."

"I cannot imagine, Maria," said the young widow, carrying a frame of candles to the drying rack. "But was this so bad?"

Maria wiped the sweat from her eyes and added wood to the slow-burning fire. "When Papa's fortune vanished, my friends came no more and the bishop no longer recognized us. Things can change so quickly, Erlinda."

Erlinda grasped Maria suddenly by the shoulders and pulled her close, whispering, "How well I know. How well I know!"

"Erlinda, I did not mean to cause you pain," Maria said.

Erlinda shook her head, silent until her voice was under

control again. "It is nothing, Maria." She smiled, the tears shining in her eyes but not falling. "Probably no people in this whole New World know better than we how swiftly life can change. But let us talk of other things."

They worked on through the day, Erlinda talking of mundane things, her voice light, her eyes filled with private pain.

Shadows were long across the yard before they finished the last candle. Erlinda extinguished the fire under the tallow vat and surveyed the day's work. "As much as I dread candle-making, Maria, it was not so bad this time. Only think how well we will work together next year."

The candles, white and gleaming, hung from the drying racks. Maria ran a finger gently over the nearest one. "Do you know, Erlinda," she said suddenly, "I enjoyed it."

Erlinda stared. "We spend an entire day bent over a tallow vat, we smell like farm animals, our clothes are soaked with sweat, and you tell me that you enjoyed it? Maria, the heat from the tallow has deranged you!"

"No, no, you do not understand," protested Maria, laughing. "This is the first time in my life that I have engaged in a useful task. You could not count the *varas* of lace I have made and the altar cloths I have embroidered. They were lovely but not essential."

Erlinda shook her head in amazement. "Truly, Maria, you have come to us from a different world."

"I have," Maria agreed.

As the sun sank in the west and the bell of Tesuque rang, Maria looked at Erlinda. "It is the signal to end labor in the fields. The Indians of Tesuque will return to the pueblo, and soon Diego's Indians who live here will go to their huts. We had better look to dinner."

They were joined in the kitchen by Luz and Catarina. "And what have you done this day, my sisters?" Erlinda asked.

Catarina rolled her eyes. "Oh, Erlinda, Mama made us recite catechism all day!"

"Oh, no, Catarina," contradicted Luz. "Not all day. Only until Diego rescued us."

Maria knelt by the young child. "You have a *caballero muy elegante* on your side? And what did he do?"

"He took us to the fields," said Luz. "We got to play by the river. It has been so long since we did that."

Erlinda noted the puzzlement on Maria's face. "They cannot leave the hacienda and grounds without guards to accompany. We must always be ready for Apaches." Erlinda turned to her little sister. "And where is Diego now?"

"Talking with Mama," replied the child as she set the table for dinner. "He and Cristobal quarreled awfully. Oh, Erlinda, they were shouting."

Erlinda looked at Maria, her lips set in a tight line. "Do you know what it was about?"

Catarina sat down on the end of the bench and stuffed napkins in the rings. "Diego struck one of the Indians who would not work."

Erlinda sat next to her sister, her hands tightly folded in her lap. "A year ago that would not have bothered Cristobal, but now he is changing. He was always a man divided . . . now he is torn."

She said no more. Diego came into the kitchen with his mother leaning on his arm.

"Mother will eat with us, my sisters," Diego said. "Let us begin soon."

"Do we not wait for Cristobal?" Erlinda rose and led her mother to the head of the table.

"No," said Diego and nothing more.

Dinner was eaten in silence. Cristobal came into the kitchen halfway through the meal, and Erlinda prepared him a bowl of meat and chilis, which he ate, sitting next to Diego. When the brothers' shoulders touched, they moved away from each other, the space between them pronounced, uncomfortable.

Diego rose first. "I will write in my journal, then we will have prayers," he said, his voice full of weariness.

Maria felt the same weariness in her bones. Her shoulders ached from bending over the tallow vats, and the little burns on her forearms from splattering wax throbbed. She wanted to sweep aside the dishes, put her head on the table, and sleep long and deeply.

Cristobal looked at her. "You are tired, Maria," he said.

She nodded.

"Do you have any other tasks this night?" The kindness in his voice took some of the ache from Maria's back.

"I think not," she replied, "but I did promise to take the kitchen scraps to the pigs."

"Come, then. I will go with you."

He carried the small bucket of scraps to the pigs. Maria walked along beside him, enjoying the fragrance of the newly turned earth in the fields beyond the *acequia*.

"Ready for the planting," Cristobal said, reading her thoughts. "Another year has turned." He poured the scraps in the trough and leaned on the fence, watching the pigs fight for them. "And what do you think of Las Invernadas after a day's work here?"

"It will do, Cristobal," she said, resting her arms on the fence. "It will do very well. There is something about this place and these people."

He grunted. "How well put," he said dryly. "You say nothing and yet much. I think that in better times you never would have come within a league of a pig sty." He sighed, turning around and leaning against the fence. "Perhaps neither of us belongs here," he said, more to himself than to Maria.

Before she could answer, the bell rang from the hacienda's interior. "Let us go to chapel, Maria," Cristobal said, offering her his arm.

She took his arm, struck by the incongruity of an evening's stroll, with a half-breed Indian, by the pig pen. As she and Erlinda well knew, times change.

Silent, they walked into the hall to the chapel at the far end, through the wide doors carved with the keys of Peter and the crowns of Castile and Aragon. La Senora knelt already at the front of the chapel, praying her private prayers. Diego knelt beside her, saying his rosary in a low voice. He glanced behind him at Cristobal's firm footsteps. There was no warmth in his eyes as he turned back to the altar.

Maria knelt beside Cristobal, too tired to pray. Cristobal pulled out his rosary. Head bowed, he whispered to Maria, "Just close your eyes. No one will know you are not praying. I do it all the time." He gazed down at the beads in his hand and crumbled them into a tight ball, his knuckles white.

Luz and Catarina, scrubbed and ready for bed in their nightgowns, came in with Erlinda, who glided silently, her eyes lowered and her hands folded in front of her. They knelt in front of the altar, crossed themselves, then sat behind Maria and Cristobal. Diego's Mexican servants filed in last, kneeling and praying on the hard-packed earth, then sitting cross-legged by the doors.

When everyone was in the chapel, Diego rose and closed the doors. He led the family and retainers in several psalms, the words memorized in a lifetime of evening prayer. His voice was pleasant to Maria's ears, soft as she had heard it first when he pulled her into his saddle on the river's flood plain. The gentleness of it was soothing and restful. Her eyes closed.

When they had finished the psalms, Diego prayed for them, a homely prayer asking for rain in this time of dryness; blessing flocks and fields; exhorting Catarina to watch her tongue; praying for the Lord to bless Old Martin with his gout, Flacca the cook with her toothache, the seamstress in childbirth, and thanking God for another day of life on the Rio del Norte.

With the same gentleness that made Maria smile, Diego asked the Lord's blessing on the Viceroy in Mexico, praying for God's bounties to fall on him as rain and asking that his decisions—particularly those pertaining to the river colony—would be wise. And if not wise, at least not harmful.

And finally, he prayed for the king of Spain, Carlos Segundo, His Most Catholic Majesty, living and ruling in a land none of them had ever seen, and probably never would, but which was home in some mystical way.

Then he was finished. He led his mother to the altar and knelt next to Maria as the household's oldest member led them all in the Rosary.

Before she began, Diego took another rosary from his pocket and handed it to Maria, closing his fingers around it. "Here," he whispered. "You may have this one."

She smiled at him, feeling at the same time Cristobal stirring restlessly on the other side of her.

Then it was over. They all rose from their knees, genuflected and filed from the chapel, pausing to kneel again and kiss Diego's hand. Cristobal knelt and kissed his brother's hand, rising quickly and leaving the chapel without a word. Diego looked after him, but said nothing.

Senora Masferrer was the last person to leave the chapel. Diego knelt in front of her, and she made the sign of the cross on his forehead.

"Mi hijo," La Senora whispered, "my son."

She said no more. Diego bowed his head, and Maria could see the burden that he shouldered, the responsibility of Las

Invernadas. She blinked back sudden tears of exhaustion, realizing how much greater was Diego's weariness than her own.

Maria said goodnight to Erlinda and went quickly to her room. She unbuttoned her dress and let it fall to the floor, leaving it to lay there in a crumpled heap. Not even bothering to pull the pins from her hair, she fell into bed and was asleep in a moment.

Father Efrain woke her, standing and smiling by her bed, then taking off his smiling head and tossing it into her lap. Maria screamed, desperate to brush the head from her lap, yet too terrified to leap from bed for fear that Carmen de Sosa's restless fingers would pat her legs as the poor woman continued her miserable search for her bloody hair.

Maria sobbed, staring into the dark room, kneeling in the middle of the bed, careful not to touch the sides. Before she could scream again, Diego threw open the door, his sword drawn, a blanket thrown around his bare shoulders.

Father Efrain sank to the floor out of sight and the head in Maria's lap rolled off the bed. She gasped and drew another breath to scream, but Diego clapped his hand over her mouth, then pulled her close to his chest, sitting on her bed and lifting her onto his lap. When he took his hand away, Maria let out a shuddering sigh and burrowed closer to him. Wordlessly he held her, his hands gentle on her back.

Finally he let her go and stood, drawing his Indian blanket around him like a toga. He lit the candle by her bed and walked slowly around the room, the candle held high.

"Nothing here, Maria chiquita," he said in his soft voice, *"ninguna cosa.* Now say your Rosary again like a good girl and go back to sleep."

She did as he said and blew out the candle. When she whimpered, reaching out for him, he sighed and sat on the floor by her bed, muttering, *"Dios mio,"* when his bare legs touched the cold ground. He leaned his head against the bed, looking back at her.

"Lie down, Maria," he said, groping for her hand in the dark and twining his fingers through hers.

Maria pulled his hand close to her, holding it tight against her stomach until her hands relaxed and she slept.

He was gone in the morning when she woke, but he had left his sword at the foot of her bed.

He was seated in the kitchen when she entered. His hands were cupping his earthenware goblet but he was staring with heavy eyes at the opposite wall. She paused, remembering her nightmare, but he turned at the sound of her footsteps and beckoned her in, patting the bench beside him. "Sit here, Maria," he said.

"Oh, I should not," she began, her face fiery red. "I have to start on the bread."

He reached out and pulled her down beside him, looking away from her embarrassment as he spoke to her. "Do not let last night trouble you, Maria, I beg. We all of us have our ghosts."

"Even you?"

Without a word he took her hand and kissed it. "Oh, Maria, even I."

He released her hand and stood. "But I have an idea. Suppose you sleep with Luz and Catarina? Would that make it better?" She nodded. "Then I will see that your bed is moved into their room this morning."

"Gracias, Senor," she said.

"No hay de que, Maria," he replied, getting up and putting on his hat. "But do remember this. I will always be there if you need me." He paused at the door. "I forgot to tell you last night. An old friend of yours will be coming here today."

"Quien es?" she asked. "I know no one here."

"Emiliano my saintmaker will be saddened to hear that you do not remember him," Diego replied, opening the door. "He remembers you."

"What is he coming for?"

"You shall see."

Maria was shaping the last loaves of bread into round balls when Emiliano came. She watched him walk down the path from the footbridge, hurrying in that same loping gait she remembered from the night on the road. He carried a leather sack on his back this time.

"Good morning, Old One," she said, cutting a sign of the cross on the loaf before her.

"And good morning to you, Senorita," he said. "Help me with this."

She put the bread in the oven and helped him take the sack off his back.

"Look in it," he said as she stood there.

The bag was full of smaller sacks of color such as she had seen in his *santero* workshop. She put them on the table as he sat there.

"That is good, my child," he said. "I tell Diego that I am too old for this, but he insists that there is no one else yet to paint his walls, and besides, I owe him the tribute. A persuasive young man, Maria," he said. "Don't listen to him."

She laughed. "I understand now. It was for you that the walls were whitewashed not long ago?"

"Of course. Where do we begin?"

They began with a serious consultation with Erlinda, who chose the colors that would decorate each room this year. With a grunt of assent, Emiliano set to work, mixing his colors in wooden troughs and readying his brushes. Maria watched him from the doorway, drawn to his splash of colors as she had been drawn to his painted saints. The *sala* walls would be red this year, the color to be painted from the floor up to a height of two feet. The bands of color would prevent the glittering gypsum-washed walls from showing everyday soil too soon.

Emiliano mixed the red to the shade of fresh blood, a fitting contrast to the dark furniture brought from Spain in years past, the white walls, and the Indian blankets covering the low adobe outcroppings built into the unbroken wall facing patio windows.

Emiliano turned around, his hands still busy with the paints. "Do you stand there all day or do I get some help?" he demanded.

"I would like to help," she offered, feeling shy in the presence of this saintmaker, this artist. "What would you have me do?"

"Take a brush and paint," he said, holding out a knotted bunch of yucca fibers.

She took it. "How do you know I will do well?"

He squatted on his heels, facing the wall. "I remember how you looked at my *santos* when I brought you to Tesuque. You seem to be one who is interested." He paused, searching her face. "Am I right?"

She nodded and dipped the brush in the red paint, red the color of a flowing wound, a beating heart. She applied the color in long, flowing strokes under the direction of the saintmaker.

"Besides," he continued, after the silence of nearly an hour. "The master said you would be inclined to this work."

She smiled but said nothing as she silently blessed Diego Masferrer and brushed on the beautiful paint, watching it soak into the skin of the adobe. Together they painted the lower portions of each room's walls, some blue like the kitchen, others the yellow of the sun, some the redbrown of the earth itself.

After an even more serious consultation with Luz and Catarina, and after considerable coaxing of Erlinda, Maria painted the girls' bedroom the rich red of the *sala,* reserved for important persons. And when the red was waist-high on the walls, Maria bordered the color with a rim of design she had noticed on a Pueblo cooking pot.

"Oh, Maria, no one else has such a design," said Catarina, almost reaching out in her delight to touch the wet wall.

Luz pulled Diego away from the noonday meal and dragged him down the hall to the room. With mock seriousness that made the little ones giggle, he flourished his napkin across his mouth and stalked around the room, surveying the design from every corner. He grabbed Luz suddenly and picked her up.

"I like it, *hermana mia,"* he declared, nuzzling her with his beard until she shrieked. "But who do you think you are, children of our king himself, that you should have so noble a room?"

"We are Masferrers," said Luz proudly when he set her down.

"And that," he said, ruffling her hair, "is infinitely better."

Maria watched the two of them, a lump rising in her throat. To be part of such a family, of such a pride rooted deep in love.

"It will do," agreed Erlinda, who had heard Luz's laughter and stood in the doorway. "Just as long as you do not become too grand for us, small ones."

"Oh, Erlinda!" exclaimed Catarina, "it is only a decoration! Maria told me we are special." She smiled at Maria.

Diego spoke up, helping Maria to her feet and taking the brush from her hand. "Next year you will do this in the *sala,* too."

The other bedrooms would wait until tomorrow. Although her knees ached from so much time spent on them, inching along the floor, Maria was sorry to see Emiliano cord up his fascinating bag of colors. He had said little to her during the painting, but she knew he was not displeased with her work.

"Well, Maria, you are a painter," he admitted as he shouldered his leather sack and prepared for the walk to Tesuque in the late afternoon. "But are you an artist?"

"I do not know," she said.

"Return with me to Tesuque," he asked, "and we could see this evening."

Maria looked at Erlinda, but the widow shook her head. "Not this evening, Emiliano. My mother has need of Maria."

"Very well. Pry Diego away from this place sometime and have him walk with you," Emiliano told Maria. "I would like to talk to him, too."

"I will see to it," said Erlinda as he left. She turned to Maria. "Mama told me last night that she wished you to visit her this day. Come along."

Erlinda led the way down the hall, stopping to knock on the blue door.

"Come in and God's blessings on you," said the voice within. Erlinda opened the door for Maria but did not enter herself.

The room was dim and cool, smelling strongly of candles. Maria hesitated, then went to the small woman sitting in the chair by the bed.

"Ah, Maria, wait, wait," La Senora said. "You did not pause before Our Lady of Remedios. Go back and do as you should to our colony's patroness."

Maria returned to the wooden figure by the door. It was a *bulto*, a statue fashioned by Emiliano, crudely carved, with arms held stiffly in place by gypsum-covered cloth hinges. Maria knelt in front of the statue, noting with appreciation that the saintmaker had copied the face of La Senora on the *bulto*, the deepset unseeing eyes, the hair closely curled, an imitation of tight ringlets. The statue's body was short and compact, possessing none of the grace of a Spanish madonna, but overflowing with endurance and generosity.

Maria prayed what was in her heart at the moment, and then rose and seated herself on the stool by La Senora.

"If you look here on the table by my bed, you will see the library of Las Invernadas," said La Senora, a slight smile playing around her mouth.

Maria picked up one volume, a grim collection of the lives of the saints that she remembered from her father's library. There was an ecclesiastical history of Rome, a Latin Bible, and nothing more.

"If you can find the time, you are always welcome here to read. I cannot say that the books will always keep us awake, but surely they will do us no harm."

"Do you wish me to read now?" Maria asked.

"Yes, but not these. There is another book. Go fetch it from Diego's room. I believe he keeps it by his bed."

"In his room?" Maria asked. "I could not go in there."

"Of course you can, my child. He is never there during the day, but if you are timid, knock."

Maria left La Senora and went down the hall to Diego's bedroom, pausing to knock before entering. His room was stark with a crucifix at the head of the narrow bed, an unpainted table and stool, a clothes chest, and a pair of boots in the corner.

As spare as it was, and totally unremarkable, the room was filled with Diego's presence. It may have been the lingering smell of well-worn leather, or the scent of sage from the clothing chest. Maria felt her timidity replaced by a rush of feeling.

She took the journal off the table, pausing to straighten the blanket and pillow on the bed, smoothing out imaginary wrinkles.

She returned to La Senora, pausing this time for a small curtsy in front of the Madonna before seating herself on the stool.

"This journal is our pleasure," said La Senora, reaching out to touch the worn leather cover. "If you were to turn to the very front, you would read what Tomas said on the occasion of our marriage more than twenty years ago. And on to the record of crops, of failures, of fires, of raids, of sparrows found homeless in corn rows, of loose teeth and new teeth. It is all here. A record of our lives."

La Senora leaned back in her chair, her hands resting in her lap. "Everyone has favorite entries. When he has time in the winter, Diego likes to gather us all in the *sala*, sit the girls on his lap and read until the candles gutter out." She chuckled. "Luz likes the time Catarina made mud pies in the *sala*. Catarina enjoys reading about her brother Francisco's departure for Mexico City, when he cried because he had to go, and Diego cried because he could not go!" She paused, remembering, then touched Maria's knee. "Such a day that was! I think Catarina likes to know that Diego can cry, too." She leaned forward. "But now, I would have you turn to December 18, 1661," she said.

Maria turned to the year, leaning forward in the shadowy room to decipher the spidery handwriting of Diego's father. She read slowly, her fingers following the words. "'December 18, 1661. My son Cristobal was born today. I will call him my son, for he is. All the confession and penance cannot change the fact. He is strong and healthy and seems destined to live.'"

Maria looked up. La Senora's expression was inscrutable. "Why did you have me read this?" she asked.

"I feel you should know something of Cristobal, my child. And lately, he has been on my mind, for reasons I cannot explain even to myself. But what was I saying? Yes. Cristobal was born about six months after Diego, the son of my husband Tomas and my Tewa maid. No, no, not the maid I have now, but another. Tomas never made any pretense about the birth, although I knew that he could have and I never would have been the wiser. And I had not the heart to blame him. What good would that have done?"

"Cristobal was raised here, then?"

"Yes. At Tesuque and here. Cristobal's mother died when he was three, and he was raised then with my own children. My husband loved him. And there has always been a closeness between Diego and Cristobal. But lately I wonder."

She looked at Maria suddenly. "Is this so? I sense a restless spirit in Cristobal lately."

"I cannot say, my lady," said Maria, choosing her words with care. "At times Cristobal looks at Diego in such a strange manner, and at others they are laughing and talking." She stopped. "I do not know what I am saying. I have been here only a few days, and I do not know anyone well yet."

La Senora stood. "Close the book, Maria. We will read in it again later. After you have returned it, come back and help me to the patio. I set Luz and Catarina to working their samplers." She laughed, and her sudden laughter reminded Maria of Diego. "They are vexed that I can feel their work and pronounce it a disaster!"

Maria returned the book to Diego's room. She set it on the table, then opened it to one of the last entries. Diego's handwriting was sprawling and large compared to his father's meticulous script. She ran her finger down the page. There it was. "Maria arrived at Las Invernadas. I wonder what will come of this."

That was all. She closed the book.

Cristobal

he night had been a restless one. Maria woke in the spring dawn with the sheets twisted around her and the pillow on the floor. Her head throbbed, and there were tears dried on her face. Diego was not in the room, sitting on the floor by her bed or resting in the window alcove, so she must not have cried out. She sat up slowly, pained by the beating against her temples, but grateful that she had not roused Diego Masferrer from sleep this time.

The smell of smoke was in the room. She sniffed the air like an animal, fighting down the urge to scream, to leap up and run.

The window alcove opened onto the hall. Carefully she got out of bed and peered through the opening. The patio was cool and still in the early light. Reflecting against its walls was fire, distant, faded fire. Maria hurried into the hall. She heard a sound behind her and whirled, gasping in fright as a white-robed figure glided toward her. "Carmen?" her voice quavered.

But this figure was tall and fair. Maria reached out for her. "Erlinda?" she pleaded.

79

Erlinda let go of Maria only long enough to brush her hand across the girl's face. "Oh, Maria, why are there tears?"

"I smelled smoke . . ."

". . . and you were afraid?" finished Erlinda, leading Maria toward the kitchen.

"Before God, I was. I am," Maria replied, her voice low. "You cannot know."

There was a catch in Erlinda's voice when she spoke. "But I can, Maria. I know what it is to fear." She hesitated, then went on. "I, too, know what it is to lose everything."

She led Maria to the back doorway of the kitchen. The bolts were already thrown open and the door stood ajar, letting in the cold of early spring. Erlinda released Maria and closed the door, murmuring, "Men are so thoughtless sometimes," under her breath. She opened the shutters and they looked out.

The ditches were alive with fire. Lines of fire marched around the fields and orchard. Maria drew back in surprise, and Erlinda's arm went around her again.

"Do not fear," said Erlinda, her own voice calm and steady again. "It is the day of San Isidro, the patron of our farms. Have you lost track of time? Here in the river colony we burn weeds out of the irrigation ditches before sunrise on this day. It is a homely task, no more. When the men are through, they will turn the water into the *acequias* again."

Maria sat on the bench by the table, her eyes still drawn to the flames outside. "Will there ever come a time when something like this will not remind me of the caravan massacre?" she asked softly.

She had never spoken of the massacre to any of them, and she said nothing more, but Erlinda sat quickly beside her on the bench, her eyes wide with understanding.

"You will never forget it," she said, and even though her words were hard, there was something in the saying of them that calmed Maria's fears. "It will be there all your life. Some things are never to be forgotten." Her voice was distant, her mind on other things. "And perhaps they should not be."

Maria watched as the flickering lights played across Erlinda's face, touching it here and there, exposing pain greater than her own. Erlinda smiled faintly, but the bleakness in her eyes wrenched Maria's heart.

"I shall never forget Marco's death. It will always be with

me, even as your caravan will always march across your mind. But it is what we make of our experiences that matters." She sighed. "Or so Diego tells me."

They sat together in silence as the ditches burned and the sun rose to compete with the fires on the land. When the flames died down and the ditches became nothing more than black ribbons circling the fields, Cristobal and Diego came in, dirty and smelling of burned grass.

Erlinda and Maria sat close together. Diego looked at them as Cristobal crossed to the water barrel to dip a cup of water. "Is all well here?" he asked quietly, his words not so much disturbing the peace as adding to it.

"Oh, yes, Diego mio, we are well," said Erlinda, her arm around Maria in a protective gesture.

Diego went to the barrel, leaning against it next to Cristobal. "It is finished for another year, Erlinda," he said. "One less thing to do."

"Does the water flow in the *acequia* again, my brother?" Erlinda asked.

"It does. But there is not so much of it as last year, or the year before," he replied, accepting the cup of water from Cristobal. He held up the cup, the hard lines around his mouth etching deeper. "We must be sparing of it. The rains do not come."

"Then you have only to pray harder, Diego," said Cristobal.

Diego looked at him but said nothing. Maria glanced at Cristobal, who was smiling at some special amusement of his own.

"We have had so little rain in the last four years, Maria," Diego explained, "but we will endure."

"Indeed," remarked Cristobal. "Nothing kills Spaniards." He laughed. "Perhaps, I, too, will live forever. Or at least half of me will—the Spanish half."

Diego left the kitchen without saying anything. Cristobal watched him go, his smile gone as quickly as it had come, then followed his brother outside.

"Why does he do that?" Maria asked Erlinda. She blushed. "I know all this is none of my business, but why does Cristobal bait Diego like that?"

"I wish I knew," said Erlinda. "Cristobal has changed lately. He spends much of his time in Tesuque. When he returns, he is moody and restless. He takes particular delight in goading Diego." Erlinda rose. "I do not pretend to understand it. But there is much to do. Let us rouse my sleeping sisters and get on with this day of San Isidro."

After breakfast and prayers, Diego told Maria to follow him to the cornfield, where the Indians, his Indians, worked. "Ordinarily, you would not be needed here, Maria, but today I must use the older sons and fathers to help me plant the beans. I want you to supervise the little ones as they weed the small corn."

The children were already in the field. They stood silent between the rows, small brown statues watching Diego Masferrer approach. The only movement was the wind ruffling their long black hair. Maria smiled at them, but their eyes were on Diego.

"This is Maria," he said, speaking slowly to them in Spanish, taking her by the arm. "She will see that you weed the rows. Let there be no laggards, and I will give you bread to take to your mothers in Tesuque." He repeated himself in Tewa, and the children bent quickly to their work.

"It is well," he said to Maria. "Just watch them and make sure they do not skip a row by mistake. I will be in the field beyond."

He left her then, walking north to the distant field where the Indians waited to plant beans. Maria turned back to the children, who weeded diligently, their fingers moving quickly through small shoots of corn. They observed her with darting glances, but did not stop.

One of the young girls carried a baby on her back, probably a younger sister or brother. She was agile and worked steadily, but began to lag behind the others. Maria went to her. "Here, let me take the baby. If we put it down here at the end of the row, you can keep up with the others. I promise to watch."

She repeated herself, wishing she could speak Tewa like Diego. After a moment's hesitation, the girl straightened and unwound the bands that strapped the sleeping child to her back. Maria took the sleeping baby and carried her to the end of the row. There she removed her own shawl and wrapped the child in it. She smoothed the black straight hair, so soft to the fingers, and wound the shawl more securely to protect the baby from the breeze. Pleased that the child slept safely on the soft earth,

Maria returned to watch the Indian children as they traveled down the rows. She followed them, listening to their low-voiced singing, admiring the shine of the sun on their hair so dark that it looked like the blue of midnight.

The freshly turned earth was warm on her bare feet. She laughed to herself as she remembered the scolding from Mama, when as a child she strayed far enough from watchful eyes to remove her shoes and prance around the family patio. Times change, Mama.

The insistent ringing of a bell disturbed her. The children stopped their work suddenly and stood straight, their faces watchful. She heard the bell again. It was the church bell from Tesuque, ringing with an unaccustomed clamor.

One of the guards fired his gun from the roof of the hacienda. Maria ran to the children, who were clustered together, their eyes big with fear.

"What is it?" she asked, alarmed by the firing of the weapon.

A second report was heard from the roof. She turned toward the bean field. Diego and his Indians were running toward them at a crouch, carrying their hoes. One of the children tugged at her dress. "It is Apaches," he said in Spanish.

Maria clutched him by the shoulders, then turned him loose, pointing him toward the hacienda. "Then run, all of you!" she cried, shepherding them ahead of her out of the cornfield.

As the men ran from the bean field, some of them picked up the smaller children, throwing them over their shoulders like sacks of grain. Diego took her hand and pulled her along with him. Cristobal came toward them on horseback. Diego picked up Maria and tossed her to Cristobal, who grabbed her around the waist without a word and raced toward the hacienda. He dumped her unceremoniously on the ground by the back gates and stood sentry as the children and men streamed in.

Maria ran into the haven of the enclosure, looking around to make sure the Indian children were inside. They stood with their older brothers and sisters, silent and watchful. Maria looked back across the fields. She could see distant figures by this time. Someone had set fire to a small shed just beyond the bean field, and smoke was beginning to curl over the roof.

The gates were closing when one of the young girls shrieked and ran toward them. With a sickening weight in her stomach, Maria remembered the baby she had put to rest at the end of

83

the corn row. Without thinking, she wrenched a hoe from one of the men and ran out the gate.

The bells of Tesuque were silent now. Diego ran out of the gate after her, grabbing the back of her dress and ripping off the apron she wore as she tugged against his hands.

"The baby!" she gasped. "I left an Indian baby in the cornfield!"

"You must come back inside, Maria!" Diego shouted, trying to grab her again as she darted out of his reach. "Leave the child!"

He lunged at her and she turned and struck him with the hoe. The wood cracked against his temple, and she sobbed out loud, but she grabbed up her skirts and ran into the field, the hoe tight in her hand. Some of the Apaches were already in the bean field, running toward the hacienda. She ran toward them, trying not to think how close they were as she looked around for the sleeping child. Panic washed over her as she heard the gates slam shut behind her, the heavy wooden beams dragged through the iron bars. She ran on, hunting for the brown baby lying on the brown earth.

There were more guards on the roof now, and they fired steadily just over her head. The Apaches crouched low in the bean field, held there by the firing. They yipped and howled like coyotes as Maria crouched on the edge of the cornfield, her knuckles white on the splintered hoe handle, searching for the baby.

Then she saw it, crawling along a corn row. The baby saw her and sat up, holding up its arms, wailing in fear. With a cry of her own, Maria ran across the rows and scooped up the baby, which clutched her neck in a stranglehold that left her breathless and dizzy.

An Apache ran toward her, his face split by a fierce grin, his hands describing obscene gestures in the smoke-filled air. Tearing the child from her neck and setting it back on the ground, Maria lunged forward with the hoe. The sharp blade bit deep into the Indian's arm, slicing it to the bone. He fell to his knees and she picked the baby up, turned and fled.

The Indians followed her, their shrieks of rage competing with the cries of the baby in her arms. The hoe was cumbersome so she dropped it and ran faster. The guards on the roof continued their steady firing. The balls whistled close over her head as she clutched the baby to her and ran for their lives.

The gates were closed, but as she pounded toward them, her breath coming in painful gasps, she heard the rapid grind of wood on metal and saw them open. Cristobal rode out, bent low over his horse, his hand tight around a long Spanish lance.

Maria ran toward him, but tripped on the hem of her long dress and sprawled in the dust. The child fell from her arms, but she scrambled toward it and fought to her feet, the child in her arms again. The baby clung to her as she staggered toward the man on horseback.

"Keep going, Maria!" hissed Cristobal. "I will keep them here."

The blood from her bruised knees ran down her legs, the child's tiny fist clung to her neck. With safety in sight, she dared to glance back. Cristobal stood between her and the Apaches, his face fierce in its composure, his lance ready. Enraged at being cheated of a woman and child, the Indians charged against the bullets that kicked up dust and tore at their flesh.

Maria ran through the gates, tripped over her dress again, and fell in the dirt. The baby's sister ran forward and grabbed the child, crying and hugging the little one to her. Maria laid her head on the earth, her eyes closed, her sides heaving. She heard Cristobal ride in and dismount, the gates being closed and barred again.

Diego jerked her to her feet. "How dare you do such a thing!" he shouted at her. The side of his face bled from the blow she had struck him with the hoe. He wiped the blood on his shoulder and shook her.

He was so angry that his skin turned sallow under his tan and his breath came in short gasps. Maria had never seen such anger before, but some curious emotion deep within her compelled her to reach out and touch his face where she had hit him.

He grabbed her hand in a painful grip and forced it against his head, then pulled it away, wet with his blood. Savagely he wiped her hand across the front of her dress.

"There! If you ever do such a thing again, the blood of Las Invernadas will be on you!"

Cristobal thrust himself between them. "It was only an Indian child, is that it?" he screamed at Diego, their faces only inches apart.

"You know that is not so, Cristobal," said Diego, his anger cooling as his brother's mounted higher. "The rule is the same for all of us. When the Indians attack, no one goes outside. Not for anything."

In a sudden motion, Cristobal snapped the bloody lance he had been carrying in half. "Could you have watched the Apaches tear apart that baby and done nothing?"

"Yes."

Diego motioned to the guards on the roof. Several of them climbed down the ladder at the corner of the house, while the rest knelt to reload, remaining where they were. One of them called to Diego below. *"Mira,* my lord, they return to Tesuque. They run."

Diego passed his hand in front of his eyes, looking older than the oldest man in the stronghold. He bowed his head and looked at his feet. "None of you, no, not even you Cristobal, understand what it is to be responsible for Las Invernadas. The lives of all here and at Tesuque, too, are in my hands. Maria," he said suddenly, looking directly at her. "The first rule of this place is that no one leaves the enclosure once they have been summoned in by the bells. You knew that, for I told you earlier. It is the first rule and the hardest sometimes. Especially today." He looked around him. "If the Apaches had breached our walls, we would all be dead. I have seen it before. Where is Erlinda? *Que barbaridad!* It is too much, too soon for her. Ay!"

Cristobal dropped the broken lance at Diego's feet, but the challenge was gone from his eyes, replaced by confusion. Diego smiled faintly, the smile barely touching his lips and eluding his eyes. "Perhaps Maria's own particular saint was with her." He turned on his heel and motioned his *vaqueros* toward the corral, where the horses milled restlessly, anxious with the smell of battle.

The baby had stopped crying. The Indian girl held the child tight to her, rocking back and forth as she knelt on the ground with the baby. Maria walked slowly toward the girl and child, rested the back of her hand on the baby's cheek, patted the young girl, and started toward the house.

The kitchen was filled with chattering Mexican women who fell silent when she entered the room. Her eyes cast down,

Maria passed them without a word and went into the hall. She took a deep breath of the piñon wood mingled with sage, closing her eyes in the comfort of familiar things. Her elbows and knees ached where she had scraped them. The skin was raw and wet through the fabric of her dress, but she had nothing to change into.

She saw the chapel doors open at the far end of the hall. Diego wore the key to the door on the sash around his waist, but another key hung high in one corner of the kitchen. Someone must have opened the doors. She peered into the cool darkness. As her eyes became accustomed to the gloom, she saw Erlinda sitting on the bench, her head tilted slightly upward as she contemplated Christ in his agony on the cross above the altar.

Maria came silently down the aisle toward her. "Erlinda?" she asked. *"Qué pasa?"*

Erlinda stared steadily ahead, but she grasped Maria's hand. "What you did, you must never do again. You must heed Diego." She hung onto Maria's hand as though it were a rope thrown to a drowning man.

"Erlinda, what is it?"

Erlinda transferred her gaze from the cross to a space past Maria's head. "I have never spoken of this. All know except you, so there was never any need. But . . . but. . . ." Her lips trembled. "I am compelled to speak of it finally. I must! You must understand!" She gasped and bent double, as if in physical pain.

Maria put her arm around Erlinda. "My dear, my dear," she whispered, "what is it?"

"That was how Marco died," she whispered. "Caught in the fields. He went back to pick up something I had dropped. I cannot now even recall what it was. I ran, because ever since we were small children here, Papa taught us thus. But Marco, growing up in Santa Fe, had not been trained so."

Her voice rose and fell as if the pain of remembering ebbed and flowed like waves on a shore. *"Dios,* Maria, the Apaches took him. There was nothing he—or we—could do. They stripped him and roasted him over a small fire while we watched from the walls."

"Dios mio, Erlinda," said Maria, her own face white.

"When I saw you run out of the gate. . . ." Erlinda's voice

faltered, and she clung to Maria's hand. "I could think only of Marco. I am glad you were able to save the baby, but swear to me by the saints, Maria, that you will not disobey Diego again! Swear it!"

Her voice rose, then she collapsed against Maria, the sobs wrenched from her very heart, choked and terrible.

Maria's instincts told her to cradle Erlinda in her arms and let her cry. She crooned to the young widow and rocked with her, as the Indian girl had caressed her baby in the kitchen gardens. She could think of nothing to say, and so was silent.

Erlinda cried until the front of Maria's dress was soaked through, the tears mingling with Diego's blood and turning the rough fabric a tragic pink that soaked through to her skin, then deeper into her body. *Dios,* she thought, her arms weary with the burden of Erlinda. Is it possible to cry so many tears?

She heard footsteps behind her and turned to see Diego in the chapel doorway. He wore an old-fashioned armor breastplate of the last century that was Moorish in design. He walked down the aisle and knelt by her side.

Diego crossed himself, bowed his head in prayer, crossed himself again, then rose and rested his gloved hand on Maria's shoulder. "We go to Tesuque to see what we can do for the Pueblos. There are guards sufficient here." He leaned over and spoke in her ear, his beard touching the side of her face. "She has never cried about Marco. It will be better now." He sighed and patted her shoulder. "When I return, Maria, we will talk."

She looked at him then, noticing with shame that his eye was blackening from the blow she had struck his head. "Oh, Senor, forgive me!" she whispered.

"Later, Maria chiquita. I must go now."

"Then go with God," she said softly, and kissed his hand formally as it lay on her shoulder.

"And thou, likewise," he said. He reached over and touched Erlinda's head, giving her a silent benediction, then hurried from the chapel, his spurs scraping on the hard-packed earth.

Soon, through the thickness of the walls and Erlinda's sobs, Maria heard mounted horsemen leaving Las Invernadas, riding east toward the Pueblo village.

Erlinda cried until there were no tears left. Exhausted, she rested her head on Maria's lap, her eyes closed. The morning was gone and the afternoon deep when she stirred again.

Erlinda sat up. Her eyes were red but her voice peaceful. "And so I have kept you prisoner all day, Maria," she said in apology, a rosy blush rising to stain her dead-white cheeks.

"It is nothing, Erlinda," Maria said.

"How kind you are," the widow replied, rising only to kneel at the altar, then rise again. "There is much to do, but I have not the energy for anything. Can you see to my duties this evening, Maria?"

"I will, with pleasure."

"Then take my arm, and let us leave here."

The two young women joined arms and left the room, Maria pausing to turn the key still in the lock. The gates were still barred, the outside windows of the hacienda shuttered. Catarina and Luz sat silent on the patio with La Senora, sewing their samplers. Luz dropped her embroidery and ran to Erlinda, who hugged her, then sat next to her mother. La Senora felt her daughter's face, touching the eyelids puffy from tears. "It is the will of God, Erlinda."

"I know that now, Mama," the widow said. She folded her hands in her lap and raised her eyes to Maria's. There was peace in Erlinda's eyes now, where before there had only been pain. Maria thought of her parents, dead of cholera, of the mission supply caravan, of her sister's rejection, of the Masferrer brothers and their short, sharp confrontation. The will of God. How did anybody know what that was anymore?

Maria left the ladies of Las Invernadas on the patio and withdrew to the kitchen, where she supervised the preparations for the evening meal. It was eaten quietly and quickly, everyone's hearts and minds on the men. Prayers in the chapel were also subdued. A pragmatic people, the Spaniards saw no reason to thank the Lord until all were returned to the safety of the hacienda. La Senora led them in the Rosary, but there was no longer prayer. That was Diego's domain, and his absence was felt by all. Maria wondered how one man, a man so young, could inspire so much love and trust.

When La Senora was through, the Masferrer women and the Mexican Christian Indians of the household remained in the chapel for several moments of silent meditation. Maria had no claim on any of the absent men, but she lifted her heart with the women who waited and prayed for them all.

The hacienda settled itself for slumber, the guards for a long vigil. All was shuttered and barred except the kitchen door. Maria went to sleep, listening to the guards pacing slowly back and forth on the roof over her head, speaking to one another in low tones, ever moving, ever watchful.

Long after the hacienda was dark, Maria heard men's voices in the kitchen. The door was closed and bolted from inside. Diego was home. After a moment, the guards on the roof resumed their steady watch.

Maria sat up carefully in bed, moving slowly so as not to disturb Luz, who had crept into her bed. She put Erlinda's long robe over her chemise and went down the hall on bare feet to the kitchen, where the light of one lantern still shone.

Diego straddled one of the benches, his head on the table, his eyes closed, as if trying to get up the energy to pick up the bread and cheese. At the sound of her footsteps, he opened his eyes and sat up.

"I didn't mean to disturb you, Senor."

Diego took off the red scarf that covered his hair and wiped his face with it. "Do not fear," he said. "You are never a disturbance, Maria. Come sit. We need to talk."

She pitied his exhaustion and was suddenly aware of how alone they were. "Perhaps we should talk in the morning, Senor."

"No, no," he insisted. "I have discovered that tomorrow never comes. I will be too busy then, and so will you. Let it be now, Maria chiquita."

He was a long way from the angry man of that morning. As the lantern light played over his face, Maria recognized that old look that the river colony etched on young men's faces. How peculiar, she thought as she watched him. At one moment he is harder than diamonds. At another, he is even more vulnerable than I am.

She sat next to him. His curly hair was damp with sweat and she wanted to touch it, to trace the tousled curls from top to root, the intricacy of the curls fascinated her. But she sat motionless, her hands in her lap as she had been taught from infancy.

"What of Tesuque, my lord?" she asked.

He broke the cheese into bits while he spoke, but did not eat them. "The Apaches ran off some sheep, stole some women and children, killed an old man at his loom. We beat them back and chased them quite a distance, then they split up into thirty different directions. It was the usual pattern." He covered her hand with his. "We did come upon the Indian you hoed. He bled to death down by the river."

They were both silent then. Diego looked wearily at the bread, but made no motion to reach for it.

"Where is Cristobal?" she asked finally.

Diego would not look at her. "He is staying in Tesuque. He is angry with me, so it is just as well."

Maria stared at her hands and said in a low voice, "I want to apologize for this morning, my lord."

He leaned toward her again. "I wish I could explain, Maria," he began.

"You needn't," she said quickly. "I was wrong." She made an impatient gesture with her hands. "And yet I wasn't. I must tell you why I went back to the field."

She got up and poured Diego a cup of wine from the cooler. He dipped the bread in it and ate, his eyes on her.

"You do not understand, Senor. It was a matter of honor. I told the Indian girl that I would watch the baby. My honor dictated that I return, no matter what the consequences."

"Well, then, Maria chiquita," he said, drinking the wine, "we should not be at odds with each other. I could never accuse you of being less worthy of honor than I."

"No, you could not, Senor," she replied proudly. "In this respect, we are no different."

"Indeed we are not," he murmured, smiling, "Maria *La Formidable*. I will never again have the audacity to think a woman's honor to be of less value than a man's." His hand went to his head. "But do promise me this. If you must strike me, do not use a hoe again."

Maria blushed a deep red and did not look at Diego, but he went on, his tone changing. "I wish I could make Cristobal understand. He thinks I am a heartless one—an ogre who would sacrifice an Indian child. He cannot see that I must think of everyone here."

Diego was sitting so close that she could smell his sweat, mingled with the sage he stored his clothing in. He was seeking consolation from her. On impulse she leaned against his shoulder and rested her head on his arm.

He sighed. "I am glad you saved the baby. But such actions

could lead to fearful consequences for all of us. We are lucky the Apaches were no closer."

He closed his eyes in weariness. They sat close together for another minute, then Maria stirred and he opened his eyes. "I am sorry, Maria," he said, rising and brushing the dust off his leather doublet. "See now, your hair is dirty."

"It is nothing," she said, pulling Erlinda's robe tighter around her. "But I should be going to bed."

"We both should."

Diego checked the bolts on the kitchen door, then blew out the lamp. He led her to the door and walked with her into the dark hall. She could not see, but she heard him brush his hand along one of the saints painted on leather, hanging on the wall.

"Things will be better, Senor," she said, touching his arm.

"No, I fear they will not," he answered. "I cannot share your optimism." He paused at her doorway. "But I like to hear it anyway. Goodnight, Maria."

"Goodnight, Senor," she said and went quickly inside, shy again.

Tesuque

In the morning, Maria hoped to see Cristobal back in his proper place in the kitchen, laughing with Diego as the brothers sat at the table, planning out their day. She dressed quickly, after taking a look at her skinned knees and elbows. When her dress was buttoned, she shook Luz awake, watching in amusement as she twisted and turned like a puppy, then settled back into sleep. She patted her again and made sure the child's eyes were open before she went into the hall.

As she passed Erlinda's door, Maria heard humming inside. She knocked. Erlinda opened the door, her pillow in her hand. *"Dios bendiga,* Erlinda," she said, noting that Erlinda's eyes were clear, her smile genuine.

"And God's blessing on you, Maria," she replied, turning back to making her bed.

Diego was alone in the kitchen, leaning on the sink looking out the window he had unbarred and opened. Cristobal was nowhere in sight.

"Another day, Maria," he said without turning around. "Perhaps this will be a better one."

93

"Dios bendiga, Vuestra Merced," she said formally, her eyes downcast. "How did you know it was I?"

He turned around with a smile. "Your step is so light. It's almost as though you skim the hall as you come into the kitchen. Erlinda plods in the morning, Mama is naturally more hesitant, and Luz and Catarina usually stomp. Haven't you noticed?"

"No," she said. "You're more observant than I."

"Only about some things. And Cristobal, I can never even hear him when he comes."

"He is not back yet?"

"No. And I don't expect him. I fear the burden of work is mine for the next few days, or at least until he is through being angry with me."

He picked up his scarf from the table, folded it into a triangle and wound it around his head, tying it tight in the back. Then he settled his flat black hat on his head and pulled the string under his chin, tipping his hat so the crown of it did not rest on his cut.

"Will you not have breakfast?" she asked.

"I haven't time. There is too much to do. We still have yesterday's beans to plant. And my shepherd came in early to tell me that the ewes have started lambing. Spring has come with a vengeance."

He smiled, watching her as she checked the level of the water barrel. "When I was young, it puzzled me that lambs were born in the spring, and Masferrers in the fall. Every one of us." He sat down to pull on his boots. "I asked Papa about that once. At first he would not say, but then he told me— quite solemnly mind you—that December is the farmer's only chance for love. In November he is finishing up the harvest and butchering the hogs, and by January he is already worrying about the spring rains." He opened the door. "I did not understand him then, of course, but I do now."

He waved at her and closed the door on her embarrassment. She watched him go down the garden path and pause by the *acequia*, looking at the water flowing in the ditch. After a moment's reflection, he turned toward the corral, calling to his *vaqueros*.

By then the Mexican cook was in the kitchen waiting for Maria to come with the corn meal so she could prepare the breakfast mush. As she hurried, Maria remembered how Mama had once, in a burst of confidentiality, told her that men were as clear as water. Mama, you did not know Diego Masferrer, she thought, measuring the corn meal into the boiling water, or Cristobal.

Breakfast and prayers were quickly over with. Luz and Catarina escaped to their play tunnel by the *acequia* before Erlinda could think of something for them to do. Maria dried the last of the dishes and turned to the widow, who was finishing her hot chocolate.

"What would you have me do today, Erlinda?" she asked.

Erlinda considered. "If you do not object to a task which I loathe, there is much mending. My brothers get more thread-bare every day. Diego has assured me that he will never get a wife if he cannot go courting in a shirt without holes. Not that he has any plans. Still, if I mend some of his clothes, his prospects might improve. Yes, the mending today."

Maria thought of Diego courting with a flash of pain. "I will do the mending. Does Diego have plans for marriage?"

"Oh, yes, as long as I keep reminding him. He promised me last week that this winter he would consider the matter. After all, he will be twenty this fall. He must find someone who strikes his fancy."

Erlinda went into the sewing room off the kitchen and Maria followed. "And we must consider you, Maria," she said, tugging the mending basket over to the chair by the window. "I hope you will not be like Diego. 'This one is too tall. I will look like her child.' Or 'This one is too homely. How can I face that every morning?' Or 'She has a moustache darker than mine,' or 'That one has no conversation. We cannot make love all the time.' And on and on." Erlinda pulled out several shirts. "He is too demanding," she sighed. "And too busy."

"Do you think I could find someone here?" Maria sat down and took the shirts from Erlinda.

"I think so," she said, looking at her with a critical eye. "You have no fortune, but you're such a pleasant person." She sighed again. "It might have to be a widower with several children half-grown. It would be easier if we were not such a poor kingdom. How I am rattling on! I haven't talked so much since . . ." She stopped, twisting her wedding ring. ". . . in a long time. Let me get the needle. We keep it locked up with the silver."

Maria sorted the shirts, holding Diego's to her face for the pleasant smell of sage. She fingered Catarina's dress, torn at the knee, and the thought of her own childhood, spent in perpetual evasion of Mama and her homilies. They've freedom to climb trees here, she thought, and play in ditches.

Erlinda returned with the needle and thimble made of silver. "Do not leave these lying around. If you need me, I will be in the chicken yard. It is time we had something besides mutton for dinner."

Maria settled in the high-backed chair and threaded the precious needle. The room was warm with the sun of early spring, the walls brilliant white. She heard the soft slap-slap of hands molding tortillas in the kitchen and the outraged squawk of the rooster as his domain was plundered. The terrors of yesterday might never have happened, except that Cristobal was not there and her scraped knees ached. She darned a patch under a torn buttonhole with dainty stitches, remembering how Cristobal had placed himself, lance ready, between her and the Apaches.

And I never even thanked him, she thought, picking up another shirt. She quickly made her way down the pile of shirts, taking extra care on a fine white linen shirt with the underarm seam ripped out. So Diego could go courting this winter. In December, she said out loud, laughing to herself as she twisted a knot in the thread, and feeling strangely sad.

A shadow moved in the doorway and she looked up. Cristobal stood leaning against the doorframe watching her. She jabbed her finger with the needle, staining the shirt.

"You startled me!" she said.

"I have been standing here for five minutes. How could I startle you?"

"Then you are too silent, Senor," she said, sucking her finger, vexed with herself for bleeding on Diego's best shirt.

Maria set the shirt aside and stood. Cristobal stepped into the room. "Come with me," he said, holding out his hand.

Maria did not take it. "Where?" she asked.

"There are people who wish to meet you. At Tesuque. Let me take you there." When she still hesitated, he took her hand. "I spoke with Diego."

She let him hold her hand. "What did you say to him?" she asked quietly.

"I did not apologize, if that's what you mean. And he did not expect me to. We both know we are right." He looked at her. "Maria, I hate to quarrel with Diego. It's almost as though I'm arguing with myself. Or at least part of myself."

He let go of her hand and looked out the window. "Erlinda triumphant!" he declared, motioning to Maria. She came to the window and he put his hand on her shoulder. "The chickens didn't have a chance. I hope Diego returns in time for dinner. He likes chicken."

"Where did he go?"

"He finished with the beans and said he was going to the north pasture where the sheep are. I asked if he needed help, but he said my hands are too big for lambing." He smiled. "It is an old joke between us. I am glad he can laugh."

Maria moved away from the window and Cristobal followed her. "Come with me. We will walk to Tesuque. My horse threw a shoe yesterday when we were chasing Apaches."

"Is it safe now?"

Cristobal shrugged. "One can never tell here. Diego has told me on more than one occasion that he is glad he does not have to worry about the Pueblo Indians." His face twisted into a peculiar smile. "We are such *good* Indians."

"Let me put away these shirts and return the needle." She folded Diego's shirts and took them to his room, where she put them in the wooden chest by his bed. She ran her hand over the altar and knelt for a brief moment on the worn stool in front of it. Then she hurried to put the needle away carefully in the silver cabinet, setting the thimble next to it.

Erlinda was in the yard, plucking chickens. "We are walking to Tesuque," Cristobal said. "I have a matter of business there that concerns Maria."

"Very well," she said, her eyes on the chicken in her lap again. "Do try to return in time for dinner."

"We will, my sister," he said, watching as she flinched.

They passed the first mile in strained silence, Maria's eyes on the ground, her whole being intensely aware of Cristobal's presence.

He cleared his throat. "I think that if you did not stare at the road, you would still know where to put your feet."

She looked up and laughed.

"That is better."

"I took the children home yesterday evening," Cristobal said, as if reading her thoughts. "Thank you for what you did, Maria. You could not leave the baby to die. Even if others could."

"Be fair," she said. "I know that for me, it was right to save the baby. But it was also right for Diego to be angry. I disobeyed him."

"Can we both be right, Maria?" he asked. "How is this possible?" He slowed down so she could keep up with him better.

"I don't know. The whole thing is confusing to me," she answered. "In your own ways, both of you are right."

He was silent as they walked together, a profound, watchful Indian silence. I do not dare pretend with this man, she thought, hurrying to keep up as he unconsciously lengthened his stride again.

When they came to the river, Cristobal scooped her up and carried her across. She knew it was useless to protest, so she tightened her arms around his neck and said nothing. He set her down on the opposite bank, pausing while she straightened her skirts around her again.

"You hardly weigh anything, Maria," he said, then was silent as they continued the walk to Tesuque.

The red brick adobe rose before them, handsome against the spring sky. The Tesuque pueblo was unlike anything Maria had ever seen. She put her hand to her heart and wished with all her mind that she could paint it. She had last seen Tesuque at night, dark and brooding. It teemed with life now on all the levels, as the homely tasks of weaving, pottery and cooking spread out before her.

"How beautiful it is," she said, stopping him with a hand on his arm.

"Yes, it is," he agreed, "just the way we see it now. Even if there are those who seek to change it." He tilted his head and surveyed her, his voice earnest. "I realize you are Spanish, but does it not strike you as strange? Although nothing about us has changed in a thousand years, and no one ever complained before, now we must pray to a white man's God, one who has not wit to decide if he is Father, Son or Holy Spirit."

"Cristobal!" Maria exclaimed, shocked enough to call him by name.

He looked as though he wanted to argue with her, but he closed his lips firmly and led her toward the nearest ladder. "Follow me," he said.

She gathered her skirts in one hand and awkwardly mounted the ladder. Cristobal pulled her up when she neared the top. "And now, you must meet a mother who has much to say to you."

He led her to the end of the terrace, past men at their looms who turned to watch as she walked by and past children who were suddenly silent at their play.

"Look out for your head," he said as he ducked inside one of the rooms.

She ducked her head too and opened her eyes wider to accustom herself to the sudden gloom. The room was small and neat, the cooking pots stacked in one corner and bedding in the other. An Indian mother sat cross-legged, nursing a baby. It was the baby she had pulled from the cornfield yesterday. She smiled at the mother, and her eyes suddenly filled with tears.

Gently the mother disengaged the baby from her breast and handed the child to the young girl sitting nearby. The woman arranged her cotton dress about her, then knelt at Maria's feet. Maria burst into tears, crying louder as Cristobal's arm went around her in a tight grip.

She turned her face into his shoulder. "Oh, tell her not to do that!" she said.

He rested his hand on her cheek for a moment, then spoke to the woman, who rose and gathered Maria into her arms. The women clung to each other, their tears mingling. The baby began to whimper and the mother released Maria, picking up the child and crooning to it. Maria wiped her eyes on the hem of her dress, smiling through her tears at Cristobal. The woman spoke to him, and he turned to Maria.

"She says to tell you of her gratitude." He wiped her face with his sleeve. "She says all she has is yours."

Maria shook her head. "I want nothing. I am only glad I was able to undo something that I caused in the first place. Tell her that."

He did. The woman motioned for them to sit. They did, and Cristobal leaned toward Maria. "She will offer you food.

Please do not accept. They have so little, and they will give it all to you."

"Oh, I could not take their food!" Maria exclaimed.

"Others do," said Cristobal. "My brother among them."

The woman was speaking again. Cristobal said, "She wants to feed you. Tell her no."

Maria shook her head, stroking the baby's head and smiling.

"She says, 'Very well,' but she has something more for you," Cristobal translated.

The woman handed the baby to the girl, rose from the floor and went to the corner by the bedding. She returned with a blanket, which she handed to Maria, bowing and then taking the baby again. Maria fingered the blanket, noting the elaborate design, the colors muted and restful in the gloom of the pueblo.

"Her husband made it. She wants you to have it as a token of her gratitude."

Maria held the blanket to her. "Tell her thank you for me."

"Tell her yourself," he replied, and had her repeat the phrase several times until she could approximate the sounds.

Maria thanked the mother who held the baby close to her. Cristobal got to his feet and helped Maria up. They stood close together in the small room as the mother began to nurse the baby again. The small sucking noises filled Maria with a contentment she had not felt since before the death of her parents. The flow of life was all around her and she marveled at the peace it brought to her soul.

"Come, Maria, let us be off," said Cristobal.

After patting the baby again, Maria ducked out of the small opening and into the sunlight. She held the blanket in front of her, smoothing it as she admired the design and texture.

"How curious," she said.

"What?"

"I came here with no possessions except my dress, and Diego burned that. And now I have something of my own, and it is Indian."

"I would call that a good sign."

They walked the length of the terrace, Cristobal stopping to speak to the Pueblos at work, touching a child, remarking on the design of a blanket on a loom, accepting a handful of pine nuts. The air was crisp and smelled of cooking and piñon wood. Maria wanted to hold out her arms and gather it all to her. Instead, she fingered the blanket folded over her arm and watched Cristobal with his people.

While Cristobal squatted by an old man making arrows, Maria remembered Emiliano *el santero* and continued toward the end of the pueblo, peering in open doorways, seeking the dancing saints on their deerskin hides.

And there they were. A saint carved of cottonwood beckoned to her from the window ledge. It could only be San Pedro, holding his keys of gold and iron, one to open the gates of heaven, the other to open the gates of hell. Maria looked inside the door.

Emiliano glanced up from his place on the floor as she peered inside. "Come in, come in," he said. "I am carving San Pedro's other arm, so do not fear that he has met with an untimely accident."

She touched the statue. "What do you call this?" she asked, walking around to view the saint from behind.

"It is a *bulto*. I have carved San Pedro for my own pleasure, but he will probably end up at Las Invernadas. Diego Masferrer is always fondest of those clear-cut saints whose purpose is straightforward. And what is your pleasure, Maria?" he asked. "San Miguel with his sword? Rafaelo and his fish?" Emiliano looked outside at the tall man kneeling by the arrowmaker. "Or perhaps San Cristobal, he who carried the Christ Child?"

She blushed. "I do not know, Emiliano." She looked at the painting of Christ on the deerhide opposite her. The mouth was open in agony, the eyes anguished at the pain of crucifixion. These people know something of suffering, she thought. Their *Cristo* did not hang bloodless on a cross. He suffered and struggled, even as they did. She turned away.

"Before you go, Senorita," said Emiliano. "Do you want to paint?"

"Not today, Emiliano."

"Come to me when your mind is more settled, Maria, and we shall see if you can look inside a human heart and paint what is there."

As she left, her eyes flickered to the agony on the cross, then back to Emiliano, who was whittling again. She went into the sunlight, turning back for a last glimpse of San Pedro.

Cristobal waited for her. "I thought I had lost you," he

remarked, following her gaze to San Pedro. "All those keys. Such a busy man is San Pedro. Almost like Diego."

"We should be on our way," Maria began, then stopped at the sound of shouting. She hurried to the edge of the terrace and looked toward the road they had traveled. A line of Indians walked slowly toward the pueblo, followed by a ranchero on horseback, cursing at them to hurry.

"Are those Indians returning from Las Invernadas?"

"No," he said briefly. "From the land of Lorenzo Nunez. We passed his place just before the river. Do you not remember?"

She nodded.

"The Pueblos from Las Invernadas will be along soon, then the Indians from the Gutierrez estancia, farther to the south and west. The men will eat, if there is anything left here to eat, then they will hurry into their own fields, to race against the sun while they and their women plant and hoe their own crops. And when the harvest comes, Senor Masferrer, Senor Nunez and Senor Gutierrez will take a share of their crop."

"But why?" Maria asked.

Cristobal shrugged. "It is the *encomienda* system. The conquered must give to the conquerors. The children are hungry and they follow you with their eyes, but still the senores come and exact their tribute."

Maria followed Cristobal down the ladder. "But I do not understand. The *encomienda* was abolished long ago in Mexico."

"But not here. We are too far away from Mexico City. The only ones who complain are the Pueblos, and they cannot write the viceroy."

They approached the Indians returning from the fields. "And there is Senor Nunez himself. I wonder what he wants. He likes young girls. And young boys, some say. When they return from his hacienda, they do not smile anymore."

"Oh, Cristobal!" Maria said, again horrified into calling him by name.

"I do not lie to you, Maria. Senor Gutierrez is a better man, but I have seen the backs of the children who do not polish Senora Gutierrez's silver to her satisfaction."

Cristobal stared at Lorenzo Nunez. "Watch him now. He will march into Father Pio's church, toss some coins in the poor box, fling himself to his knees and pray, assured that he is a benevolent man, a kind master." He turned to Maria in sudden anger. "Is your God blind, as well as witless, that he can ignore the blows on the backs of children? And are we to pray to this two-faced being? I marvel, Maria, what you Spaniards expect of us."

Maria turned pale in stunned surprise. "And what of..." Maria could not go on.

"Diego? I have prayed with him long enough to know that he is an honest man. But you will agree that we eat much better at Las Invernadas than the children do here. I have seen the young ones prowling around our dump out behind the wall."

"This is not right!" Maria said. "Let me return this blanket. I cannot take what is theirs." She made to climb the ladder again, but Cristobal stopped her.

"Keep the blanket. It will just go to Nunez or Gutierrez. We are helpless, Maria."

As they walked past the Indians, Lorenzo Nunez swiveled around in his saddle to watch Maria. Cristobal cursed under his breath. "And that is what we live with. We used to be masters of the earth, but now we are less than dust underfoot."

On the walk back to Las Invernadas, she saw nothing but the thin children with their hollow eyes and men returning discouraged from others' fields. She understood now the agony in the eyes of the *Cristo* in the saintmaker's shop. Emiliano had painted his own people.

They arrived at the hacienda just as Diego was returning. *"Hola, amigos,"* he called out. The front of his shirt was stained with the blood of birthing ewes, and the lines on his face were more pronounced than ever, but he was cheerful as he wiped down his horse Diablo and turned him loose in the pasture by the orchard.

Luz ran from the hacienda to meet Diego. He kissed her and ruffled her hair, then reached into the wriggling sack on the ground by his saddle. "Look what I have for you. A lamb to mother."

"How did it go, Diego?" Cristobal asked as Luz took the lamb carefully from her brother, holding it to her and looking at Maria with delighted eyes.

"Well enough. A ewe decided that one child was enough,

so Luz will see what kind of a substitute she is. What have you, Maria?"

She held out the blanket and he fingered it, a smile on his face. "Beautiful. Is it from the parents of the baby?"

Cristobal answered, "Yes, my brother. They are grateful to Maria, even if you were not."

Diego made no comment. He turned, picked up his saddle and carried it to the stable.

"Are you coming, Maria?" Cristobal asked.

"No. I want to talk to Diego." She stood where she was, watching Luz nuzzle the little lamb that butted against her stomach and made her squeal.

"Take it to the cook," Diego told his sister when he returned to them. "She will show you how to feed it with a rag dipped in milk."

Luz staggered toward the house with her burden. Diego laughed. "Catarina got an orphaned lamb last year. It became such a member of the family that it would follow her to evening prayers." He peered closely at her face. "But you have not stayed behind to laugh about lambs, have you, Maria? I was afraid this would happen if Cristobal took you to Tesuque. Out with it. What have I done now to add to my catalog of unforgivable sins?"

He walked with her slowly toward the house, crossing the footbridge and standing at the top of the garden.

"There is so little to eat at Tesuque, Senor," she began, trying to fathom his emotions from his calm expression. "Could you not, perhaps, release the Pueblos of Tesuque from the allotment they must give you this year?"

"I cannot."

"But, my lord," she burst out, all control gone, "if you could but see the children!"

"I have seen the children," he shot back. "I see their big bellies and their deep-set eyes. But Maria, Maria, to stop the tribute they owe their *encomendero* would be a sign of weakness I cannot afford!"

She said nothing. The tears welled up in her eyes and Diego turned away.

"It was never so hard before you came, Maria chiquita," he said quietly. "You must think I am a wretched person. I cannot begin to express to you the personal agony I feel when I see

104

the children. Although I am their *encomendero* and bound to exact tribute from them, I am also bound to defend them and protect them. Of late, I have not been doing so well."

"Forgive me, Senor," she said softly. "I do not understand this place."

"No, you do not," he agreed, turning to face her again. "Do not judge me so harshly."

He left her and went into the kitchen. She followed a few minutes later. Several chickens roasted on the fireplace spit, revolving slowly as the cook turned them. Maria watched the juices drip onto the coals, hissing and steaming.

She went to her room, put the Indian blanket at the foot of the bed and sat down next to it. If there were someplace else she could have gone, she would have left Las Invernadas, not out of unhappiness but out of confusion. She felt torn between two rights, between Diego's vision and Cristobal's. But she had no place to go, so she sat where she was, touching the blanket and thinking of Emiliano's *Cristo*.

The Awakening Heart

*M*aria *could never put her finger* on the moment when she began to love Diego Masferrer. Her feeling was as natural and necessary as the water flowing in the *acequia* or the moon rising full and gleaming over calm fields. Her love for Diego Masferrer was as much a part of her as her very breath. As she had never known a time when she did not breathe, so now she could not imagine a moment not loving Diego.

He had none of the handsomeness of his brother Cristobal. He did not go out of his way to help her with small tasks, to see that she was happy, as Cristobal did. Diego teased her as he teased his sisters. He touched her as he touched them, his hands sure and firm on her shoulders. He did not realize that his careless arm around her became a thing almost of pain to Maria, because she knew that he did not love her as a woman, only cared for her as a sister.

He liked and admired her, calling her Maria La Formidable when she stood up to him, or Maria chiquita in moments of fondness, but nothing about him indicated that the well of his soul was filled to overflowing, as hers was. When she knelt to kiss his hand each night after evening prayers, she longed to hold his hand against her cheek, then place it between her breasts, where he could feel the beating of her heart. But she did nothing.

She tried not to think of it, even to herself. She would have continued ignoring her own emotions if Cristobal had not come courting.

Maria sat in the sewing room one summer afternoon, looking out the window at Luz and Catarina, who sat in the pepper tree playing with their dolls. Cristobal had hammered a crude platform for them in the tree, over Erlinda's objections. Maria could watch them from the window, and it gave her pleasure to look up from the darning of endless socks to see them sitting there, their legs dangling over the edge companionably.

Cristobal knocked and she looked around.

"You seemed to be elsewhere."

"Just in that pepper tree."

He came to the window and leaned over her, watching his little sisters at play. "Diego and I had a tree like that. Over by the corral. I could always beat him into it, because his legs are short. But he had more staying power." He chuckled, resting his hand on the back of the chair. "I would tire long before he was ready to come down. It became a matter of pride to outlast him in the tree, but I never could."

His face was close to hers. "Are your eyes blue or green, Maria?" he asked. "They have the most amazing depth to them."

She leaned back. He was too close. "They are blue," she said firmly, "only blue."

He was holding a shirt. She took it from him, anxious to take his mind off her eyes. "What have you for me?" she asked.

"A shirt. I have pulled off two buttons and it is my best shirt. Can you fix it for me before tonight?"

"Are you going courting?" she teased.

He looked at her quickly. "Yes, I am," he said with a dignity that made her wish she had not made a joke of him. "It is an important thing I do tonight."

She was oddly touched by his manner. "You are a lucky man then, sir. Do I know the young woman?"

He hesitated before answering. "Yes, perhaps. But possibly not as well as you think you do."

"You speak in tongues," she said.

"It is no matter. If you do not have any buttons, take two off another of my shirts. I must help Diego shoe a horse now. Will you put the shirt in my room when you are through?"

"Yes, of course," she replied, a little awed by his serious manner.

After another look out the window, he left her. She could not find any buttons to match, so she rearranged the remaining buttons to put the two odd ones at the bottom where he tucked the shirt into his breeches. In her mind's eye, Maria could see Cristobal sitting in the *sala*, speaking his heart and mind to the father of the woman he loved. She smiled and lined the buttons up carefully, pleased in some small way to further the prosperity of his cause, which surely in his position must be a different one. He was a Masferrer, but he was also an Indian.

When she was done, she smoothed the shirt with her hands and folded it, carrying it down the hall to Cristobal's room. It was even smaller and more sparse than the other bedrooms, with only a bed and chest in it. There was no altar, and only a bare nail over the head of the bed where a crucifix should have been. Maria sighed. Perhaps when Cristobal had a wife and children of his own, he would come to understand the abundance God had given him.

She met Erlinda in the hall. "I think Cristobal is going courting tonight," she said, and told the young widow about the shirt and the buttons.

"It would be a fine thing, Maria," she said. "The hacienda seems too small these days for both Cristobal and Diego. They remind me of two stallions, squaring off at each other."

"Erlinda!"

"Well, they do. They intrude on each other's territory more and more, and I confess it does not make me easy. And I am happy for Cristobal—despite our differences."

She touched Maria's arm. "You will understand what I mean someday. It was that way with Marco. We had spent time in each other's company, but suddenly something changed."

Erlinda pulled Maria out to the patio. "This is not a subject one should talk about, but Maria, I can understand Cristobal in this matter." They sat on the sun-warmed bench by the tile fountain. "You can know somebody for years and then one day, instead of seeing Marco Castellano, you see a husband, the father of your children." She paused in embarrassment. "I can understand Cristobal. He has reached that moment in his life, and it is a special feeling."

Maria looked away. I already know that feeling, she thought.

But Erlinda was speaking. "He has not said anything, but I think Diego could be persuaded to see that you are provided for."

"I cannot expect that," said Maria, her voice low.

"I do think he will always have your interests at heart," insisted Erlinda, "for you are one of us now."

Maria could say nothing. Struggling with tears, she rose and left the patio. She spent the afternoon in the calm of La Senora's room, reading to her from the book of the saints. As she read the words on the page, her mind traveled in circles. She read of Santa Catarina de Alexandria spurning an earthly crown because she aspired to a heavenly one. Oh, Catarina, you foolish woman, Maria thought. The things of this earth are precious, too.

She was beginning the chapter on Santa Clara when La Senora put her hand over the page. Maria looked up. "Child, your mind is not on what you are reading today," said the woman. "Are you unhappy?"

Maria shook her head, closing the book. "No, not really. I feel at odds with myself, and I do not know why." To her horror, she burst into tears.

La Senora patted her knee while she cried and protested through her tears that she did not understand her turmoil. Through her stormy tears she heard the door open. "Not now, *hijo*," said La Senora quietly, and the door closed. Maria dried her tears on her dress and blew her nose on the handkerchief La Senora gave her.

As she rose to leave, La Senora rose with her, tucking her arm through Maria's. "My husband Tomas used to tell me that this time of year is hard on tender young things. I always thought he meant plants and small animals. Perhaps I was wrong. Maria, we love you here. If you wish to talk to me, I am always ready to listen."

Maria hugged her. "How kind you are, Senora. It must be the weather, or the time of the month. It is nothing that will not pass."

La Senora smiled. "Are you so sure? Well, never mind. Just remember what I said."

"I will." Maria kissed her forehead and left the room.

Cristobal ate dinner in his usual clothes, then excused himself before everyone was finished. Erlinda leaned toward her brother.

"Maria sewed two buttons on his best shirt this afternoon."

"And?" asked Diego, holding his fork between the bowl and his mouth.

"He is going courting."

Diego smiled to himself. He shook his head and continued eating. Erlinda picked up the dishes and headed for the sink. "Some men know nothing of the heart," she said over her shoulder.

Diego laughed and threw his napkin at her.

Maria washed the dishes while Erlinda visited with her mother. Diego still sat in the kitchen, his head resting on his arm, his eyes closed. But Cristobal came into the kitchen as she swirled the dishwater at the sink.

"Diego, wake up."

Diego opened his eyes and looked at his brother. "Cristobal, *que guapo!* How elegant you look tonight."

Cristobal had laid aside his usual leather breeches and was resplendent in black wool. His doublet was black, too, with silver and turquoise beads down the front that winked in the firelight. He wore his best boots pulled high on his legs and polished to a gloss in which Maria could see her face. She noted with satisfaction that the two odd buttons on his shirt did not show.

"Diego, I would speak with you in the *sala,*" Cristobal said formally.

Diego shoved away his dinner and stood up. "Yes, of course."

"You can advise me."

"Then let us go."

They left the room without a word to Maria. She carried Diego's dishes to the sink and washed them. Erlinda came into the room.

"Did you see Cristobal?" she asked.

"Was he not superb? He is speaking to Diego in the *sala.* Diego is advising him in his courting."

"I would almost risk perdition to listen at the door, so let us put temptation behind us and get far away from this place!"

She dried the dishes while Maria carried the dishpan into

110

the garden and let the water run slowly to the ground by the tomatoes. She set the dishpan by the back door and walked to the *acequia*. Erlinda joined her with two towels and the soap.

"It is dark enough and the guards have not yet climbed to the roof. If we are in the water, it will keep us from the keyhole!"

Laughing, Maria unbuttoned her dress and stepped out of it. Shivering, she hurried out of her chemise and stepped into the water. Erlinda followed, gasping as the water touched her skin. She sank into the ditch. "Turn around, I will scrub your back," she said through chattering teeth.

Maria did as she was told. The rough soap felt good on her skin. She sighed. Erlinda flicked water at her and laughed. "You scrub my back now."

The cold soon drove them from the water. They toweled off rapidly and pulled on their clothes. "Do you think Cristobal is through?" asked Erlinda, walking ahead of Maria toward the house.

As if in answer, the back door banged open and Cristobal strode down the path. He was dressed in his everyday clothes again. He said nothing to Erlinda as he passed her, but stopped by Maria, who was hurrying to button her dress.

He made as if to speak, then took both her hands in his. Without a word he kissed her hard on the mouth, released her and ran to the stables. In shock, Maria saw him leave the stable on horseback, take the fence in a graceful leap, and race north on the road to Taos. She stood where she was, her feet rooted to the ground, her hands to her lips.

Suddenly Diego stood in the doorway. "Maria, I would speak with you," he said. "Come into the *sala*."

Numb, Maria wrapped her wet hair in the towel and followed Diego into the *sala*. "Sit down." She sat. Diego faced her. "I do not know how to begin, Maria." He paused and unwound the towel on her head. "You look silly with that on your hair."

"But my hair is wet," she protested.

He ignored her, removing the towel and draping it over the back of his chair. A flush rose to his cheeks and he looked away from her. "Cristobal asked me for permission to marry you."

"You cannot be serious," she said when she found the words to speak.

"Of course I am serious. He says that since I have appointed myself your guardian, I should speak for you."

"What did you tell him?"

"Need you ask? I told him no." When Maria said nothing, his tone softened. "Was I wrong?"

"No, you were not wrong," she whispered, and he leaned closer to hear her. "No," she said again. "I do not love Cristobal."

He leaned back in his chair. "He accused me of wanting you for myself. I told him that was ridiculous—you are like one of my sisters—but he just laughed."

Maria closed her eyes. Diego's words lashed at her heart, but she said nothing to him.

"I was hasty with him. I suggested that he go away for awhile to give himself time to think." Diego got up, walked to the middle of the room and leaned on the narrow table there, his back to her. "If he still feels the same way, well, perhaps this had better become a matter between you and Cristobal. He is my brother and I love him, but he is also half Indian and you are a well-bred Spanish girl, Maria."

He turned around. "On the other hand, Maria, you are fifteen. You have no dowry. You are a pretty thing, and you have such dancing eyes. . . ." He stopped, shaking his head and smiling. "I can provide land for Cristobal, though as an Indian he is not permitted to own it in his own name, and he has always had a share in the livestock, although I have never told him. Maybe you should think about this. He will return in a month or so. Then you both must act carefully and, above all, wisely."

Maria rose and walked to the door. "But is this not a matter for the heart?" she asked.

He came to her and leaned against the door. "I do not know. I have never been in love," he said, "and I know few people who have, Maria. This kingdom has made us calculating. We must plan our every move. To achieve certain aims, I must move in certain directions. If I am to expand my herds, I need land nearby. Lorenzo Nunez has a daughter. She is young, but she will grow. When she is old enough, I will declare myself to Senor Nunez. He will slap me on the back, call me a fine fellow, and we will seal the matter between us with wine. Then he will tell his daughter. That is how it is."

"Let me leave, Diego," she said, chilled to her bones by his words.

He moved away from the door, his hands in his pockets. "You do not approve, Maria?" he asked. His voice was devoid of emotion. "We must survive in this harsh land."

Maria opened the door. "That is what my sister said. Are you no different than she?"

Her words had the force of a slap. Maria left the room without another look at Diego. She went swiftly to her room and sat silent before the altar. When the bell sounded for prayers an hour later, she remained where she was.

Summer brought an uneasy peace to Maria. Life was hard in the river colony of New Mexico, the land all-consuming. There was little time for personal thoughts. There was only the shocking blue of the cloudless sky, the red-brown earth the color of an old wound, the purple mass of mountain and mesa, the brassy yellow of the sun. There was only work.

A dozen times a day, Maria thought of Diego's words. This *Nuevo Mexico* was not a place for softness or romance. And yet with each passing day, she fell deeper in love with Diego Masferrer. He was an imperfect human being, even as she was, struggling daily against the harshness of his surroundings and losing. The drought deepened that summer and she watched him walk his fields, measuring the height of the corn against his body with his hands, kneeling by the *acequia* with desperate prayers. It tore at her heart, but she had no consolation to offer him.

She turned to the saints of Las Invernadas, pleading with them silently as she passed them daily in the halls, pausing also to admire their lines and texture. Diego caught her at it one morning. "So you like our holy ones here?" he commented, coming up behind her as she ran her hand over San Isidro in the hallway.

They had not spoken alone since their confrontation in the *sala*. She put her hands behind her back like a small child, and he laughed. Maria relaxed at the easiness of his laughter but she knew, with a hollow feeling that emptied her soul, that her love was destined to go no further than her own heart.

"Truly, I did not mean to startle you," he said.

"Well, you did." The last person she expected indoors was Diego Masferrer. He spent his days in the saddle, overseeing his cattle and sheep. And with Cristobal gone, his work load had doubled.

He was dressed in his usual work clothes, his legs from the waist to knee covered with the kilt-like leather apron all the New Mexican rancheros wore. His calves from the ankles up were wrapped with leather leggings that tied behind each knee. Then she saw it. The scarf he usually wore around his head was held to his forearm, which was covered with blood.

"What happened?" she asked, following him to the kitchen.

"I would prefer not to say," he began, "but I suppose I must. I fell off Tirant and landed in a bed of cactus." His eyes smiled at her.

"I hardly think it something to joke about," she murmured, holding the door open for him.

"Oh, you do not? You should have heard Teruel, my *vaquero*. I am only grateful that Cristobal is not here." He coughed and looked at his boots. "I didn't mean to remind you. I mean . . ."

"Oh, Diego," she interrupted, unconsciously using his Christian name. "He is your brother, and I have driven him away."

"So he is," he replied heavily. He sat down at the table and stretched his arm out in front of him. "Well, I have come on other matters. Can you find the turpentine and pincers?"

Maria hurried into the storeroom for the jug of turpentine. She found the pliers and seated herself at the table next to him. Diego turned to face her on the bench, crossing his legs Indian-style and taking the pliers from her. He began pulling out the thorny spicules, swearing under his breath.

When his hand became slippery with blood, Maria took the pincers from him and pulled out thorns. Some were in so deep that she had to press the skin down with a knife to reach them. "It would seem to me, Senor," she said, "that everything in this land either bites or tastes bad."

"I never thought of it that way," he replied, gritting his teeth.

"Of course you do not. This is your home."

"Do you think I would not like your Mexico City, Maria chiquita? *Aiye, ten cuidado, hermana!* Have a care!"

She paused while he wiped the blood off with his shirttail.

"No," she reflected, "you probably would not. It would be much too tame."

He closed his eyes as she dug away at his arm again. "So you admire our saints, Maria?" he asked, changing the subject. "Jesus, Maria, have a care! I must use this arm again!"

"Sorry. You have to hold still. Yes, I admire your saints. At first I thought they looked foreign, but the longer I am here, the more they seem to fit."

"Like you?"

"I could wish that, but who knows?" she countered, dabbing at his arm with her apron.

He opened his eyes. "Hand me the pincers."

"No. Just hold still."

"Oh, very well, very well. There must be some penance for falling off a horse."

She smiled.

"About our saints," he continued, straightening his arm. "I am sure we are the only family upriver with a *santero*. After Father built this hacienda, the Apaches burned it down. His Indians managed to drag out the carved chests in the *sala*, and some of the chairs, but everything else burned including our Spanish saints. I remember Mama wailing about that. Here, give me the pincers. You find a clean cloth."

She got up and found a clean dishcloth, tearing it in a long strip while Diego dug away at his arm, still talking. "So Papa put Emiliano to work painting new saints. I scarcely remember it. I've grown up with Emiliano's saints. I know our neighbors laugh at us, but where can you find Spanish saints? The supply caravans come every other year, when they come at all."

He held his arm out while Maria swabbed it with turpentine. *"Sangre de Dios,* Maria!" he exclaimed, "can you not be more gentle?"

"You requested turpentine," she said, and he laughed. She wiped the skin and dried it with her apron. Holding his right arm against her side, she began winding the strip of dishcloth around it. "Tell me, why Emiliano?" she asked, pausing to dab at the sweat on his forehead.

"Gracias, chiquita," he said. "I am relieved you have humanity. Why Emiliano? He told Papa that before he was converted to the True Faith he used to paint the *kachinas* in the pueblo."

"*Kachinas?*"

"You will doubtless never see any. The priests have destroyed them all. I suppose you could call them Pueblo gods. Large masks, and also small figures, given to the young ones for instruction." He straightened out one layer of the cloth. "I think Emiliano is my only Tesuque Indian who is really a true believer."

"But what can you mean?" Maria asked. "What about the servants who come to family prayer every night?"

He shrugged. "My house servants are descendants of the Mexican Indians my grandfather brought from Mexico, and I know their allegiance. As for the others that come sometimes, my Pueblo Indians, I cannot say." He shifted on the bench. "It is just a feeling, really, but in odd moments I wonder how deeply our ways have penetrated in this place. The priests destroy the *kivas* and burn the *kachinas* when they can find them, but I wonder."

Maria finished bandaging Diego's arm, ripped the end of the cloth with her teeth and tied a knot securely in place. "*Gracias, Maria chiquita,*" he said, getting up. "If you and Teruel have finished laughing, I shall gather my dignity around me once more and go back to work."

"Before you go, Senor, have you heard from Cristobal?"

There, she had said it. He turned in the doorway. "No, I have not. I was thinking of riding to Taos this week to speak with him. It has been too long."

And he was gone. Maria cleaned the pincers, wiped off the table and replaced the jug in the storeroom.

That evening at dinner, Diego announced that he was leaving for Taos in the morning.

"This is sudden, my brother," Erlinda said, passing him the bread.

He took a slice and buttered it. "I know. But I am concerned about Cristobal. It is time he came home." He shook his head. "We can never work out our differences if he is there and I am here."

He sat with his elbows on the table until Catarina reminded him. Absently he took his elbows off the table and ate the bread. "I will visit with our Uncle Robles, too, and see if he has any horses to trade."

Diego was gone before sunrise. When Maria came into the

kitchen the next morning, rubbing sleep out of her eyes, all she found was a half-filled cup of cold chocolate. Maria held the cup in her hands a moment, then drank it, pausing to rest her cheek against the rim.

Diego was back in four days, alone. He rode in slowly after dinner, the barking of his dogs the only signal of his return. Erlinda dropped the mending she was struggling with and ran to meet him. He came into the kitchen with his arm around his sister's waist. She helped him out of his dusty cloak and shook it off outside the door.

"Come, Maria, some food for Diego."

He waved her away. "I am too tired. I just want to sit here." He rubbed the back of his neck, discouragement tracing itself in every line of his body.

"Is all well?" Erlinda asked. "You came back so soon."

"Certainly all is well, Erlinda. What could be wrong?" he answered quickly, too quickly. He reached into his pocket and pulled out a small cloth sack. "Here, Erlinda, take this to Luz and Catarina. Tia Robles sends her love and some *dulces*."

She smiled and took the bag. Maria returned to her mending again. Diego spoke. "Maria, it is good to see you. Cristobal asked about you, and I told him you were well."

She made no reply. Without thinking, she put down her mending, and began to massage his shoulders. He stiffened in surprise, then relaxed, sighing deeply.

"What is the matter, Senor? Please tell me."

"Can I not fool you, Maria?" He was silent for a moment, turning his head quickly as she struck a tender spot. "Cristobal is different somehow, Maria. But then, so is Taos. There is a trouble that has no name in Taos."

He shifted slightly and unbuttoned his shirt so she could reach under it. His skin was warm to her fingers, the muscles tense.

"I confess I always feel uneasy in Taos. I do not speak their language. Taos has a brooding air about it. Always has, for that matter, as though they wait for something. I will take you there someday, and you will feel what I mean." He tipped his head back to smile at her. "Maria, for one so small, your fingers are strong."

"I have been kneading bread in the household of Diego

Masferrer for several months now," she said with a smile of her own.

"So you have. Well, as I was saying, Tio Robles tells me of an Indian in Taos, large of body, black of face. Tio does not know his name, but said he was stirring up trouble. The usual things—blaming us for the drought, saying that we Spaniards are the cause of the land's unrest, things like that. We have heard it all before, but now. . . ." He left the sentence unfinished, closing his eyes as she rubbed his back.

"And Cristobal?" Maria asked. Her shoulders ached, but she needed to go on touching Diego Masferrer.

"He has none of his usual warmth. We visited for several hours, but he kept looking at me as though I were the enemy." He bowed his head over the table and Maria took her hands from his shoulders. "He is an Indian. I forget, but he is an Indian."

"He is your brother, Senor," she said quietly, sitting beside him.

"Not in Taos." Diego ran his fingers over Maria's hands folded on the table in front of her. "Such strong hands."

He got up from the table suddenly. "I had better speak to Mama. She will want to hear the news of Taos I bring from her sister."

Two days later, as suddenly as he had left, Cristobal Masferrer returned. Maria was down at the *acequia* with the leather buckets, hauling water, when she looked up to see him standing on the other side of the footbridge. He stood as he always did, one leg bearing his weight, head angled to one side.

Without a word, he crossed the bridge and took the buckets from her, dipping them in the *acequia*, then carrying them into the kitchen, ignoring the stares of the Mexican servant girls. Maria stood and watched him. He made enough silent trips to fill the water barrel.

"Thank you, Senor," she said when he came back outside.

"It is Cristobal, Maria, only Cristobal. Some of us will never be 'Senor' around here." She had heard him speak sharply before, but this time the anger was barely concealed beneath his words.

"I know what you mean. I used to be a *'Senorita muy elegante.'* "

He leaned against the beehive oven. "Does it not bother you to come down so in the world?"

She considered his question. "No. I would wish I had a dowry still, for I would like to marry someday. . . ." She stopped in confusion, remembering his offer and his kiss.

He leaned his head against the oven. Maria noticed for the first time that his hair was unbound, worn the Pueblo way. "Ah, you have been talking to my big brother. Land and sheep and cows marry land and sheep and cows. Indians are traded and sold, bought and paid for. Those of us who do not have these things do not fare so well."

"Oh, but surely you are different from the other Indians."

He stalked toward the footbridge, and Maria followed. "I did not mean. . . ."

He turned and put his hands on her shoulders. "You do not hurt me, Maria. I do not think you ever could. But I learned something in Taos. I am no better than my brothers in the fields." He gestured toward the cornfield and the Pueblos stooping over their short-handled hoes. "All that I have is at the sufferance of others."

"It is the same with me," Maria said softly.

"And does this not bother you?" he lashed out.

"No," she replied. "I am glad enough to be alive."

He took his hands off her shoulders, looking at the Indians in the waist-high corn again. "Poor Maria," he said softly. "What choices does a woman have? But a man is different. Sometimes when my brother says 'my Indians' in that possessive way of his, I want to tear his heart out. If he has one." He left her then, and she watched him walk back to the stable where his horse was tied. "Oh, Cristobal," she whispered. "What has happened?"

He was sitting in his usual place at the dinner table that evening, speaking of inconsequentialities to Erlinda and telling his little sisters of their Taos cousins. Diego relaxed visibly as he listened to him. Cristobal even joined them in the chapel for evening prayers. Sitting beside Maria, his responses were firm, though he refused to kneel and kiss Diego's hand when he left the chapel. If Diego was surprised, he did not show it.

Cristobal stopped Maria in the hall. "Come with me to Tesuque tomorrow. I saw Emiliano when I was there this after-

119

noon, and he says he has something for you. I think the man is an old fool, but perhaps he means well. Will you come?"

"Yes," she replied without hesitation.

Maria watched him walk the length of the hall to the kitchen. When he did not come back with the candle for his bedroom, she knew he had left the hacienda. She turned to go to her own room, but Diego stood behind her.

"*Dios,* you are silent!" she uttered.

"Am I? That may be a virtue I am learning from my brother." Diego took her by the arm and led her toward the *sala*. He had already gotten his candle from the kitchen. The small flame flickered and almost went out as he opened the door and pulled Maria inside, closing the door behind him.

"What is it, Senor?" She remembered their last interview in the *sala* and felt a growing uneasiness.

He motioned her to a hard chair. The seat was so high that her feet did not touch the floor.

Diego smiled. "Ridiculous furniture. Is it any wonder that we never use this room—except for unpleasant discussions?" He set the candle down and pulled a chair up until he was sitting close to her.

"I need your help," he said. "I have pondered this since speaking with Cristobal this afternoon, and my thoughts do me little credit." He shook his head. "Even now, I do not know quite what to say."

"My lord?" she asked.

"I wish you would not call me that," he said absently, admiring the way the light of the candle brought out the gold sparkles in Maria's hair.

"I know you do," she replied, "but when I kneel to kiss your hand each night, it seems to follow."

"The effort was too great for Cristobal tonight," he said.

"I saw. You are right. He has changed. But what is it you need of me?"

"Only a small thing, Maria chiquita," he said, the sun-wrinkles deepening around his eyes as he smiled. He ran his hand over his close-cut beard. "When you are in Tesuque tomorrow, keep your eyes open."

"What do you mean, Senor?" she asked, sitting up straight.

"There is a cunning about Cristobal now that worries me. He looks at me as if he were measuring me for a coffin."

"Surely you are imagining this," she said, thinking as she did so of Cristobal's words to her by the *acequia*.

"You are probably right. But watch for me, please. In Tesuque you must be my eyes." He held out his hand.

She hesitated, then put her hand in his and shook it. "I will."

He walked her down the hall to the door of her room. Catarina bounded out when she heard their footsteps.

"Catarina," said Maria, "you are supposed to be asleep."

"I could not," she insisted. Diego put his arm around her shoulder, and she leaned against her brother. "Besides, Maria, you promised us another story." She looked up at Diego. "You can come in, too. Maria takes off her dress and we all sit cross-legged like Indians while she tells us stories."

"Oh, I could not," Diego said.

"You could. Maria would not mind," Catarina insisted.

"No," said Diego, taking his hand off her shoulder and giving her a small push. "Now go to bed. Maria will join you in a moment."

"Do as your brother says," admonished Maria. Catarina went into her room.

"I shall not keep you," Diego said to Maria. "But you will not forget our pact? And you will speak of it to no one?"

Maria gave her word, then went into her room and closed the door softly behind her. She took off her dress, shook it out and hung it on her clothes peg, putting her petticoat next to it. Quickly she took the pins out of her hair and brushed it with one of Erlinda's old brushes. When she got in bed, Luz cuddled next to her. Maria put her arm around the child, delighting as always in the small one's warmth.

"What would you like to hear tonight?" she murmured, marveling at how much Luz looked like Diego.

"The story about El Cid," declared Catarina. "The part where the men strap his corpse to his horse and he rides out of Valencia."

"*Santos,* Catarina! You like all the gory parts!" said Maria, propping her pillow against the wall and snuggling down with both sisters. "Besides, I told you that one last night."

"But I like it," said Catarina.

Maria looked down at Luz. "And what about you, my darling? What would you have?"

"If you please," said the smaller one, her voice already full of sleep, "I like the story about the poor girl who marries the rich prince. Tell us that one, but put in some good parts for Catarina."

"Very well," said Maria, and wove a story, complete with Apaches and a daring rescue, that the girls had heard many times. They huddled close to her as she told of the Indians and sighed with pleasure when the prince declared the lack of dowry was no obstacle to his love and, on bended knee, swore his undying devotion.

When she was finished, the candle was guttering low in its socket. Catarina looked up and dragged herself into a sitting position. "Tell us the part about the Indian raid again."

"Oh, Catarina," said Maria, "you are so bloodthirsty. Perhaps you should have been a man."

Both girls giggled. Luz looked at Maria. "But is it true, Maria?" she asked, her eyes on the storyteller. "Do things like that happen? Do princes marry poor girls?"

Maria pinched the candle's light out with her fingers. "No Luz, they do not. Not ever. At least, that I know of."

The Demons of Tesuque

Marie did not see Cristobal at breakfast. After finishing her chores, she took off her apron and stepped outside the kitchen door. The sun was warm on her face after the coolness of the hacienda. She slipped off her shoes and walked down the row of beets to begin her weeding. The children of Diego's Mexican servants who usually tended the kitchen garden were busy in the fields this morning, weeding the growing corn. She could see them on the far side of the *acequia*, working alongside Diego's Indians from Tesuque.

She knelt between the rows and pulled weeds, humming to herself, filled with a contentment she could not have explained to anyone who had known her in Mexico City. Here was Maria Luisa Espinosa de la Garza, gently reared descendant of *conquistadores*, grubbing about on her knees in someone else's garden patch. She who used to dress in velvet and satin now knelt barefoot in her homespun *jerga*. Her hair that used to be so carefully arranged hung long and braided, caught at the ends with rawhide strips. Her face was tanned and freckling, her hands rough with work.

123

Maria patted the soil around the beets, enjoying the feel of warm earth between her fingers.

Cristobal was standing at the end of the row, a dark shadow against the clear sky. Maria smiled and thought that it would be nice to paint him. She stood and wiped her hands on her dress. "Let me get my shoes and tell Erlinda where I am going."

Cristobal snorted. "Do not tell her! She will find another fifty things for you to do to keep you from me!"

His words startled her with their vehemence. "Do not be absurd." She went inside to put on her shoes. Erlinda was there, instructing the servant women how to clean the glass in the windows, something they did several times a week, but never to Erlinda's complete satisfaction.

"Erlinda, I am going to Tesuque with Cristobal."

"Does Diego know?"

"Yes, of course. I told him last night."

"I have nothing to say, then. *Vaya con Dios.*"

Maria went back outside, joining Cristobal, who stood by the *acequia,* watching Luz and Catarina in their play tunnel.

"I must admit, I wondered if you would come with me," he said, turning to watch her approach.

Maria stood next to him. Her head came only to his shoulder, and she looked up at him. "I said that I would, did I not?"

"Yes, I know. But why?" he asked, staring at her in a way that made her wonder if he was serious or merely teasing.

"I wanted to see Emiliano again," she replied, matching him look for look, amazed at her own boldness. She admired the elegant curve of his high cheekbones and the easy way he stood.

He took her arm and led her across the *acequia* and along the path that paralleled it. "I left my horse in the orchard." She paused to look back at Catarina and Luz, who dabbled their feet in the water by their small tunnel. She blew them a kiss and then walked beside Cristobal to the orchard.

"The apples are so small, even for this time of year," she said.

"We have not had a good rain, a really good rain, in several years, Maria." He paused, looking away, then spoke in a softer, more tentative voice. "I think the gods are angry."

She looked at his profile. "Gods? I do not understand."

He turned around so suddenly that she stepped back. "Yes, the gods! The *kachinas* that rule this land."

"Cristobal? I still do not understand. I thought you followed the True Faith."

"So they think!" The words spilled out of him in an angry flood.

He waited for Maria to catch up with him, the anger covered now with a smoother tone. "Explain to me why I must pray to a god I cannot see, one who hangs like a weak man on a cross and does nothing about it. Why can I not pray to the sun anymore? I can see the sun. And what about the clouds? If we do not honor them, there is no rain. Is there something wrong with these things that were so right before?"

He looked down at her and touched her cheek, his hand gentle on her face. "But you do not understand, do you, Maria? You do not understand anymore than they do." There was unmistakable sorrow in his voice. "And what have the saints done for you, little one?"

She lowered her eyes and he stopped. "I do not know," she said at last. "But I have hopes that the saints are there somewhere."

"I know they are not." His voice took on a musing tone. "And these people who have raised me so kindly have given me nothing but expectations. Do you think for one moment that I will ever inherit any of this land? Do you really believe that Diego would grudge me even one *hectare?*"

"I believe he will."

"Ah, then you do not know him very well, for all that he calls you Maria chiquita. I am still half Tewa, and in this place I amount to less than dung." He took her by the shoulders, his hands heavier this time. "Listen, Maria, if there were something I wanted and Diego wanted it, too . . ." he paused, then smiled grimly. "I shall prove it to you soon. You will see what I mean." He stopped then and let go of her shoulders. "Never mind, never mind." He untied his horse's reins from an apple tree. "There are times coming," he said, half to himself, "and things will change for all of us."

She stood where she was, her hands folded in front of her, watching Cristobal Masferrer. She wanted to hurry back across the footbridge and into the safety of the hacienda, but she could not move.

Then his mood changed, as quickly as clouds moving across the face of the sun. He held out his hand to her. "Come, Maria. I promised you Emiliano today, did I not?" Before she could say anything, Cristobal mounted his horse's bare back and pulled her up behind him.

"Put your arms around my waist," he said, and they trotted out of the orchard.

As they skirted the cornfield, several of the Pueblo Indians looked up to watch them, then stooped silently to their work again. As soon as they reached the road in front of the high-walled hacienda, Cristobal touched his heels to his horse's flanks. Unlike Diego, he wore no spurs, but the animal leaped forward. Maria tightened her grip.

As the horse galloped toward Tesuque, she felt the wind on her face. She had ridden bareback once as a young child on her grandfather's estancia south of Mexico City. The horse then had been an old respectable mare with more prudence than daring, but she'd still been wild with excitement. Maria sighed and leaned against Cristobal. She could feel the vibrations of the horse's hooves and the warmth of Cristobal's body. She closed her eyes.

When he slowed his horse, talking to him in Tewa, Maria opened her eyes and sat up straight, loosening her grip on Cristobal's belt. Ahead and to the south of them was the now familiar pueblo of Tesuque, its two- and three-terraced levels rising beside the river. The color of the red-brown adobe, contrasted with the blue of the sky, drew a sound of appreciation from her.

As she remembered, there were people on all levels of the pueblo, weaving, making pots, grinding corn with a steady back-and-forth motion of *mano* on *metate* that was the heritage of centuries long before Spain ever dreamed of new lands beyond the earth's end. Dogs barked, naked children squealed and chased each other, and the old men sang at their tasks.

Cristobal reined in his horse and handed Maria down. He jumped off his mount Indian-style and dropped the reins. "You get such a look in your eyes when you see this place."

"It's beautiful," she said.

His eyes held hers. "I believe you are Indian in spirit."

She turned away to the ladders leaning against the lowest terrace, noting that there were no entrances on the first level.

"Did you not notice that the other day? It is for protection."

"Against whom?" she asked.

"The Apaches, of course," he replied. "The Spaniards would never do anything to hurt us, would they now?"

She smiled at the children gathering near them, and they scattered. "Oh, I do not want them to be afraid of me," she said.

"They run from all Spaniards," Cristobal said. "They are taught to from birth."

He climbed a ladder to the second level and Maria, tucking her skirts around her legs, followed him.

"Do they add on to the pueblo for new families?" she asked.

Cristobal gave her a hand up. "Yes. The interior rooms are used mainly for storage now, the outer, lighter rooms for living. The pueblo can rise higher still."

They climbed another ladder and crossed a long terrace. The Indians stopped to watch them without appearing to do so, a mannerism that Maria found more disturbing than a blatant stare. Cristobal looked around. He appeared to be searching for someone. Like the Indians watching her, his eyes darted here and there, his head scarcely moving. "Wait here," he commanded.

She stood where she was and he quickly climbed another ladder to the next level and spoke to an Indian with a white-painted face who watched them. As they spoke, their heads together, both men glanced her way.

It was as if a chill wind blew suddenly across the terrace, setting Maria's teeth to chattering. Suddenly she wanted to leave the pueblo and forget about Emiliano.

After a few more words, Cristobal descended the ladder. "I will take you to Emiliano now," he said. "Follow me."

He led her into the pueblo and they walked from room to room, through storage spaces and family dwellings. Cristobal knew everyone. He greeted men and women and patted the children, and they welcomed him into their homes.

"Are these people your relatives?" Maria asked as he helped her through one of the openings, high off the floor.

"Yes, many of them. They are my mother's people, and the pueblo belongs to the women. I have many cousins and aunts here."

They descended an interior ladder. The darkness in the middle of the pueblo was complete. Maria put her feet carefully on each rung, afraid to miss a step and plunge into total blackness. Cristobal took her hand, and she hung onto him.

"We could light a *farol*, Maria, but I know the way, and we are almost there."

They approached the front of the pueblo from the inside. Maria sniffed the air. It smelled of piñon and juniper wood like every other dwelling in the river kingdom, with the familiar smell of animals intermingled. She heard a mother humming to her crying baby, and the wordless song filled her with an inexpressible loneliness. She stood still, pulling Cristobal to a stop.

"Listen," she said.

"It is a sound that you hear in your heart," he whispered. They remained there side by side until the baby stopped crying. The mother's voice continued for a beat longer, then softly died. There was silence for a moment, and they heard the scrape and grind of corn on stone again, the rhythm of the Tesuque pueblo.

Cristobal tugged on her hand, and they walked toward the sound. They stepped outside again on the second level, and Maria blinked her eyes. She let go of her companion's hand and walked to the edge of the terrace.

"I know where I am now," she said.

"Then I will leave you," Cristobal replied. "When you are through, wait for me with Emiliano." Then he was gone, stepping back into the dark interior. Maria walked to the opening next to the one Cristobal had entered. She pulled back the skin and peered in. It was the *santero*'s workshop. San Lorenzo roasting on his grill did a slow, dignified dance of death in the light breeze that blew from the west. Maria and her child Jesus fluttered nearby, stiff dancing dolls painted on deerskin. From across the workshop, San José frowned at his young wife and small Son, engaged in such frivolity.

And there was Emiliano, his back to the open doorway, hunched over a flat piece of wood, a *retablo*. As Maria came closer, he did not turn around, but he raised his head from his work.

"Is that you, Maria Espinosa?" he asked.

"How did you know, Emiliano?" she asked, coming closer to look over his shoulder.

He did not answer. He was carving a lunette at the top of the *retablo,* a delicately fluted ornamentation. Below the shell-shaped decoration, a saint was outlined in black. He held out the work for her to see.

"Santa Teresa de Ávila."

Maria examined the wooden tablet, crude, yet full of possibility, ripe with potential. "What color will her dress be?" she asked.

"Whatever you wish. This is yours to paint. And when you have finished, carry it home to Diego Masferrer. I promised him something of the sort, for he is fond of her poetry."

Maria tried to hand the tablet back. "Emiliano, I am not yet accomplished enough for such a task."

"And can you learn without doing? Besides, my fingers are stiff." He got up from his low stool and motioned for her to sit down. She placed the *retablo* carefully on the workbench and sat down, pulling the stool closer.

Emiliano busied himself in another corner of the small room, tugging a buffalo hide off a stack of them and trimming the edges of it with a small knife. Maria picked up a brush. Teresa from Avila, the walled city of the Spanish central highlands. Teresa of the vision, of Christian ecstacy, of a poetry deep as the soul. How to paint this? And for Diego, too.

I will give her closed eyes, thought Maria, dipping the brush in an earthenware pot of dark pigment. And her hands will be folded in front of her.

She stroked the brush on the *retablo,* pleasuring in the feel of paint on the smooth wood. When the eyes were painted, with drooping eyelashes, Maria put the brush on the table and picked up one leaning in a red pot. The mouth should smile slightly, as if she is thinking of the goodness of God.

Maria felt she could paint that smile. She had smiled that way only this morning as she weeded her way down the beet rows. How Saint Teresa would relish the small task, the little act of service to honor God. But do I work to honor God, she asked herself, or to please the lord of the hacienda?

What color was Saint Teresa's hair? She could paint her with her hair hidden by the severe lines of a wimple, but surely there were times in Teresa's youth when her hair was unbound, floating free behind her. I will make it the color of Erlinda's hair, she decided, adding the smallest dab of brown pigment to the yellow.

The result was the rich honey color of Erlinda's beautiful hair. Sometimes at night Erlinda would call her into her room, and Maria would spend a pleasant interval pulling the hairbrush through Erlinda's thick hair.

She spoke of Marco once. "Do you know," she said, "Marco used to brush my hair."

"He did?" asked Maria. She tried to imagine Diego brushing her hair but could not.

"You think it amusing?" Erlinda asked, a smile on her lips. "Men are different, Maria, when they are away from their daily concerns. You will see."

And so Maria colored Teresa de Ávila's hair honey-brown, knowing that the saint would take delight in a simple task like hairbrushing.

Her gown would be blue. Maria blended several colors, wishing she knew the art of texturing paint to make it look like velvet. She remembered the statues in the churches of Mexico City, fairly glowing with a life of their own, so rich was the paint's texture. The more favored statues wore dresses of material dipped in *yeso* and dried to a starched finish. Some of the truly pampered saints had a different dress for each Sunday, their doll's wardrobes kept in gilt-covered caskets and possessing more wealth than many of the people who sought saintly intercessions.

But here she sat, dreaming of rich clothing for the saints of Spain while hunched over a small slab of wood in an Indian pueblo. As she held board and brush, pausing in artist's anticipation and dread, she was struck again by her unity with this place and these people.

Maria filled in the outline of Santa Teresa's dress, careful to stay within the lines Emiliano had traced. Then she drew Santa Teresa's hands clasped in front of her, like any proper lady of careful upbringing. When the hands were painted, she outlined a small book in the corner. After all, she reasoned, without her volume of poetry, it was entirely possible that Diego would not be able to tell which saint it was.

When she painted Teresa's feet bare, peeking out from under the long folds of her gown, she turned the tablet over.

"Wait, Maria," said Emiliano. She had thought he was still

trimming the buffalo hides, but there he was, peering over her shoulder. "Do not write your name on the back. Let it be for the glory of God alone."

She turned the *retablo* over and laid it down on the workbench. Santa Teresa glowed up at her, the heavily lashed eyes downcast, contemplating some inward journey of the soul.

"It will do, Maria," Emiliano said. "Now, let me show you how to mix a little gold dust with the *yeso* to paint the lunette and trim."

She watched as he took out a leather sack and put a pinch of its contents in an empty pot. He added *yeso,* and told her to stir the gold-gypsum combination. The sparks of gold danced before her eyes as she whirled the paint around in the pot, admiring the flashes of color.

Emiliano painted one side of the *retablo,* dipping his brush in after every stroke, careful to get the bits of glitter on the bristles. When it was half-done, he handed her the brush and sat down again with his buffalo hides. "There now, you finish the trim and paint the lunette. It will dry before you are done."

Maria's brush strokes were not as steady as Emiliano's, but she filled in the scallops on top, pausing often to admire the sparkling effects.

At last it was done. Maria stood up. Emiliano watched her. "You will come back again?"

"If you would like me to."

"Next time I will show you where to gather wood for a statue, a *bulto.* And see if you can bring Diego with you then. I would like to talk to him."

"I will," Maria replied, picking up her saint from the workbench. She held it in front of her, careful not to rub it against her dress.

"And Maria," Emiliano continued, his eyes on the buffalo skins again, "do not stay away so long next time."

She stepped over the high doorsill and into the sunlight, happy for the warmth of the afternoon. When she saw the sun's position in the sky, Maria realized how long she had been gone from the hacienda. She looked around for Cristobal, but he was nowhere in sight. It was late and she had kitchen duties. Perhaps she should go look for him.

Maria set her *retablo* down on the window ledge of Emiliano's room. "I am going to look for Cristobal."

Emiliano put out his hand quickly. "No, Maria," he began, "he will show up."

But Maria did not listen. "I have to get back to Las Invernadas." Before Emiliano could stop her, she went through the entrance where she had last seen Cristobal.

She had not gone through many doors when she realized her mistake. The darkness grew deeper inside the pueblo, even in the rooms that were lit with *farols*. And the women in the rooms did not regard her with the same equanimity they had shown when Cristobal was with her. "Cristobal?" she asked over and over, receiving only blank stares or shrugs in answer.

She tried to retrace her steps to the outside, but was lost. As she leaned against one of the ladders, she realized another strong point of the Tesuque pueblo. Even if any attackers could gain access to the pueblo interior, they would be lost, wandering in semidarkness.

Maria stood still. Perhaps she could follow voices to the outside terraces, where most of the daily activities took place. She listened. Not too far away she heard drums. The beat was low and steady, accompanied by rattles shaken in ponderous rhythm. She strained to hear the low voices of men chanting. She set out to follow the sound to its source. Cristobal would be there.

She felt her way from room to room, all of them empty or partly filled with large woven baskets of dried corn, the remnants of last year's harvest. An army of mice scurried around her feet.

The singing grew louder. She felt the pulse of the drums under her feet now. Perhaps a few more doors would take her to the source. She groped her way into the next room, then the next. She stumbled through room after room, banging her knees against the high openings of the doorways. Tears filled her eyes, her pulse beat as loud as the drums. Then suddenly she could see a light ahead, a thin strip of light such as would shine around the edge of a door flap. She staggered toward it.

Her hand pulled aside the hide flap. The drumming stopped. Unknown hands yanked her into the room.

Maria blinked in the light. *"Salvador santo,"* she whispered in terror.

The sight before her was more frightening than her worst nightmares. Terrified beyond speech she stared up at the enor-

mous figures that stood in front of her, great tall creatures
covered with feathers of fantastic colors and masks frozen in
vivid expressions of violence, beasts from a long-forgotten age
of giants. She looked from one figure to the next, with a
compulsion that was hypnotic. The demons were covered with
a dull white paint the color of dead skin. In the murk of the
smoky, stifling room, they seemed to float in the air.

Indian eyes watched her from behind immobile masks. The
dancing had stopped. The dancers came closer, the jingle of
copper Spanish ankle bells the only sound in the room.

In panic Maria dropped to the floor, her legs unable to hold
her. She lay in a heap on the dirt floor, staring at the tall figures
in front of her.

A demon came closer, reached out a hand to her. She shuddered and drew back. The Indian lifted off his headpiece. Cristobal.

"You!" she gasped, scrambling back against the wall. His
face was filled with anger, his eyes harder than she had ever
seen them.

"I told you to wait for me with Emiliano." He yanked her
to her feet. "Why did you not do as I said?"

"It is getting late. I must return to Las Invernadas." She
managed to force her words past the growing lump in her throat.
He let go of her then, and she knelt in the dirt in front of him.

The anger went out of him in one sigh. "Maria, it would
have been better if you had done as I said."

"Please forgive me," she whispered, her head bowed, her
voice scarcely audible. "I meant no harm. Please believe me."

He knelt beside her and she drew back unconsciously, re-
gretting her movements as soon as she looked at his face. He
had reached out to her, but now he pulled his hand back. "I
believe you, Maria," he finally replied, the hurt betrayed by
his voice and his averted face. "I believe you. I only hope the
others will."

He stood and turned to speak to the other men in masks.
The three largest demons retreated to the far side of the room,
looking like gigantic birds of prey. They did not remove their
masks. The remaining figure took off his headpiece and set it
on the ground.

"This is Popeh," said Cristobal to Maria. The man said

nothing, only stared down at Maria, his expression unfathomable, his eyes glittering.

Maria gazed back at him in terror. He was enormous, taller than any man she had ever seen, and burned nearly black by the sun. His eyes were a curious yellow, and they bored into her face without blinking. She stared at his eyes like a bird trapped in a rattlesnake's trance.

The Indian spoke to Cristobal, who answered him after uncharacteristic hesitation. The men argued back and forth in Tewa, Popeh demanding, Cristobal answering. All the while, Popeh's eyes never left Maria's face.

Suddenly, Popeh stepped forward and yanked Maria to her feet again, ripping her dress under the armpit. He pulled her close as if memorizing every pore and freckle on her face. He shook her off then, like a terrier does a mouse.

Maria slumped against the wall. Her legs still would not hold her up. Popeh spoke again to Cristobal, then folded his arms, as if waiting. Cristobal approached Maria again. She did not back away from him this time.

"Maria, he told me to tell you that members of his own family have died for less than this."

Maria straightened, her back against the wall. She clasped her hands in front of her to stop their trembling. "I have done nothing wrong. I beg his mercy and his permission to go."

Cristobal repeated her words to Popeh, who uttered a string of harsh phrases. As he turned away, Maria saw that his back was covered with a mass of scars and welts, as if someone had beaten him. The deep furrows between his shoulders ran with sweat, smearing the white *yeso* paint. He turned to face Maria again, his eyes on her like a hound harrying a rabbit. She forced herself to look away, to concentrate instead on Cristobal, who was reaching for her.

He took her gently by the arm and pulled her toward the opening, speaking in a low voice. "Just keep walking. Do not look back. And hurry when we get outside. I cannot account for Popeh. Not ever. I have saved you for the moment, but the moment may pass."

She took a few tentative steps, walking as if in a dream. Cristobal pulled her out of the room then, snatching up a lighted *farol* as he ducked through the low doorway. With Maria in tow, he hurried through the empty storerooms, pausing only to listen for pursuers. He loosened his grip on her arm finally. "I hear the drums again, Maria. You will be safe now."

They continued in silence from the pueblo's interior and her fear gradually gave way to confusion. Cristobal was deliberately choosing the longest way around the Indian maze. Does he honestly think I would ever, ever go back inside there again? she asked herself.

Back at the *santero*'s workshop, Emiliano was nowhere in sight, but Maria picked up the *retablo* still resting on the window ledge. She touched the paint. It was dry. Santa Teresa's gentle gaze still rested on her folded hands. She had not seen the evil Maria had.

The sun was nearly below the rim of the horizon. "You must walk back," said Cristobal. "I must return to Popeh."

Maria shook her head and held onto his arm. "Do not go back there. Please."

He shook her hand off his arm, smiling slightly, the smile vanishing quickly. "Look, your fingers are white now."

She wiped her hand on her dress. "Cristobal, please!"

Cristobal sighed. "I must go back. It is Popeh's will." They descended the ladder. "I will walk you to the edge of the trees," he said, as if reluctant to let her go. "You know the way to the hacienda."

She walked beside him to the cottonwoods, her legs still shaky but her mind full of Popeh and Cristobal. They stood together at the edge of the trees. "Cristobal," she began, unsure of his reaction, "you do not worship those demons, do you?"

He wouldn't look at her. "You do not understand."

"But what about the True Faith?" she persisted, driven on by demons of her own.

"Maria, I follow *my* true faith." He took her by the shoulders and gave her a gentle shake. "Everyone seems to have forgotten that I am Tewa."

"Only part Tewa," she argued.

"It is enough," he concluded. "Go now. You will be back before dark, if you hurry."

He released her and after a long look at him, she hurried up the road toward Las Invernadas, holding Santa Teresa tightly to her, as if to ward off the demons of Tesuque.

Cutting the Cloak to Fit the Cloth

When she was out of sight of the pueblo, Maria slowed to a walk and looked behind her. No one followed. She paused to take a rock out of her shoe, then started walking quickly to Las Invernadas. She knew she should feel comfort in the knowledge of the strength and power of the Masferrer hacienda but, for the first time, she felt none. One look in Popeh's compelling eyes convinced her that there was no safety in the river kingdom of New Mexico.

She could still see his peculiar yellow eyes measuring her face, compelling her to look at him. Almost as though he were trying to hypnotize me, she said to herself.

The hate in Popeh's eyes had been unmistakable. He hates me because I am Spanish, she thought, stopping in the road and looking down at the serenity of Santa Teresa cradled in her arms.

She looked back once more, then walked on more slowly. All her life she had taken for granted the servitude of Indians. They were there, those slim, dark-skinned people, to serve her and those around her. In exchange they were rewarded with

Spanish ways and the True Faith. They were as little children, looking to their white lords for guidance. But were they really?

Popeh was not childish. If Cristobal had not been there, Popeh would have killed her. *Simply because I am Spanish. What has gone wrong?*

Diego would tell her that nothing was wrong. He would speak of his land and his Indians, as if they were personal possessions, bought and paid for. And yet even he sensed trouble brewing. Why else had he asked her to keep her eyes open?

And then there was Cristobal, equal in all things, according to Diego, except the things that mattered. *He can eat with us, pray with us, dress like us, and even ride horses—Spanish privilege,* she thought. *But he cannot own land, he cannot inherit.*

As Maria stood still in the road, terrified of Tesuque, strangely apprehensive about Las Invernadas, she heard a horse and rider approaching. Instinct drove her off the path and into the cottonwoods lining the road. Then she saw Diego. She returned to the road, her *retablo* held tight against her.

"Maria," he called out, reining in his horse and dismounting quickly. "I have been searching for you. Erlinda said you have been gone since midmorning. I thought it was time to start worrying." He peered closer at her. "What is the matter, Maria chiquita? Where is Cristobal?"

She gestured back toward Tesuque. "He is still there. He told me to leave without him." She hesitated, unwilling to expose Cristobal to Diego, and afraid not to. Fear of Popeh was sharp as a knife pricking her conscience to speak, fear for herself and fear for Cristobal.

Steadying himself against his horse, Diego removed his spurs, dangling the spiked rowels from his gloved hand as he walked beside her. "Tell me, *por favor*. Something is wrong, is it not?" he asked. When Maria would not answer him, he nudged her shoulder. "Come now, Maria. I must know what is going on. Besides, we shook hands on it."

She walked beside him, looking straight ahead. "Do you know an Indian named Popeh?" she asked suddenly.

"No. He is not one of my Indians." He waited for her to continue.

"He is tall and very dark. His eyes are the most curious

137

shade of yellow. . . ." Her voice trailed off as she remembered those eyes. With an effort, and another nudge from Diego, she said, "His back was covered with scars, as if from a flogging."

Diego frowned. "Is this my Taos Indian?" he asked himself out loud. He stopped walking and his horse nuzzled him. He put up his hand and absently stroked the animal's nose. "Your description does remind me of something, the more I think of it. It was just before Papa died, about five years ago. He was too sick to travel but the rest of us had gone to Santa Fe for a hanging."

"Hanging?"

"Yes. Sixty or so Indians were caught practicing their old religion. Remember the *kachinas* I told you about? Three Pueblos were hanged."

"And you went to see it?"

He nodded. "Our governor's command. He thought such spectacle was educational. I suppose it was. I was never tempted to worship a *kachina*. As I was saying, they were hanged, and their bodies left dangling between Santa Fe and Analco. A warning. Thirty or forty other Indians were beaten quite soundly and then thrown in prison. I think this Popeh was one of them. It would seem, Maria, that our Taos trouble is moving south."

"You're sure?" she questioned.

"No more than you are. But I seem to remember that Taos Indian. He was a born leader—and a trouble maker."

Maria took a deep breath. "I saw Popeh, and Cristobal with him. They were wearing enormous headdresses that covered their faces—and they were dancing."

Diego stopped again. "Dancing?"

She nodded. "The room was filled with smoke and there were other Indians chanting and dancing."

"Where was this?" he asked quickly.

"Inside the pueblo. I went in search of Cristobal, got lost, and there they were."

Diego juggled the spurs in his hand. "A *kiva*," he said.

"What?"

"An underground, circular room where the Indians used to summon their gods. I thought the *kiva* in Tesuque was destroyed years ago by the missionaries." They started walking again. "The Fathers have gone to great pains to eradicate all signs of the old ways. I wonder if Father Pio knows?"

"I do not see how he could," replied Maria. "Their *kiva* was in the middle of the pueblo. Cristobal led me out by such a roundabout way that I know I could never find it again." She rubbed her arms, suddenly cold. "As if I would ever look for it."

"You're sure Cristobal was there?" Diego asked, his voice colder than the gathering evening. "You saw him?"

"I told you I did. He was wearing one of the masks and dancing, too."

Diego let out an explosive sigh. "Cristobal! A Spaniard! My brother!"

She remembered Cristobal's words that morning. "Half Spaniard. And half Indian. Also half-brother. He is troubled. Torn."

"But still my brother. A Masferrer does not dance at pagan ceremonies. And the Indians are forbidden to dance."

"You ask me questions and rage at the answers!" she snapped.

He turned away and began walking again. She fell in step. They covered nearly a mile in uncomfortable silence. With each step Maria regretted her words more. He spends 18 hours a day in the saddle, then I keep him awake nights with my nightmares, she brooded. And how much he has done for me. I should not speak harshly to him. "I am sorry," she whispered.

"Accepted. And I am sorry."

"Accepted."

They continued in silence until Maria remembered the *retablo* she carried. She held it out to Diego and he took it, examining the wooden plaque carefully. He tried to hand it back, but she shook her head.

"It is for you, Senor," she said. "Emiliano wanted me to paint it for you. It is supposed to be Santa Teresa de Ávila," she added, afraid that he would not know who it was if she did not tell him.

"Oh, I can tell, Maria," he said, tracing his finger around the outline of the poetess-saint. "You have done a good job. Can it be that Diego Masferrer, *hacendado* of Las Invernadas, *encomendero* of Tesuque's Indians, possesses not only a *santero*, but a *santera* as well? He is a wealthy man indeed."

She could tell that he was teasing her, trying to make her feel better, but his words still spoke of ownership, and they rankled. "I enjoyed painting it."

"It shows, Maria, it shows. I will hang it in my room," he said, putting the *retablo* carefully in his saddlebag, choosing to overlook the coolness in her voice. They continued in a more compatible silence, walking side by side down the narrow road.

A breeze freshened from the northwest, and Diego turned to face it. The rustle of the wind in the cottonwoods, mingled with the chirp of crickets and the peep of tree frogs, brought a smile back to his face.

"Was there ever another place like this, Maria?" he asked, and then laughed at himself, looking down at the ground. "I suppose you think I am now adding foolishness to acquisitiveness on your list of my sins."

So he knew how she felt, even if she had said nothing. "No, never that," she murmured.

"We have none of the wealth of the Indies, nothing really to recommend us. The work here will always be harder than we are. But this is my land, Maria chiquita, and I love it."

She did not add that it was others' land too. Instead, she touched his arm lightly in understanding. He looked at her, then glanced away when she blushed.

When they were in sight of the high walls of Las Invernadas, he cleared his throat. "Maria, I was planning a trip to Santa Fe to take Erlinda and the other girls. We usually go every year at this time. They like to look over the goods that come in on the supply caravan, and visit with friends." He noted the questioning look on her face. "I realize there is no supply caravan this year, but we are going anyway."

"And?" she prompted, when he fell silent.

"Perhaps you would come with us? I want you to speak to Governor Otermin of what you saw in Tesuque."

"Do you feel there is danger?" she asked, feeling the familiar tightness in her stomach.

"Oh, no," he said quickly, then nodded his head. "Why is it that you command the truth in me, chiquita? It is a feeling I have. I have noticed things, and others have too. Now you tell me of Popeh and the *kiva*. I do not want to alarm you, but I believe there may be danger. Perhaps if you and I speak to Otermin. . . ."

"I understand," Maria said. "I will go with you. Who stays with La Senora?"

"The servants. She does not like Santa Fe."

When they were at the front gates of Las Invernadas, Diego's dogs bounded to greet them, nearly knocking their master down in their delight. Diego put his spurs on again and swung into the saddle. "Go on in, Maria. I shall be along later."

She went through the gates and into the hacienda, noting with new eyes the thickness of the walls and the strength of the doors that constituted the only break in the wall. Her hand rested on the heavy iron bolts for a moment, then she closed the door, pushing the bolts in place.

When she entered the kitchen, Erlinda rushed to her. "Maria! I was so worried when the sun got lower and you did not return! Was something wrong?"

"No," Maria lied, amazed at the ease of her prevarication. "I became intent on what I was doing at the saintmaker's and forgot the time." She said nothing about Cristobal, hoping that Erlinda would not mention him. She knew how Erlinda felt about her half-brother.

"Well, you are safe." Erlinda hugged Maria to her.

Supper was long over. Maria rolled some cheese and beans in a cold tortilla and sat down at the table. Erlinda poured her a cup of hot chocolate, stirring the steaming mixture until it foamed.

"Diego found you?" Erlinda asked. "When he saw that you were not here at the table, he got up and left his dinner."

"Yes, he found me. He said he would come in soon."

He entered through the back door just after she spoke, hanging his hat on the peg by the door. Motioning to Maria to stay seated, he fixed himself some tortillas and beans. Erlinda poured him chocolate, and he warmed his hands on the earthenware cup.

"There is a chill in the air," he said.

"Oh, Diego," said Erlinda, "it is only July!"

"I know it!" he exploded, slamming down the cup. "I know it!"

Erlinda was silent, staring at her brother. Diego ran his hand over his beard. "I am sorry, Erlinda. I think I am speaking of a different kind of chill." He took his tortilla in one hand, the chocolate in the other, and stalked down the hall to his room. The door slammed behind him.

Erlinda watched him go, then turned to Maria, appraising

her with the careful glance that missed nothing. "Something is wrong."

Maria got up quickly and walked to the open back door. She looked at the garden, peaceful in the moonlight, and rubbed her arms as if she, too, felt the chill. How could she explain to Erlinda that this chill went deeper than the skin? She shook her head, and Erlinda sighed. "If neither of you will talk to me, I suppose it is not my affair."

When Maria turned back to the table, Erlinda was gone. Maria carried her half-eaten tortilla out to the chicken pen beyond the garden and put it on the ground. She leaned against the fence and stared into the distance until she heard the bell for prayers.

Although Cristobal was not in his place for evening prayers, he was sitting at the table with his brother before breakfast. His back was to Maria as she stood in the doorway tying on her apron. She was fearful of entering the room, unsure of her reception.

Cristobal looked at Diego and without turning around said, "It is all right, Maria. Come in."

"So you know her light step, too?" Diego said, pushing a cold tortilla toward his brother as he looked around to smile at her.

Cristobal picked up the tortilla and rolled it into a cylinder. "I listen for it, the same as you do, Diego. It's just that you won't admit it."

Diego flushed a deep red and got up. Without looking at Cristobal he went to the outside door. "I will be in the corral."

After he left, Cristobal motioned for Maria to sit down. She shook her head. "I have to prepare the baking, Cristobal."

"As you will, then."

The room was crowded with the silence between them. Cristobal finished eating and came to her where she stood over the wooden *batea*, measuring flour. He put his hand on her shoulder.

"You think I should not tease my brother? I should not tease the master of the earth?"

She did not answer. The touch of his hand on her shoulder was warm, but his fingers pressed roughly, almost painfully, and he was standing too close.

"We used to make mudpies together. We shared the same

bed. Can I not tease him if I choose? Or did I hit a nerve that time, eh, Maria chiquita?"

She shook off his hand. "Do not call me that."

"Why not? Diego calls you that."

"It's . . . it's different." She poured flour into the wooden trough, losing count of the measure.

He took the measure from her hands and stepped in front of her. "How?"

The room was so quiet that she could hear her own heartbeat. Or was it Cristobal's? He was standing so close, looking at her. Maria backed against the *batea*.

"Do not ask, Cristobal," she said quietly.

He backed away in turn and leaned against the kitchen table again. "We are much alike, Maria. We both want things we cannot have. You do not belong here any more than I do. Hush now, let me finish," he said, waving her to silence. "Do not think my big brother will ever forget what he owes Las Invernadas. If he cannot acquire more land, more cattle and more of *his* Indians"—he spit the words out—"by marrying well, then he will not bother. Diego does not love—he owns."

She looked at him. "I do not know what you are talking about."

He took his hat off the peg by the door. He was across the room from her, but he still seemed close. "Perhaps you do not . . . yet. But perhaps we are more alike than you care to consider. I asked for permission to marry you once. Perhaps I will do it again. Good day, Maria." He put on his hat, adjusted the ties under his chin and was gone, moving silently down the garden path.

Maria wanted to slam the door after him, to let him know that she did not care for his words. Instead, she turned back to the *batea* and thumped more flour in, coughing as the white dust rose in her face. She stopped, staring at the flour. "By the saints, what am I doing?" she said and began shoveling the unneeded flour back into the sack.

While she measured the liquid ingredients into the *batea*, Cristobal's words were clear in her mind. She did not belong at Las Invernadas. But did she belong anywhere? She knew she should have died in the cholera epidemic. Failing that, she should have perished in the Indian raid on the supply caravan, or in Diego Masferrer's cornfield. And now here she was, by some curious twist of God's grace. But did she belong?

Cristobal's words had brought her back to her senses. If she had ever thought of Diego as husband instead of master, she would not do so again. Princes married poor girls only in the stories she had told Luz and Catarina.

"Foolish Maria," she murmured out loud, dumping the bread dough onto the table. "Silly girl."

Cristobal sought her out more than ever. If Maria had thought he was courting, she would have discouraged him, but how could these harmless walks with the children or simple conversations between friends be called courting? Even if Diego, whose scowling eyes sometimes followed them, thought it was courting, Maria knew it was not. She and Cristobal were two foreigners at Las Invernadas, two half-members of the Masferrer clan, dependent on Diego's generosity—and sufferance.

Maria often walked with Luz and Catarina around the cornfield after the evening meal, while the sky was still light. She loved to watch impetuous Catarina test the limits of her surveillance, while Luz followed shyly. The children liked to play hide-and-seek among the corn rows, grown tall enough now to shelter them from each other's eyes. Diego would not allow them beyond the walls alone, so Maria was content to lead them out and sit by herself as they darted in and out of the rows, chasing each other and shrieking with laughter.

And Cristobal joined her there often, to sit cross-legged, saying nothing. One night, after considerable soul-searching, she turned to look at him. As usual, he was watching her, observing her face with the same leisurely air that characterized most of his actions. He had none of the driven nature of Diego. He did not appear to hurry from task to task, as did his half brother. He had the time to sit in silence and observe Maria. How different the brothers were. Maria smiled to herself.

Cristobal leaned back and propped himself up on one elbow, his eyes still on Maria's face. "Why do you smile?"

She shook her head, still smiling. "I was just thinking about you and Diego. You appear to be standing still, even when you are busy."

He laughed, and the laughter pleased her. It helped banish a different Cristobal—Cristobal the savage in thrall to Popeh.

"You compare me to Diego Masferrer, who always looks busy, even when he is standing still!"

She joined his laughter. "And why is that, do you suppose?"

Cristobal looked away then, his mood changing, his face suddenly serious. "Because all this is his, and he knows there are not enough hours in a day to get everything done." His mood changed again, like a cloud passing over the sun, and he smiled. "You should have known him when he was younger, before our father died. He was different then."

Cristobal paused. "I should qualify that. Don't I sound like Diego? He and I were both busy, even from the time of our early youth. You see how it is around here. But when the inheritance fell to him—and the burden—he went from being my brother to being my master."

He said no more, and she did not press him. She was becoming used to his Indian silences. They sat together and watched the Masferrer sisters until the bell sounded for prayers.

Cristobal got up, reaching down his hand for Maria, and tugged her to her feet. "That bell," he said, "that bell. It follows me everywhere."

"It's only prayers," she said, motioning to the girls.

Again he was silent, leading the way down to the *acequia* and across the bridge, moving with the wonderful grace that made him part of his surroundings. Maria thought again how much she would like to paint Cristobal Masferrer.

He met her often at the cornfield and she found a certain peace in his silence, a security in his quiet that made her think of him often during the day. But she learned the impenetrability of that silence when she tried once to talk to him about Tesuque and Popeh.

They had been sitting as they usually sat, at the edge of the cornfield, Maria with her legs drawn up close to her body and chin on her knees, Cristobal lying beside her, just at the edge of her vision.

"Cristobal, tell me about Popeh."

She had said it suddenly, quickly, and the words hung on the cooling air. She did not turn to look at Cristobal, but sat staring straight ahead into the cornfield. When several minutes of silence passed, she turned her head slightly to look at Cristobal. He was gone. He had risen silently and left her.

It was several days before he joined her again at the cornfield, and then he spoke of other things. Maria never asked him about Popeh again, even though she longed to know more, to understand the feelings of fear that came to her when she remembered Popeh and his eyes full of hate. But Cristobal would not speak of what went on at Tesuque.

And then something happened, and he never came to sit with her again.

Maria remembered the date, July 15. She knew that she would never forget it, that each July 15 to come, some corner of her heart would go out to Cristobal Masferrer. And she knew that she was not the only one who would remember.

The day began as all others. The rhythm of life at Las Invernadas had worked itself into Maria's senses. She rose now by instinct, dressed, spent a moment in prayer before the room's altar, then hurried to the kitchen, tying on her apron or smoothing her hair back with impatient fingers.

But this morning she did not enter the kitchen. The brothers were inside as usual, and they were quarreling. It was a loud, shouting argument. She knew she should not listen, knew she should go back down the hall to her room and wait there until there was silence again, but she heard her name spoken.

It was Cristobal, his voice strained with tension, filled with a desperation that both surprised and saddened her. "You are sure you know what Maria wants! Do you ever ask her, eh? Do you ever slow down long enough to think about people?"

"You know I do, Cristobal," replied Diego, his voice low.

"I do not! We are not people to you. You pat us on the back as you fondle your dogs, a pat here, a kind word there, and then you presume to run our lives!"

The bench scraped back and tipped over as Diego leaped to his feet, all patience gone. "What would you have me to do, brother?" he roared. "Do you think it was my idea to take over Las Invernadas so young? Do you think I like working so hard that I fall asleep at the dinner table? Somebody has to run this place!"

Cristobal too was on his feet. "But must you run our lives as well? I do not ask your advice or permission this time. I love Maria," he said, the bare pleading in his voice going to Maria's heart. "You told me once to think about it. Well, I have! All I want to do is ask her. She will say yes."

"I do not think she will," said Diego. "But you are not going to ask her anything. I will not allow it, not while she has committed herself into my care."

Maria flinched at the sound of broken glass, followed by a resounding slap.

"Don't you ever strike me again, Diego," said Cristobal, his voice heavy with menace. "If you want her for your own, just say so, my brother. Let her choose for herself. Who knows? Maybe she prefers someone who is too tired to love her." His voice rose then, "But she does not come with cattle or nails or land or fenceposts, so I think you are just playing the same game you have always played, you and all of you Spaniards. If you cannot have it, then nobody else will either! We have had a bellyful of your games!"

Someone sat down heavily on the table. "Then I have failed you, Cristobal," said Diego quietly.

"You were bound to someday," Cristobal shouted.

"So be it then," snapped Diego, the spark leaping into flame once more. "But Maria is not for you."

"Not for your bastard Indian brother, eh? I know her better than you ever will, Diego mio." Cristobal's voice was low, scarcely audible.

"No, you do not, Cristobal, for all the time you have spent with her. And you never will, because you are Indian and we are not. It has finally come down to that."

Then the brothers were silent, drained by the passion of their argument. Cristobal spoke at last. "You will regret this morning's work, my brother."

The outside door slammed. In the silence that followed, she heard Diego weeping, his sobs heavy, dragged out of his body with great pain. Her own heart heavy, she turned and fled to her room.

Diego said nothing to Maria of the incident with Cristobal, nothing to anyone. He was silent and withdrawn, in the evenings moving restlessly from room to room or sitting by himself in the unused *sala*. On the mornings when she was at work in the kitchen before him, Diego would enter quickly, looking around for Cristobal. When he did not see his brother, he would eat in silence, ignoring her presence. Often at night she would hear him walking back and forth in the hall.

Cristobal did not return to Las Invernadas until late July, and then one morning he was sitting in the kitchen beside

Diego, the two of them dipping yesterday's bread in last night's chocolate, together as in earlier days. Maria entered the kitchen to begin her day's work, too shy to look at either brother, excited by the presence of both of them.

"Dios bendiga, Maria," said Diego as usual.

"And to you, Senor," she answered as usual.

Cristobal rose, wiping his hands on his shirt. "I will be with the cattle today, my brother," he said. "Several have strayed beyond the Gutierrez place."

"I am sure they have, my brother."

"What? You do not know, down to the last horn and hide, where they are?" said Cristobal. His words were teasing, his tone harsh.

"Don't, Cristobal," whispered Diego, pushing back his cup and looking up at his brother.

"Very well, master," said Cristobal with a sweeping bow.

Maria watched the anger rising in Diego's eyes, but still he said nothing. With a laugh, Cristobal waved to her and left, closing the door gently behind him.

Maria bent over the *batea,* kneading the bread. Diego poured himself another cup of chocolate and sat there, watching it grow cold.

"Why did he come back, Maria?"

She shook her head, unwilling to look at him. She was crying into the bread dough, unable to control her sobs. She wanted to wipe her face, but her arms were sticky to the elbow with flour and water.

Diego got up, pulling out his handkerchief. He tipped her head back and covered her nose with it. "Blow." She blew, then he wiped her eyes with a corner of the handkerchief.

"Don't cry, Maria. I cannot bear it. It isn't your trouble."

She looked up suddenly, her eyes full of anger. "Oh, yes it is!"

His voice rose. "It cannot be helped!"

"Not now. The thing has gone too far. I am to blame, and I know it."

"You are not to blame," Diego said, pocketing his handkerchief and sitting on the edge of the table. "I stare at my own sins when I look at Cristobal." He paused, looking away carefully. "So what should we do?"

"I should leave here, Diego."

He smiled. She had never called him by name before. "And where would you go, Maria chiquita?" he asked softly, his eyes kind again. "You belong here."

"I do not. Cristobal belongs here."

He made no reply. She wiped her hands on her apron and stood with them folded in front of her, torn by gratitude and guilt, love and despair. "I wonder why I did not die in that Indian massacre."

He leaned toward her and touched her arm. "I have wondered that, too, Maria. From the little, the very little, you have told me, I wonder, too. It is one of God's mysteries, and it does us no credit to question it."

She sighed and returned to the bread. After watching her a moment, Diego went out into the garden. He stood on the path, looked around him at the morning, stretched, rubbed his back and walked toward the footbridge. Maria finished the bread dough while the Indian servant girl swept the dirt floor. Usually Maria enjoyed the homey sound of the broom on the dirt, but today the whispering sound filled her with sadness. I will go to Margarita, she thought, although in her heart she knew that wasn't the answer.

Maria was interrupted by Erlinda, who came into the kitchen with her sisters. "Here, Maria," she said, "let us put these worthless ones to work."

Luz and Catarina grinned at her. Erlinda held them close so they could not dart away. "Come, you scamps," she said. "We shall help Maria gather the dirty linen. If we can get the washing done today, then it will not be staring at us when we return from Santa Fe."

Her words were magic. Luz and Catarina scattered to collect the laundry. Erlinda and Maria pulled the wooden *bateas* from the storeroom and into the kitchen yard, where they started a fire in the large copper kettle.

"I suppose you do not think Santa Fe is much, Maria," Erlinda said, "but to us, it is all we know of towns and cities."

Maria picked up two leather buckets and started for the *acequia*. She looked back at Erlinda who followed, buckets in hand. "Mexico City is a grand place, and I miss some of the excitement, but the air smells cleaner here, and I like to listen for the frogs at night."

Erlinda made a face. "You sound like Diego. You will not

believe this, but I have seen him sit outside, just listening to the crickets. And he has the most pleasant expression on his face." She laughed. "Although lately he just falls asleep after dinner. How like an old ranchero he grows!"

Maria dipped a bucket in the *acequia*, watched it fill and felt it grow heavy in her hand. "Erlinda, he is so overworked."

They spent the morning over the washtub, scrubbing the soiled clothing with yucca root and stirring the shirts, dresses and stockings in the boiling water before dipping them in the cool water in the *bateas* to soak. The work was hot and hard, but Maria did not tire. She was growing accustomed to the drudgery of the river kingdom. As she squeezed the water out of Diego's clean shirt, she thought of her mother, who never in her life did anything more strenuous than embroider altar cloths.

You would never know me, Mama, Maria thought as she piled the clothes into a Pueblo basket. She felt no bitterness against her parents, only resignation. She had thought for a time that there might be a place for her in the upper colony of the Rio del Norte, but her sister's rejection and Diego's words about land and nails and fenceposts sealed her fate—and her heart. As much as she abhorred the calculation of his words, she could not fault his honesty. She possessed nothing of worth to tempt him, and he had never given her any reason to hope.

Erlinda leaned over the *batea*. "Maria, your face is so solemn. Of what are you thinking?"

Maria rested her hands in the cool water. "Of nails and fenceposts," she replied quietly, her eyes on Diego's shirts floating in the rinse water.

Erlinda's eyes went to the water, too, and she made no reply.

They left for Santa Fe before the sun was up the next morning. The full moon was still big in the sky, so it was an easy matter for the Indian servants to hitch the oxen to the four-wheel cart. Diego lifted his sisters and Maria into the wagon and mounted his own horse. They moved slowly down the road from the hacienda, the wagon creaking and rumbling, guided by the Indian servant who walked alongside with a long whip.

The little girls hovered on the edge of sleep. Luz leaned against Maria with her eyes closed as Erlinda finished braiding her hair. As soon as her hair was done, Luz plopped her head down in Maria's lap and Erlinda swung the child's legs up onto the hard seat.

Maria leaned against the side of the wagon, her head resting on her arm. Erlinda finished Catarina's hair, tying the ends deftly with a small piece of lace. "Ah, Maria," she said, "you look so low."

Maria glanced up. "You cannot imagine how tedious that *entrada* was from Mexico City to Santa Fe. I suppose I suffer from remembrance."

"We will be in Santa Fe by noon," replied Erlinda, plaiting her own hair. She wound her hair on her head, securing it with pins. "Perhaps you wonder why we use such a cart?"

"I do," answered Maria. "I have seen no proper coaches since I left Mexico."

"It is impossible to bring such a thing so far," Erlinda explained, raising her voice to be heard above the squeaking wheels. "And no one has the skills here—or the time—to make one." Erlinda reached across and covered Luz with the end of Maria's light cloak. "Papa did try to bring one here. He wanted Mama to have a fine coach." She giggled like a young girl at the memory. "He managed to get as far as Chihuahua before the whole thing fell apart."

Maria laughed and Erlinda continued. "Papa was like that. He would try things no one else would. I suppose it has given us a local reputation for eccentricity, but we do not care."

"What was he like?"

"Papa? Oh, like me, like Diego. You would have enjoyed him, Maria. He has been gone from us more than five years now, but I still miss him with intensity." She looked at Diego, riding to the front of the wagon. "Life would have been different for Diego, had Papa lived."

"How do you mean?" asked Maria, gentle in her intrusion. Erlinda did not often speak of the past.

"Diego always wanted to go to the university in Mexico City. The plans were made, that summer of his fourteenth year. Then Papa became ill. So ill. When it looked as if he would not get well, Diego sent our little brother Francisco in his place." Her eyes clouded at the memory. "Dear Francisco. He was only thirteen. He cried all the way to Santa Fe, begging Diego to go in his place. But Diego could not, even though he wanted to."

"And what did your father look like?" Maria asked.

"Much like Francisco and me," she replied. "Tall and blond, with big feet," she laughed. "As Diego will remind me forever!" She leaned forward in confidence. "Did you know that Diego still keeps Papa's boots in one corner of his room?"

"I have noticed the boots there when I get the journal for your mother," Maria replied. "I thought they were Diego's."

"Oh, no. Diego has never spoken of them, but they are his reminder."

"That he must fill them?" said Maria.

Erlinda nodded solemnly and looked at her brother. He had spurred on ahead to greet an early riser from the Gutierrez hacienda just beyond Tesuque. "There is no finer man in all the Rio Arriba than my brother," Erlinda said, her eyes on Maria again. "The day Papa died, Diego became a man. I do not think he has ever resented his duties, no matter how hard they are. I do not suppose he even regrets Mexico City anymore." Erlinda reached over and touched Maria lightly on the knee. "Besides, the crickets probably do not sing New Mexican songs there, and who can ever vouch for frogs?"

Maria joined in Erlinda's gentle laughter, then she was suddenly serious. "And were it not for him, I would not be here." She did not tell Erlinda the rest. How morning after morning, even in Luz and Catarina's room, she would wake to find Diego's sword across the foot of her bed, a cold reminder of restless sleep, restless ghosts and warm protection.

The dreams came to her now dimly in a troubled night, but she must still cry out in her sleep, because Diego would be there, sitting on the floor by her bed until she passed into deeper sleep. His sword in the morning was the only reminder. And after she left her room for her early morning duties in the kitchen, he would reclaim his sword before Luz or Catarina woke. She knew because once she had seen him, but she did not understand the meaning of his actions.

Erlinda closed her eyes and leaned back, then sat up suddenly. Maria could scarcely hear her voice above the noise of the wagon's wheels. "Maria, take good care of them," she said.

Maria leaned forward too. "What do you mean, Erlinda?" she asked.

"I do not know," said Erlinda, embarrassment in her voice.

"It is a feeling I have, nothing more. And look now, I have startled you. Forgive me."

She was silent then, and soon her eyes closed in sleep. Maria pulled Luz closer to her, wondering at the impulsive words. The morning air took on a chill that she felt all the way to her shoes. She thought then of the third person in her dreams, a person dimly glimpsed, as through a haze of smoke. A person tall and black with yellow eyes.

Unlike Father Efrain and Carmen de Sosa, the demon of Popeh pursued her in daylight as well as sleep. He was a sudden sound causing her to whirl about, her heart hammering against her rib cage. He was never there, of course, but he lived in her mind. Having seen Popeh once, she dared not dismiss him. She looked at the sleeping Erlinda. "I will take care of them, all of them," she whispered, then crossed herself. She looked toward the Sangre de Cristo Mountains, a gloomy heap to the east that darkened further as the sun rose slowly behind them in glorious contrast.

The journey to Santa Fe took six hours. Diego relieved the tedium of travel for his little sisters by taking turns holding them before him in the saddle, laughing and singing old songs, some of which were familiar to Maria from her own childhood, others of which were Tewa Indian songs, learned long ago from his Indian servants.

Diego could make even the solemn Luz chuckle, her hands before her mouth like a proper Spanish lady. Luz sang almost as loudly as her brother, sitting close to him, holding the reins in her hands. Tirant ignored her tugging and sawing on the reins, responding instead to the pressure of Diego's legs and spurs. Maria laughed to watch Luz, who thought she controlled the black horse of Spain.

"How much alike they are," said Maria to Erlinda.

"Yes. Luz looks like Diego and Mama," said Erlinda. "I wish we had more time for this. Luz and Catarina see him so seldom."

And soon there was Santa Fe to watch for. Even Luz abandoned her efforts with Tirant to look for the red-brown villa that seemed to appear out of nowhere, the color of the adobe blending so well with the earth that they were almost upon the town before anyone realized it. Smoke curled from the chimneys into the startling blue and white of the noonday sky.

Maria watched the smoke rising. "What will you do here?" she asked.

"Ordinarily, we would go to the shops," answered Erlinda. "It takes several months for the goods from caravans to reach the shelves. They must be unpacked, counted and taxed." She chuckled. "And then taxed again, I vow! Of course, there was no caravan this year, so there is nothing on the shelves we have not already seen. But we go. It is a good time to visit."

"Where do you stay?"

"At the home of my parents-in-law, Marco's family. We have always stayed with the Castellanos. Even before my marriage. Things are different now since . . . well, they are different now, but still we visit."

The oxcart followed Diego into a quiet side street and stopped before a low adobe building. It was built like all the other houses in town, great or small, with a windowless wall on the street's edge, broken only by a stout door. The door was open, and Maria saw a welcome glimpse of courtyard and flowering plants, then people coming out with smiles and exclamations of greeting.

The Castellanos met them on the street, greeting Erlinda with cries of delight. They embraced her, Luz, and Catarina in welcome. Maria remained by the wagon, aching with a loneliness she had not experienced since the death of her own parents. She watched the Castellanos and the Masferrers and was filled with a yearning to belong to someone of her own again. She felt a great lump rising in her throat and she would have turned away, but Diego was prodding her forward.

"And this is Maria Espinosa de la Garza," he introduced her to the Castellanos. "She has been honoring Las Invernadas with a visit these past months."

Don Reynaldo Castellano extended his hand and drew her toward him. "Then our home is yours." He touched his chest with his other hand.

Only Diego's hand resting lightly on Maria's shoulder kept her tears from falling. "Thank you," she managed, "thank you."

"You must excuse Senorita Espinosa and me," Diego said to Don Reynaldo. "We have a matter of business to attend to. Do not wait dinner for us." Don Reynaldo and his wife protested, but bowed to them as they left the courtyard, La Senora

Castellano promising to keep something hot for them to eat later.

"I am sorry," Diego said as they crossed the street. "We did not mean to make you sad."

She shook her head. "It is nothing. I was homesick for a moment, sad about not belonging."

"I think of you as such a part of my own household that I do not call it to mind anymore."

It was a gracious thing to say. Cristobal would have called his words another example of Diego's acquisitiveness, but Maria could not agree. She glanced at Diego shyly. "Thank you, Senor."

"Watch where you are going," Diego warned as he steered her around a pig rooting in the street. "This is not a large city, but it is the only one I know, and I have learned to look out for pigs."

They crossed the street. Another block, walked in silence, took them to the plaza fronting the palace of the governors. Maria stopped, in spite of herself. She remembered La Dona Margarita and her reception and could not bring herself to go any closer.

"Come, Maria," said Diego. "I will not leave you alone this time. We must speak to the governor about Popeh."

The plaza's midsummer color was fading already into the brown of drought, but the fountain bubbled with water from the *acequia* close by. Women stood around the water with their large jars, gossiping with each other and watching the passersby. Several of the older women greeted Diego, stopping him to ask about his mother. He paused to exchange a few words with them. The young women eyed him with slow, sidelong glances.

Maria looked toward the governor's palace. Indians were selling food and notions on the wide portal that shaded the walkway around the building. They squatted, their goods displayed on blankets in front of them. Though they looked asleep, they came to life with surprising swiftness when a browser knelt to examine their wares.

After bowing to the ladies, Diego took Maria's arm and they walked toward the wide, open *zaguan* of the palace that led to the large interior courtyard. The entrance was guarded by two brass cannons, both of which showed visible signs of neglect.

"I think these weapons have not been fired since Noah's flood," Diego said.

Her glance was attracted to the outside walls. There were rows and rows of curious brown circles, misshapen and shrivelled. She walked closer, then gasped, turning back to Diego for explanation.

"Apache ears," he said. "Did you not notice them the first time you came here?"

She shook her head, thinking of Cristobal and the woman softly crooning to her baby in the Tesuque pueblo. But, of course, they were good Indians, not Apaches.

"Well, I have tacked a few there myself," he finished, carefully overlooking the tightness around Maria's mouth and eyes. "Apache, Maria, remember that. And now, shall we go inside? I cannot see any guards to stop us. In fact, I cannot see any guards at all."

The courtyard was the same. Maria could almost see herself sitting on the far bench, eagerly waiting for her sister, La Dona Margarita. So long ago it seemed. But it was only a few months, the time of the early planting, when Maria had sat there, expecting her sister to make things better.

She followed Diego inside the palace. The wide corridor was cool and smelled of pine and wax. Diego went to an open door, peered inside, then rapped on the wooden frame.

Governor Antonio de Otermin was seated behind a large desk, writing. He looked up in surprise when Diego entered, then half rose from his chair and extended his hand across the desk. Diego kissed it as Maria dropped a curtsy.

The governor seated himself carefully, folding his hands in front of him. "Diego Masferrer," he began, fixing Diego with a stare that made Maria move uneasily from one foot to the other. "Diego Masferrer. I have been expecting you. Indeed, I have." He motioned toward the chair in front of his desk and they sat down.

"How is this, my lord?" Diego asked. "I did not know you wanted to see me."

"Oh, I do. I do. We have a small matter to discuss." The governor eyed Maria and she drew back involuntarily. "This small matter," he continued, watching her.

"But first." He looked back at Diego and then at his desk. "For Father Pio, in Tesuque," he said, handing a small book to Diego. "Would you see that he gets it?"

"Of course, your honor," Diego replied, pocketing the book. He started to say something else, but the governor interrupted.

"And I have something more for you, Diego. Of a more serious nature. Except I wonder if you will think it serious. I wonder if you Masferrers think like the rest of us." He held out a sheaf of papers, bound with red cord and sealed with red wax.

Diego frowned and did not reach for the document. "Take it, Senor, indeed you must," the governor insisted, holding the papers, "although I do not wonder at your hesitancy. Take it!"

Diego reached across the desk, his gloved hand closing around the paper, the seal crunching in his grip. He took off his gloves, pulled the string from the paper, flattened it out and read.

Maria stirred uneasily in her chair as the veins in Diego's neck stood out and his face darkened. "What is the meaning of this?" Diego spoke softly, and Maria's uneasiness increased. She knew that tone of his.

The governor had gone back to his writing, his pen scratching on the paper. He looked up leisurely. "Unless residing in this dusty kingdom has completely deranged me, Senor, I suspect that someone has issued a warrant for your arrest."

As Maria rose from her chair, Diego motioned her to sit down, but she continued to stand. The governor gave her a curious glance. "It is from your sister, La Dona Margarita Espinosa de Guzman."

When she continued to stare at the governor, the color draining from her face, he went on, looking this time at Diego. "She calls you all manner of dreadful things, Senor Masferrer." He leaned across the desk in a conspiratorial manner. "I enjoy the part where she says you are a lecher and a womanizer, ready to take advantage of a lonely orphan and a poor, helpless widow. Have you come to that part yet?"

Diego raised his eyes to the governor, and Otermin looked away. "Poor, helpless widow indeed!" murmured the governor. "How grateful I am that I do not have two in my kingdom like Margarita Guzman." His glance rested on Maria again. "You look like a ghost, child. Sit down, do."

When she had lowered herself into the chair again, Otermin spoke to Diego. "But the presence of Maria Espinosa in your company does require some explanation. I am willing—nay, I am eager—to listen to your side of it. I fully suspect it will prove to be as interesting as La Viuda Guzman's story, and it has been a dull summer."

Diego rose so abruptly that his chair fell crashing against the dirt floor. He leaned across the governor's desk, his eyes boring into the governor's. Then he deliberately ripped the arrest warrant in pieces.

"Now, Diego," said the governor, less assurance in his voice. "You know I have copies in triplicate, perhaps even quadruplicate. Our country runs on red sealing wax. I insist that you sit down and tell me of this little—shall we call it—adventure of yours. You hardly seem the womanizing type, although the Widow Guzman would persuade me otherwise."

Diego pounded on the governor's desk, overturning the inkwell which spilled onto the floor.

The governor frowned, but did not move. "I think you go too far, Masferrer."

"Not I," replied Diego in that quiet, rock-hard voice that Maria dreaded. "The Widow Guzman goes too far, and she will hear from me before the sun sinks much lower. But first, Maria, will you tell this man how you came into my household? One moment, Maria. Governor, perhaps you should call in your scribe to take this down. I see him peeking around the door there."

The governor motioned to the man standing just outside the door. He was dressed in black like all scribes, the white collar around his neck wilted and brown with sweat. The scribe sidled into the room, reminding Maria of the solicitors who had picked over and plundered her home in Mexico City. She thought also of the vultures at the caravan massacre.

The scribe picked up the chair Diego had tipped over and then seated himself on a stool by the governor's desk, hitching himself and the stool closer to the window and farther away from Diego Masferrer. He readied pen and ink from the writing table he carried. The ink from the governor's desk continued to drip to the floor, soaking into the dirt.

"Your Excellency," Maria began, "your Excellency, it is not Diego's fault." Otermin's smirk was eloquent. "You have no right to make accusations against the only friend I have in this whole, miserable Rio Arriba," Maria continued. "After you and Diego left me with my sister, she told me that she could not support me, or take me into her household. She said she was too poor to afford another mouth or a sister without a dowry."

"She is poor like Croesus," commented the governor, half to himself. "No, no, Juan, do not take that down, you block-head! Only Maria Espinosa's words. But do go on, my dear."

"That is really all there is," said Maria, sitting farther forward on the edge of her chair, gripping the arms. "She left me there."

"But where did you go?" asked the governor. "I went back to the courtyard, but you were gone."

Maria's voice fell to a whisper. "She said I would have to be made a ward of the town. I just could not stay. It would have been too humiliating." She squared her shoulders and spoke louder. "I have honor."

Diego smiled for the first time, and his fingers went to the scar by his ear.

"I remembered that Senor Masferrer said he lived north of Santa Fe near Tesuque. I started walking."

"You walked to Tesuque?" asked the governor.

"Yes. How else was I to get there?"

"How, indeed," replied Otermin. "Were you not afraid?"

Maria's eyes softened at the silliness of his question. "Oh, yes. You cannot fully comprehend how frightened I was, Your Excellency. But I told myself that since I was still alive, after all that I had been through, that I would survive."

"And did you not wonder about your reception?"

Maria thought a moment, not looking at Diego, who stirred beside her but made no comment. "Not really. I did not think he would turn me away. Do you know Diego Masferrer, Your Excellency? I know you are his governor, but do you *know* him?"

"Perhaps I do not," admitted Otermin.

Maria smiled at Diego, her love illuminating her expression from within. As Diego bent to right the inkwell, the flush rose in his face.

"And so you have lived there ever since. In what capacity, may I ask?"

"As a servant. Senor Masferrer would not hear of it at first, but I told him that those were my conditions."

"You told *him?"* said the governor, a new respect rising in his eyes.

"She has a mind of her own, Excellency," Diego interjected.

Maria looked from one man to the other. "I told him that since I had no one and nothing, I would earn my own way."

"And does she?" the governor asked Diego. There was no malice in his voice this time, no innuendo. The scribe's scratching pen was loud in the quiet room.

"Yes, and then some," Diego replied. "She tends to household chores, reads to my mother and helps with my little sisters. I might add that she has taken much of the burden from my sister Erlinda."

Otermin folded his hands together on the large desk, looking at Diego. "And you, sir, have you felt no slight, tiny twinge that perhaps the Widow Guzman might be concerned about the welfare of her sister?"

"None, Governor Otermin. After Maria knelt at my feet and pleaded with me to give her shelter, I never gave La Senora Guzman another thought."

"So it would seem," murmured the governor. "But it appears now that La Senora Guzman has entertained second thoughts. It puzzles me, Masferrer, how a stiff-necked ranchero like you, and I might add, like all the stiff-necked rancheros in this Godforsaken land, would not have considered the question of honor."

"La Viuda Guzman has no honor."

"Indeed she has," said the governor. "Do not we all? Sometimes I think it is our Spanish curse. Of course she has honor," continued Otermin. "I strongly suspect she was just toying with Maria. It is a regrettable habit she has. She is a whimsical woman. She came to me in tears, real tears, mind you, after Maria was discovered gone, to plead with me to do something about the situation."

"I do not believe the Widow's tears," said Diego.

"You must be more charitable, Diego. She has come to me to right things. It would be best for Maria to leave your household."

"No!" shouted Diego. The governor was silent. Diego could

not look at Maria. "That is, not unless Senorita Espinosa wishes to go."

"Of late, I have been considering it," Maria told the governor quietly.

"It seems that your sister wants you now," replied Otermin.

"Maria!" Diego said. "How can you?"

She raised her eyes to his. "It would end a situation at Las Invernadas that can only grow more dreadful, Senor."

Otermin waved to the scribe to stop writing. "I must say, Maria, you are telling me what I want to hear, but why do I feel so uncomfortable all of a sudden? Nonetheless, because you have not the protection of a husband, I think that you have no choice."

The room was silent again. The scribe looked up from the paper on his lap, his eyes eager for more. He dipped the quill in the ink, ready. Diego walked to the window and stood there, looking into the courtyard, his hands behind his back.

"And what if I marry her?" he asked.

Maria gripped the arms of the chair, wondering if she had heard him correctly. The scribe bent over his record, his smile broad. He could scarcely wait to leave the room and tell someone, anyone. The idea of Diego Masferrer marrying a penniless nobody would flame the fires of gossip long past the first frost.

The governor leaned forward as if he had been struck from behind. "Well, Senor," he said, when he found his voice again. "I suppose you could do that."

"Then I shall," said Diego, turning around.

"But, Diego," continued the governor, "do not be hasty! Have you considered? She is a pretty little thing—provided one is partial to freckles, of course—but she has no dowry, no family connections here, no . . ." he paused, at a loss. "The people of Santa Fe will think you have been wandering around in the sun without your hat."

"Of what possible concern is that to me?" Diego asked.

"None, obviously," snapped the governor, his patience receding. "But what would your father have said?"

"He probably would have said 'Congratulations, long life, and many children,'" replied Diego, "because you see, Excellency, the possibility lingers in the back of my mind that I am not really good enough for Maria. Perhaps she will make me better than I am."

"Oh, Diego," murmured Maria. She could not raise her eyes to his face.

The governor stood and walked to the window to stand close to Diego. "Now I am not a romantic man, Masferrer, but you say nothing of love."

"I am a realist, too, Excellency," said Diego. "I do not have the time to sit down with my feelings, to think of love. I know there is no survival in this brutal place unless one marries well." His eyes softened again as he looked at Maria.

"Then why are you saying this now?" asked the governor.

Diego looked out the window again. "I do not know. It was just an idea. And not a bad one, for all that you think me crazy." He turned suddenly. "But in the meantime, no matter what we decide, I will not cooperate with your warrant, I will not give up Maria." He went to Maria and pulled her to her feet. "And now, good day to you, Excellency."

Outside in the plaza Maria looked at Diego, then lowered her eyes. "Senor, what you said to the governor, it isn't necessary. I know that you do not love me." There, she had said it.

He stood still before her. "And is that so important?"

"Senor, twice in the last year, three times, I have not died when I was supposed to. I think I see life, my life, differently now. What remains of it must surely be a gift to me. Perhaps you think me foolish, or greedy, to want another gift as well, but I do want it. I even dare to hope for it." She hesitated, then plunged on boldly. "And as you do not love me, let us not waste each other's time. We can give each other nothing of what we require to survive. You need land and I need love."

"That is true. But still. . . ."

"Senor, you have amply spelled out your requirements—your cattle, nails and fenceposts," she continued in a rush, embarrassed beyond endurance and entirely out of patience with this man that she loved.

Diego burst out laughing. "Cedar fenceposts, Maria chiquita! Only the best!"

"Oh, will you not be serious?" she raged, stamping her foot.

Diego took her arm again and headed down a quiet side street. "Maria, this is becoming so tangled. Let us speak no more about it. Now, I think we should pay a call of courtesy on your sister."

Maria hung back. "Must we?" It was one thing to be humiliated by her sister with no one else present. It would be quite another thing with Diego there.

"Well, it will not be a pleasant interview," Diego agreed. "But she cannot say such things about a Masferrer."

As they approached the Guzman house, the Widow Guzman stepped from her courtyard into the street. She came toward Diego and Maria rapidly, the cross she wore about her neck swinging vigorously from side to side. Diego tightened his grip on Maria's arm, forcing her to stand where she was.

Margarita scarcely glanced at her young sister. She faced Diego, who was slightly shorter than she, and stared down at him. "Senor, you are a scoundrel!"

Diego bowed and smiled, the coldness in his eyes matching Margarita's. "I would say the same to you, Senora, if you were a man."

"I wonder that your mother and sister would allow you to treat my poor sister in such a manner," she continued, darting a fierce glance at Maria.

"I advise you not to speak of my women," Diego hissed.

"I suppose we cannot expect much from a blind woman who floats on dreams, but I did think Erlinda Castellano was not so lost to virtue that she would allow you to bed with my own sister at Las Invernadas."

"You have gone too far now," whispered Diego in his deadly quiet voice.

Maria's hands were clammy and cold, and her throat threatened to close off completely, but she was filled with her own fire. "Margarita, when you left me, I went to the only person in all of New Mexico that I knew would not cast me off! Did you really expect me, your sister, to throw myself on the mercy of this town? Do I not have honor, too?"

Margarita rounded on her young sister, grabbed her by the shoulders and shook her until Maria's hair came loose from its pins and fell about her shoulders. With an oath, Diego wrenched Maria away from Margarita, who turned and raked her long fingernails down his face, drawing blood.

"Hechizera!" he muttered, wiping the blood off his cheek, his eyes blinking.

A crowd of residents who had heard the commotion and left their dinner tables was beginning to form. Others ran for the governor. Margarita looked around her but did not stop. "I hope it was a warm bed, Maria!" she screamed.

Diego slapped Margarita, his gloved hand making a cruel noise on her face. "You go too far, you witch!" he roared. "Maria has been working for us as a servant!"

Margarita gasped as though she had been struck again. Her mouth opened and closed several times. She looked from Maria to Diego, and then back to her sister. "A servant! You, the daughter of *hidalgos* and *conquistadores*, scrubbing floors, washing walls! *Ay de mi,* the humiliation!" She dropped to her knees in the street, wailing and rocking from side to side. Maria knelt by her sister and tried to put her arms around her, but the widow pulled away.

"I thought for a while that I would help you after all," she shrieked, "but if you are so dead to your own position. . . ." She left her sentence unfinished, moaning and holding her head in her hands.

Maria got to her feet, tears filling her eyes. "Margarita, I had to eat, I had to survive. No one would help me except Diego Masferrer. Not even you, my sister."

Margarita shook her head. "Better you had died in that Apache raid than to be found serving in the kitchen of a stranger."

The crowd had swelled, but no one stepped closer, either from fear of Diego, who stood with his hand on his sword, or from fear of the Widow, who moaned and pulled at her hair.

Diego looked at the woman on the ground and whispered to Maria, who drew closer to him. "We should not have spoken of your servant duties. I think she might have tolerated fornication, but washing walls is out of the question."

"Diego, be still!" cried Maria. "How can you jest at a time like this?"

He passed a hand over his face, pausing at the scratches around his eyes. "A thousand pardons, chiquita, but I sometimes have cause to marvel about the human mind and what it values." He looked over his shoulder. "It is over now. The governor comes."

The widow began to cry louder when she saw the symbol of Spanish authority shouldering his way through the crowd. She redoubled her efforts, moaning and sobbing and clutching at her hair. *"Ay de mi! Pobre Viuda! Qué miserable! Ay de mi!"*

The governor, breathless from running, leaned foward to help her to her feet, but Margarita would not stand. Instead, she raised her eyes to Diego, who watched her with mixed anger and amusement on his face. She slowly extended a shaking arm and pointed her finger at him.

"That man struck me!" she screamed. "And I have many witnesses!"

"Is this so, Senor Masferrer?" asked the governor.

"I was provoked beyond endurance," Diego said, looking Otermin in the eye.

"Put him in irons!" Margarita sobbed. "Arrest him! He is a vicious man!"

Otermin turned to Diego. "What would you have me do?"

"Let us leave in peace." The widow was wailing louder than ever. Diego raised his voice. "I have been insulted, my family has been insulted, and Maria has been greatly misjudged. All because she had the effrontery, the gall, to survive an Indian raid!" He paused, and even the widow ceased her wailing. "There can be no justice here today, Governor."

"There is always justice here, Diego," the governor replied. "Someone needs to teach you rancheros that you cannot assault people with impunity. You cannot play with the law. You do not own this river kingdom!"

"Excellency," began Diego in a weary voice, "I am accustomed to assume control over my own affairs. If I did not, if we did not, we would have been run over years ago by the Indians, for all the protection we have ever had from the Crown."

Margarita gasped. "And now he adds treason to his crimes," she cried. "How can you just stand there, Governor Otermin?"

"And let me add," continued Diego relentlessly, "that I will always defend those weaker than I, and also my own people who look to me for protection. I can do no less. And now you must excuse us."

He started to leave the circle of townspeople, which by now included most of the residents of Santa Fe. The Castellanos and Erlinda stood silently in the circle, Erlinda twisting her hands together, her face white.

The governor put a hand on Maria's arm. "What say you, Maria?" he asked.

She looked at her sister, who was slowly getting to her feet. "I cannot stay here, Excellency," she whispered, and he leaned closer to hear her. "I fear a terrible wrong has been done to me and to Senor Masferrer."

Margarita's renewed cries drowned out her sister's words, and the governor held up his hand. "Please, please, Widow! I will write of this matter to the viceroy in Mexico and he will instruct me further."

He turned to Diego. "You may go, Senor, but you must pledge to me that you will not leave this kingdom. And I would request you not visit Santa Fe again for awhile, on pain of jail."

"You have my word," said Diego, his voice low and dangerous. He bowed. "Again we kiss your hands, Governor Otermin," he said and pulled Maria after him. Erlinda and the Castellanos followed.

"Oh, Diego," said Erlinda. "How could you strike that woman?"

"Sister," he began, biting off each word, "I was goaded beyond endurance!"

"Diego, it is so unlike you," said Don Reynaldo.

Diego let go of Maria but he did not stop walking. "No, it is not so unlike me, Senor. I struck someone much dearer to me than the Widow Guzman not long ago. Someone much closer to my heart. Do not ascribe to me virtues I do not have. The thing is done."

"And so it is," agreed Don Reynaldo. "I will send the servants to prepare your wagon. You should be on your way."

Diego nodded. "Accept my apologies, Senor, for any embarrassment I have caused you. We will meet again, under better circumstances I hope."

Don Reynaldo hesitated, then spoke. "As to Maria, you may leave her here with us, if you wish. Perhaps it would be best."

Diego smiled bleakly and shook his head. "No, no. I could not. What none of you seem to understand is that Maria is my responsibility. She put herself under the protection of the Masferrers and I will not betray her, no matter what other virtues I lack."

They left the Castellanos within the hour. Luz and Catarina would have protested the early leave-taking, but one look at Diego's stark face silenced any objections. They sat still on the board in the wagon, their hands folded quietly in their laps. Luz edged closer to Maria, who sat staring straight ahead.

Diego lifted Erlinda in, then put his hand on Maria's cheek for a moment. "We will talk later, Maria, about the other matter. I know it must be discussed."

Erlinda watched them both, a frown on her face, but she made no comment.

The journey home was a silent one, each of them occupied with private thoughts. Maria found a long piece of string and the girls played cat's cradle. Diego rode ahead of the wagon, his back as straight as ever, seldom looking behind.

They arrived at Tesuque as the sun was setting. The sky was still light in the west, the underside of the few clouds tinted a delicious pink. Diego directed the teamster to lead the wagon through the pueblo's plaza.

As they rode into the plaza, Diego reined in his horse suddenly and sat motionless. The wagon creaked to a stop behind him. Erlinda and Maria stood up, then the young widow sat back down heavily on the wagon seat, her hand at her throat. "*O Dios,*" she whispered, her eyes wide. "The Indians are dancing!"

La Afortunada

*M*aria *sat down slowly on the* wagon seat, watching the spectacle before her. The Indians had come out of their hidden *kiva* and were dancing in the plaza to the slow beat of drums and the rattle of gourds. Their feathered headdresses swayed with a grace and beauty that made Maria catch her breath.

There was none of the smoke and the fear of the *kiva* where she had first seen Popeh. There was instead a terrifying majesty about the stately movements of the *kachina* dancers. Most of the men were painted white. They turned slowly and gracefully, naked except for their white cotton loincloths and enormous headdresses. They were like spirits rising from troubled graves on All Soul's Eve, wheeling and spinning until Maria felt dizzy and disoriented. She was afraid to watch, afraid to look away.

Luz whimpered and slid toward Maria. She pulled the child closer, speaking softly in her ear. "All will be well, Luz, *querida mia*, my darling. Diego will not let anything happen to you." Like all the Masferrers, Maria now trusted Diego for safety. Luz nestled closer and shut her eyes.

Diego remained on his horse, watching the dancers. Maria

could not see his face, but she could tell by the sudden stiffening of his back and the careful way he moved his hand to his sword that he was alert.

A black figure ran toward the wagon. For one terrible moment, Maria thought of Popeh and his compelling eyes. She clung to Luz, shielding the child with her own body. But it was Father Pio. He ran to Erlinda, who was sitting like a statue, her hands clenched in her lap. "Senora Castellano," he managed, "you should not be here."

Diego looked around at Father Pio. Slowly he dismounted and walked toward the priest, his spurs making a firm ringing sound in the sudden quiet of the pueblo. Maria clung to Luz with one arm, and pulled Caterina down on the wagon bed with the other, forcing her to sit on the straw-covered floor.

"Father Pio," said Diego, his quiet voice sounding like the roar of a mountain lion in the stillness of the pueblo. "What is the meaning of this?"

One of the dancers took off his headdress and approached Diego quietly. Maria whispered to Diego, "Behind you."

In one motion, Diego whirled and drew his sword. The blade gleamed for a second as it caught the last rays of the sun. The Indian stood still.

"Diego, put away your sword," Cristobal spoke, his face dripping wet, his eyes dark pools in his handsome face, the Indian standing behind him.

Diego immediately sheathed his Toledo blade. "Cristobal," he said. As the Indian came closer, he stood there with his weight on one leg, his head to one side, in unconscious repetition of Cristobal's stance.

Maria's palms were wet. She kissed Luz's hair and twined her fingers in the dark curls, covering the child's ears with her hands. Luz burrowed into her lap like a small animal seeking shelter.

The Indians all moved closer. Maria closed her eyes, her mind leaping back to the burning caravan, the circling vultures, the terrible carnage.

Cristobal stood facing his brother. They were very close to each other, but Diego would not back away. They stood boot to toe in the silent plaza.

Father Pio spoke. "They have been dancing since early morning after you left, Senor Masferrer."

Diego did not turn around. Still staring at his brother, he addressed the priest. "And where are the soldiers garrisoned here? All two of them? What of them?"

"I do not know, my son."

"I will tell you where they are, Diego," said Cristobal. "They fled."

"Cristobal, you know this is forbidden," said Diego.

"These are my people," Cristobal replied. "We are dancing for rain."

"Only God brings rain," countered Diego.

Cristobal laughed and spoke in Tewa to the Indians crowding around them. They hooted and banged their drums. Luz whimpered again. "Hush, *querida,*" Maria said.

Cristobal leaned even closer to his brother. "God and Mary have done us no good, my little brother."

"I am not your little brother, Cristobal," snapped Diego, breaking off each word. "You go too far, son of my father."

"I do not go far enough, Diego. We will dance if we choose."

"You will not," said Diego. "It is an abomination before God and the saints, and it is forbidden. I would remind you of that." The Indians moved about restlessly, whispering to one another.

Diego stepped away from his brother and walked alone into the center of the pueblo's square. He spoke in Tewa, his voice firm, his tone reasonable. Maria looked toward Father Pio. "Father, what does he say?"

"He tells them to remember whose Indians they are, and to go to their homes."

Diego stood where he was. Then Cristobal was beside him, speaking to the dancers. The Indians left the plaza, quickly climbing the ladders into the pueblo. In seconds, the square was deserted.

Cristobal turned to his brother. "They go only because I tell them to."

"Be not so sure, Cristobal," Diego replied, turning on his heel and striding back toward his horse. "I will speak to you later."

"We have nothing to say, Diego."

"You owe me an accounting," said Diego, his voice rising for the first time.

"An accounting!" shouted Cristobal. "For what? For the

sheep and the cattle I cannot have? For the horse that is not my own? For the woman you keep from me? I owe you nothing. I am not your Indian!"

He raised his hand to strike Diego. The Indians in the pueblo had come out to the terraces again and were watching in eerie silence.

Diego stood where he was, his feet wide apart in the sand of the plaza. "Strike me and you are a corpse, Cristobal," he said.

Cristobal's hand remained upraised for another long moment, then he lowered it to his side and turned on his heel. He looked around suddenly, and Diego started, in spite of himself. "There is a time coming, Diego! A time when the angels of your heaven will turn their backs on you."

"And how is this?" asked Diego, his voice steady.

"You will see, my brother, you will see." Cristobal disappeared into the gloom of the pueblo.

When he had gone, Diego heaved a sigh and walked to the wagon. Maria pulled Catarina up to the seat and brushed off her dress. "You made me miss the best part!" the child scolded, even as her hands trembled.

"Hush, Catarina," Diego said. "Maria only wanted to protect you. Come, Luz, come. It is over now."

Maria sat back on the wagon seat with Luz still in her lap. As the little girl began to cry, Maria rocked her back and forth, her hands still entwined in the curly black hair. Absently, Diego picked the straw off Luz's serge dress, his hand shaking like Catarina's. Maria looked away, the fear in her growing greater. It was as Cristobal said, they had much to fear.

"Father Pio," said Diego, "what has been happening here?"

The father pressed his hands together. "It has been a terrible day," he began. Diego smiled faintly and nodded. "Truly a dreadful day," continued the priest, unable to interpret Diego's expression.

"You were not harmed?" asked the ranchero.

"Oh, no. Never," the priest assured. "They are my little flock. They would never raise a hand to me. They are as little children."

"I wonder," Diego mused, ruffling Luz's hair. His hand touched Maria's.

"Indeed they are, Senor," continued Father Pio. "They are

upset, as we all are, by the continued drought. And there have been disturbing elements in the pueblo of late. But he is gone now."

"Who?" asked Diego quickly.

"I do not know his name. A large Indian, quite black of face, with curious light eyes. To look into them—ah, it is hard to tear one's glance away. But he is gone now, and I think all will be well, especially if you do not go to Santa Fe again soon."

"Our governor expressed the same hope to me only this afternoon," Diego said, then hesitated. "But I will not bore you with the details now. I fear you would require a confession. One I am not yet ready to give."

Erlinda reached inside the wagon and handed Father Pio the package from Governor Otermin. "Are you sure you would not rather stay with us a few days, Father?" she asked.

He accepted the small package with a smile and a shake of his head. "No, no, my child. I am quite safe here."

"Very well then, Father," said Diego, "we will continue our journey."

"Go with God, my son," replied the Father, making the sign of the cross. "And come to see me when you can make that confession."

"In time, in time," replied Diego, mounting his horse and taking a last good look around. He laughed then, the sound echoing in the deserted plaza. "Be of cheer, Father. There are always other sins."

Erlinda sat facing Maria in the wagon. As they approached the hacienda she leaned forward and touched Maria lightly on the knee. "Remember what I said this morning, Maria. My brother and sisters need your special care."

When they drew up to the hacienda, Diego sprang from his horse and raced into the house. Maria glanced around the property. There were no guards.

La Senora sat in the darkening hall, an old sword resting in her lap. Diego knelt by her side. "Mama, what is it?"

She groped for his hands and held them tight within her own. "Drums, Diego. I have been listening to them all afternoon."

"It is over now, Mama," he said, then looked around suddenly. "But what of my servants? Is no one here?"

"No one, my son. Only I."

Diego leaped to his feet and turned toward the main hall. "Juvenal!" he shouted. "Pablo! Endalecio! Come at once!"

There was only silence. He looked back at his mother. "What has happened?"

"I have heard no servants," she replied, reaching for Diego's hands again. "And yet there was one, someone I do not know. Large. Striding through the rooms, as only a big man can. He came into my room."

"*Dios mio,* Mama," Erlinda breathed, sitting down close to her mother on the bench, her face white. "Who was it?"

"I do not know. He did not speak. I could only hear his breathing. He walked around my room. I heard him walking around all the rooms. As if. . . ." She paused, raising her hand in a helpless gesture. "As if he were measuring the place for his own."

Diego drew his sword and walked through all the rooms of the hacienda. Maria sat down on the earthen ledge where she had sat on her first night at Las Invernadas, holding Luz and Catarina close to her. Even Catarina was silent for once, her eyes big, one finger in her mouth.

After what seemed like hours, Diego returned, his sword sheathed again. "There is no one here now."

But even as he spoke, they heard voices coming from the direction of the kitchen. Without a word, Diego slapped his dagger in Maria's hand, wrapping her fingers around the handle.

"Use it if you have to," he whispered, his lips close to her ear. He took off his boots and pulled his sword slowly, silently from the sheath again. Then he was gone, his feet noiseless on the dirt floor.

Maria followed him to the archway where the hall branched off toward the kitchen. She stood in the shadows with her back against the wall, watching him go and feeling an emptiness that made her practically hollow. Erlinda thrust Catarina and Luz behind her as she crouched by the front door. La Senora's hands tightened around the sword in her lap, and her lips moved in prayer.

Maria gripped Diego's knife. The handle was well-worn and smooth in her hands. She held the knife with both hands raised to chest level. Luz began to cry again, a thin wailing sound, full of all the fear in the world. Maria wanted to go to her, to comfort her, but she dared not move.

There was a rustle of clothing. Maria stiffened and grasped the knife tighter. She heard loud voices now, coming toward them. She took a deep breath and stepped out of the shadows.

The voices stopped in surprise at her sudden appearance. Then she heard Diego's words. "It is well, Maria, Erlinda. Mama, be at peace. The men are back. Are you all right, Maria?" She sagged against the wall and dropped the knife. She could only nod, still leaning against the wall. Cold all over, she hugged her arms to her body and looked at Diego. Their eyes met and held for several seconds. "Thank you, Maria," was all he said.

Erlinda and her sisters rushed to Diego, who put his arms around them. "Where was everyone?" Erlinda asked.

Diego gestured to the men behind him. "They were tricked out of the hacienda, perhaps by that someone Mama heard. They said they went in pursuit of him." He glanced at his men. "We will talk in the morning." His voice was quiet, but firm. "Never again will this hacienda be left unguarded, not for a moment."

The men bowed to him and left, speaking softly among themselves. "Where are the women?" La Senora asked as Diego took the sword off her lap and leaned it against the wall.

"They fled when the men ran to chase whoever—or whatever—was in the rooms. They are coming back now. My men do not know what they saw. Someone large, someone black." Diego glanced quickly at Maria. "I suppose by morning it will have sprouted wings and grown a tail. Who is to say? Hush now, Luz, I am here."

I am here. The quiet words were loud in Maria's ears. How we depend on him. She looked at La Senora, who still sat with her hands folded in her lap. It is a wonder that Diego can bear all that we put on him.

"And now, Maria, if you will take Luz and Catarina to their room and help them change for dinner, we will get on with things. Go now. I will help my mother."

But Luz would not let go of her brother. As Erlinda helped her mother, Diego picked up the child and followed Maria and Catarina down the dark hall. Outside the door to their room,

Diego paused with his hand on the latch. "Would you have used that knife, Maria?"

"I think so—yes—why do you ask?"

"I just wondered." He shouldered the door open and went into the room, sitting on the bed with Luz in his arms while Maria lit the branch of candlesticks by the altar. "Erlinda would not have used the knife, or so I think. But you would?"

Maria looked beyond Diego to the saint on the wall, its inward smile calming her. "When I came here, even before I left Santa Fe," she said, choosing her words with care, "I told myself that I would live." She stopped, looking down at Diego. "I could not give up easily. Not now."

"I called you La Afortunada—the lucky one—then, did I not?" Diego said, his eyes on her face. "I have wondered—perhaps we all have—if you are our gift from God." He paused and looked down at his little sister resting in his arms. "I treasure the care you take of my sisters, and the love you have for my mother. For them, I thank you."

He said no more, but sat Luz on her bed and left the room. Maria closed the door after him and leaned against it. He had thanked her for her kindness to his women, but he said nothing of himself, or of the words he had spoken in the governor's office.

Perhaps I should have stayed with my sister, she thought, looking at Luz and then helping her off with her travel-stained dress. But she knew she could not stay with her sister. She did not belong there, not as a sister or as a servant.

"And where do I belong, Catarina?" she murmured out loud, going to the chest and helping the older sister pull out another dress.

"Here, of course, where we love you," Catarina replied, almost brusque in her appraisal of a question that really needed no answer.

Her words startled Maria, who did not realize she had spoken out loud. "Do you really?" she asked in surprise.

But Catarina would say no more. She blushed and smiled at Maria.

Such shy people we are, Maria thought. We never say what we think or feel. As she buttoned up Luz's dress, she hummed an Indian tune she remembered Diego singing that morning. On impulse, she kissed Luz on the top of her head. Luz looked around in surprise, the same pink glow covering her delighted face.

Dinner was a silent meal. Luz and Catarina were unusually quiet, eating without having to be reminded by Erlinda to chew with their mouths closed or to use their napkins. Diego rose more than once and went to the kitchen window. The shutters were still open and he listened to the night sounds that ordinarily never would have caused him to leave the table. Erlinda watched him, her eyes big, her fingers tight around her fork. She only pushed the food around her silver plate, toying with it until she felt Maria's eyes on her. She put down her fork. "I am not hungry tonight, Maria."

"But you always tell us to eat everything, Erlinda," said Catarina, running a tortilla around the *salsa* on her plate.

"I know, my dearest, I know. I will be better in the morning."

Catarina turned to Diego, who was leaning on the table with both elbows, running the rim of his earthenware cup along his lower lip, but not drinking. "Diego, Juanita Castellano says that you are in trouble with the governor. What does she mean?"

He sat up straight then, looking sideways at his little sister. "*Ay de mi,* Catarina, why are your questions always so... piercing?"

Erlinda laughed and Catarina plunged on, encouraged by her brother's smile. "Juanita whispered that Maria has got you into trouble. How could Maria get anyone in trouble?"

"How indeed?" he said, teasing her. Diego threw up his hands. "*Caramba!* The Inquisition!" he exclaimed as he stood up. "It is a matter between Maria and me. When I need you, Catarina, or you, Luisita, to help me with my affairs, I will tell you."

His words were hard, but his eyes smiled at his sisters, and they grinned back. "And now excuse me, all of you. I will retire to write in my journal. This has been a day of some event."

After the dishes were washed and the silver plates locked back in their cabinet, Maria took the leather bucket from the hook and walked to the *acequia.* The night air was cool, the slight breeze chilly on her cheeks. The crickets sawed and buzzed in the cottonwoods, and the horses made their usual snuffling sounds in the stable beyond the *acequia,* but tonight there was little comfort in familiar things.

She wished again they had had the chance to tell the governor about Popeh. Maria climbed down the side of the ditch to the water, noting as she dipped in the bucket how much lower the water was. If only God would bring us rain, she thought, then paused, remembering Diego's words to Cristobal in the pueblo.

"I am afraid," she said out loud, then looked around to make sure no one was near. She sat where she was, her knees drawn up to her chin, her arms tight around her legs, feeling cold in July.

She thought of her sister again, trying to divine the reasons for her strange behavior. Diego had said something about the hardness of the country, and also about the cruelty of Margarita's husband. Maria could testify to the hardness of the land, but the husband? Maria did not know. How little she knew of men.

But I do know it would be better, much better, to be loved and then marry, rather than to marry and hope to be loved. She knew no one, not one of her friends, who had loved first. It was a thing not done. She tried to recall Felix de Guzman's application for her sister's hand, but she only knew stories of the wealth and property that had exchanged hands as Margarita went from one master to another. That was the way it was, the way it always was.

She sighed. She would never know what had made Margarita as brittle as glass, but she knew enough to fear what Margarita would do now. Maria understood the ways of her country. As soon as the governor wrote to the viceroy for his advice, and as soon as the reply came, she would be under the control of La Viuda Guzman. Instinct told her that Margarita would use her hard. A hundred times a day she will tell me how grateful I should be for a sister's concern, and forget how shocked she was that I should scrub someone's floors.

It wasn't the work that saddened her. She was used to work now. It was the abiding knowledge that she belonged nowhere in the river kingdom of New Mexico. She had come as an intruder, and she remained one, a survivor who never should have lived.

Like a tongue worrying an inflamed tooth, her mind darted back to Diego, always to Diego, and his words to the governor. He would marry me to keep me away from my sister, she mused, but is this right? Is this fair? And who was to say, when she was his wife, his property, that he would treat her any better than Felix de Guzman had treated Margarita? There must be love, she thought, looking across the *acequia* to the dark fields beyond. If only he loved me as I love him.

Maria stood and picked up the bucket, bending down for more water. She looked out across the rows of corn and remembered Cristobal sitting beside her evening after evening, saying nothing, thinking his secret thoughts.

Perhaps she should have married Cristobal. At least he loved her. She remembered the brothers' shouting match in the kitchen and tears came to her eyes. La Afortunada, indeed, she thought, walking slowly back to the hacienda. A girl of fifteen with no husband, no prospects and no dowry.

Evening prayers were the same, and somehow different. Diego's Mexican workers huddled in the back. The young girls, scrubbed clean, wriggled through their devotions with giggles and nudges. Erlinda glided in and knelt in her usual place. She closed her eyes and her lips began to move as she fingered her rosary. La Senora's face was troubled, her brown eyes, so like Diego's, dark pools of ruffled water. The serenity had vanished from her, stripped like husk from corn in one swift motion.

Cristobal's place was empty, his voice missing as Diego led them in the Psalms. Maria turned anxious eyes to Diego, then lowered her gaze before he looked her way. Already the room was full of questions. How unfair it would be to raise another.

Diego's prayer was the same, the invocations and blessings on the land and its people. If he paused in his prayer for the governor and for the viceroy in Mexico City, and those others in authority, perhaps it was her imagination. He prayed for the king with his usual fervor. And there he would have ended his devotions on any other night, but he went on. Although her eyes were closed, Maria felt everyone in the room lean forward to hear him, so eager were they all for some solace.

"And now, Father Eternal, bless this house. Watch over my lands, protect my Indians, my flocks, my herds, my loved ones," Diego continued. "Oh, Father," he began, and paused again. Maria wondered what father he prayed to. Was it the All-knowing Father, or his own who had died too soon, leaving heavy burdens on young shoulders? "Oh, Father, protect us each according to our needs. Grant Luz peace. Let her know there are those who hold her dear. Teach Catarina to school her tongue, to know when to be silent. Give Erlinda a heart to take in even those who would cause her fear. And help Maria to understand what she is to us." He paused and cleared his throat. "Father, help me to know my friends from my enemies. And teach us love and understanding, for without them, we are as dust."

He said amen. They crossed themselves, rising swiftly from knees accustomed to prayer. Maria could not look at Diego as he walked to the back of the chapel. Her eyes were wet, and she wiped them on her sleeve, then extended her arm for La Senora to grasp.

The Indian servants filed past their master, kneeling to kiss his hand. Catarina kissed his hand and slipped out quickly, but Luz kissed his hand and clung to him for a moment. Diego smoothed back her hair, kissed her, and sent her after her sister. Erlinda knelt next and rested her cheek on his hand for a moment. She rose without looking at his face and hurried out.

Maria knelt at Diego's feet as she did each night and kissed his hand. Instead of drawing back his hand when she finished her obeisance, Diego reached forward with his other hand and cupped her face. There was no one to see him. The others had gone ahead, and only La Senora remained behind to bless her son.

Maria looked up in surprise at Diego. He looked down at her, more serious than she had ever seen him. "I meant what I said, Maria." He let go of her and turned to his mother. Maria rose and hurried out of the chapel.

What did he mean? Was he speaking of his words in the governor's office? Of his prayer? Or were they somehow one and the same thing? Maria slipped into the storeroom off the kitchen and wiped her eyes on the dishtowel drying there. Luz and Catarina would want a story before sleep, as always. She could not come to them in tears.

The children had abandoned their bed for Maria's that night. The three of them crowded close together, their arms around each other. Luz whimpered when Maria blew out the candle, but by the time Maria had finished her story of the poor girl and the prince who loved her, embellished this time with jokes and bumbling suitors, Luz was content. The three of them lay together in close companionship. Maria believed that she would

179

not rest, not after the events of the day, but the warmth of the small bodies on either side of her soon put her to sleep.

It was a night of troubled sleep. Father Efrain put his head in her lap again, but when she looked down, it was the face of an Indian with curious yellow eyes that refused to close, even when she ran her hands over and over his face to shut the lids. And Carmen de Sosa whimpered and searched for her hair, or was it Luz, nestling close to her, who cried in her sleep?

Maria woke at dawn, exhausted. The girls still slept, so she raised herself carefully on one elbow. The sword was there at the foot of the bed, as she had known it would be. She stretched and felt the heavy metal with her toes.

She glanced at Catarina's bed. It was empty, but someone had slept there all night. Maria got up slowly, careful not to wake the little girls. She tiptoed on bare feet to Catarina's bed, where she sat and felt the indented pillow. It was still warm. She leaned forward and sniffed the pillow, breathing in the scent of sage. She put her head down on the pillow and closed her eyes again. When she awoke, the girls were dressing and the sword was gone.

Catarina pulled her dress over her head and ran her fingers in her hair. "Ay, Maria, you are the sleepy one this morning. I can already smell chocolate from the kitchen."

Maria sat up and tugged her nightgown down around her knees. Luz looked at her from the bed where she still lay, both pillows propped behind her head. "Diego came in here, Maria. Did you know?" She giggled. "He wasn't even dressed! He got his sword. Did you know that he left his sword here?"

Maria smiled. "You ask more questions than Catarina."

Luz continued, snuggling deeper in the pillows. "He told us to be quiet and let you sleep. We promised that we would, then he pulled your nightgown down around your ankles and covered you with that rug from the floor." Her eyes were big. "Why would he do that?"

"I expect he did not want me to be cold, Luz, and did not want to wake me," said Maria, touched and embarrassed at the same time. "Heavens, let us dress and get to the kitchen. The sun must be almost up."

"I am already dressed," declared Catarina. "Perhaps I will tell on Luz."

Maria laughed, "If you go outside this room looking as if you ran backward through a bush, Erlinda will laugh! Come, my child, and let me braid your hair."

The sun was up and warming the patio in the hacienda's interior before they finally left their room. Erlinda was sitting alone in the kitchen. She shook her head over her sisters. "Mother in heaven!" she exclaimed, "it must be six of the clock! You three must think you are the viceroy's children, to lie in bed after sunrise!"

Luz and Catarina looked at each other and covered their mouths, giggling behind their hands. Maria stood behind them, her hands on their shoulders, enjoying Erlinda's gentle joking. The morning sun was warm and inviting in the long room, and the delicious aroma of piñon and juniper wood in the fireplace was pleasing to the senses.

She went to the kitchen door and looked out. Maria had seen Diego's Tesuque Indians at other sunrises, raising their arms to the morning sun, singing a wordless song to it, their invocation to the dawn as meaningful in its own way as the prayers in the chapel. The thought struck her suddenly that she would like to stand in the middle of the garden and lift her arms to the beckoning sun, praising the bringer of dawn.

"Maria, how like Diego you grow!" Erlinda chided. "How many mornings have I seen him to do just what you are doing. He surveys his beans and tomatoes, gives some sort of silent benediction to the ovens and hives. A lord surveying his lands! You would think he commanded vast domains in this new world!"

Maria turned around. "Life is made up of such small things, I think. And I do count each day as special." She sat at the table, looking down at the plate the Mexican servant girl put before her. "Besides, I like the morning."

Erlinda rose from the table. "Perhaps I have lived too long in this kingdom to appreciate what you and Diego see in it." She laughed, brushing her hand against Maria's cheek. "All I see here is work to do!"

And they worked that morning, weeding the garden, baking the day's bread, hauling water from the *acequia* for La Senora's bath. After their midday bread and milk, Maria set her young charges to stitching on their samplers in a comfortable corner of the patio, and she and Erlinda began to wash the family silver.

"Maria," began Erlinda after a long, companionable silence, "what would you say if I went to Santa Fe to stay with the Castellanos?"

Maria's hands were deep in yucca suds and water. "Erlinda, we would miss you."

"And I, you. But while we were there yesterday, Don Reynaldo and La Senora Castellano asked me to visit them. I mentioned it to Diego this morning, and he thought you could manage without me for a while."

"You would like to go, wouldn't you?" Maria asked as she wiped the knives clean of polish and set them in the cool rinse water.

"Oh, I would. I love the Castellanos. And I feel that I owe them something of myself." She paused as she dried a spoon in her hand, rubbing it over and over.

Maria removed the last of the knives from the rinse water and spread them on a towel. "Erlinda, how old were you when you married Marco?"

"I was your age. Fifteen." Erlinda sat down on the bench by the table, the spoon still in her hand. "Let me tell you how it was, the day that Don Reynaldo and Marco rode out here to our holdings. I was not supposed to know about it, of course, so Diego sent me to read to Mama. You should have seen Diego. He was only just turned seventeen then, but head of the household. He tried so hard to act older than he was, but I knew he was scared, too."

She put down the spoon and took a handful of the knives Maria held out. "Poor Mama! I think I must have read the same sentence over and over to her, so distracted was I, wondering what was going on in the *sala*." Her hands continued to polish as she spoke. "After they left—with never a word to me, of course—Diego teased me and said that nothing had happened. I shouldn't have done it, Maria, but I pushed him down, sat on him, and tickled him until he told. He is very ticklish."

"I cannot imagine your doing such a thing, Erlinda!"

"Well, it was more than two years ago, and we were both much younger then—in many ways."

"Tell me what happened then," Maria asked.

"After Diego pushed me off, we sat there on the floor in the *sala* and he told me of my forthcoming marriage. He showed me the paper with all the marriage arrangements." Erlinda picked up another knife. "I had no idea of our worth until then. I was to take 300 sheep, 10 horses, 250 cattle, blankets, pottery, furs, cloth, and yes, 500 nails and an entire blacksmith's shop. Diego also said I could choose twenty Indians to take with me. It was quite a list."

She paused then, glancing shyly at Maria. "Why do you allow me to wander on like this?"

"I just wondered what it was like," said Maria, taking the knives from Erlinda and replacing them in the deep drawers of the cabinet. "I have often thought it would be special to love the man you marry."

"It is," Erlinda replied simply. "We were of one mind about things that mattered. Even here, this is not often the way of it. I know I was lucky." She stopped then, no sadness in her eyes, only a remembering look. "You will know how it is someday, Maria."

"I cannot see how," Maria answered, sitting down on the bench. "I have no dowry, not even one of those nails Diego gave away for you."

"It is a problem," Erlinda agreed. "Do you think the Widow Guzman would ever. . . ."

Maria interrupted. "No, she would not. I cannot imagine her ever providing the wool of one sheep, let alone the whole animal."

"How curious," murmured Erlinda. "But I do not doubt that you will make a happy marriage someday."

"How could I possibly, with no dowry?" Maria asked. "No, if I marry, it will have to be to someone as poor as I."

"Diego might . . . Diego might provide you with some dowry. It would be like him."

"I could never expect such a thing, Erlinda."

"You could. You do not have to live here long to discover what a big heart he has. Besides, he likes you. Sometimes he gets such a look in his eyes when he watches you. I think he would like to . . ." Erlinda broke off, laughing. "He told me once that he thought you had the most beautiful hair."

Maria's hands went to her hair. "He did?"

"He did. Something about the way it shines in candlelight.

'Copper and gold,' that was what he said." Erlinda stood up. "Come now, think of the time we are wasting! Let us see how my sisters are doing. It is much too quiet on the patio."

"How can you let me daydream out loud, Maria?" she continued as they walked toward the patio. "Still, let us consider the Castellanos' offer. Perhaps this winter I can go to Santa Fe."

Maria went to read to La Senora from the book of saints. She had read the work many times over, but she cherished the time spent in quiet with La Senora.

After only a few pages, La Senora's head dropped forward and she slept. While the woman dozed, Maria thought again of marriage. Cristobal wanted to marry her, but Diego would not give his permission. Cristobal called his brother greedy. Erlinda said he had a generous heart. Which was it? Or could a man be both? She had cast herself on his mercy, and he had protected her, yet Diego was dogged when it came to defending what he considered his own. Even after all these months and all their closeness she could not pretend to know him.

"I have not seen Diego," Maria said to Erlinda, as the two of them hurried over dinner preparation that evening.

"He left early this morning, just as I came into the kitchen. We had time for only a few words. Here, taste this," she commanded, skimming some broth off the pot she was tending.

Maria leaned over the pot, blew on the spoon and sampled the offering. *"Ay de mi,* Erlinda," she exclaimed, as the fiery liquid burned its way down. "You certainly have a way with *chilies!"*

Erlinda laughed and swung the kettle back over the low flames. "I do not think we will see much of Diego from now until the harvest, especially now that Cristobal. . . ." She stopped and turned away. "Well, we may not see Cristobal around here again. And so the burden falls heavier on my brother."

Maria nodded. All the more reason for her to speak with Diego and make him understand she did not hold him to his hasty words.

"But you remind me," Erlinda continued. "He told me this morning on his way out to tell you that he had something to ask you. Today or tomorrow."

Maria felt the heat rise within her and knew it was not from the chili.

Diego did not come in for the evening meal until Maria was clearing the table after dinner. He looked more tired than she had ever seen him, and she remembered with a pang the indent of his head on the pillow that morning.

He sat down at the table and spoke briefly to Erlinda as his sister shepherded Luz and Catarina out of the room and down the hall to La Senora's room. He followed his sisters with his eyes until they were out of sight, then turned around and leaned on the table with both elbows. He sat there in silence, his eyes closed.

Maria brought a bowl of stew and a plate of tortillas. Diego opened his eyes, but did not move. "Maria, I cannot find Cristobal anywhere. Some say he has gone to Taos, others shrug their shoulders. How ignorant Indians can be when it suits them. And several of my Indian farmers from Tesuque are missing."

He sat up then, as if impatient with himself, running his hand over his headscarf in the gesture that was familiar to her now. He took off his scarf and put it on the bench beside him. He slammed his hand down on the table, and she jumped.

"I am sorry," he said immediately. "I have no business coming in here and pouring my troubles on you. I would never tell Erlinda," he said, looking down at the food. "She worries so much. And yet, sometimes. . . ."

"Sometimes you have to tell someone, Diego," she finished, sitting down across from him.

His eyes looked into hers with an eagerness that pleased her and was oddly unsettling at the same time. "You have called me Diego," he interrupted.

She looked at him, startled. "What?"

"Oh, you call me Senor," he said, smiling at her, "or Vuestra Merced, if you are upset with me, but mostly you do not call me anything. And now for the second time you have called me by my name."

She looked down in confusion. "Perhaps I was being presumptuous."

"No, no," he insisted, reaching across the table and taking her hand. "I wish you would do it all the time."

Maria withdrew her hand quickly. "I should not."

Diego picked up his spoon and ate a mouthful of stew. "Maria, you silly girl," he said, his mouth full.

In spite of her embarrassment, she was pleased to see the exhausted, discouraged look leave his eyes. "But there is another matter," she began carefully, then the words rushed out. "Surely you do not need to wake up every night I have a nightmare. I know that once I wake up, I always go back to sleep. I do not wish to disturb you. It cannot be fair of me to rob you of sleep."

Diego put out his hand again to stop the rapid motion of her gesture. "I do not mind, Maria, really I don't."

"You cannot mean that," she contradicted, "especially when you look so tired."

"But I do mean it. And it is a small matter. I hear you stirring and mumbling in your sleep. If I rise quickly, go to your room and pat you on the shoulder, you generally go right back to sleep. If I am slower, you are usually sitting up and looking around." He paused, reaching toward her to brush his fingers briefly across her cheek. "Ay, such a look in your eyes then, Maria chiquita!" He lowered his own gaze as she stared down at her hands. "I wonder what it is you are seeing. And then I have to hold your hands and talk you into lying down. Sometimes we recite the Rosary together. And you remember nothing of this?"

She shook her head. He ate a few more bites, then rolled a tortilla, holding it between his fingers. "One night I came in and you were standing behind the door. *Dios mio*, what a surprise you gave me!"

"I remember nothing of it."

"Not even when I picked you up and carried you back to your bed?" he asked. "When I tried to put you down, you would not let go of my neck."

"I am sorry," she whispered, almost overcome by mortification.

He laughed and took both her hands in his as she started to rise. "I did not mind. I sang you some of my Indian lullabies and you went back to sleep. See there, what a nice fellow I am!"

She was silent, unable to move.

"Besides," he continued, his voice warm, low, "your hair smelled so sweetly of clover and woodsmoke. How prettily it curled around your shoulders." His eyes went to her face. "You should wear it that way in the daytime, instead of braided." Never before had he sat still with her long enough for so many words. It pleased and worried her at the same time. Perhaps she should take a light tone. "Long hair would be impractical," she countered with a smile of her own, "even if it is my only good feature."

"Oh, no," he contradicted quickly, "not your only one. I like those silly freckles on your nose. Like cinnamon. Have you never been tempted to count them?"

"Heavens, Senor," Maria exclaimed, rising from the table.

"Senor, is it?" he asked.

"If someone could hear you, Senor," she said, "they would think you were crazy."

He picked up his spoon again. "Possibly. But I meant what I said about your dreams."

Maria gathered the dishes from the table. He continued after a few minutes of silence, speaking in a voice half to himself. "I know I carry a heavy load, but you are no part of the burden. You serve to lighten it."

She carried the dishes to the sink, and when she turned back to him, she saw he was staring beyond her, over her shoulder out the open window. Before she could say anything, he leaped to his feet, knocking over the bench, and ran to the open door.

She whirled around. The sky was alive with fire. For one sickening moment she was back in the grove of trees, watching the mission supply caravan burn. She ran to Diego and grabbed him around the waist. "What is it!" she cried.

He shook her off and grabbed the bucket by the door. "The wagon shed!" he shouted. Even as he spoke, the warning bell in the garden beyond the beehives began to clang. Diego was halfway down the path before he turned and shouted to her as she stood transfixed in the doorway. "Don't let Erlinda or the girls outside!" he called. "And don't allow the Indian women to leave the house!"

She nodded, her eyes on the flames. She heard Diego pound across the *acequia* footbridge, following his Mexican servants, who were already running toward the shed.

Erlinda ran into the kitchen, her eyes big with fright, her face as pale as her hair. "Is it Apaches?" she shrieked.

Maria came away from the door and grabbed Erlinda. "No,

no! Not that! The wagon shed is on fire. Diego said you were to stay with La Senora and your sisters. He said you were not to leave your mother." She shook Erlinda, who continued to stare at the stabbing flames. "Do you hear me?"

Erlinda clung to her for a moment, then darted for the door. "I will keep everyone inside," she said, pausing with her hand on the door. "Oh, Maria, what is happening here?" Then she disappeared in the hall, and Maria heard her speaking softly to Luz and Catarina. Maria thrust her feet into her slippers by the back door, gathered up her skirts with one hand and ran down the garden path. She stopped by the *acequia* long enough to retrieve the bucket left there by the girls that afternoon. Rather than take the time to cross on the bridge, she waded into the *acequia*, the water coming only to her knees. She lost one of her shoes in the mud, but did not stop for it.

The smoke was already choking her. She coughed and wiped her eyes, feeling the acrid smoke settling in her throat like a layer of glue. As she ran closer, Maria could see that the shed was already a total loss, and the wagons underneath it. The wooden roof blazed away, the popping of the flames sounding like firecrackers on All Souls' Eve. The heat drove her back a step, then she hurried forward, her head down.

Diego had already ordered his servants into two lines, one to pass buckets of water to the flames, the other to send the buckets back to the *acequia*, where they were refilled and passed on again, almost thrown from hand to hand.

Diego and his *vaqueros* had let the horses out of the stable next to the wagon shed. The animals milled around the corral, whinnying and bumping into each other in their fright. Diego knocked down part of the fence to let them out and, their eyes rolling in terror, the horses streaked across the fields.

The flames from the wagon shed were fanning up a hot wind. Maria shaded her eyes with her hand and ran closer, the bucket knocking against her legs. The legacy of drought was all around her as she listened to the parched timbers crackle and watched them burst into flame spontaneously. The play of light on dark held her in dreadful fascination as she stopped to watch.

Diego was forming another fire line, this one for the roof of the stables. He climbed onto the roof as Maria squeezed her way into the line, her eyes on him. He propped his feet against the wooden poles that ran the length of the stables and leaned back against the roof. Several Indians joined him, and they poured water on the dry timbers of the roof, working to stay ahead of the flames on the wagon shed that threatened to jump the gap and fire the stables, too.

The men worked in silence, the only sound the crackling of the flames and the roar of the fire as it billowed upward, carried higher and higher by the fiery drafts of its own creation. The heat nearly knocked Maria down. Sweat rolled off her chin but she could not pause long enough in the fire chain to wipe her face.

Diego called from the roof, his voice strained and loud, ordering the Indians to take poles and knock down the walls of the wagon shed. The walls were adobe, but the wooden-framed windows were bursting into flame from the heat of the burning roof and the wagons inside. Indians rushed forward with long poles, poking and prodding at the walls.

Diego climbed higher on the stable roof until he was straddling the peak. The Indians followed him, inching along, as they dumped bucket after bucket of water on the timbers.

And then she saw Cristobal climbing to the roof, moving slowly toward Diego. He had appeared suddenly out of the dark.

Cristobal edged slowly along the roof. He paused behind Diego and touched him on the shoulder. Diego glanced back, motionless, waiting, for a long moment. Then he handed Cristobal the empty bucket. After another pause, Cristobal took it, passing it back along the line. Maria sighed and turned her attention once more to the man next to her, who was shouting at her to speed up.

The workers were soon able to force out enough adobe bricks to bring the wagon shed roof down. It feel on the blazing wagons with a whoosh that sent a cascade of flames and sparks soaring even higher into the darkness. A sparkling shower of flaming wood winked down onto the stable roof, but the wood was soaked through and it did not ignite, except in isolated patches, where the men hurried to beat out the sparks with their bare hands.

Maria's hands were blistered by the rough leather straps of the buckets slapped from hand to hand. Her back ached from bending forward to receive the full buckets, but she stayed in the fire line until the wagon shed was a smoldering heap of coals.

An hour later, the men climbed off the stable roof, coming down slowly and awkwardly like old men. Diego and Cristobal were last. They leaned against the adobe wall of the stable, their faces blackened by smoke. Diego took the last bucket handed to him and drank out of it, coughing and spitting out the water. He handed it to his brother.

The Indians put down their buckets and gathered around the ruined shed. No one said anything as the men watched the red embers flickering in the ashes. Maria set down her bucket and wiped her face with her sleeve. Her throat was raw and hot and her eyes ached. She rubbed them, then walked slowly toward the stable.

Diego and Cristobal were sitting on the ground, leaning against the wall. Diego looked up at her and coughed. "I thought I told you to stay with Erlinda."

She shook her head. "No, Senor, you told me to tell Erlinda to stay with your mother."

The words stuck in her throat, and she coughed until her eyes watered. Diego got slowly to his feet and handed her the bucket. She drank from it. The water was the only coolness in the whole wagon yard.

"Maria," Diego said carefully. She waited for his anger to explode. "Maria, you are a mess," he said softly.

She looked at him. His face was as black as his hair. His homespun shirt was burned through in several places, and even the leather of his breeches bore holes from the sparks. There was an angry red streak on his cheek. On impulse, she reached out and touched it. "Erlinda has some salve for that," she said.

"Later," he said. "I have to round up the horses."

"I will do that, brother," spoke up Cristobal. He had been silent, watching them standing close together. "With a few of your Indians." Diego stared at him hard, but he continued. "I can have them back by morning."

Diego turned from Maria. "I suppose it is the least you can do, my brother."

The brothers faced each other. Cristobal put out his hand, but Diego shook it off.

"I saw the flames from Tesuque," said Cristobal.

Diego was silent.

"But you do not believe me," Cristobal continued.

"Why should I, Cristobal?" Diego asked. "Why should I believe a man who hates me and all I stand for?"

Cristobal smiled. "Why would I start such a fire, Diego?"

"Perhaps someone told you to," said Diego, his voice old and tired. "I wonder if you have a mind of your own any more."

Cristobal lashed his hand across Diego's face, slamming him against the stable. Diego's eyes rolled back in his head as he slid down the wall.

"Don't touch him, Maria," Cristobal shouted as Maria darted forward. "If he gets up again, I will kill him."

She stopped where she was, her eyes on Cristobal.

He did not see her. "He is like all the rest, my own brother! He will not take the word of an Indian. Not even an Indian he calls brother."

Maria stood watching him. Cristobal took her arm, his touch gentle. She raised her face to his face.

"Come with me, Maria. It will not be safe here soon. And do not ask me how I know. Just come with me. Perhaps—perhaps I can protect you." He was holding her with both hands now, his fingers warm on her arm.

Maria looked down at Diego, who was beginning to stir, then back to Cristobal. "I cannot," she said.

"Maria, you are the only particle of goodness in this cruel place. Come with me."

She tried to move away, but he held her. She leaned forward then, resting her head against Cristobal's chest like a tired child, and he encircled her with his arms. "Cristobal, I cannot leave Diego, not after all he has done for me." She did not add, "And I cannot go with you." She loved Cristobal, as a friend, a brother, a Masferrer, but not as a lover.

Cristobal released Maria and turned to his brother. "I will find your horses," Cristobal spat out. "Let it be the last deed I do for you, the last time I am ever *your* Indian." He turned to leave the wagon yard as silently as he had come, but paused, looking back at his brother. "You are a curious man, Diego mio," he said, his tone almost conversational. "You cannot believe a gesture of honor in someone who is not Spanish." With a curse, he walked back and jerked Diego to his feet, peering close into his eyes for a moment, then letting him go with a grunt. "You will soon," he said. With a nod to Maria, he left the wagon yard. After a look at Diego, several Indians followed him.

With a slow shake of his head, Diego staggered to the fence and leaned against it. Maria joined him. Feeling someone's eyes on her, she turned to see Cristobal still watching. She raised her hand in farewell, and he was gone.

In silence she turned back to Diego. "You need to put cool water on that, Senor." She touched his bruised scalp gently.

For a brief moment while her hand was searching through his hair, he leaned against her shoulder with his eyes closed. Then he straightened, putting his fingers to his head. "Say nothing of this to Erlinda. She would only worry more."

They stood close together, their shoulders touching. "Does it matter that she worries?" murmured Maria. "Why can you not share your troubles?"

His only answer was to turn away from her and start toward the burned wagon shed. Maria remained by the fence as he walked around the still-smoking shed, idly kicking dirt and mud onto the embers. He went around the building twice, then walked back to Maria, his hands shoved deep in his pockets.

"Pues, bueno," he said, as they started slowly back toward the hacienda. "The harvest will be difficult this year." In an almost unconscious gesture he put his arm around her shoulder, hugging her to him as they walked. She hesitated a moment, thinking of everything her mother had ever taught her, then put her arm around his waist, hooking her thumb into his sword belt.

Halfway to the hacienda he stopped, standing still to cough until Maria thought he would turn himself inside out. "Ay, that smoke," he finally gasped. "I feel as dirty on the inside as I do on the outside." He felt the back of his head again and swore.

They started walking again, slowly, almost leisurely, as if this were the end of an evening stroll out beyond the *acequia.* "But do you know the worst part of this fire, Maria?" he asked suddenly.

"What is it, Senor?"

"We really cannot leave this place now. The wagons are all burned, and the only way out is on horseback—if Cristobal finds the horses. Do you think he will?"

"Yes."

"Why?"

"Because he gave his word," she burst out. She faced Diego, compelling him to stop. "And I do not believe Cristobal lies."

Anger rose, then died in his eyes. He looked at the ground. "Do you love him, Maria?"

She could not have heard him right.

"Well, do you?" he asked again, still looking at the ground.

Her feelings were too complex for an answer. There were many kinds of love. There was also the prospect of her spinsterhood, since she had no dowry. "I was not raised to answer such a forward question."

"And I was not raised to ask it," he said sharply, looking at her. A slight smile, a caressing smile, crossed his face. "But I am asking."

Before she could answer, the kitchen door banged open, and Erlinda and her sisters ran down the garden path. They crossed the footbridge, the little ones flinging themselves at Diego as he stood facing Maria. Erlinda stood watching them, a thoughtful expression replacing the fear on her face.

"Mama is so worried, Diego mio," Erlinda said.

"I will be in. Tell her all is well."

Erlinda went back inside, and Maria followed. She was conscious again of her smoke-blackened face. She had lost a shoe in the *acequia* and her dress was in ruins, scorched, wet and muddy. She looked back at Luz and Catarina, who crowded close to Diego.

"We were so afraid, Diego," said Catarina, plucking at his sleeve. "But Erlinda told us that all would be well. And it is, is it not?"

"Yes, of course, sister," Diego replied, his eyes on Maria as she walked alone toward the kitchen.

The Saint in the Wood

$\mathcal{M}$ *aria woke in the morning to* the smell of smoke hanging heavy in the room. Out of habit, she felt with her toe to see if the sword was there. It was not, and she sighed. *Pues, bueno,* she thought, curling her legs close to her body again and snuggling against Luz. She closed her eyes again, then opened them, determined this time not to oversleep. As the room lightened, she could see the smoke in the room. The air was stifling. She cleared her throat. It was sore from smoke.

She got out of bed and dressed quickly, pulling on her remaining dress that had not been ruined by the fire, wincing when the coarse material brushed against the burns on her arms. She ached from the labor of the night before, from the constant motion of bending and passing the buckets. Her hands were blistered and painful to touch.

The room had no mirror. None of them did. Erlinda said once that her father had not approved of mirror-gazing by his daughters, and La Senora had no need of them. Maria ran her hands over her face, feeling the small burned spots where cinders had nicked her last night. In sudden panic she felt her hair, but she could find no burned spots.

She brushed her hair, letting it fall around her shoulders, turning her head this way and that to watch the effect of her chestnut curls arranging themselves on her breast. She would love to wear her hair down again, pulled back slightly to show her ears, but Mama had never allowed her to show more than the tips of her ears after she became a young lady, and besides, she had no earrings to slip into her earlobes anymore. The solicitors had taken them all, even the small gold hoops she wore as they had spoken to her of chattels and goods and indebtedness and compensation.

But how pretty her hair would look pulled back with the pin that Papa had claimed was made from pearls found by Balboa himself. The pin was gone, too, lost in the Indian attack on the supply caravan.

Maria sighed. There was a soft knock at her door and, after making sure that all her buttons were done up the front, she opened it.

Diego stood there. *"Buenos dias, chiquita,"* he whispered. Her hands went to her hair again. "But, Senor, I am not. . . ."

He took her hand and pulled her into the hall. His eyes were deep brown in the early morning dimness of the corridor.

"A woman's crowning glory," he murmured, his eyes on her hair. "At least, in your case."

The burn on his face was darker still against his swarthiness. It looked hot to the touch. When he remained silent, looking at her, she spoke. "Yes? Is there something you need, Senor?"

He paused, as if to consider the question at length, looking away when an unruly blush rose to her face.

"Oh, not really. But I do have a proposal to make." He let go of her hand, and she looked at him. "It is a small thing, really, but something I have been meaning to do. Indeed, I promised Emiliano."

She let out her breath. "And?" she prompted.

"I promised him I would take you to Tesuque. Would not today be a fine day?"

"But you have so much to do. Surely I could go alone." She spoke quietly, her voice low, so as not to awaken the sleeping sisters.

"Maria, I will always have too much to do." He took a deep

breath and coughed. "But this place wearies me, and I would go with you."

The place wearied him? His livestock, his buildings, his land wearied him? She did not believe him for a minute, but suspected he wanted to find out what was going on at Tesuque.

When she was silent, he continued. "Two of the horses have returned. I have set all my Indians to work on new wagons. *Dios mio*, how can we harvest without wagons! But never mind. I want to leave this place today, so I will take you to Emiliano."

"I will go with you," she said, "but first I have kitchen duties."

"I have discovered something about duties," he commented, running his hand over the back of his head. "They are always there when you return to them. No one runs off with them while you are gone."

"Very well, Senor," she said, and he laughed.

"Come, let us go, Maria chiquita. Everything will keep."

She returned to her room and wound her hair in a hurried knot on the top of her head, sticking the chestnut mass here and there randomly with hairpins. She turned to slide her feet in her slippers, then remembered that one of them was still probably stuck to the mud in the bottom of the *acequia*. She sighed and left the room on silent bare feet.

Diego met her in the still-dark kitchen. He held something soft out to her. "Here," he said, "try these on." It was a pair of Indian moccasins, velvet to the touch. "They are Apache. We used to have an old Apache slave who made them for me when I was younger. I think they will fit you."

Maria sat on the bench and pulled on one of the moccasins. They were higher than Pueblo moccasins, reaching to her knees. Diego knelt in front of her.

"See? You lace them up like so. Very good for walking through brush. I will have our cobbler make you more shoes, but I have put every man on the wagons right now and cannot spare him."

She pulled on the other moccasin and sat still as Diego laced it up, his fingers working quickly in the dim room. "It is hard to see in the darkness," he said as he crossed the rawhide laces back and forth. "Someday I would like to sleep till after sunup."

It was the closest thing to a complaint Maria had ever heard from him. "Diego, you are tired," she murmured.

He looked up at her, smiling at her use of his name. "Oh no, not really. I will feel better after today." He finished lacing and rocked back on his heels, squatting Indian-style in front of her. "I used to do things like this with Cristobal. We would take a couple of tortillas and spend the day fishing at the river. Or making rabbit snares."

Maria stood up, enjoying the feel of the soft leather on her legs. "Where is Cristobal?" she asked quietly. "Was it he who brought the horses back?"

Diego shook his head. "I do not know where he is." He turned to the storeroom off the kitchen. "But tell me now, where do my servants keep the cheese?"

He did not want to speak of his half-brother, so Maria did not press him. She went to the pantry and found a slab of cheese. Diego cut off two hunks with his dagger and wrapped them in coarse cloth. He took a handful of tortillas and stuck them in his shirt front.

Maria watched him. "I think you should leave a note, Senor. Erlinda will wonder where I am," she said as she watched Diego wind his silk scarf around his hair and put on his flat Andalusian hat, drawing the cords up under his chin.

"Very well, chiquita. We cannot have her thinking that you became discouraged with the Masferrers and ran off to your sister's mercy." He went across the hall to the *sala* and returned with paper, pen and ink. He wrote quickly, propped the note against the large silver salt cellar that stood in the middle of the table, and returned the writing materials to the *sala*. When he came back, he looked closely at Maria. "Do you have a hat?"

She shook her head. "It cannot matter, really. I have so many freckles by now that I have given up worrying about my skin."

He peered at her face in the rising light. "And you have never been tempted to count them all? It would be nice sport some winter evening."

"Oh, Senor," she murmured, shy again. He laughed and took her arm, pulling her after him into the kitchen garden.

He stopped suddenly, and she bumped into him. He pointed toward the mountains. "Look how beautiful the sun is, Maria. I never tire of my view."

They crossed the footbridge. Diego walked over to the burned rubble of the wagon shed and stood looking down at the still-warm embers. He remained there a long time. Maria walked to him and touched his arm lightly. He looked at her, remembering where he was. They went to the stables. There were only two horses in the corral. The stables were lonely in the dawn's light.

"Praise God that Tirant came back," said Diego, leaning on the fence and watching his horse. "I will probably have to go to Santa Fe and barter for more horses."

"But did not the governor tell you to stay away from Santa Fe?" Maria asked.

"Damn!" he exploded, striking the fence and causing Tirant to shy away. "I forgot." He climbed the fence and sat on the top rail, looking at the empty stable. "Perhaps one of the other rancheros around Tesuque will do a little horsetrading. We should thank Our Father that the oxen were not lost, too."

He sat in silence on the fence until his horse came back to him, nuzzling his shirt front. Diego took out the roll of tortillas, peeling one off and holding it out to Tirant. "That is one of yours, chiquita," he teased Maria, putting the others back.

Maria smiled, leaning her arms on the railing. How cheerful he is, she thought, and he has nothing to be cheerful about.

"What are you so pleased about?" Diego asked, watching the smile playing about her lips.

"I was thinking. Remember the proverb—Fortune is like bread, sometimes the whole loaf, sometimes none?"

He mounted Tirant. "And looking around you, what would you say we have now?"

She thought a moment. "The whole loaf, Senor, the whole loaf."

He reached out and touched her cheek. Then he rode Tirant into the stable, where he saddled the stallion and returned to the fence. "Here," he commanded, holding out his gloved hand. "Climb to the top railing."

She did as he ordered, careful to keep her dress tucked around her legs. He took her around the waist, pulling her into the saddle in front of him. They left the corral, Diego leaning over to open and close the gate. They started at a slow walk toward Tesuque. She could feel his warm breath on her ear. Suddenly, he blew on her neck.

"Maria, your hair tickles my nose."

"You could have saddled the other horse," she said sensibly.

"I did not say I was complaining," he added, and blew on the fine tendrils that curled around her neck.

She laughed.

"You don't do that very often," Diego said.

"Little is funny, Senor, these days."

"But today we have the whole loaf, eh?"

As they watched, the sun rose over the Sangre de Cristo Mountains. Maria shielded her eyes with her hand, and Diego tipped his hat forward. "We will be there soon."

They rode into the quiet morning. The air was clean and the birds sang into the peaceful stillness. Diego hummed one of the Indian songs that he sang to his sisters. Maria leaned against him and settled her head in the hollow of his shoulder, feeling his song more than hearing it, for his voice was low. She remembered when they had ridden together away from the Apache massacre. How long ago that seemed, yet it was no more than six months. Now it was August. Time flowed through the days and nights like the river beside which they rode. She closed her eyes. "Where did you learn your songs?" she asked.

He shifted in the saddle. "From Cristobal's mother. She used to sing to him all the time when he was small. And when she died, we learned from others."

"Even Erlinda?"

"Certainly Erlinda. Although she would never admit it, I suppose. But I think that if she had babies of her own, she would sing the Pueblo songs, too. What will you sing to your small ones?"

She shrugged. "I learned the lullabies that everyone learns, but mostly no one sang in our house."

"Ay, pobrecita," he said, his lips close to her ear. "You may be the only person who ever came to our river kingdom for an education!"

"And what have I learned?" she teased in turn. She knew she should sit straight, but Diego made a sturdy support.

He guided Tirant down into the river, reining in, and allowed the horse to drink. "You tell me what you have learned," he said finally.

After they rode out of the water, Diego turned in the saddle and looked behind him. "How low the water is! Why does Our Father not hear our appeals for rain?"

"I have given up trying to fathom the ways of Our Lord," Maria said quietly.

Tesuque lay red and solid in the sunlight. The sky was a breathtaking blue, and Maria delighted in the contrast of colors, even as she tried to overlook the brown grass and wilting cottonwoods. She smelled bread baking in the great Spanish ovens on the level ground near the pueblo, and listened to the clack of looms as the men wove their beautiful blankets, the designs so striking.

"Do you think they will ever change?" she asked.

"Never. Now and then they grow restless, but at heart they are good Indians who have always lived this way. I do not suppose a more peaceful tribe ever existed. Not like the Apaches."

"And still . . ." she began, thinking of Popeh, and the Indians dancing in the plaza.

"And still," he echoed, and she knew she was right about the real reason for their visit. "Perhaps Erlinda is right when she says we Masferrers borrow tomorrow's worries for today."

Diego handed Maria down, then dismounted, tying his horse to a cottonwood tree. "And now let us find Emiliano."

It was a simple matter to climb the ladder to the terrace above. As they stood in the doorway of the *santero* workshop, Emiliano turned to greet them. He was sitting cross-legged at the low table by the window where the light was best, putting the final touches on a small *bulto* of San José. He held it up to Diego.

"Your neighbor, the ranchero Alvaro Gutierrez, would have me create something to encourage the crops and the weather. Good day and God's blessings on you, Senor, and on you, Maria. Have you come to be a saintmaker?"

She took the small statue that he still held in his outstretched hand. "I think so, Emiliano," she said, turning the *bulto* over in her hands, admiring the staff of yucca blossoms that the saintmaker had carved with intricate detail. The arms of San José stood out stiffly from his wooden body. They were hinged at the shoulders by small wooden pegs. Maria moved the arms up and down. "As though he were blessing the fields," she said, handing the *bulto* back to its creator.

"Senor Gutierrez was adamant in his specifications." Emiliano set the figure down on his workbench. "This day, Maria, shall we see if you have the eye of an artist? And you stay, too, Senor. Perhaps we can talk."

"I will. Did you see our fire last night?"

"We all did. I must tell you, Senor, there were those who cheered, and then danced. Danced all night, in fact, so we have a sleeping pueblo this morning."

Diego squatted on the hard-packed earth in front of the saintmaker. "What do you make of it, Emiliano, old friend of my father?"

"I cannot say, except that you are not as beloved as you would think you are."

"Go on, Emiliano," said Diego quietly when the *santero* hesitated. "You know that I am fair with my Indians."

"So there it is, Senor," said the old man. "You have said it. You are fair, probably fairer than any other ranchero in this valley. You do not take the women, you do not abuse the men, the children do not work long hours for you in the hot sun. Your exchange of goods for services is fair. But you have said it yourself—my Indians. You say it all the time. So do the others. But we are not your Indians."

Maria had never heard an Indian speak this way to Diego Masferrer. He glanced at her, then directed his attention to Emiliano again. "What are you saying, Old One? If you are not mine, whose Indians are you? Tell me that? I have a paper from King Felipe himself to my grandfather, saying that whatever he found here would be his. For seventy years it has been so. For seventy years we have owned and protected you."

"It was never so!" said Emiliano forcefully. "We were not your king's to give away. Can you own another, Senor?"

"We have these rights. From the king of Spain himself."

"Tell that to Cristobal."

Diego took Emiliano by the arm. "Have you seen him?"

"I saw him. He left late last night for Taos. I know nothing more."

"Or you will not tell me more, Emiliano? But remember, the king of Spain has given us rights over you in this land."

The old man looked around him pointedly. "Show me where this king of Spain is. I cannot see him."

Diego was silent. He let go of the saintmaker. Emiliano straightened his cotton tunic. "I can truly say no more, except this one thing, Diego Masferrer. Did not one of you ever consider that what is so right for you might not be the wishes of others?" He turned back to his San José to apply careful brushstrokes to the face. He held the saint up to Maria, who smiled and nodded, captured by the painted gleam of kindness in the saint's eyes. Emiliano put down the saint and stood up.

"Come, my children. I grow older instead of younger, despite my wishes to the contrary. With this in mind—because unlike you rancheros, we Indians do not live forever—perhaps we should educate this small saintmaker, if that is what she is."

He took hold of Maria's hands, turning them over until they were palm up within his own. He traced the blisters with his finger and looked at her, a question in his eyes.

"From the fire, Old One," she explained.

"And do you fight Diego Masferrer's battles with him?" he murmured.

"She does not listen to me," said Diego.

"Independence of mind, Maria, is a valuable gift in a saintmaker. But can you pick the saint out of the tree stump? That is what we shall see. Come."

Emiliano rummaged in the dark corner next to the workbench where he kept his pile of hides. He tossed out two shoulder bags and picked up a handful of smaller sacks. Diego and Maria each took a bag and followed the *santero* down into the plaza, now sun-drenched and warming.

They crossed the plaza in front of the pueblo. Father Pio was sweeping the entrance outside the church. He waved to the three of them, calling out a greeting. Diego nodded to him, but did not stop to speak.

Maria hurried to keep up with the men. They walked along the river's edge until they came to a small *arroyo* that fed into the larger stream. Except for a weak trickle down the center, the gully was dry, littered with smooth pebbles and many branches from the cottonwood trees lining the bank.

Emiliano gestured to the fallen wood. "See there, Maria? Go, find me a saint." He sat on the riverbank, nodding to Diego, who sat next to him, grinning at Maria.

Maria put down the bag and walked to the riverbed. She was grateful for Diego's Apache moccasins as she walked over the stones, poking the wood, wondering what she was looking for. I am to find a saint, she thought, as she examined the jumble of twisted, drying wood. She raised her eyes to Emiliano, but he looked away from her, deliberately ignoring her.

A saint in the wood, a saint in the wood, she thought, walking farther away from the men lounging and chatting on the bank. Diego was pitching pebbles into the stream while Emiliano sharpened a small knife on a whetstone he had brought with him.

She turned her back on the men, looking down at the wood, picking up pieces and discarding them, tugging at larger limbs, turning them this way and that, wondering what Emiliano could have been thinking of, and feeling failure hovering over her like the buzzards at the supply cavern massacre. She felt tears hanging somewhere behind her eyes, ready to fall in a moment.

Then she saw him, San Francisco. Maria knelt by a small cottonwood limb lying half under a larger piece of brush. Using both hands and one foot, she tugged it out and held it up.

It could only be San Francisco. The chunk of wood was small, less than a foot in length, but there was a smaller branch reaching down from the sturdiness of the main limb, extended like San Francisco blessing the small animals that were his particular delight. She ran her finger over the wood and looked at Emiliano, who was smiling at her.

"Ho, Maria," he called, "have you found a saint?"

"I have," she said, hugging the piece of wood to her.

"Come show me then."

She tucked the cottonwood limb under her arm, grasped her skirts and climbed the bank to the men. "Look. It is San Francisco," she said, holding out the wood to Emiliano, who took it, turning it over in his hands. Diego watched them. He tipped his hat forward and leaned back on his elbow.

Emiliano handed the wood back to Maria. "Tell me, where is the front?"

Maria frowned, pursing her lips. "Here," she replied, after turning the wood over several times. "And see! He is blessing the animals."

"Oh, Maria!" said Diego. "And where is the skull that San Francisco always carries?"

"This one will not," she flashed back. "Not my San Francisco. If you insist on skulls, you must find your own."

He laughed, and pitched another rock toward the water.

Emiliano handed her the knife he had sharpened, a small knife with a deer bone handle, worn smooth with many years of whittling and carving. "Strip off the bark, if you are so sure that San Francisco dwells within."

Maria took the knife and set the wood upright in front of her. She carefully peeled the bark off the dry wood, marveling at how easily the outer shell fell away from the whiter wood underneath. She worked slowly around the downpointing limb, guiding the knife with her thumb. When all the bark was removed, she handed the wood back to Emiliano.

"Perhaps you are right, my child," he said, after running his hands over the cottonwood. "It could be San Francisco himself. Only think how long he has waited here for you."

She nodded. Emiliano cleared his throat, "And what say you, Maria? Can we trust that ranchero over there with your San Francisco?"

"Perhaps," she replied.

"Here then, Senor, you carry our saint."

Diego took the wood. "With pleasure." He put the small piece in his leather sack, then brushed his hand across Maria's cheek. "You're crying, chiquita," he said.

"I know. Silly, isn't it?"

To her surprise, he hugged her to him for a brief moment. When he let go of her, Emiliano took her by the arm to hurry her on.

"We must find the right colors now, Maria. No time for dawdling."

He led them along the riverbank and they walked for another mile. The saintmaker seemed to know just what he was looking for. Soon he came to a place in the river where the bank rose high above the water and a narrow path led down to the water's edge.

"Down there, Maria," said Emiliano, sitting cross-legged again, "you will see a wall of gypsum, of *yeso*. Fill your bag."

She picked her way down the slanting path. At the river she looked back at the bank and saw the glittering wall of gypsum. The *yeso* peeled away from the side of the bank in flaking handfuls. She filled her leather bag with it, then toiled up the path, the strap of the pouch biting into her shoulder.

Emiliano patted the bag and nodded. "That should do nicely."

They took another high path back toward the pueblo, away from the river this time. Emiliano stopped and pointed to a barely seen *arroyo*. "Over there, Maria, you will find color."

Diego walked with her to the *arroyo*. The sun was high overhead now, and he took off his hat and put it on her head, pulling the cords up under her chin. Maria gathered the clay of red and yellow from the side of the *arroyo*, filling the small sacks the *santero* had given her. They returned to Emiliano, who was lying on the ground, his eyes closed. He woke and peered into the sacks, nodding. "The rest we can find at the pueblo. And do not dawdle, you two! We have much to do this day!"

"Let us see what we have now," said Emiliano when they sat together again on the floor of his workshop. He shook the contents of the bags into small clay dishes on the low workbench. When he had poured in enough, he turned to the small cooking fire and lifted off the pot of blue beans simmering there. Ladling out a fair amount, he put the beans in a cloth bag, knotted it tight, and handed it to Maria. "Here now, squeeze this over the small pot."

She did as he said, even though the beans were hot and pained her blisters. Doggedly she squeezed the bag until the pot was half-full of blue gray bean water. She looked over at Emiliano, who had dumped the gypsum into a larger pot and added a small amount of water. He put more wood on his little fire until it was crackling away, then set the pot on the flames, handing Maria a paddle. She mixed the gypsum and water together until it was the consistency of cream, smooth and slightly off-white.

"Now take it from the fire. Set it down like so. Follow me."

They went outside again to the mission corral by the church where Father Pio kept a couple of milk cows with their calves. "Find me some bits of hide, horn and hoof. Especially hoof."

She climbed into the corral. It was ill-kept and littered with parts of hoofs. She combed each corner of it, picking up bits of ragged hide. Next to the feed box she found a complete hoof, still soft inside and stinking. She held it away from her, wrinkling her nose. She found another like it, and a horn, as well, and returned to Emiliano, who peered close at what she carried and chortled like a small boy.

"Good, Maria! You shall have a fine San Francisco. Now let us cook this mess. But outside. I cannot stink up the entire pueblo."

Emiliano tossed Maria's malodorous scavenging into another cooking pot, added water and instructed Maria to stir it over the flames of the outdoor fire he had started. "Until it thickens," he said. "Diego and I will eat and take a siesta."

She watched them go toward the pueblo, then turned her attention to the pot before her. The smell that climbed from the pot made her stomach heave, but she stirred the horn and hooves and hide round and round until the whole disgusting mixture boiled.

When she could hardly stir the mixture, Emiliano and Diego returned. Diego took his hat, which was hanging by its cords down her back, and set it on her head again. "Chiquita, we cannot have you falling into the pot with sunstroke. I fear no one would retrieve you. Ay, what a smell!" Diego sniffed her hair.

Emiliano watched Maria's face and laughed. "Senor Masferrer, you had better stand back. Maria feels little charity toward even you, at the moment. This is the hard part, Maria. You are almost through."

When she could turn the paddle in the pot only with real effort, Emiliano motioned for her to stop. He had carried out the pot of gypsum, which he had added to the glue. "Now stir this only a little, Maria. You will know when it is done."

And she did know. There was a magic point when glue and gypsum blended into a thick sparkling mass that caught the sun. She took the paddle from the pot and looked at Emiliano, who lifted the pot off the flames.

"Well done, Maria. Now, we will let Diego carry this up the ladder for us, and if he trips, we will laugh at him."

Once inside the workshop, Maria leaned against the cool wall. Her back ached from bending over the pot, and her already-blistered hands were rubbed raw. Diego set down the pot and looked at her, taking his hat off her head.

"Are we too hard on her?" he asked Emiliano.

"No. You cannot be too hard on a saintmaker. I think there must be a necessary pain in this work, eh, Maria?"

She smiled faintly, but said nothing.

"And now," said the *santero*, "if I may have your attention. I have carved a ring about his shoulders and given San Francisco a neck. If you will carve down his back and make it straight, we can proceed."

Emiliano handed her the knife and she scraped the small bumps of wood off the back, smoothing it down with sand. She carved the saint's waist so his long gown flared out.

Emiliano pointed to a small brush in a dish of water. "Made of yucca fibers, set to soak. Remember that, Maria. By rights, you should have made your own brush, but time is too short." He paused and caught Diego's eye. "Too short. Now, spread the white on your San Francisco. He has waited too long for this."

She sat cross-legged on the floor in imitation of Emiliano and applied the thick, gluey gypsum to the statue, beginning at the head and working down to the hem of his robe. As the white flowed on, she smiled, forgetting how her back ached and how sunburned her face was. She paused when she finished and looked at Emiliano. "What about his other arm?"

"I have carved you one. Here it is, for you to paint." He handed her a small piece of cottonwood, already smooth. "We will put a cross in it later."

She painted the other arm, and when she was done, the statue was already dry.

Emiliano looked at her work. "It never takes long to dry, not here. And now, I will get an egg or two and some chicken feathers."

Diego sat in the corner on the buffalo hide pile. Maria put down the brush and stood up. The pueblo was still, wrapped in the afternoon rest, but she heard a distant drum throbbing somewhere deep within the adobe walls.

"What does he mean, Diego?" she asked in a whisper after Emiliano left.

"*Qué, chiquita?*" Diego asked. His face had a distracted look, as if he were listening to the drums, too.

"He speaks of too little time, or that time is short."

"He is old, Maria," he said. His answer seemed evasive to her, and he shifted slightly, turning away from her.

"It is more than that, Diego mio," she said quietly, "isn't it?"

He smiled faintly at her use of his name. "I do not know, Maria. But there is something here we know nothing of. I can only hope the unrest will pass as it always has."

She sat next to him for comfort, and he put his arm around her. Their thoughts were on the drums, which had faded further, then stopped with a suddenness more disconcerting than their sound.

Emiliano returned with a handful of chicken feathers and two eggs. He cracked the eggs and separated the yolks from the whites, then looked at Maria. "I forgot something. Take the knife and scrape off the bottom of that pot. Put the shavings here in this dish."

Maria knelt by the cooking pot and scraped the blackened bottom until bits of carbon floated in the air.

"Now, then. Mix a little egg with the blackening and make a beard for our *San Francisco de Asis*. Use our Diego for your model. Of course, his vanity keeps his beard well-trimmed, but he will do today, when we have no one better."

"Thank you, Old One," grinned Diego.

Maria stirred a small portion of yolk into the blacking with a feather, soaking the feather with black paint. Her hand was unsteady as she raised the feather brush to the gleaming white statue. "It is like cutting out a piece of expensive brocade for a dress," she confessed. "I fear the first step."

Emiliano snorted. "And why should this act of beginning be any different than any other act of life? It is well that you fear. If you did not, I would take the brush from you."

She glanced at Diego for reassurance. He winked. With another dip of the feather in paint, and another glance at Diego's close-cut beard, she painted the beard on the empty white face, her hand steady. She put the brush down. "What do I mix for his robe?" she asked.

"A little more black, some of the red clay, blue bean, perhaps a touch of yellow. As you wish."

She mixed the colors, blue predominating, relishing the small swirls of brightness that spun around and around and then vanished in the emerging blue-gray, adding their bits of color and contrast. When she had the proper hue for San Francisco's robe, she stroked the color on with another chicken feather, pleased with the way the color soaked into the gypsum.

Maria set the figure down on the workbench, carefully turning it around with the tips of her finger. The *bulto* had none of the grace she associated with San Francisco. This figure was crude and primitive, carved quickly of cottonwood and painted with chicken feathers. A year ago she would have laughed and turned away from this small saint, but not now. This gentle representative of the faith had come to her, not from the belly of a great Spanish galleon, but from the earth itself. She had freed the saint from the tree limb.

The men in the room were silent, Emiliano's eyes on the saint that blessed his workbench, Diego's eyes on the woman who painted it. Maria was silent, looking at her saint. She picked up a clean feather and dabbed it in the blue bean paint. Her strokes were surer now as she painted the eyes.

"Maria," asked Emiliano, "why do you paint his eyes that way? Should he not be looking straight ahead, contemplating some eternity we know nothing of?"

"No," she replied decisively, "he is looking down at the bird in his outstretched hand. For this he must glance sideways. No one looks at a bird straight on. They fly away."

"But Maria chiquita," said Diego, his eyes still on her face, "there is no bird."

"Diego, you will never be a saintmaker. As I found the saint, so will I find the bird."

She took up the blackened feather and brushed hair on the gentle man of Assisi, careful to leave a bald area for his tonsure. She made short brush strokes, glancing at Diego as she did, trying to capture the curl of his hair on the head of the saint.

"You flatter me, *querida*," Diego said, the endearment slipping out.

Maria heard him, but sighed. Somehow, it did not look right. "Emiliano, I want curly hair, but I don't know how to do it. And I wanted to carve folds in his habit, but I do not know how."

"So you must practice. I am fifty. You are fifteen. Do you think I learned everything in one day?"

"When you are old and toothless, Maria," said Diego.

Her eyes twinkled at him as she picked up another feather, dipping it into the red clay-egg yolk mixture. She dabbed on a small mouth, a serious mouth. She could never have imagined

San Francisco as a jolly sort of man. His beauty came from within. But how to paint that glow? She put down the feather. How indeed? The technique escaped her.

"He needs a knotted cord around his waist," Emiliano reminded her.

With the whitened yucca fiber brush, she painted the cord around his waist, careful not to smear the blue-gray of his habit. Mixing a little more white with a dab of brown, she painted San Francisco's hands the color of work and summer fields, the color of Diego's hands.

She set the *bulto* on the worktable and rubbed her back. Her legs ached from sitting cross-legged so long, and she noticed that the sky was darkening. But she had one more thing to do.

"May I leave San Francisco here?" she asked.

"I was going to suggest it. I will carve a small cross for his other hand, and hinge the arm to the shoulder for you. Next time you come this way, he will be ready." There was no word of compliment or praise from Emiliano, but she did not expect any. She could read his thoughts in the small glances he darted at the little saint gracing his workbench.

"Are you ready?" Diego asked.

"Almost. I have one more stop to make, if you will," she said, getting slowly to her feet.

"Why not? We will miss dinner anyway."

Maria stepped onto the terrace. The Indian women were preparing their evening meals. Wonderful aromas rose from the cooking pot, and she remembered that she had eaten nothing since early that morning in the dark kitchen. She looked back at Emiliano's workroom and smiled. Her little San Francisco watched her through the open window, his hand extended.

Diego followed Emiliano out onto the terrace. The *santero* nodded to Maria and turned to Diego. "Go with God, Senor Masferrer."

"And you, Old One."

The saintmaker hesitated. "There is one other thing. Of late, your enemy the Apache has been visiting our pueblo. In friendship, they say. Now, is this not a strange thing?"

Diego watched him, looking for more information than the

210

old man's words provided. "It is a strange thing, friend of my father. And what do you make of such a curious circumstance?"

Emiliano shrugged. "I cannot say." His tone was guarded. "Perhaps they choose to make friends. Perhaps they want an alliance. Who can say?"

Diego carefully matched his speech to the saintmaker's, the formality of his speech reflecting the importance of the conversation. "Yes, who can say? But tell me, Emiliano *el santero*, did these 'friends' of yours and mine come on horseback?"

"They did—despite your king's regulations to the contrary."

Diego did not answer right away. He looked at Maria, then down at his boots. "It is curious indeed," he said in a flat tone that gave away nothing.

Again the saintmaker chose his words with care. "I do not know how to say this, or even if I should. There is great conflict within me, as there is within Cristobal. He is of mixed blood, I of mixed spirit. But no, say nothing. Only be careful. Do not leave Las Invernadas unguarded for any reason. Not if you value what is within. Not if you value this small saintmaker," he said, touching Maria lightly on the shoulder. "I will say no more. Go now."

They climbed down the outside ladder, Maria waiting at the foot while Diego untied his horse. He came back leading Tirant, his eyes on the terraces above. He motioned to her slowly. "Come this way, Maria," he said in a low tone, "then turn and look up to the third level. To the left there."

She did as he said. While he leaned against his horse to put on his spurs, she casually scanned the terrace. "Diego, are they men?" she whispered.

"Look away now, Maria. Yes, they are men, such men as we have never seen before."

She took one last glance at the terrace. Four men stood there, painted white and wearing long white loincloths that reached to their painted knees. Their eyes stood out like black coals on white paper.

"It would appear that we are not the only gatherers of gypsum," said Diego.

"But what does it mean? Who are they?" She hated the way her voice rose in fear. Diego took her by the arm. When she looked back at the terrace, the Indians had vanished. The pueblo was silent, even the cooking noises hushed. As they stood there, the same pueblo that had appeared so bright in the day's sun began to take on shadows that lengthened and stretched across the plaza to Father Pio's church.

"Let us leave, Maria," said Diego, a note of urgency in his voice. "Where was it that you wanted to go?"

"It can wait." She felt a strong desire to be back at Las Invernadas.

"No. I will not show fear in front of my Indians. Where is it that you wanted to go?" he repeated.

"Back to the little *arroyo* where I found the saint in the wood. It should take only a moment."

"That will be about all the time we have before it will be too dark to see." He boosted her into the saddle, and she held the reins while he mounted behind her. He gathered the reins in his hands and sniffed her hair. "You still smell of ox hoof."

"There is always the *acequia* after dark," she replied, relieved at his light tone.

"And I recommend it. Maybe this is too high a price to pay to become a saintmaker. Mama has some lavender soap she has been saving for a special occasion."

Maria jabbed him with her elbow, and he laughed, the sound ringing across the deserted plaza.

The sun was setting when they arrived at the *arroyo*. Maria swung her leg over the saddle and dropped to the ground as Diego reined in his horse. "You needn't come unless you want to," she called as she started down the rocky bank to the dry riverbed.

She heard him dismount, and heard the ring of his spurs on the rocks, but she did not look back. She walked carefully among the dry woods, searching. There it was. She picked up a small piece of cottonwood, turning it over and over in her hands.

"What have you there?" Diego called from the bank above.

She held up the piece of wood. "San Francisco's bird!" she said. "I remembered seeing a piece with wings, and here it is."

He laughed again, holding up his hand as if to ward off her enthusiasm. "It would be only a piece of wood to me, chiquita," he said.

"Oh, Senor! And I thought you had poetry in your soul," she chided, picking her way up the rocky path.

212

"Not I. I am just a river kingdom *paisano,* an itching, scratching ranchero from *más allá de la frontera*—the kind of person your family probably joked about in Mexico City," he said, squatting on the riverbank. "But if you say it is a bird, I would never doubt you, *querida mia.*"

She paused halfway up the bank, hanging onto a root from the mesquite tree. She must speak to him of his words to the governor. As she stood there looking up at him, she knew it would break her heart if he called her his darling again. Never before in her life had she felt such a longing for someone. She hung there, clinging to the mesquite root, wanting Diego Masferrer as she had never wanted anything before in her life, and knowing that she had nothing to offer him except herself. And in this place, it would not be enough. "Senor," she began, "I am not your *querida.*"

But he was not listening to her. He was standing up now, leaning forward slightly, looking to the north and up the river valley.

"Senor?" she said again.

"Hush," he commanded. He leaned down swiftly, yanked her up to level ground, and pushed her down in the concealment of a bush beside him. He sat down slowly on the rock, his face draining of color, his eyes still intent on the distant view.

She got to her feet and sat next to him on the rock, her heart pounding loudly in her chest. She leaned against his shoulder, and he shifted, encircling her with his arm. He put his cheek close to her and pointed with his other arm, whispering, *"Mira.* Look there. Do you see?"

Intensely aware of his nearness, she looked down the length of his arm, squinting against the setting sun. At first she could see nothing, but as she watched, breathing in rhythm with Diego, she saw.

Six Indians ran along the Taos road. They came slowly, leisurely, as if they had set a pace some distance away that was, by now, second nature to them. They ran with a grace that took her breath away, their long dark hair unbound and swinging from side to side with the rhythmic movement of their legs. She slid closer to Diego, and his arm around her tightened.

"Where are they from?" she whispered in his ear.

"From Taos, I would say," he answered, never taking his

eyes off the magic runners. "That is an old Taos road. I did not think anyone used it anymore."

They watched the Indians come closer, the running almost hypnotic in its effect. "They will pass behind us, where Tirant is," said Diego. He rose in a crouch and ran to his horse, pulling the animal into a small, tree-covered gully beside the *arroyo*.

Maria could not take her eyes off the Indians. As they drew closer, she saw that they were white-painted like the Indians in the pueblo. She sat still on the rock. It was full of the day's heat, but she felt none of its warmth.

"Hurry, Maria," said Diego, gesturing to her. She ran to him, and he took her hand and pulled her down next to him on the narrow incline in front of his horse. "Keep your head down," he commanded, his hand heavy on her hair. He moved his fingers down to the back of her neck, but the pressure remained. He was forcing her to stay down.

She lay with her ear against the ground, and soon she heard the Indians coming, running with the same compelling rhythm that was almost as mesmerizing as Popeh and his dancers. Maria raised her head just enough to see the Indians top the rise from the river's edge.

Except for their cotton loincloths, they were naked, their arms and legs painted a dull white that was almost phosphorescent in the dying sun's light. Each man carried a knotted string in his hand, and the cords swung back and forth in rhythm with their dark hair, unbound and floating free.

"What are they doing?" she asked.

"I wish I knew, *querida*," he replied.

The Indians were running by the rock Diego and Maria had been sitting on only minutes before. Diego's hand left her hair and inched down to his waist. She heard him pull out his dagger, which he handed to her handle first, wrapping her fingers around the bone grip. Her knuckles whitened on the handle.

His lips were on her ear. "If they should stop or discover Tirant, just follow me, and quickly."

But the Indians did not stop. Without a glance to the right or the left, they ran on, heading down the little-used road toward Tesuque, the motion of their movements unbroken by any suspicion that they were watched.

Five minutes, ten minutes. Diego sat up. He held out his

hand and Maria gave him back his dagger. He tapped it on his other hand, watching her. She looked back at him in silence.

"Could you count the number of knots on the strings?" he asked.

Maria knelt, facing him. In the scurry her hair had tumbled down around her waist and she ran her fingers through it, working out the snarls. "Five? Four? I could not tell for sure. What do they mean?"

"I think it is some sort of calendar, a time line. I have seen them before in the pueblos."

"Then something is going to happen in four or five days?"

"Yes. Something."

They looked at each other. Tirant whinnied in the draw, and Diego got to his feet. He took his red scarf from around his head and tossed it to Maria, who wound it around her hair and tied it at the back of her neck, as he wore it. Diego picked up his hat and put it on. He untied Tirant and mounted, reaching down for Maria and pulling her in front of him. They started north.

"Aren't we going back by way of Tesuque?"

"We are not," he replied. "We will take the old Taos road until it drops down to the river, then cross my lands that way."

"Through the cornfield?"

"Yes. And when we get to the cornfield, we are going to dismount and walk. The stalks will cover us."

"Someone is watching us, intending to harm us?"

"I fear this could be," he admitted.

He would say no more. There was none of the playful talk of the morning. They started out at a walk but by the time they reached the river, Diego had urged his horse into a gallop. They crossed the river without pausing and rode to the edge of the Masferrer cornfield, the rows of corn standing tall in the August evening and rustling with the breeze that came up every night.

Diego helped Maria down, then dismounted, pausing only long enough to yank off his spurs. He slapped Tirant's rump with the flat of his hand and the horse took off across the field, streaking for the stables.

"That will worry them back at the hacienda," he said, taking Maria's hand in a tight grip. "So let us hurry. Pick up your skirts."

Maria grabbed up her skirt and petticoat and held them draped over one arm. It was dark, and she could not see where she was going, but Diego held her hand, and he knew his land well.

They ran until they reached the *acequia*. Tirant was at the stable, one of Diego's Mexican servants currying him. Erlinda was standing at the end of the kitchen garden, calling for her brother, a note of panic rising in her voice.

"We are here, Erlinda. All is well," he called to her, his breath coming in gasps. He let go of Maria, and she arranged her skirts around her again.

Erlinda ran across the footbridge, her arms outstretched. She grabbed Diego's shoulders and clung to him. "Diego, how afraid we were! It was so late! And when Tirant came back. . . ."

"We were right behind him."

"Why did you do that?" she asked, then shook her head. "But never mind. It is worse than you think. Your Tesuque Indians have all gone."

They crossed the bridge and walked into the garden. Diego paused and leaned against the beehive oven. "No. Tell me here. I would not frighten the little ones. All my Indians are gone? *Válgame,* I did not expect that. At least, not yet."

Erlinda stared at him. When he did not explain, she continued. "I noticed about midday how silent the fields were, and then one of your Mexican servants came running to say that all the work on the wagons had stopped, and the one remaining horse was gone."

"So we have only Tirant."

"I thought perhaps the Indians went to look for the horses, but they have not returned yet, and their wives and children have left, too. Thank God the Mexican servants remain loyal."

Diego was silent. Maria moved to his side, and Diego reached out for her hand, holding it tight.

"I have been thinking about taking Mama and the girls to stay with Lorenzo Nunez and his family," said Erlinda, choosing her words carefully.

Diego shook his head. "Don't you remember? Nunez always goes to Santa Fe to have Masses said on his name day. They are all gone."

They walked slowly toward the hacienda. In the kitchen Luz and Catarina were still eating dinner. Luz leaped up and

216

ran to Maria, who held her close. The child quickly moved her face from Maria's dress, her nose wrinkling. "Maria, you stink," she said.

Diego laughed. He ruffled Luz's hair and set his hat on her head. "You should have seen Maria today, Luisita mia," he said. "She made a saint. Out of a piece of cottonwood."

"That is nice," replied Luz, tipping the hat back so she could look up at her brother. "But why does she stink?"

Diego sat on the edge of the table. "She had to dig around in Father Pio's smelly old corral for rotten ox hooves and cook them into glue. You would smell, too, if it had been you."

"Thank you, Senor," said Maria.

He winked at her. "And now, I am sure Mama has that lavender soap I was praising. Erlinda," he said, "go to Mama with Maria. That is her only dress. Surely Mama has something that will fit Maria. They are of the same size."

Erlinda nodded and left the kitchen, Maria following. She looked around her, grateful for the thick walls of the hacienda and the warm, inviting candlelight. She paused before a saint on the wall in the corridor, still and watchful on his deerhide. Perhaps Emiliano would show her how to paint on hide. She remembered her little San Francisco, motioned to Erlinda to wait, and went back into the kitchen.

"Senor, I think I dropped the bird when we were running through the cornfield," she said.

Diego looked up from his dinner of chilies and cheese and reached into his pocket. "You did, but I retrieved it." He put the small cottonwood piece in her hand, closing her fingers over the wood. "If you have time tomorrow, you can make some blue bean paint and fashion us a mountain jay."

She put the wood on a shelf by the door. "And I thought you had no poetry in your soul! A mountain jay, eh? And why not a blue bird?"

"Here? This is not, nor ever shall be, Spain. Now go with Erlinda and change your dress," he laughed.

La Senora was on her knees in front of her altar, fingering her rosary. She rose and faced the door when they entered.

"I am sorry, Mama," apologized Erlinda. "We can come later."

"No need. Is that Maria with you? Then has my son returned?"

"They are both back, Mama, and Maria needs a dress, if you have one."

The woman sniffed the air and made a face. "Ah, Maria! What kind of scrape did Diego get you into?"

"Emiliano the saintmaker taught me to make a *bulto* today, and I had to cook ox-hoof glue."

"That does explain it. Erlinda, look in the chest at the foot of my bed. I am sure there is something there."

Erlinda found a pale blue dress of homespun serge, soft from many washings. La Senora touched the worn fabric. "This will do, Maria. It is yours."

"Thank you, Senora."

"It is nothing. And now, Erlinda, send Diego to me. We have much to say. And something tells me, I cannot say what, that time is growing short."

"Yes, it is late," replied Erlinda, closing the chest. "It is almost time for evening prayers. I will get him for you."

"One more thing," said La Senora. "Over on that shelf, Maria, you will find a bowl of lavender soap. Use it as your own," she said, putting her hand to her mouth and laughing softly.

Maria put her hand on La Senora's shoulder. The older woman reached up and patted her. "You are a good girl, Maria. I think that each of us, in our own way, has come to depend on you. And I have wanted to tell you how I treasure the love you have for my Luz and Catarina."

The words sounded too much like a farewell, and Maria's uneasiness deepened.

There was a knock at the door and Diego entered. Maria took the lavender soap from the shelf and left the room. Before going to the *acequia*, she finished the rest of the chilies and cheese still warming over the dying fire. The food tasted good. She had not eaten since before sunrise. Her hunger was gone, but the gnawing fear lingered. She picked up the dress, admiring the mother-of-pearl buttons and tiny tucks down the front. She fingered the material. How like everything in this river kingdom of New Mexico was that dress, simple homespun with mother-of-pearl, almost as an afterthought. It reminded her of eating off silver plates in a dirt-floored kitchen, or painting the glorious Spanish saints on the hides of buffalo and deer.

Maria hurried down the path to the *acequia*. She untied Diego's moccasins and stepped out of them, stripping off her dress and shift. She got into the water, shivering in the cold, then took the soap and waded down from the footbridge to the girls' play tunnel. The water was deeper there. She sank down, and the water came to her shoulders.

First she washed her hair, enjoying the fragrance of the lavender as it drifted around her in the slowly moving stream. She had not used soap like this since her father's house. She was used to rough household soap now, but it was pleasant to remember how things used to be. Maria closed her eyes and thought of her mother and father.

She sat still in the water, remembering the advice her mother had dispensed. "Not much of it has proved useful, Mama," she whispered. "I never carry a clean handkerchief anymore, I lost my own rosary, and I cannot flutter my eyelashes behind a fan because I have no fan."

She stood up in the water, looking over her shoulder at the moon, full and golden, already rich with the promise of harvest. "But Mama," she continued, "I suppose I have never been more content."

Maria waded upstream and pulled her towel off the footbridge. She left the water and dried herself quickly, shivering in the night air. She debated whether to put on her shift again and decided against it. The fabric smelled of ox-hoof glue and could be washed on the morrow. She pulled La Senora's dress on quickly, smoothing the soft material around her hips, then doing up the buttons. She looked around, hunting for Diego's moccasins.

"Is this what you seek?"

Maria gasped and whirled around. Cristobal was sitting cross-legged by the ovens, his back to their warmth. He was holding the moccasins.

He was dressed only in a loincloth, his legs and arms painted white like the Indian runners on the old Taos trail. His hair, usually worn pulled back and tied at his neck, was long and flowing loose.

He rose and walked toward her. Maria backed toward the footbridge, her throat constricting so she could not cry out. He held out the moccasins. "Come, take them," he said. His face shone ghastly white in the moonlight. He smiled. His teeth were blackened, and he looked like a death's head.

Her fear gave way to humiliation and anger. "How could you sit there and watch me!"

He laughed and handed over the moccasins. "It was easy, Maria chiquita," he replied, mocking Diego's words, "although I must say that if Diego could see you the way I saw you, he would not call you a 'small one.' But then, who is to say that he has not already seen you thus, eh? My brother, *el santo*. Maybe that is why you refuse my offer of safety, my offer of marriage. Maybe that is why you refuse me."

He laughed again, stepping closer, and she slapped him. He reached out and grabbed her wrist. "You will wish you had not done that," he hissed as she tried to wriggle out of his grasp.

"Let go of me!"

He released her as suddenly as he had grabbed her. Maria stood still on the footbridge, rubbing her wrist. The towel wrapped around her hair had fallen into the water, but she made no motion to retrieve it.

"Go into the hacienda," he commanded. "Tell Diego that you have seen me and how I am dressed. Perhaps he will understand. Perhaps he will take the warning."

Without a word, Maria rushed past him and ran down the garden path, slamming the kitchen door behind her. Diego had heard the door slam and was standing in the hall. She ran toward him. By the time she got to the door of his room, he had his sword out. He pulled her into his room and blew out the candle with one motion.

"Qué pasa, chiquita?" he whispered.

She had told herself that she would not cry, but she could not stop the tears. "Oh, Diego, Cristobal is in the garden! He watched me bathe. *Dios mio,* I am so ashamed. He told me he has come in warning."

Diego released her and raced down the hall. She heard the door to the kitchen garden opening, then there was silence. With flint and steel, Maria lit the candle again and sat on the bed. She looked down at her hand. It was streaked white where she had struck Cristobal.

She heard Diego in the hall again. He threw his sword down

on the bed when he entered the room and sat next to her. "No one was there, Maria."

Maria stared at him, then lowered her eyes. Her hand, stained with white from Cristobal's face, was proof that she had not merely imagined his appearance. It was proof also of the anger and violence that stalked the land. "He said I was to tell you how he had come. Oh, Diego, he looked like those Indians on the road today. He didn't look like himself." She sobbed. "He was terrifying." She buried her face in Diego's shoulder.

"Cristobal is a man torn in half," Diego whispered, his hand on her damp hair. "The Indian half has won. But perhaps there is something we can do." He stood, pulled her to her feet, and led her to the wooden wardrobe in the corner of his room. "Maria, can you use an arquebus, a firing piece?"

She shook her head.

"I would be more surprised if you could, but you are a woman of some resource."

"Gracias," she replied, a ghost of a smile crossing her face.

He opened the wardrobe. A cry of rage escaped him. "Dios! Someone has already taken it!"

Maria leaned against his arm and felt him tremble. He looked at her, and the age in his eyes was even more frightening than Cristobal's death mask. He took his dagger out of his belt and handed it to her, then pulled his leather cloak out of the wardrobe, the same cloak he had worn when he had found her after the Indian massacre. He slung it around his shoulders, swiftly knotting the cords.

"Let us go, *querida*."

Erlinda met them in the hall. Her face drained of color as she saw her brother's expression. Diego put his hand on her arm. "I am going out to look for the horses."

"What about prayers?" Erlinda managed, clinging to his hand as if to stop him.

He smiled, and Maria looked away. "Pray for me tonight, Erlinda. And for all of us. Come, Maria. I will talk as I saddle Tirant."

They left the hacienda through the kitchen garden and crossed the footbridge. "After I leave, tell one of my Mexican servants to pull the water barrel inside the kitchen and fill it. Close and bar all the shutters. See if you can find my dogs and bring them inside, too." He stopped. "Where are the dogs? I haven't heard them all evening. Well, anyway, my guards will be on the hacienda roof, as they always are."

They reached the stables and Diego put out his arm suddenly, pushing Maria back. She heard him suck in his breath, then looked around his arm and grabbed it.

Tacked to the adobe wall of the stable were Diego's dogs, gutted and spread out, their heads hanging down, their blood dripping in the dust. Maria covered her eyes with her hands. When she took them away, the dogs were still hanging, their gray coats dark with blood.

"Now we know where the dogs are," said Diego quietly. He took out his sword again. "Do not follow me."

She waited in the horse corral, unable to move. Diego called to her finally, and she jumped. "Come, Maria, and quickly," he said.

She ran into the stable, staying as far away from the gutted dogs as she could. Diego was leading Tirant from his stall. He hurriedly saddled and bridled the animal, talking to her as he worked.

"Open the doors to no one—I mean no one—except me tomorrow. but if you should see any of the upper valley rancheros passing this way, going toward Santa Fe, get them to take you and my family with them. Even if you have to walk alongside their horses. Do not leave alone. But if I should not return by midday tomorrow, then go. But stay off the roads."

"Will Erlinda and your mother listen to me?" Maria asked as Diego swung into the saddle.

"I honestly do not know, and I have not time to find out. I am going back to the old Taos road. I am going to watch there and see what I can see." Before he ducked out of the stable, he snatched a coil of rope hanging by the door.

Maria ran after him into the corral. He looked back at her. "Bless you, Maria *querida,*" he said and disappeared into the darkness.

She stood there a moment in the empty corral. She looked down at her white hand. It still held Diego's dagger. She climbed through the fence and hurried across the footbridge.

The Mexican servants were all gathered in the kitchen, silent and watchful. In a voice that did not sound like her own, Maria directed two of the men to close and bar all the shutters, and another to haul in the water barrel. She told the other men to mount the roof for the nightly watch. "And bring your families into the chapel tonight," she added. "Make sure all the doors are triple-bolted tonight." She hurried down the hall to the chapel and met Erlinda coming out.

"They are bedded down, Maria," she said. "Mama is sleeping, and I told the girls a story tonight." They walked arm in arm back to the kitchen. Erlinda watched the men filling the water barrel inside by the back door. "Diego fears an Apache raid?" she asked.

Maria shook her head. "It is the Pueblo Indians that he fears."

Erlinda stared at her, an incredulous look on her face. "Maria, you are joking! Has my brother lost all reason? His Indians are not capable of mischief. Oh, they steal, they lie, but they do not raid."

Maria thought of the gutted dogs and Cristobal in his white paint but said nothing.

"However, Diego would have us safe, rather than sorry, and I bless him for that. Someday he and I will laugh about this!" Erlinda turned to the men, who, having finished filling the barrel, stood waiting. "Do as you always do, my servants. Go to your families. This will be over tomorrow."

The men bowed and left. Erlinda looked at Maria, who was staring into the glowing coals in the fireplace. "Come to my room, Maria, I will brush your hair and braid it for you."

They spent the next hour in Erlinda's room, Maria listening in silence as Erlinda chattered about her future visit to Santa Fe. She was not usually so voluble. Did she too sense the danger and seek to ward it off with words? Did she believe her counterfeit cheer would cheer Maria?

Finally Maria went to her own room. Luz and Catarina were sleeping in the same bed, curled up close to each other. Maria pulled the blankets up higher around their shoulders and made sure the small fire in the grid was properly banked. Closing the door behind her, she went into the hall again. All was quiet in the chapel, so she went to Diego's room, picking up his dagger from the hall table where she had left it.

She lit the candle in his room and sat down on the bed, propping his pillow behind her head and leaning against the wall. The fire had not been lit in his room that night, and the air was chilly. Maria pulled her legs up tight against her body and rested her chin on her knees. She heard the Mexican guards on the roof as they walked back and forth, watching. She closed her eyes finally on the reassuring sounds of the guards.

Maria roused herself at intervals throughout the night, her heart pounding as she listened for the slow steps of the guards. Finally dawn illuminated the Sangre de Cristo Mountains.

El Terror

$\mathcal{S}$*he woke with a start, sitting* up in Diego's bed. During the night she had crept between the sheets and covered herself with his Indian blanket. Out of habit, she reached out with her toes to feel for his sword. Of course it was not there. Diego was gone, and she felt a longing for him that was both more terrible than anything she had ever known, and more wonderful.

She propped the pillow up against the end of the bed again and picked up the Masferrer family journal. It was open to yesterday's entry. "August 8," she read, squinting in the early morning light. Diego's handwriting was large and sprawling and hard to read. "A visit to Emiliano with my Maria. She learned to make a saint out of cottonwood. Trouble with my Indians, with my brother. The horses are gone, the wagons burned, the fields empty of farmers. Father, what would you have me do?"

Maria put her head down on the parchment. With his words of instruction last night, he had transferred some of his burdens to her shoulders, and the weight of it was bitter.

She wiped her eyes and set the journal back on the little

table next to a wine bottle and silver cup. She picked up the bottle and took a large swallow, thinking about her mother. "A lady drinks only from a cup, Maria." She took another drink from Diego's bottle and shoved the cork back in, thinking how he would tease her if the bottle were half empty when he returned.

If he returned. Fear pulsed in her veins and made her temples throb. She got out of his bed, straightening the pillow and arranging the covers. The pillow smelled of lavender now, but she did not think he would mind.

She went into the hall. The Mexican servants were up as usual, the women making their familiar kitchen clatter as they prepared breakfast, the men attending to their chores outside. As she approached the kitchen, she saw that the shutters were open already. The steady rap of hammers and whine of saws from across the *acequia* told her that they were at work on the wagons again.

Erlinda was setting the table for breakfast. "God's blessing on you, Maria," she said as always, her cool blond serenity camouflaging the difference of this day.

"And His Mercy on you, Erlinda," Maria answered as always, struck by a feeling of unreality as if she were floating through a nightmare of her own creation.

"Mama is asking for Diego," Erlinda said. "Would you see if he has returned?"

Maria hurried through the kitchen, admonishing the women to close and bar all the shutters again on her way. She heard the servants giggling behind her back, but she had no authority to make them obey her.

Maria went into the garden, her eyes going immediately to Diego's Apache moccasins, lying where she had dropped them when she'd slapped Cristobal. She looked at her hand, but the white paint had worn off. She sat down on the ledge by the oven and put on the moccasins, doing up the laces rapidly, then hurried through the garden and crossed the footbridge, toward the stable.

One of the Mexican servants had cut down the dogs, and the animals now lay on the ground in a puddle of dried blood. Maria looked around and swallowed. She had not noticed in last night's darkness, but the unknown butcher had draped the animals' entrails over the fence. A servant was now removing the offal, looping it over his arm and dropping it on the pile by the stable doors.

"Have you seen Senor Masferrer?" she called, shading her eyes against the rising sun.

"No, Senorita, he is not here."

She hurried back to the hacienda, pausing only long enough to fish her towel out of the *acequia,* where it had snagged on a cottonwood limb. In the kitchen, Luz and Catarina looked up from their morning mush and chocolate. Maria flashed what she hoped was a reassuring smile. "Girls, Diego has asked that you play indoors today. Something quiet on the patio. If you are good, I will tell you stories in the afternoon."

She expected an argument from them, some words of protest at confinement on such a beautiful day. Instead, they followed her quietly down to the patio. Luz turned to her Indian doll that Cristobal had carved for her, picking up the toy and patting the Pueblo blanket, bright with design, around the wooden figure. Catarina picked up her embroidery, watching Maria through troubled eyes. When Luz sat down next to her, crooning to her doll, Catarina edged closer on the bench. Clearly the children sensed something.

Maria left the girls and walked to the front of the hacienda, throwing back the bolts on the door with difficulty and walking into the coolness of the portal, where honeybees were already gathering around the opening flowers. She could see no movement on the road passing the hacienda. She walked down to the big iron gate, but did not open it. The road was deserted. By this time of morning, there were usually laborers trudging to the fields, children hurrying to small labors, women carrying market goods from Tesuque to the nearby haciendas. Today there was no one.

She looked north past the cornfields. No sign of Diego. She would wait until midday for his return. If he was not back by then, they must follow his instructions and leave. With a great weight on her heart, she went back inside, locking the front door behind her and throwing the bolts in the cool silence of the foyer. She paused, leaning against the door, all strength gone.

When she had gathered her ragged emotions into some imitation of serenity, she returned to the kitchen, where she could see Erlinda from the window, heating water in the yard for the washing. Maria walked past her without speaking and crossed the footbridge again, looking to the cornfield, willing Diego to appear, even as she despaired of seeing his dear face again.

And then she saw him. She ran past the stable, ignoring Erlinda's cries. She gathered her skirts around her and ran into the field, crossing it at an angle. Her mother would have been shocked at such a display of legs and petticoats, but Maria did not care.

He was riding slowly down the Taos road, tugging two Indians after him on a rope. She ran to the road and waited for him. The Indians were white-painted, their hair long. One of them stared at her hard, then looked away. The other walked with his head down, scuffing at the dirt.

Diego dismounted and walked stiffly toward Maria. His clothes were covered with dust and there were deep circles under his eyes. Maria ran to him. She put her hands on his arm, but said nothing.

"I heard them early this morning, Maria. Not long before sunrise. They tripped over the rope I had stretched across the road. There were three of them. One got away. He ran back toward Taos. Look here, Maria." He reached into his shirt front and pulled out two of the curious cords they had seen yesterday. She took them from him gingerly, as if they were living things. Each cord was about a foot long, woven tightly of maguey fiber. She fingered the knots. "Four knots?" She glanced back at the Indians, who were watching them with an intensity that made her stomach turn.

"Four days, Maria. Four days until there is an uprising. I am sure of it now." He looked south down the road and sighed. "Do you suppose Governor Otermin will believe me if I tell him? Or will he throw me into prison for returning to town against his orders?

"I do not have time to stop at Las Invernadas. Tell everyone not to worry. I will be back from Santa Fe before sundown. I will try to bring some help with me, some horses, a wagon. At any rate, we will leave here tomorrow morning. No later." He paused and leaned against his horse. "Maria, Maria," he said, his eyes closed, his face half-turned to Tirant.

She put her hand on his arm and he reached for her, hugging her. *"Dios mio,* I am afraid, *querida,"* he said in a whisper. She leaned against him, and he stroked her cheek with his gloved hand. Then he straightened, glancing behind him at the two figures now squatting in the dust.

"If there is time," he began, not meeting her eyes, "I will return through Tesuque and persuade Father Pio to join us here."

"Diego, if there is any way, could you . . ."

"Could I collect your little saint?" he finished for her, the smile crossing his face at odds with the bleakness in his eyes. "I will try, Maria, you know I will. We will need all the blessings of all the saints. And we have but four days."

"Go there only if it is safe, Diego," she insisted. "After all, it is only a possession."

"You have another possession, Maria, one which will always be with you."

"Tell me what it is, Senor."

"You have my heart, *querida,* my heart," he said, his voice low. "I took the time to think last night while I was keeping myself awake." He touched her face again. "I thought only of you."

The Indians rose and began to walk toward Diego and Maria. She jumped, and he pushed in front of her and pulled out his sword. The Indians squatted in the dust once more.

"When I mount Tirant again, stand clear, Maria," he said. "God in heaven, if I close my eyes to kiss you, those Indians would be on us in a moment! Remember that I love you, Maria. God forgive me for discovering it so late."

He motioned her away then and mounted quickly, jerking the Indians to their feet and keeping the rope taut. He blew her a kiss and tipped his hat.

She stood watching until Diego and the Indians turned the bend in the road toward Tesuque and the river, then walked slowly back to the hacienda.

That day was longer than any Maria had ever lived through, even longer than her wait by the smoldering ruins of the mission supply caravan. She sat in the cornfield in miserable silence until she felt she could face the others. Then with a calmness that amazed her, she told Erlinda about Diego and the Indians. Erlinda extinguished the fire under the wash water and went inside to pack.

Once during the afternoon Erlinda came to her. "Tell me, Maria, do you love my brother?"

"I do," she said simply, continuing to fold clothing into the trunk. "I love him so much that it is not something I can talk about, not even to you, who are more than a sister to me."

"Gracias," said Erlinda. "And does he love you? Tell me that, at least."

"Yes. He told me so this morning."

"Then I wish you had left with him," said Erlinda savagely. Her eyes widened in horror. "We are going to die here, and you will never know him!"

Maria held out her arms to Erlinda. The widow sank into them, and they cried together.

La Senora asked for Maria during the middle of the silent, endless afternoon. She went into the still room, dimly lit by the small candle burning near the *bulto* of Our Lady.

"What should we read today?" Maria asked, her voice steady, her hands clenched tight in front of her.

La Senora closed her eyes. "You sound so tired, my child. Did you not sleep well?"

"I slept well, Senora," Maria said, "but we have been busy today with the washing."

"Maria," said the woman, her voice taking on a distinct tone of command. "You should not tell lies. You are terrible at it. What is the matter here, and why does Diego not come?"

"Senora," said Maria, sitting close to her, "he is in Santa Fe. On urgent business."

"And what of Cristobal?"

"He is gone. I saw him last night. Only he . . . left." She knew she was not making any sense, but her voice was rising in panic, and she could not help herself.

La Senora groped for Maria's hands and held them in a surprisingly strong grip. "Maria, calm yourself! We have been through hard times before. I remember a famine when all I had to feed my children was ox hides—the smell of your dress last night brought back memories, my child. I remember when Apaches even breached our walls and killed some of the servants. This is a terrible place we live in, sometimes I think. But we survive."

Maria covered her face with her hands. "Forgive me, Senora."

"It is no matter. But promise me this. No matter what happens, keep Luz and Catarina close to you. Erlinda will look after me." The blind woman patted Maria's hand. "Perhaps my time would be better spent in prayer this afternoon. But there is one more thing you must do for me."

"Anything, Senora," said Maria.

"Anything, is it? How simple you make my task. If, by chance, my son should ask you to marry him, oblige him."

Maria leaped to her feet. "Oh, but I could not!"

"Sit down, Maria, for heaven's sake," ordered La Senora crisply. "Do you feel that you could not learn to love him? He loves you. He told me." She paused, making an impatient gesture with her hands. "Of course, I asked. I had to drag it out of him. *Dios mio,* why are men so reticent these days! It was not so when I was young!"

Maria sat down slowly. "You do not understand, you, of all people. I have nothing to offer him, or any of you Masferrers. Absolutely nothing."

La Senora made a sound in her throat somewhere between a laugh and a snort. "And what is that to any of us?"

"It is everything to me!" Maria burst out. "I see how it is here in the river kingdom. This family marries into that family—to join fields, to expand herds, to build empires. But I have no wealth, no possessions, no family even."

La Senora held up her hand, waving Maria to silence. "All this aside, I have only one question. Do you love him? Eh?"

Maria looked down at her hands. "I do," she said simply, "and it is such a wrenching thing. I did not know love could hurt like this."

La Senora reached for her hands again and patted them. "How curious. Diego said nearly the same thing to me." She rose then and walked to her altar, her step sure. "That is all I wanted to know. Go now, and let me pray. There is work to be done here."

Maria went out quietly and spent the rest of the afternoon on the patio with Luz and Catarina, telling and retelling their favorite story of the foolish prince who fell in love with the poor girl. She was rescued by Erlinda, who pulled the girls away to take the leather buckets and help fill the water barrel in the kitchen.

"She will not even let us play outside at the *acequia,*" Luz grumbled, "and if there really were Apaches, we would have heard the bell at Tesuque first."

"Do as she asks, girls," said Maria, anxious to be alone

with her thoughts. Diego should have been back by now. The nine miles to Santa Fe were easily covered by noon, the return by midafternoon. As evening approached, she made several trips to the main road, to stand behind the heavy gate, peering south. No one. Nothing.

He is probably in jail in Santa Fe, she finally forced herself to admit. The governor warned him about coming back to town, and they have put him in jail. Her eyes went back to the empty road.

Dinner was a quiet meal, eaten quickly as darkness fell. The Mexican servants returned from their evening chores to report that the sheep in the distant pasture beyond the cornfield had been run off. They had managed to corral the other sheep next to the stable.

The servants spoke to Maria. In some peculiar fashion, Diego's power had been transferred to her. Erlinda sat, withdrawn and silent, by the fireplace, mechanically stirring the chilies simmering there for Diego. Her expression was inscrutable.

"There is nothing more we can do about the sheep tonight," Maria said to the men. "Stay with your families again this night in the chapel, and make sure the guards are on the roof."

"As always," replied one of the servants.

Madre de dios, thought Maria, what he must think of me! I, who know so little of Indian attacks, telling him! Diego, I am trying to remember everything.

She smiled at the servants. "Let me thank you for Diego Masferrer. Any man would be lucky to have you as servants."

They nodded to her and looked at one another in embarrassment. The ringing of the chapel bell summoned them.

After evening prayers in the chapel, crowded close together with the families of the Mexican servants, Maria shepherded Luz and Catarina to their bedroom, told them a quick story and tucked them in bed. She kissed them goodnight as Diego would have, and hurried down the hall to his bedroom. She would write an entry in the family journal, recording the events of that endless day for Diego to read later. Holding her candle high, she opened the door to Diego's room.

She stopped on the threshold, nearly dropping the candle. The journal was lying open on the bed, the pages ripped out and scattered all over the room. The bedding lay in long strips on the mattress, slashed repeatedly with a knife or sword. The pillow's feathers floated about, mingling with the journal's pages. "Oh, *Dios,*" Maria whispered. She went into the room quickly and shut the door. Forcing herself to move, she crossed to Diego's wooden wardrobe and flung open the doors. Inside, the folded clothes were slashed and torn, ripped apart by a madman.

She slammed the doors shut and leaned against them, staring across the room to the altar. The deerhide painting of the Madonna was also in shreds, with deep gouges in the plaster behind the picture. The ebony Spanish crucifix over the altar was broken in half, the pieces lying like kindling on the floor.

Maria blew out the candle and went to the door. For one long moment she could not work the latch. Panic overcame her, and she forced herself to stand still and try the door again. It opened and she stumbled into the hall, shivering convulsively in the cool August evening.

They must leave Las Invernadas. But they could not leave at night, alone, without Diego. They could not cross the land on foot in darkness, a pathetic band of women and children. Maria made up her mind. First thing in the morning. They would leave at dawn.

She went to her room. The girls were already asleep, their soft breathing a familiar rhythm in a night that was different from all others. Maria felt under her side of the bed for Diego's knife, picked it up, and lay down to wait.

If I can just rest a moment, she thought, her eyes already closing, then I will watch until morning and get everyone out at first light. She closed her eyes and slept, the knife dropping from her hand.

Sometime later, Maria awoke suddenly, sat up and listened. She leaned back against the cold wall, listening for the familiar sounds of the guards on the roof, pacing back and forth. There was only silence.

She felt for Diego's knife, groping by the bed in panic until her fingers wrapped around the bone handle. She slowly swung her legs out of bed. She had not taken off her moccasins, but the floor was still cold under her feet. She padded quietly to the door and opened it, grateful that the leather hinges were silent. Slowly she stepped into the hall, then drew back in horror.

She must have been dreaming, for Carmen de Sosa crawled down the shadowy corridor, coughing softly, lurching toward her on all fours. "Diego, help me," Maria whispered, "Diego." This dream was more real than all the others, and he was not there.

Maria forced herself to look down the hall again. Still Carmen de Sosa came, but now she was whimpering, something she had never done before. And as Carmen de Sosa approached, moving more slowly now, but still coming, Maria heard a dripping sound.

The crawling figure came closer. Maria flattened herself against the wall. The figure stopped and tried to speak. It was the gargle of a drowning man. It was not a dream, but something a thousand times worse than any dream that had ever jerked her from sleep.

Clamping her teeth to keep from screaming, Maria knelt on the floor and crawled toward the man who was now swaying in the middle of the hall. She reached out and touched him, her hand coming away wet and warm.

"*Quién es?*" she whispered. "*Quién es?*"

As her eyes adjusted to the gloom, she could see it was one of the servants who had bedded down in the chapel at the far end of the hall. As he turned toward the sound of her voice, she saw that his throat was slit from ear to ear. The blood glistened in the dim light and splashed to the floor. Maria put her hand on the man's shoulder again and he fell forward.

Maria crawled back to the chest against the far wall and crouched beside it. Now she heard sounds from the chapel, the screams of children, the muffled cries of women.

So it had begun. Maria crawled back to her room, not trusting herself to stand. The sounds coming from the chapel were muffled, as if the large double doors were still shut. Perhaps the dying servant had crawled out undetected and shut the doors after him. He had bought her a few precious seconds, and she could not waste them.

Her hands shook so badly that she could not light the candle, but it was just as well. Her hands were bloody, and her dress was damp, too, soaked with the blood of the man in the hall. She shook Catarina gently, calling her softly, "*Despierta, mi niña,* wake up." She said it over and over, her voice low and

234

soothing, her bloody hand cupped just over the young girl's mouth in case she should cry out.

Catarina sat up, rubbing her eyes and looking around her. Maria hurried to Luz and shook her awake. Luz cried out, and Maria clamped her hand over her mouth. "Hush, my darling, *querida mia,*" she said, taking her hand away slowly.

Catarina pulled the blankets up tighter around her and settled back down. "Is it morning, Maria?"

Maria compelled herself to speak calmly. "You have always told me that you are an adventurous girl, Catarina. Is this not so?"

They heard a crash from the chapel. Catarina edged closer to Maria in sudden fear.

"Never mind, my dear, never mind. I want you to come with me. I am going to pick up Luz and carry her to the kitchen. I want you to hold onto my skirt—don't let go—and follow me. Can you do that?"

Catarina nodded, her eyes wide with terror now. Maria shook her head and put her finger to her lips. "We will find Diego. Should we do that and surprise Erlinda and your mama?"

Catarina nodded again and got out of bed. Maria hurried to Luz and picked up the groggy child. "Now take hold of my skirt," she told Catarina.

"But Maria, it is wet," whispered the girl.

"Never mind that, *querida.* Just do as I say."

Maria pushed open the door. The sounds from the chapel were still muffled, but as she stood there, the doors slammed back against the wall with a bang that shook the hacienda.

"Diego!" Maria said out loud. She put Luz over her shoulder, stuck Diego's knife in the waistband of her dress and felt behind her for Catarina. She guided the girl silently down the hall, carefully skirting the corpse in the darkness.

She ran to Erlinda's room and knocked on the door, which opened before she lowered her arm. Erlinda yanked her and the children into the room. *"Por dios,"* the widow whispered, her lips to Maria's ear, "what is this I am hearing?"

"It is the Pueblos. Let us hurry!" Maria tugged at Erlinda's nightgown, but Erlinda would not move.

"No," she said, the fear of the day replaced by a strange look of resignation. "No. You will never escape with my sisters if you are burdened with Mama. I will remain here with Mama.

Our lives are over. You and the children have not yet lived."
Erlinda kissed her, patted Luz's dark curls, and shoved them
toward the kitchen. "Now go! Find my brother, and be as happy
as I was!"

Before Maria could stop her, Erlinda started down the long
hall toward La Senora's room, pausing only to square her shoulders and pat her hair into place. Maria followed with the children in tow. "I know, I know," said the blind woman, as they
opened the door. "I have been listening. We waited too long."

"Come with me now," pleaded Maria. "Hurry!"

"I cannot. I will be a burden. You must take the children
and flee."

"Erlinda says the same."

"We have always been of one mind about the things that
mattered."

"Mama!" Maria cried, forgetting herself.

La Senora smiled. "How good that sounds. But no. I will
stay here. Take my girls. They are yours now. Do as I say."

Maria kissed her, and La Senora caressed her cheek. "Go
quickly. Find my dear son. And do not look back."

Maria ran down the hall, tugging Catarina behind her. She
heard menacing cries of violence drawing closer, and then
Erlinda screamed. Maria tightened her hold on Luz and did not
look back. "Do not let go," she whispered to Catarina clinging
to her skirt.

When she reached the kitchen, Maria bolted the door to the
hall behind her, wincing at the scraping of iron on iron. Still
towing Catarina after her, she ran to the outside door and opened
the bolts. She stood there for precious seconds, too afraid to
open the door, too afraid of what might be on the other side
of it. Steeling herself finally, she edged open the door and
looked into the kitchen garden.

The moon was still up, casting its soft glow on the bean
vines and tomatoes. She saw the reassuring hump of the beehive
ovens, and heard the *acequia* flowing in the distance. She heard
two Indians shattering the doors in the hall with axes.

"Stand here, Catarina," she ordered, and ran into the pantry,
still carrying Luz, who was wide awake now and sobbing.
Maria grabbed one of yesterday's loaves of bread and stuffed
it down her dress front.

Catarina stood by the open doorway, her hands covering her

ears. Someone within the house was screaming now. Maria pushed Catarina into the garden. Luz cried out, a thin wail that seemed to hang on the night air.

"Hush, Luz! Before God, you must be silent," Maria exclaimed, and the girl was still, her fingers in her mouth, her eyes filled with shock.

Maria ran through the garden. As she looked back, the chapel end of the hacienda burst into flames. Catarina screamed, and Maria shook her into silence.

She dragged the girls to the footbridge and pulled them into the water. Catarina cried out again, and Luz's arms tightened like a vise around Maria's neck. Maria pulled them downstream to the small play tunnel the girls had dug in the side of the ditch. She swung Luz inside, peeling the girl's arms off her neck.

"And now you, Catarina. Do as I say!"

Without a word, Catarina crawled in after her sister and clung to her, wet and shaken. Maria pulled the loaf out of her dress and put it in Catarina's lap.

"And now, my darlings, you must be ever so brave."

The screams were louder now. Erlinda was howling, pleading, crying, "Diego! Diego!" over and over. The girls drew farther back into the cave, crowding against the shallow back wall in their attempt to flee the nightmare.

"Do not leave us, Maria!" sobbed Catarina.

"I must. There is not room for me, too. Now listen to me and do not talk. I am going for help. I am going to find Diego. You must not leave this cave, no matter what you see or hear. Do not doubt that I will return for you. You may get hungry, but do not leave this place."

Maria reached out for the girls, crying with them. She hugged them, kissed them, made the sign of the cross over them, then wrenched herself away, wading back to the footbridge.

The air was filled with screams. La Senora's joined with her daughter's. Gulping back her own tears, Maria climbed the bank, gathered up her sodden skirts and ran into the cornfield.

What now? She sank down between the rows of corn. She did not know where to find Diego, where to seek help. She looked south over her shoulder. There was no fire at the Nunez hacienda. Diego had said that they had gone to Santa Fe, but surely not everyone in the large family had made the trip.

Perhaps one or two of the family's sons remained. Perhaps they would take in her and the children.

She stood up and took one last look at the Masferrer hacienda. Flames licked around the chapel end, spreading toward the rest of the building. She started for the old Taos road where she had last seen Diego.

The road was deserted. She crossed it running and jumped into the brush beside the trail. Staying in the undergrowth, she followed the road toward the Nunez holdings, half a league distant. She picked her way carefully around the scrub brush and dry tree limbs, thinking of other saints resting in cottonwood limbs along the nearby creekbed. "Then intercede for me now," she said out loud as she skirted the bare limbs, "and for my girls."

As she approached the Nunez hacienda, instinct compelled her to stay in the shadows off the trail. All appeared calm. She saw small lights flickering in one of the barred windows and smiled with relief. Not everyone had gone to Santa Fe.

But as she watched, the lights turned into a blaze that roared up along one entire wall. Maria shrank farther into the shadows. Coming from the hacienda was the whole Nunez family. That could not be. Her hand to her throat, she watched.

The younger Nunez daughters were followed by Pueblo braves dressed in the clothes of their parents. Maria blinked back her tears. By the light from the burning building, she saw blood on the girls' faces where their eyes had been. They were led stumbling and silent to the road. The older child tripped and fell, and the Pueblos were upon her, tearing her clothes as she blindly tried to fend them off with her fists.

Maria turned away, sickened, as the other girl was tossed from spear point to spear point. She thought of Luz and Catarina and buried her face in her hands.

"Senorita Espinosa!" a voice whispered.

Maria froze. A hand reached out for her, touching her hair. She turned slowly.

An Indian woman leaned toward her. Maria peered closer. Another figure crawled from the shadows of the deep underbrush. Maria drew in her breath in sudden recognition.

"You are the girl from the cornfield!" she exclaimed, then looked around in fear of being overheard. The Indians by the hacienda were paying no attention. One of the Nunez sons was now in flames, impaled on the gatepost.

She turned back and put out her hand tentatively to the older woman. "And you are the mother," she whispered. "I remember."

The Indian woman watched Maria for a long moment, weighing her, measuring her, then spoke to her daughter.

"Senorita," the young girl said, "we have been following you. We have known of this thing for several moons now. My mother could not forget what you did for my small sister." She paused, looking back at her mother. "We have told no one. We would both die if our people knew."

The woman spoke to her daughter, who inched closer to Maria. "Come with us. We can keep you safe."

Maria crawled toward them and they drew her further into the brush. "But where?" she asked. Her head throbbed from the screams and laughter of the Indians on the trail.

"To Tesuque."

Maria shook her head and tried to draw away, but the Indian mother took her hand.

"You will be safe," the girl said. "It is the time of my mother's uncleanness, and no man enters our quarters. My mother says perhaps we can get you to Santa Fe."

Maria looked around her at the tree limbs and thought of Diego and the saintmaker in one aching rush. Her San Francisco was in Tesuque. But Santa Fe? It seemed so far away. She nodded finally and followed the Indian women away from the road.

They kept to the streambed east of the road, walking carefully over the stones. Maria was grateful for her moccasins. She hurried after the others, her eyes on the clouds over the Sangre de Cristos as they turned pink with the threat of dawn.

They were approaching Tesuque when Maria realized someone was following them. It was only a feeling at first, a feeling that someone's eyes were on her. When they stopped, Maria whirled around quickly and glimpsed a flash of white on the higher bank. She pulled the knife from the waistband of her dress and walked faster, hurrying to keep up. Whoever it was made no pretense of silence but strode along with arrogance.

They hurried into the cottonwood trees before the pueblo.

The ladders from the upper levels had been let down, but she saw no one.

"Walk between us, Mother says."

Maria obeyed the girl, matching her steps to those of the two women, hoping for some trick of fading moonlight to blend her bloody Spanish dress into their cotton tunics. They crossed the plaza and climbed the ladder, the mother pulling her up and leading her quickly into the welcome darkness.

The room was dimly lit with one small torch. Maria felt her way to the pile of blankets in one corner. "Tell your mother that your father's blankets are still without equal."

The young girl smiled and whispered to her mother, who ducked her head in shyness, then sat down beside Maria.

"We will rest here a moment and then think," said the girl.

Maria leaned against the cool adobe wall. She looked at the Indian mother, who had turned to her still-sleeping baby in another corner. I have no right to endanger their lives, she thought.

Maria leaned forward to speak to the girl, to tell her that she would have to leave, when a voice like a snake hissed at her from the dark doorway leading to the pueblo's interior.

"Maria. Maria."

That was all. Maria closed her eyes and held her hands tight against her stomach. The mother crawled away from her sleeping baby and looked at Maria, her eyes pleading, sorrowful. Without a word, Maria rose and ran out the door she had come in.

The voice hissed again, then was silent. Waiting. Maria climbed down the ladder, panic close at her heels. Ahead of her was Father Pio's church. The sun was rising. It was time for Mass, but she knew there would be no Mass this morning. Perhaps there would be no Mass in this land ever again. She hurried toward the church. Diego had said that he would go to Father Pio if there was time. Time. She spit the word out of her mouth like venom. And if only Father Pio were there, at least she would not be alone.

She slipped inside the chapel, then fell on her knees in homage to terror.

The chapel was filled with Indians, Indians painted like Cristobal, Indians wearing the tall, feathered headdresses of the *kachinas*, Indians dancing and swaying to a rhythm only they could hear.

They did not see her. All eyes were on the altar. Maria stared up at the large crucifix above the altar, the one Father Pio was so proud of, and blinked her eyes in disbelief.

Father Pio hung from the wooden cross above the altar, dressed in the robes of this holy day, San Lorenzo Day, the red of the martyrs. But there was another red as well. His stole and alb dripped with blood from a hundred knife wounds. Even now the Indians standing around the altar were throwing knives at him, while others stood naked below the cross, raising their arms to the droplets of blood that fell in a gentle shower.

Maria raised her eyes to Father Pio. She could not tell if he was alive or dead. His tonsured head drooped over his chest. His hands were riveted to the cross by spears, but his feet dangled free.

Clutching Diego's knife in one hand, Maria crawled out of the chapel. She huddled in the doorway until two Indians in the plaza disappeared into one of the lower openings, then she forced herself to walk slowly and deliberately across the plaza toward Emiliano's workshop. She started to skirt carefully around what appeared to be a woodpile, but stopped short, her breath coming in little gasps.

It was Tirant, lying twisted and stiff with a gaping chest wound. Maria knelt by the black horse and ran her hand over his hide. As she patted Diego's horse in the killing silence of Tesuque pueblo, she knew that dawn was coming on a more terrible day than she had ever known before. And she was alone.

Where was Diego? Still Maria crouched by the horse, telling herself to think, to reason her way through the horror that threatened to block her very breathing. She sat back on her heels. If I cannot find Diego alive here, she decided, I will go back to the *acequia* and stay there with my girls until the Indians find us. I cannot leave them to die alone.

She stood up with unexpected resolution and walked to the ladder. A loud roar rose suddenly from the chapel, and she looked back to see the first flickers of fire at the church's high windows. Indians were pouring from the chapel now, carrying Father Pio's clothing and vestments and smashing the plaster saints in the plaza.

Maria reached the first terrace. Crouching low, she ran toward Emiliano's workshop. She stumbled over Emiliano, lying dead in the doorway, his eyes open, staring blindly at the lightening sky.

"Oh, *Dios,*" Maria whimpered, picking herself up and groping for Diego's knife which she had dropped. She looked up then and saw her San Francisco, still standing where she had left him in the *santero*'s window, his arm extended. Emiliano had hinged on the other arm, but it was unpainted, waiting for her to finish. She crawled into the workshop and sank down on the dirt floor. Great gulping sobs escaped her. She reached up and pulled San Francisco off the window ledge, hugging him to her. She thought of Luz and Catarina and rose to her knees. She must go back to them.

She heard a rustling noise in the corner of the *santero*'s workshop and turned toward it, her hand tightening around the knife. A figure rose out of the pile of buffalo skins, white and moving slowly. Without a sound, Maria pitched forward on her face, unconscious.

Day of Death

S*he came to consciousness only a* few minutes later. She had been pulled into the corner near the hides. Someone was stroking her hair and saying her name over and over. The voice was familiar, but she feared to open her eyes, feared to look on one more nightmare.

"Maria chiquita," the voice pleaded, "look at me!" His fingers tapped her cheek in a familiar gesture. She opened her eyes, and her tears flowed.

Diego Masferrer wiped her face with the scarf he usually wore, dabbing gently at her tears. His face was as grim as her own, with the same dazed look, the same curious blankness. A large bruise started at his temple and ran down to the point of his jaw. She reached up and touched his face. He winced and drew back slightly, then gathered her closer to him.

"Diego." She had so much to tell him, but she could say nothing more.

"So it has begun, Maria," was all he could say in return. He hugged her closer to him and she put her arms around his neck.

"Diego," she finally whispered, "I have been searching for

you." She touched his face again, and he held her hand to his cheek.

"What happened to you?" he asked. "Tell me. I must know now. What of my family? What of Las Invernadas?"

She started to cry again, and he was silent until her sobs subsided against his chest.

"What of them, Maria?" he asked quietly. His eyes were full of tears, and she could not bear to look at him. She turned her gaze toward the hide painting of San Pedro on the opposite wall.

"I woke to the sound of Indians killing your servants in the chapel. They must have surprised the guards on the roof and let themselves down some way. I only had time to grab Luz and Catarina and hide them. Erlinda and La Senora would not come." The words were wrenched out of her. *"Dios mio,* Diego, they sacrificed themselves to save us."

"Hush, Maria," he said, kissing the top of her head.

She had told him what had happened, but she knew she would never tell him how Erlinda had called his name over and over, pleading for his help, though she would remember it always.

"We heard the Indians behind us, so I hid the girls in their play tunnel in the *acequia.* Then I went for help." She burrowed closer into Diego's shoulder. "But there is no help," she sobbed. "There is no hope."

She was crying harder. Diego put his hand to her face and held her tight against his chest, pulling her farther back into the gloom of the workshop. The sun was up now, but the room was still deep in shadow. In answer to her unspoken question, he began.

"I arrived in Santa Fe around noon, as you would have thought. The governor would not see me. Refused me, Maria. *Dios,* he will pay someday. So I sat there with my Indians— *Dios, my* Indians—in his anteroom until close upon three o'clock, watching others come and go. Finally I bashed in his door and threw the Indians into his office."

Her hand went to his face, and he kissed her fingers.

"Ah, Maria! I forced him to listen to me. It appears he had received other warnings, one from Santo Domingo, another from the south and west. But he had no troops to spare. He must guard Santa Fe. Even Santa Fe is in danger. So my mission was futile.

"I rode Tirant hard, and, fool that I am, I thought Tesuque would still be safe. I thought we had four days. I went to Father Pio and tried to convince him to join me at Las Invernadas. 'Oh, my son, these are my Indians, my little children,'" he mimicked. Maria put her fingers to his lips again, and he stopped. "Ah, *querida,* I once spoke the same way, but they are not our Indians. Emiliano was right. *Pobre* Emiliano. Well, Father Pio would not leave, so I ran to Tirant and tried to leave the plaza."

He stopped, pulling her closer, reliving the moment. "I suppose they were hiding in the shadows. The Indians felled Tirant with an ax. I was thrown off onto my face. But I killed those Indians. Then I ran in here. Emiliano was already dead, and his workshop ransacked, but I am thinking now that it might be the safest place in the whole river kingdom."

"Not quite, my brother."

In a single motion, Diego tumbled Maria off his lap and leaped to his feet. Cristobal stepped out of the shadows, laughing softly. He was dressed as Maria had seen him last, in loincloth with white paint on his body. His legs were red from the knees down, as if he had waded through a river of blood. Maria rose up on her knees, her hands clenched in tight fists. She knew whose blood he had waded through, and who had followed her from the burning hacienda.

He looked at her, his head tilted to one side in his characteristic pose. "Maria, how clever you are! Who else would have thought to hide my little sisters in the ditch?"

Maria jumped up and lunged toward Cristobal, but Diego held her back. She leaned over Diego's outstretched arm, all fear dissolved by terrible anger. "If you have touched them, Cristobal . . ." she hissed.

"You'll do what?" He held his hand up as if to ward her off. "I would never bother them now. I will wait until they are good and hungry, and then I will go back."

"Cristobal, you really are a bastard," said Diego slowly.

"Oh, we always knew that, Diego mio," Cristobal replied quickly. "But do not fear for the little ones. They are still young, young enough to learn the Indian ways. I will keep them as mine—just as you kept me as yours, Diego. Now, Erlinda, ah, Erlinda, she is a different story. Erlinda. . . ." He paused, his eyes on Diego. "Diego, she was still calling for you when my Indians—*my* Indians—cut off her arms."

Maria sank down on the buffalo hides and covered her face with her hands. "And what about my mother, Cristobal? Could you find enough ways to hurt her, she who helped raise you?" Diego said.

Cristobal stalked closer to his brother. "I thought of something entirely fitting. You are not the only clever one."

Without another word, Cristobal threw Diego against the wall and stabbed him in the arm, digging his long dagger into the adobe, pinning his brother to the wall. "And now you will hold still, my brother," Cristobal commanded. "You will die last, after you have watched me kill your chiquita." He looked at Maria, a smile on his face. "Or whatever it is I finally decide to do to her."

Diego wrapped his fingers around the knife, trying frantically to yank it from the wall. His face was a mask of pain. "Cristobal, you will die for this!" he shouted, and Cristobal laughed and turned to Maria.

She backed up against Emiliano's workbench, feeling behind her for the small carving dagger he kept there. Her hand brushed across the table but she could find nothing. She felt a piece of broken pottery jab her leg and she clutched it just as Cristobal turned around suddenly and kicked Diego. The writhing, bleeding man swore at him in Tewa.

His back was to her for only a heartbeat of time, but Maria lunged at Cristobal. He half-turned when he heard her, but she raked the sharp piece down his bare back. Twice she dragged the broken shard down his skin before he slammed her away and put his hand to his back. Maria leaped to her feet and yanked the knife from Diego's arm.

Diego gasped with pain and threw himself on Cristobal, jumping on his back and wrapping the scarf he still carried tight around his brother's neck. Cristobal clutched at his throat, clawing at the silk scarf. In a frenzy, he backed up against the wall and shoved hard, trying to shake Diego off. Diego only pulled tighter. His hand was slippery with his own blood, but he hung on, tightening his grip with every second that passed.

Maria scrambled to find Emiliano's dagger, pawing among the broken pots and bits of splintered wood. In desperation she grabbed Emiliano's small pot of gypsum and pounded Cristobal over the head with it. The white paint oozed over his head and mingled with the blood from the wounds on his back, turning an incongruous pink. Cristobal gasped as he struggled to breathe. The blood vessels in his eyes broke as Diego hung on grimly.

Then Cristobal fell to his knees, his face turning a dark purple. He tried to rise again, but he could only lurch from side to side like a wounded animal, his head drooping lower and lower.

In one brisk movement, Diego got off Cristobal and stood up, planting his knee firmly in the middle of the swaying man's back. With one sharp crack that made Maria retch and turn away, Diego snapped his brother's spine. Cristobal went limp, paralyzed. His hands flopped to his side and he hung from the scarf that Diego continued to tighten around his neck.

"Diego!" Maria implored, "he is dead! Stop, I beg you!" She grabbed the uninjured arm and tugged on it. He looked at her with glazed eyes and dropped the scarf. Cristobal fell forward into the white paint that covered the floor.

Diego drew a ragged breath and slumped down next to his dead brother. His hand went to his bleeding arm, and he looked up at Maria.

Without a word, she lifted her skirt and ripped off a large swatch of petticoat. Working quickly, she bound the bloody strip around his arm, holding the flap of lacerated skin tight against the wound. "What do we do now?" she asked, wiping Diego's face with her dress and smoothing back his dark curls.

He looked at her again. "Since I never considered the possibility that I would live through this, I have no idea."

"I would recommend that we dispose of Cristobal." She stood up and brushed her dress off, the same automatic gesture that had struck at Diego's heart so many months ago when she came walking to his hacienda in the middle of the night. "If you can take hold of his feet, Diego, I propose that we pull him underneath the buffalo robes. Then I recommend that we join him there, at least until nightfall." Suddenly she burst into tears, great wracking sobs that shook her entire body. Diego wrapped his arms around her waist, holding her until she was silent. He wiped her nose on his one remaining sleeve and stood up, swaying a little. "Come, Maria, take his arms."

Breathing deeply, she grabbed Cristobal under the arms.

Diego picked up the legs and they carried the body to the corner of the workshop where the buffalo skins were stacked. Maria pulled aside the hides and Diego pushed the body into the corner and dropped the skins over the corpse. By the time he finished, his face was white, and he had to sit down with his head between his legs.

"Diego, you have lost so much blood," she said.

"There is no remedy now," he answered, his voice muffled.

She looked around the room. There was blood everywhere—on the wall where Diego had been pinned, on the buffalo-hide *santos,* and smeared with the paint on the floor, where it had turned the color of a pink sunrise. Her little San Francisco was smashed on the floor, both arms broken off. She thought of Erlinda and closed her eyes.

Diego raised his head slowly, cautiously. "Let us join Cristobal," he said. "Help me to my feet, *querida.*"

She pulled him to his feet and led him to the corner where Cristobal lay, buried under the mound of buffalo skins. Maria pulled back the hides, turning her face away from Cristobal. Diego found his dagger and lay down next to the corpse. Maria took a small deerhide and smeared it over the bloody floor to erase their footprints. She arranged the skins around Diego, then lay down, pulling the hides on top of her.

The weight of the skins was suffocating, claustrophobic. She fought a strong urge to throw back the hides and run screaming into the plaza below. And why not? Their chances of survival were almost nonexistent.

She thought of the children in their cave by the *acequia.* "Diego, what will become of Luz and Catarina?"

He was silent a moment, arranging his wounded arm carefully around her. "*Querida,* they may be safe there. I am thinking that the Indians have burned all the haciendas between here and Santa Fe, and probably north to Taos, too, and are going to march on the capital. If this is so, they are probably safe where they are—or safer than anywhere else." She felt, rather than heard his small laugh. "Safer than we are, anyway." He kissed the side of her head. Soon his breathing was regular and deep. Maria rested next to him, her head on his arm. The weight of Diego's arm around her was comforting, even though his hand still held the dagger and it was only inches from her.

She tried to ease the knife out of his grasp, but his fingers were as tight as death around the handle.

She slept then, lulled by the close air under the hides, the warmth of Diego, and the fact that she had not slept for two nights. Reason told her to be watchful, but she could not stay awake.

She woke hours later to the sound of footsteps. Diego was awake. His hand was covering her mouth, so fearful was he that she would awaken with a scream or sudden movement. She kissed his fingers to let him know she was awake, and he moved his hand only far enough to grasp his dagger again.

She lay absolutely still, listening to the footsteps prowling about and the boom of her heart. It was as loud in her ears as thunder. The beating of her heart joined with the pounding of drums in the plaza as the Indians danced out their victory over murdered women and children.

The voices of men were loud in the next room, and for one wild, irrational moment, Maria thought they were rescuers. But they spoke Tewa, and she knew there was no help. They were two isolated people in an ocean of blood. Maria reached for Diego.

The footsteps entered the *santero* workshop, pausing for a long time in the doorway, the unseen prowler taking in the pillage and blood. The Indian moved around the room, kicking rubbish here and there. Then he walked toward the buffalo skins.

Maria closed her eyes. The blood in her veins ceased to run when the Indian began removing skins from the pile, one, then two, another skin, and another. Then the drumming in the pueblo stopped, and the unknown figure stayed his hand. Maria could almost hear his breathing now, and she held her own breath. She was drenched with her sweat and Diego's.

One of the buffalo skins flopped back, and they heard the sound of someone dragging the other skins from the room. Diego was silent for a long moment, not relaxing his grip on the dagger. After a time, he let go. "Let us pray he does not come back to steal again."

Maria cried then, her tears turning to mud under her cheek. She felt Diego's tears on her neck. His body was hot, and she knew he had a fever.

They stayed under the buffalo skins through the long day.

The drums pounded again, the same monotonous, hypnotic rhythm she had heard before in the *kiva* and in Father Pio's desecrated church. She could feel the vibrations of many feet stomping out a pattern of celebration. The trillings and songs were muted, but unrelenting.

Maria dozed off and on through the hot day. She could hear Cristobal's body making wheezing, gaseous noises. Diego moved closer to her and whispered in her ear, "Before God and all the saints, Maria, he is cold. Such a coldness I have never felt." He shuddered now and then, whether from fever, or from some primitive reflex of fright, she did not know. The drums in the plaza were soothing her back to sleep.

When she awoke, the plaza was silent. The quiet was so enormous that it hummed in her ears. By some sense, she knew that darkness had finally come. "Diego," she whispered, "are you awake?"

"Yes," he whispered.

"The Indians?"

"I think they have gone. We will wait a little longer."

Diego was so warm. She felt his face. He was burning with fever, his skin hot and dry. And yet he shivered off and on, his body exhausted by shock and loss of blood.

After another endless hour, Diego shifted and groaned softly. "Chiquita, my arm is asleep. Can you pull back the hides?"

Slowly she wriggled out from under the weight of the hides, her body nearly as stiff as Cristobal's. The room was dark, but the moon shone through the small door and window, casting its bright reflection on the gypsum paint smeared everywhere. The particles of gypsum sparkled on the floor. She began pulling the hides off Diego. When she reached him, he turned over on his back slowly and held up his good arm. She tugged him to his feet only to have him collapse on the *santero's* workbench.

"You look terrible," she said.

His eyes flickered over her. "You don't look so good yourself," he replied. Both of them were stiff, sweaty, and covered with white paint and blood. "We look like *kachina* clowns," Diego said, patting his wounded arm with his fingers. *"Ay de mi,"* he muttered.

She touched his arm. It was swollen and hot. "I can loosen the bandage," she offered, her fingers already on the knot.

"Not now, Maria. Let us leave this place first. Cover up Cristobal."

But she stood staring down at the body. Diego got up from the workbench and knelt by his brother. Tentatively he reached his hand out and touched Cristobal. Maria's heart turned over as he began to cry.

She laid her hand gently on the back of his neck as he sobbed, his tears wrenching her very soul as she remembered Erlinda's similar outpouring in the chapel after the Apache raid. His were the tears of a proud man.

She wiped his eyes with her hand. He sighed and was silent, kneeling by his dead brother. She covered up Cristobal and made the sign of the cross over him.

Diego watched her. "Did you love him?" he asked softly.

"In some ways I did. Just as you did."

Diego got up and went to the doorway. She followed him, looking over his shoulder. The plaza was littered with the remains from the church, which still smoldered. Smoke was heavy in the air, mingled with the odor of cooked flesh. The combination was oddly tantalizing, and Maria's mouth watered. She couldn't remember her last meal.

The ladders were already pulled up, but the pueblo appeared to be deserted, or caught in the grip of an exhausted, satiated slumber. Maria looked at Diego, a question in her eyes, and he shrugged. Motioning to her to remain where she was, he tiptoed to the edge of the terrace and looked down. He waved for her to join him, picking up one side of the ladder and indicating that she take the other.

She shook her head. "Wait, Diego. Take off your boots."

"You are right. If anyone should see Spanish bootprints, they will track us."

Her eyes went to Emiliano, his corpse lying where she had first seen it early that morning. She knelt by his body and removed his moccasins. "Here. They are probably too small, but it would be safer."

Diego sat down and tried to remove his boots. He looked at her and shook his head, and she tugged them off, carrying them back into the *santero* workshop and stashing them under the buffalo hides.

"They almost fit," he whispered when she came out. "Now, let us be away from here."

251

They picked up the ladder and inched it over the edge of the terrace. When it was in place, Diego handed her his dagger and climbed down the ladder as quickly as he could. She followed him, grabbing up her skirt, stiff with blood and gypsum. When she was down, Diego took her arm and hurried across the plaza. He paused in the shadows to look around.

"There aren't even any dogs here," he said.

"It is as if everyone has packed up and gone to . . ." she stopped.

"To Santa Fe," he finished.

They reached the shelter of the cottonwood trees lining the river, Maria helping Diego, who staggered as he walked. She put her arm around him and curled her fingers under his sword belt, supporting him.

They took the old Taos road out of Tesuque, walking in the tall brush at the edge of the stream and avoiding the road itself, which looked as deserted as the pueblo. When they had gone some distance, Diego stopped.

"I have to sit down, chiquita," he said. He sounded drugged.

She pulled him down to the water's edge and he collapsed on the ground. "No, no," he said, "don't touch me. Just let me lie here."

She went to the small stream and ripped off another hunk of her petticoat, dipping it in the water until the gypsum was rinsed out. She laid the cloth on a rock and leaned over the stream, lapping the water like an animal. She drank until her stomach felt tight, then wet the cloth again and went to Diego. She pulled his head into her lap and dribbled water into his mouth. When the cloth was only damp, she wiped his face with it, then kissed his forehead, pulling him to her breast. He closed his eyes and slept.

She leaned against a rock and shut her eyes. After the heat of the buffalo skins, the cool air felt like lotion on her skin. She breathed deeply of the familiar smell of juniper. Listening to the water murmur over the stones, she bowed her head over Diego and slept.

When she woke, the sky was beginning to lighten around the horizon. The familiar bulk of the Sangre de Cristo Mountains shielded the valley from daylight, but it was coming.

Diego still slept, so she gentled his head on the grass and inched away. She stood up and stretched, her eyes on the stream. The area was familiar to her. She had gathered gypsum not far from where Diego lay. After another look at him to make sure he was sleeping, she walked north toward the gypsum wall. With her fingernail, she peeled off flakes of gypsum. Perhaps it would be possible to make a poultice for his arm. She knew it would harden quickly when mixed with water. Her skirt was still stiff with the gypsum and blood from the *santero*'s workshop.

She held her skirt out in front of her, and with one hand peeled off handfuls of gypsum from the cliff wall. When she had enough, she walked carefully back to Diego.

She had nothing to put the gypsum in, so she piled it by the stream and scooped out a shallow depression in the mud by the bank. When it was deep enough, she put water into the hole with her hands and waited for the mud to settle. While it was clearing, she took Diego's knife and ripped through her dress, taking the material off at her knees.

Diego jerked awake at the sound of the tearing cloth. He groped for his knife, then sat up, watching her. She handed him his knife, then took the long strip of cloth to the stream where she washed the material, soaking the blood, dirt and gypsum paint out of the fabric. The water was cold on her legs and she was soon shivering.

Maria anchored the material in the stream with a rock and turned back to her makeshift basin of water, where she dumped in handfuls of gypsum, stirring it with a stick and trying not to mix up the mud on the bottom. When the water was white and thick, she retrieved the material from the stream and laid it in folds in the gypsum water.

Diego understood what she was doing. He began to work at the knot on his bloody bandage. His fingers were unsteady, and with an oath he looked at her, his arm extended.

She sat down next to him and made him lie with his head in her lap again. She worked the knot out of the drenched fabric and gently unwrapped the dirty, blood-encrusted bandage, biting her lip as Diego groaned and closed his eyes. The wound looked even more ghastly in daylight, long and ragged where he had struggled against the knife. The bone was laid bare, the muscles torn.

She paused for a minute. Diego was shivering uncontrollably. "I am sorry, *querida,*" he managed, "but I cannot help myself."

"Shh, shh, Diego," she answered, her voice a murmur like the stream. "I will try not to hurt you."

When he was still, lying with his eyes closed and sweat pouring off his face, she dipped a small square of her skirt in the river water and cleaned the wound, wiping gently around the lacerated edges. Then she leaned over to her basin of gypsum water and slowly pulled out the coated fabric. Working as quickly as she could, she wrapped the gypsum-coated material around Diego's arm from shoulder to elbow. The blood quickly soaked through the first layers, but by the time she finished, the bandage was already beginning to harden.

Maria leaned back against the rock and looked at Diego. He opened his eyes and smiled. "Now tuck me in bed with a hot rock and I will be fine in a day or two."

"Of course," she replied, a smile of her own playing around her lips. "And I will fluff your pillows and bring you hot chocolate and tortillas. With or without cheese and onions?"

He considered the matter as she wiped his face. "No onions."

"Ah. Will you be a good patient?"

"Probably not. Why should my convalescence make me any different?"

Without a word, she leaned forward and kissed him on the lips. His good arm went around her waist and he kissed her back until he started to laugh.

Maria sat up straight, her face on fire. "I shouldn't have done that," she said, her eyes wide. He lay back with his head in her lap, laughing softly and wincing every time his shoulder moved.

"Oh, Maria, Maria," he finally gasped, "how strange we are! We're probably the only two *paisanos* left in all of New Mexico, we're going to starve to death before noon, and I require Last Rites, but all I want is for you to kiss me again."

"Well, I won't," she said, her hands on her red cheeks. "Whatever was I thinking?"

"I am sure I do not know," Diego replied, "but perhaps you can show me sometime when I feel better."

"I would not dare!" she said, lowering Diego's head to the grass again and getting to her feet. He stared at her legs with a smile on his face, and she tugged at her shortened dress. "I only did it for you," she muttered, grateful she still wore his Apache moccasins that laced to her knees.

"Gracias, senorita," he murmured.

She looked around her. The sun was over the mountains now, although shadows were still heavy in the valley and the grass was wet with dew. She knew they were less than a mile from the Masferrer cornfields. They had to reach shelter of some sort. "If I help you to your feet, do you think you could walk to the cornfields? We might be safer there."

In answer, Diego held out his hand and she pulled him to his feet. He sank to his knees immediately and she hauled him to his feet again, her hand tugging at his sword belt. He managed to straighten up, and they walked slowly along the streambed.

When they came to the point where the stream crossed the trail, she made him sit down in the shadows while she walked to the old Taos road. Maria knelt by the side of the road in the tall grass and watched to the north. Indians were coming down the road on horseback. She had never seen Pueblo Indians riding before. They must have taken the horses from the dead landowners around Taos. She knelt in the grass, her mind finally registering the enormity of yesterday's revolt. She watched their approach in stunned silence, then backed down the slope to Diego.

"Well?" he asked, sitting there with his eyes half-closed.

"Many Indians. They are all mounted, Diego. All of them."

He contemplated some distant scene beyond her vision. "I wonder how many dead men, women and children have paid for that ride!" He struggled to lie down in the weeds and Maria lay down next to him, watching the road.

All morning the Indians rode by. Maria started counting the riders, but gave up after the total passed one hundred. The men and boys were dressed in loincloths, but most of them carried Spanish shields and arquebuses. They rode silently, purposefully, heading south.

Diego watched the riders for several hours, then put his head down. Maria thought he had fainted. She put her lips to his ear and whispered, "Diego? Are you all right?"

He nodded, but would not raise his head until the last group of horsemen was a cloud of dust in the distance. When he looked at her, his face was streaked with tears. She turned away, overcome again by the specter of yesterday's killing rampage.

When he could finally speak, he looked years older, and somehow different to her. "Maria," he faltered, and could not continue.

She leaned closer, her cheek against his wet face. "Diego?"

"My Taos friends, my relatives," he managed, then shook his head. "The rancheros up the valley. I recognized their horses, their saddles, their bridles. Maria, are these people *all* dead?"

"*Pobrecito,*" was all she could say. She patted his back, then leaned her head on him. As she had listened to the horses and riders passing she had known that she was hearing the death of an entire colony. Ultimately, the colonists had belonged no more than she had.

Diego took hold of her hand, and they sat close together as the sun rose higher. No words passed between them, for neither knew what to say. They were alone in the depth of terrible trouble, of times neither of them could have predicted yesterday, could still not comprehend today.

The land around was silent again. With a gasp of pain, Diego pulled his dagger from his belt and looked at it. "Maria," he said slowly, "it would be easier if I killed you and then killed myself. I think we can expect no other future."

Without thinking, Maria wrenched the knife from his hand and held it behind her back. "Listen to me!" she said harshly, hating herself for speaking with such hardness to Diego, feverish, bleeding and dazed by the events that had altered his entire world. "If you think for one moment that I am going to give up, then you do not know me!" She grabbed his good arm and shook him. Diego drew back slightly and turned away. He was silent for long minutes. "La Afortunada," he finally said, still not turning around to face her. "The Lucky One," he repeated, wiping his eyes with the end of his bloody shirt and facing her again. "I called you that. Do you not remember?"

"I remember," she whispered, "maybe that is why I cannot quit. I will not. It isn't in me." She touched his arm. "Not now. Especially not now."

He met her gaze again. "If we live through this, I will always

256

wonder why I waited so long to love you. Cristobal was right, of course. It is possible to be too busy to notice the things that matter. I wish I could tell him that."

"Don't, Diego," she said. "You did what you had to do."

"Perhaps, but I never stopped to think."

"No. But could you have stopped being what you are?"

He smiled and held his hand out for his knife. She handed it to him without hesitation, and he put it back in his belt. "Perhaps not." His eyes clouded over with pain.

"Where does it hurt now?" she asked, her hand on his forehead.

He pointed to his heart as his eyes filled with tears. "In my soul, *querida*. Only there."

Maria kissed him and held him to her while he cried. When he was through, he wiped his eyes and looked down the road, then across it to his cornfield. "Well, let us go find my sisters."

Maria rose and pulled Diego up. He wrapped his arm around her waist and they walked across the road and into the rows of corn. They reached the shelter of the corn as other riders from the north appeared on the road. Maria pulled Diego down and he landed heavily on her, gasping when his arm hit the ground. The cornfield showed evidence of trampling by many horses. Maria whirled around to face the riders on the road, knowing that if they decided to cross the field as others had done, she and Diego would be trapped like rabbits.

But the horsemen passed. Diego sat up, looking toward the hacienda of Las Invernadas. "I thought you said it was on fire yesterday," he said, squinting toward the buildings.

"It was, at least the chapel end of it. Does it still stand?"

"What I can see of it. Can we not get closer?"

She pulled him to his feet again, and they crossed the rows of corn, both of them glancing back to watch for more horsemen on the Taos road.

The roof of the hacienda was still intact, but little else remained. "Look over there, and there," gestured Diego with his head. "My livestock, my sheep, all dead."

All the animals at Las Invernadas had been slaughtered, even the chickens and ducks butchered and left to rot. The beehives had been slashed open, the bees left to circle and circle in the ruin of hive and honey.

"Did they hate us so much, *querida?*" Diego asked in dismay. More horsemen galloped down the Taos road. Diego watched them. "And still they come," he murmured as Maria pulled him down.

The Indians continued to straggle down the Taos road. To Maria's terror, several groups skirted the cornfield and prowled through the half-burned hacienda. But no one stopped, or even glanced at the cornfield. She was grateful it was only early August, and not September, when the corn would be ripe and tempting. Maria listened for sounds from the tunnel by the *acequia*, but all she could hear were bees humming about the shattered hives at the end of the garden, and the drone of many flies rising from the slaughtered farm animals.

The sky darkened and it began to rain, small pelting drops that laid the dust of long drought, then fell heavier and heavier on the thirsty land, running in muddy rivulets toward the *acequia*.

Diego looked up at the leaden sky as rain pelted his face. "Cristobal's rain. From his gods, I suppose."

Maria felt his forehead. He still burned with fever. He put his hand to hers and brought it down to his mouth, kissing her fingers. She smiled down at him, trying to shield his gypsum bandage with her body and shivering as the rain fell on her back. It was the cold rain of August and she was soon soaked through.

"Let me sit up, Maria," Diego said finally.

She put her arm under his neck and pulled him into a sitting position. He leaned against a cornstalk and patted his arm. The gypsum came away on his wet hand.

"I must cover your arm," Maria said. "Turn your head. I am going to take off my petticoat."

He smiled briefly. "No."

She didn't argue, but reached under her dress and undid the string of her petticoat, wriggling out of it as he watched. "And I thought you were a *caballero muy elegante*," she murmured, her face red.

"I never said I was," he pointed out as she draped the petticoat around his arm and tugged her soaking skirt as far down as it would go.

The rain continued to pour down. They sat close together, their arms around each other, shivering in the cornfield, watching the Taos road. When no Indians had passed for some time, Diego turned to Maria. "Let us take our chances now, *querida*. We need to find my sisters before it grows dark."

Maria helped Diego to his feet. She felt under the petticoat on Diego's arm. It was dry. She tugged the material higher up on his shoulder. "Do not lose that," she ordered. "I want to put it on again when the rain stops."

They left the shelter of the cornfield and sloshed through the muddy field toward the footbridge. "Diego, suppose they are dead?" she asked, not looking at the irrigation ditch.

"Then there is no remedy, Maria *querida*," he replied.

Diego could not go into the water. Maria dropped down into the *acequia*. It was even colder than the rain. She waded down the muddy ditch, calling softly, "Luz? Catarina? *Cómo están?*"

For a long moment she heard nothing. She could feel the lump growing in her throat. She looked back at Diego, and he slid into the ditch, too, coming toward her, his bandaged arm held high.

Then she heard the girls. They were both crying, thin wailing sobs torn from throats so hoarse with crying that she could barely hear them above the rain on the water. She waded quickly toward the hiding place, calling their names.

The children had tunneled back farther into the side of the *acequia*, and some of the dirt in the front had fallen across the entrance, shielding them. Maria pawed in the mud and reached inside. She felt Catarina's arms around her neck, tightening to a stranglehold. Maria pulled her out of the cave, muddy and shaking in her nightgown. Diego reached inside for Luz. For one small heartbeat the child held herself away from him, looking at him closely, running her fingers over his face, feeling the contours so familiar to her. With a tiny sigh that made Diego Masferrer sob out loud, she enveloped her brother in an embrace surprising in its strength.

Maria smoothed back the muddy hair from Catarina's eyes. "My darling, how brave you were! You did just as I said."

Catarina nodded through her tears. "I wanted to leave, especially when we heard all the screaming, and then saw the house on fire. But Luz told me you would return. And you did."

Tucking Luz on his hip, Diego carried his sister to the footbridge and sat her on it. He heaved himself up onto the bridge and held out his arms for Catarina. Maria pulled herself up to join the Masferrers.

Catarina looked at the hacienda first. "Oh, *mira*, Luz, look! It is still standing! Can we not go inside?"

She started to get up, but Maria restrained her. "No!" she burst out, louder than she intended.

"I will go inside," said Diego, getting to his feet slowly. "Perhaps I can find something to eat."

Maria was on her feet in front of him, blocking his way down the garden path. "Diego Masferrer, the only one going inside that hacienda is I!" she shouted, trying to push him back to the footbridge.

He stood where he was and pushed back, jabbing her in the shoulder with his fingers. "You cannot keep me out of my own house!"

"Oh, yes I can, Diego!"

They were both shouting at each other. "It will not do you any good to go in there!" cried Maria, pleading now. "If you think I dragged you all the way from Tesuque to go inside and see what you will see, then again I say you do not know me very well!"

They stood glaring at each other, looking into the fire in each other's eyes. "I mean it, Diego," said Maria more calmly. She was short of breath and weary of the sound of her own shouting.

Diego looked away first, turning back to his sisters on the footbridge. "Very well," he shot back. "Although I do not like it."

Maria walked toward the darkening hacienda with a cold feeling in her stomach that grew chillier with each footstep. She began to shudder, but forced herself to keep walking. If Diego went inside, it would be worse, much worse, and someone had to look for food.

She was shaking so badly that it took both hands to raise the latch on the kitchen door. She went inside, leaving the door open. She paused on the threshold, sniffing the air. It was heavy with smoke and the smell of charred flesh she remembered from the mission supply caravan. She gagged and raised her dress to her mouth.

The room was in deep shadow, but as she stood there, her eyes became accustomed to the gloom. She knew before she looked that all the silver would be gone, and it was. The beautiful wooden cabinet that Erlinda had so prized was smashed in two, as if by an ax. The long kitchen table they had sat around only days before had been rammed into the fireplace and burned along half its length. The floor was gritty with spilled corn meal. Maria peeked into the storeroom. The shelves were bare, but she scarcely noticed them. Her eyes were riveted on the meathooks where hung the charred bodies of Diego's servants, killed in the chapel. She stepped back in horror and slammed the storeroom door shut.

She sat down weakly on the ruined cabinet, her eyes on the storeroom door. It swung slowly open on its own weight and she leaped up and ran into the hall. She stood there until her eyes were adjusted to the deeper gloom, then edged her way along the wall. The only other food in the hacienda was on the patio, where she had set out several pans of apricots to dry in the sun. She inched down the corridor, stopping every few feet to listen.

It was the silence of a tomb, a charnel, a repository for all the tragedies, real or imagined, of mankind. She could make out bodies lying in the hall, some the small bodies of children who must have dragged themselves still-living from the burning chapel. Other bodies were sprawled in heaps on the hard-packed earthen floor. Her feet, still wet from the *acequia,* were sticky with the blood of Diego's servants.

She stopped at La Senora's room. The door was open, sagging inward on torn leather hinges. The wood in the paneling had been smashed to kindling, as if the woman had barricaded it in a futile attempt to slow down the butchers in those early morning hours.

Maria paused on the threshold and covered her mouth and nose with her dress. The roof was partly burned and she could see in the room clearly. Blood was spattered everywhere, the floor drenched with it. La Senora was sitting in an iron-red nightgown, her head sagging to one side. Maria stepped back and put her fingers to her mouth. Cristobal had been true to his word. La Senora's eyes had been pried out. As Maria looked away, her horrified glance fell on the familiar wooden statue of Our Lady of Sorrows. The *bulto*'s deeply indented eyes bulged with La Senora's own. The dead eyes stared back at Maria, unblinking, all-seeing.

Maria stepped backward into the hall, screaming. She turned to run, and saw Erlinda sprawled on the chest on the other side of the hall, her arms ripped from their sockets, her blond hair hanging in bloody handfuls from her ruined scalp.

Maria screamed again and again, unable to help herself, too terrified to run. Everywhere she looked were bodies, even when she closed her eyes. Above her screaming she heard Diego in the kitchen, shouting her name. She stumbled toward him, holding out her arms.

He met her at the door to his mother's room, took one quick glance inside, then picked her up, tossed her over his shoulder like a sack of meal and whirled toward the kitchen. He stopped short at the sight of Erlinda, then with a groan, ran through the kitchen and out into the clean air of the garden, where he dropped Maria and fell to his knees, retching.

Maria leaped to her feet and ran to the footbridge. She grabbed Luz and Catarina and ran with them back to the corn-field. She wanted to keep running, but she could not carry both girls any farther. She sat in the corn row, her head down between her knees. Luz and Catarina huddled on either side of her, seeking warmth.

Maria raised her head in a few moments and gathered the girls closer to her. Her mind overflowed with images of La Senora, Erlinda, the small burned children, the dangling bodies in the storeroom, and she was speechless with horror. The rain stopped and she watched the hacienda until Diego Masferrer crossed the footbridge and trudged toward the cornfield like an old man, calling her name.

"We are here, Diego," she said, her voice hardly above a whisper. He found them huddled together, sank down next to Maria and put his arms around the three of them. His lips were close to Maria's ear, his voice thin with pain. "I carried Erlinda into Mama's room and then set fire to it. The interior was dry, and I think it will burn now."

She looked toward the hacienda and saw the points of light rising from the roof. The flames stabbed the sky.

Diego got to his feet and reached for Catarina. "We must leave quickly. The blaze is sure to attract attention. Maria, you take Luz. Let us go."

Catarina looked at her brother. "But Diego, we have only our nightgowns. What would Erlinda say?"

A great wave of pain crossed Diego's white face. He looked at Maria for help. She knelt by Catarina. "Catarina, she would call it a great adventure. Come now, and let us do as Diego says."

The four of them started through the cornfield, heading south, away from the burning hacienda.

Journey

*T*hey walked in silence for over an hour, moving slowly across the fields. Catarina wanted to know at first why they did not take the road. When neither Diego nor Maria answered her, she was quiet, holding Diego's hand. Luz walked beside Maria, taking little skipping steps to keep up. She began to lag back, and Maria stopped and put the child on her back. Her arms were tight around Maria's neck, but finally her head flopped forward and she slept.

They walked in a southwesterly direction, away from Santa Fe. Maria looked at Diego. He caught her glance. "You wonder where we are heading? Not far from here is a cave," he explained. "Cristobal . . ." he began, then stopped, the weariness of too many troubles in his voice. They walked farther, and he continued, "Cristobal and I used to play there when we were younger. If he were still alive, I would never hide there, but I think it will be safe enough now."

Maria nodded and shifted Luz higher on her back. She couldn't remember a time when she had been so tired, or so hungry. Diego staggered as he walked beside her. Maria felt a rush of anxiety for him, but he held tight to Catarina's hand and did not stop.

They reached the cave when the moon was high overhead. There was a small opening hidden among the juniper trees, well back from any trails. Diego boosted Catarina up to the rocks and she clambered inside. He lifted Luz off Maria's back and put the child over his shoulder. When he was in the cave, he held out his hand to Maria, who followed him in. Then he went back outside, sweeping away their tracks beyond the rocky approach with a tree limb.

Maria helped him back inside the cave. Luz and Catarina had already arranged themselves close to each other for sleep. The cave was cool and dark, and the girls huddled together for warmth.

Diego sat by the entrance, too tired to move. "Come here, Maria," he said, motioning to her with his good arm. She sat next to him, and he put his arm around her. "We can watch the valley pretty well from here," he said. "Cristobal and I used to come here to play 'Pueblo.'"

"Don't, Diego."

He was silent then and they sat together, watching the valley. They could not see the flames of Las Invernadas, and the night sky was peaceful, the stars glittering, the fireflies winking among the trees by the cave's entrance. Maria closed her eyes.

But Diego was awake. "I was thinking, Maria," he said, then looked at her. "Maria? Wake up."

She opened her eyes.

"That is better. Now, just for a moment. I was thinking I could walk ahead to Santa Fe tonight. You and the girls are safe here, and perhaps I could bring back help, or at least horses."

Maria shook her head. "No. We must stay together. Suppose you were killed? Suppose you could not go any farther? How would we know what had happened?"

He sighed. "I suppose you are right. It was just an idea. I am not so sure I could leave you, anyway. I have had enough of leave-taking."

"And I, too. Let us stay here tomorrow and start walking again after dark. Besides, you saw all those Indians on the Taos road."

"So I did. Do you imagine . . ."

". . . there is anyone left in Santa Fe?" she finished.

"Querida, we could be the only Spaniards left in the entire province."

"I have thought of that, too," she replied, snuggling back down in the hollow of his shoulder.

"Well, what happens to us?" he asked, leaning against the rock wall and resting his head on Maria's.

"I do not know, Diego mio," she replied, her eyes closed. "Let us think about it tomorrow." They slept then, while the moon crossed the sky and gave way to a new day on the river kingdom.

Maria woke first. She opened her eyes, wondering why she wasn't in her own bed, smelling hot chocolate brewing in the kitchen, listening for the rattle of pans. Her head was in Diego's lap and his arm was heavy across her body. Then it all came back to her. She sat up carefully, trying not to disturb Diego, who still slept. He did not wake when she pulled herself out from under his arm. She felt his forehead. He was hot with fever.

"Is he dead, Maria?" whispered Catarina from across the cave.

"Oh, no, no, child," Maria replied quietly, stifling her own fears in front of the children. "Just ill. Let us come away and not waken him." She went to the sisters and sat with her arms around them.

"Maria, I am hungry," said Luz. Her eyes were big in the gloom of the cave.

Maria pulled her close and kissed the top of her head. "You know what your brother says. This is one of those times we have to cut our cloak to fit the cloth."

Luz was silent a moment. "But I'm still hungry, Maria."

Maria smiled. "I know. Words are cheap, especially when your stomach speaks a different language. We will find something to eat tonight."

"But that is a long time," argued Luz.

"Then go back to sleep," said Maria, coaxing Luz to lie down. "The time will go faster then, will it not?"

Luz put her head in Maria's lap and sighed. "Perhaps. I am so hungry I would even eat bread pudding."

Maria patted the child. "Well, that tells me something. But

think of it this way, my child. Think how good whatever it is
will taste tonight when we do find something!"

Luz nodded and closed her eyes. Catarina curled up on
Maria's other side, looking up at her. "And you, Catarina,"
murmured Maria. "How goes it with you?"

"I find adventures are not as much fun as I thought, Maria."

"They seldom are, my child."

Maria closed her eyes and dozed restlessly. She awakened
to Diego, standing over her. He sat down and pulled Catarina
gently to his lap, stroking her shoulders as she slept on. "Maria
querida," he said softly, looking at his little sister, "do you
think we will ever sleep like that again?"

Maria's eyes filled with tears. She bowed her head over Luz
and tried to gulp back her sobs. Diego quickly pulled her close
to him and put his arm around her. Catarina stirred but did not
waken. Diego's fingers were gentle on Maria's neck.

"I am sorry," he whispered. "But I think I will never close
my eyes again without seeing Cristobal hanging at the end of
my scarf. My own brother. *Dios*, what a sin I have committed!
Or Erlinda, lying on that chest. Or Mama's eyes." His voice
faltered, and he hugged Maria tighter. She put her arms around
him in wordless attempt at solace, and they slept again.

When Maria woke again, the shadows were lengthening
across the cave front, and Luz and Catarina were gone. She
jumped up, waking Diego, who grabbed her ankle in a sudden
reflex as she tried to run.

"Hold still, Maria," he ordered, "don't run out of the cave!"

"But Luz, Catarina!" she implored, trying to pry his fingers
off her ankle.

"You listen to me, Maria, for once!" She stopped struggling
and he let go of her ankle. He looked around the cave, then
crawled to the front, where he found his dagger. "Stay here,
Maria. I will find them."

She squatted on her heels by the cave entrance. She could
almost see the girls running slowly across a field, their hair
floating behind them, followed by Indians, all the Indians in
the river kingdom. Indians large and dark like Popeh, Indians
slim and graceful like Cristobal. But not Cristobal. He was
hanging dead at the end of Diego's scarf.

Diego was back almost before he was gone, shepherding
his two sisters in front of him. The girls carried something

between them, and they called to her even as Diego hissed at them to be quiet.

They carried honeycomb. As the girls clambered up the rocks toward the cave, Maria saw that one of Catarina's eyes was swollen shut, her face puffy. In spite of her obvious discomfort, she grinned at Maria.

Maria stepped out of the cave, braced herself against a boulder and reached for Luz. Diego boosted both sisters up to her and followed them in. The girls set the honeycomb down on a rock by Maria carefully, as if it were gold. They stood together, their backs straight, their hands behind them, looking up at Diego. Maria saw the muscles in his face working as he tried to control himself. He turned away, quivering with anger.

Maria put her arms around the girls and shook them. They were sticky everywhere she touched. "Luz, Catarina, how could you!"

Tears rolled down Luz's sticky, dirty cheeks. "Maria, we did not think Senor Gutierrez would mind if we took just a little honey. It was a beehive by itself in his field."

Diego let out an explosive sigh and turned around. His face was white under his growth of beard. *"Niñas . . ."* he began, but could not speak.

"My darlings," said Maria, shaking them again, and then pulling Luz to her. "I am sure that Senor Gutierrez does not mind." He will probably never know, she thought. There was little hope that any Spaniards survived. "But suppose an Indian saw you! *Niñas,* we would all be dead now."

Catarina burst out, "Like Mama and Erlinda?"

It was the first time either sister had mentioned the events at Las Invernadas. Catarina exploded into helpless sobs that came from deep within her. Diego drew her to him and held her close. "Go ahead, *hermana mia,*" he crooned, all anger gone. "You will feel better." He rocked her in his arms, humming one of his Indian tunes.

Luz looked at Maria. "I want some honey," she said simply.

Maria smiled in spite of herself. "Well, then, you shall have some. Get your brother's dagger and choose your own slice."

Luz took Diego's dagger from his belt and knelt by the honey. She frowned, holding the dagger first this way, then that way. She hesitated and looked at Maria. "Erlinda would say I should be fair," she explained.

"Erlinda taught you well," replied Maria, the words almost sticking in her throat. "Make it even, and then you say the blessing."

Luz glanced up from her effort. "Me?"

"You know the words. Diego will not mind."

Luz brought the dagger down, separating the honeycomb into lumpy fourths. She put the dagger on the rock and crossed herself. "Bless us, O Lord, and these Thy gifts," she prayed, her eyes shut tight. "And please do not let Senor Gutierrez be angry. In the name of the Father and the Son and the Holy Ghost, Amen."

She crossed herself again and picked up the honeycomb in one swift motion. Catarina sat up on Diego's lap, watching her sister eat. She wiped her eyes and joined Luz, picking up a section of honeycomb.

"After you, Maria *querida*," said Diego, wiping his knife on his leather breeches and putting it back in his belt.

Maria picked up the honeycomb with thumb and forefinger. It was dusted with a fine coating of grit, but she pulled off a piece and put it in her mouth, enjoying the flavor of Senor Gutierrez's honey.

Diego sat cross-legged on the floor of the cave and put the remaining piece in his mouth. He closed his eyes and chewed on the wax. "I haven't had anything to eat since the night we came back from making your San Francisco, Maria."

"That was long ago, Diego," she said, licking her fingers.

"Seems like years." He chewed and swallowed, then flashed a wolfish grin. "The governor did not even offer me any wine when I threw myself into his office."

"I can't imagine what he was thinking." Maria handed Diego the rest of her honeycomb. He shook his head, but when she continued to hold the gray lump out to him, he took it from her with a smile. "I'll pay you back someday," he said.

"No need," she replied, and quickly wiped her sticky fingers in his hair. Catarina whooped with laughter, and Luz's eyes were wide as she watched her brother anxiously.

Without missing a beat, Diego grabbed Maria with his one good arm, turned her on her back and sat on her. Maria freed one hand and began to tickle him.

Giggling, Catarina came closer, while Luz stuck two fingers

in her mouth and continued to stare at her brother. But gradually she started to laugh, too.

"I surrender!" Diego finally gasped and flopped down next to Maria on the ground, still laughing. Then he grabbed her again and pulled her over on top of him. Her hair came undone from her few remaining hairpins, and his hands tangled in its thickness as he kissed her on the mouth. He tasted like honey, and Maria started to laugh again.

"Will you never be serious?" he murmured, then tried to let go of her hair, but it clung to his hands in sticky patches. He pulled her close again. "I vow we are yoked together, Maria," he said, his voice caressing. "Marry me."

She sat up quickly. "Oh, no," she said, tugging at her hair even as he drew her close again.

"What possible objection can you have now, *querida?*" he asked, pulling her down until her head was on his chest again. "I am poor. You are poor. We have not one possession between us, so it cannot be money anymore. Can it be that you do not love me?"

She didn't answer, lying there with her cheek against his doublet, a smile on her face. Luz and Catarina had turned back to the flecks of honey remaining on the rock.

"Well?" he said. He tried to tip her head up, but she would not look at him. She lay listening to the steady rhythm of his heart, her eyes closed.

"Well?" he prompted again.

Maria sat up. "I love you, Diego," she said.

His eyes opened wide. "Somehow, I did not think I would ever live to hear you say that," he said. "So you will marry me," he said, pulling her hand to rest on his chest.

"I didn't say that," Maria replied. "I said that I loved you."

He sat up suddenly. *"Dios mio!* You are a difficult woman!" he shouted, and then looked around him as the sound echoed in the cave. Luz and Catarina were still seated by the rock, picking at the honeycomb. Diego lay down again, whispering in her ear. "Will you marry me, Maria?"

She turned to look at him. "And I have a question for you, *querido*. Do you really think we will live much beyond to-morrow or the next day?"

He was silent, looking at the stone shelter above them. "I

270

doubt it, Maria, but do answer me this: If by some miracle we get to Santa Fe and find a priest, will you marry me?"

"Of course," she replied promptly. "My grandfather—and he knew what he was talking about—always used to say that it is poverty that makes the man."

Diego laughed. "So you think I will be better for being poor? Make you a better husband, eh?" he said, his hand caressing her hip.

She put his hand back on his chest, her voice suddenly serious. "I think it will be a long time before you presume to call anyone *your* Indians again. I only hope your education does not begin too late."

"Aiyee, you have stabbed me. But perhaps your *abuelo* was right. Perhaps I have learned something."

Maria ran her fingers over the gypsum bandage on Diego's arm. His skin was still hot to her touch, but his arm was not as swollen. He touched her sticky face, then licked his finger. "You are sweet to me, Maria, and in spite of everything, I am a happy man." He held her close to him, gently rubbing her neck. "A day at a time, a sunrise, a sunset, another day. Do not think beyond that. And I am a happy man. Who would have thought it?"

They sat that way for a while, happy to be, however temporarily, alone together. Then Diego rose and went to the entrance to the cave. "Let us wake the girls," he said. "We are close to the Gutierrez estancia. Perhaps there will be something to eat. Then we will follow the river and branch off toward Santa Fe."

Maria shook Luz and Catarina awake. Both girls sat up quickly and rubbed their eyes. Luz put her hands out to Maria, who grasped them.

"Maria, I dreamed of Indians," she said.

Maria kissed her. "Never mind, Diego is here."

Diego looked over his shoulder at her. "And Maria, too, Luz. I would not tinker with Maria."

"Oh, you would not," she murmured.

He laughed and motioned to them. "Let us go now. Catarina, you walk with me, and you, Luz, stay with Maria. Do not say anything, no matter what you see or hear. Do you understand?" Both girls nodded, impressed by the steel in his voice. "And do not ever, ever leave us," he added quietly. "Let us go."

Diego let himself down from the cave, holding his good arm up for Catarina and then Luz. When the girls were standing beside him, Maria followed. She took Diego's hand and steadied her way down the rocky pile. When they were on level ground again, Diego put his arm around her waist, leaning toward her. "Over there, across the river, is the Gutierrez place. Can you see it?"

She shook her head.

"Well, it is there, or I suppose it was there. I propose that we cross the river, hide the girls in the Gutierrez cornfield and look around."

The silence of death was on the land. Maria shivered in the cool night air. The stars bright overhead seemed to dangle just on top of them. The trees thickened as they neared the river, the smell of piñon almost overwhelming. But along with the piñon was another smell, a sweetish odor. The smell was death.

They crossed a little-used road. Maria could make out several large whitish lumps lying across the narrow path. Diego drew closer to examine the bodies and then returned to his women. Maria covered Luz's ears. "The Gutierrez family?" she whispered.

He looked at her, then glanced away. "No. Cousins of my mother's from Taos."

They reached the river quickly. Diego and Maria had to hold the girls back to keep them from rushing to the stream to drink. "It is such actions that will see us all dead, Catarina," Diego whispered to his sister as he held her back. "I will go ahead and look around first, and then you will follow with Maria." He disappeared among the trees.

The girls crowded close to Maria, shivering in the cool of the night. *"Pobrecitas,"* Maria said, "and still you wear only your nightgowns."

"Well, it *is* night," said Luz, her teeth chattering.

"Ay, you have hit on it," Maria replied. "And how you sound like Diego!"

Diego was coming back through the trees. "I see no sign of anyone at the river, although there were some tracks from a fairly recent crossing. I would beg you to move silently."

They hurried to the river. Although the water was still low with the season of drought, it was swift, and came to the girls' waists. Luz gasped when she stepped into the water. She bent

272

forward for a swift drink, lapping like a small animal. Catarina crossed the stream, then knelt at the water's edge for a drink.

"While we are here, get the honey out of your hair," Diego said to Maria. She knelt in the stream and ducked her head under. Diego waded slightly downstream where the water was deeper. Maria followed him, calling to him, "Diego, don't put your arm under or the gypsum will melt."

"Then help me," he said.

She followed him to where the water was waist deep and held his bandaged arm while he put his face in the water and worked the wetness through his curly black hair. They walked slowly upstream together, dripping wet, their arms around each other. "That is better," said Diego. "I think I would rather be wet than sticky. Now, if we can only find some. . . ."

The word died in his throat. He was looking at the bank behind his sisters and pushed Maria down in the water.

An Indian stood watching them from the riverbank. He was standing behind the children, who huddled together by the water's edge, staring up at him. Diego lumbered upstream in the water, calling to his sisters, his voice agonized. He took out his knife as he struggled through the water. Maria stood and followed him, pausing only long enough to pick up a rock from the streambed.

As she watched in helpless fear, the Indian slowly pulled an arrow from the quiver on his back, placed it against the bow he raised, and aimed at the girls.

Luz rose suddenly and pushed Catarina in the water, where she floundered and drifted slightly downstream toward Diego. As the Indian watched, Luz started up the bank toward him, her teeth bared, her expression terrible. She paused to pick up a stick and her face went pale with anger as she struggled up the riverbank, and the Indian began to laugh at her.

Diego was still struggling against the swift current, his arm raised with the knife in it. Maria snapped her arm back and threw the rock, sobbing in fury because she was sure she would miss him.

The rock hit the Indian in the stomach. At that moment Diego threw.

All five of them watched the knife spinning end over end through the air. It struck the Indian between the eyes. He dropped to his knees. Luz gasped and put her hands to her mouth as she scrambled out of the way. With his fingers still clawing at the handle that protruded from his forehead, the Indian tumbled down the bank, a dead man.

Luz stumbled back to the river's edge, reaching for Catarina. The two girls stood in the water as Maria waded toward them. "He was going to kill you, Catarina," Luz said simply.

"But what of you, Luz?" Catarina finally managed to say when she found her voice again.

"But you don't understand," Luz insisted, the same doggedness in her eyes as when she climbed the bank with her puny stick. "I love you!"

Diego bent over the body, toeing it with his moccasin. He put his foot on the Indian's chest and tugged at the knife, working it this way and that to pull it out. Then he sat back on his heels and looked at the Indian. Slowly he twined his fingers in the Indian's loose-flowing hair and raised the head, bringing his knife close to the scalp.

Maria grasped Diego's shoulder, her fingers digging into his flesh. "Don't do it."

"Tell me why not," he said, his voice flat, devoid of feeling.

"For me. And for your eternal soul."

He sat there, squatting on his haunches, for a full minute before he let the Indian go. The head lolled to one side and the blood spattered on the rocks at their feet.

Diego wiped his hands on his doublet, climbed the bank and picked up the bow. Looking back at Maria he said, "Get his arrows."

Without a word, she turned the Indian on his side and pulled off the quiver. Dangling from his loincloth was a string of scalps—white hair, blond hair, gray hair, black hair curly and damp like Diego's, chestnut hair like her own. "Mother of God," she whispered, unable to tear her eyes from the bloody offerings that hung limp from the dead man's waist. She touched one of the scalps, running her finger down the length of a blond tress so like Erlinda's, then got to her feet, swaying a little as her head cleared. She wiped her hands on her soaking dress and beckoned to the girls. They ran to her and the three of them joined Diego.

She held out the quiver of arrows to him, but he shook his head. "You put it on and stay close to me. If I have that on my back, I can't reach my arm around to get an arrow."

Her eyes went to his wounded arm. It was bleeding again, the blood and gypsum flowing steadily down the tattered remnants of his shirt.

"I must have opened it when I threw the knife," he said. "You keep the arrows, *querida*." He sat down with them, his face white. "We dare not stay here. Someone is sure to find that Indian. And we dare not go much farther. Surely he was not alone." He was talking to himself.

"We go on," Maria said. "Perhaps we can hide in the Gutierrez hacienda."

He was silent a moment, leaning his head against the tree and gazing up at the stars that still glimmered in the lightening sky. "Of course you are right," he murmured, covering her hand with his own. "But where do we get the strength?"

"From each other," she replied, her eyes on his face. "Diego, I love you."

"You already told me." He kissed her fingers, closing his eyes as she caressed his cheek.

"And so I tell you again," she said. She felt the tears on his cheek and leaned closer to him, kissing his face. "Come, *mi corazon*," she said, "let us be off before the sun rises."

The four of them stood up, Maria straightening her dress and smoothing it down with that decisive, womanly gesture that never failed to move Diego.

They walked through the narrow stand of trees, skirting the open fields that surrounded the Gutierrez hacienda. Maria could see the house now. It appeared, like Las Invernadas, to have been partially burned. They followed the general course of the river through the trees until they came to an irrigation ditch. Diego lifted Luz and Catarina into the dry *acequia* and Maria followed.

"Now, let us crawl along the ditch to the cornfield," Diego said. "Maria, you go first. I will be last."

Slowly they covered the distance from the river to the cornfield, working their way carefully along the ditch. Their damp clothing was soon covered with dust. Luz sneezed several times and Maria's heart pounded every time the sound exploded in the air. But all else was silence around them. Even the birds and crickets were still, so quiet was the dawn.

They crawled into the cornfield, keeping low until they were surrounded by the waving cornstalks that caught the gentle breeze of the coming morning. Maria sat on the ground, rubbing her stiff knees. Diego sat next to her, his face strained and white. The blood from his wound had melted the gypsum cast and the white and red streaks ran off his fingertips. "I am leaving a trail a blind man could follow," he muttered.

"Well, you lost my petticoat, and I have sacrificed most of my dress," said Maria, beginning to undo the buttons, "so you might as well take the rest. Wasn't I wearing my chemise when we first met?" she said, pulling the dress off over her head. She wound the material around his arm as tight as she dared, tying the whole thing in place with the sleeves. The morning breeze was cold on her bare arms and she shivered as she worked.

Diego watched her, a smile playing around his white lips. "You fill that out better than you did the first time," he said.

"It must be all the good food I have enjoyed lately," she retorted. "Keep your hands to yourself! What must your sisters think?"

"They're both asleep."

"No excuse. There now."

He touched his arm lightly. "That should at least get us to the hacienda. Wake up, my sisters—*despiertan, mis bienes, despiertan.*"

She smiled. "You are so poetic."

"But of course. Someday I will lie with my head in your lap and quote poetry by the bucketful, hour after hour."

She sighed, and he was silent. The girls were awake now. Luz stared at Maria. "Maria, you are practically naked! Whatever would Erlinda say?"

"She would be pleased that I am so resourceful, child. Now hush. We have to leave."

They crossed the cornfield, going silently down the rows, careful not to disturb the waving corn. Diego paused once and stripped down an unripened ear, holding it out to Maria.

"Look at that, will you? He could have bigger corn if he would weed out more of the suckers."

Maria put her arm around him. "Diego, don't be a farmer now."

When they reached the last row before the hacienda, Diego paused. "Let us wait here until we are sure that no one is about." They sat down and the girls promptly fell asleep again, leaning against each other. "Put your head in my lap and sleep, Maria," said Diego, tugging her down. "I will watch." He put his hand on her bare arm and rubbed it. "You're so cold, Maria. Perhaps there is some clothing in the hacienda."

Diego's hand was warm on her shoulder. "Dare we to move now?" she whispered sometime later.

"Yes, I think we had better. I have seen no movement anywhere."

Luz and Catarina came awake as soon as she touched them, their eyes wide, questioning. Maria put a finger to her lips.

Diego rose. "From here on there is no cover. We must walk forward like Masferrers. Come."

Single-file, they followed Diego from the cornfield, looking straight ahead at the Gutierrez hacienda. Maria prodded the girls in front of her to keep up with Diego, who was taking swift strides. Every moment she expected an arrow between her shoulder blades. The estancia was wrapped in silence.

They reached the kitchen gardens of the hacienda, so like the gardens at Las Invernadas. Diego sat his sisters down next to the beehive ovens, out of sight of anyone crossing the fields, admonishing them to stay. He held out his hand to Maria and she took it, clutching it so tightly that he looked back at her in surprise. "Just stay close," was all he said.

The kitchen door sagged inward on broken hinges. The kitchen was dark and silent and smelled of day-old death. Maria shuddered and closed her eyes, allowing Diego to tug her along. But then she opened her eyes, more fearful of stumbling over a corpse.

The bodies were sprawled across the long kitchen table. Diego looked hard at the corpses of his neighbors, bloated and fly-covered. "They were caught at breakfast, Maria. *Madre de Dios.*"

A woman's body stretched across the doorway into the main hall. Diego knelt down and pulled the woman's dress gently around her ankles again. "Angelica, prim and proper," he whispered, passing his hand in front of his face. Maria turned away. "Such animals, Maria," he murmured, and took her hand again.

They entered the hall, soaked with blood and overpowering with the odor of decay. Diego gagged and retched, and Maria put her hand to her face. It was no use. Even her fingers stank of death. The rest of the large Gutierrez family were lying in the hall, caught in various poses of death. All the women had been raped and scalped, all the men mutilated.

Diego stopped by one body, running his hand over the man's swelling chest. "Luisito, Luisito," he whispered, and looked at Maria. "Do you remember him, *querida mia?* He fetched your shoes from the grove when you wouldn't go back there."

She pulled Diego to his feet. "Don't do this to yourself," she said, her voice a low murmur, scarcely heard over the flies. Diego resumed his journey of remembrance down the hall, pausing only to cover the bodies of the women. He led her to the chapel.

As at Las Invernadas, the room had been desecrated, the chalice overflowing with urine, the walls smeared with body wastes. All of the plaster Spanish saints had been hacked to pieces like the people lying dead in the hall. Diego looked around him. "The hatred, Maria. The hatred."

She put her arm around him, and they stood together in the middle of the ruin. In her mind she could see Cristobal walking away from her, through the cottonwoods, when she had asked him why he could not believe as she did. We never knew them, she thought.

"This will have to do," Diego finally said. "I do not think the Indians will come back to the Gutierrez hacienda." He went to the altar and emptied the chalice behind it. "If we stack the benches against the door, the only entrance is that small window that opens onto the patio."

They pushed the benches against the door and let themselves out the window into the patio, crossing back to the hallway of death. Diego hurried along the blighted passageway, Maria following. She kept her eyes straight ahead, looking at the curls in Diego's black hair, telling herself over and over how much she loved him, trying to keep her mind off the death all around her.

They both took a deep breath in the garden. Luz and Catarina were still hunkered down behind the ovens. Diego knelt by them. "We are going into the Gutierrez hacienda," he said, his hand on Catarina's hair.

"But won't Senor Gutierrez mind?" she asked. "And did you tell him about the honeycomb?"

"No, no. He won't mind. He would be glad we have chosen his place, I think. But listen to me, sisters. I want you to close your eyes before we leave the garden and not open them until I tell you. Will you do as I say? Will you?" He was shaking Luz. She nodded, her eyes filled with an exhausted fright that went to Maria's heart.

Maria put her hands on Diego's head as he knelt by the ovens and pulled him back against her. He released Luz, passing a hand in front of his eyes. "I am sorry," he said with great weariness. "These are hard times."

The girls got to their feet. "Wait, Diego," Maria said, looking at the ovens. "If the Gutierrez family was at table, there may have been bread baking in the ovens. We always had our bread baking before breakfast."

Diego opened the oven nearest him, stuck his hand in and pulled out two loaves of bread. The crusts were hard and black, but it was bread. Maria opened the other oven door. The bread inside was also burned black, but her mouth watered as she pulled out the charred loaves.

"Maria, you amaze me," Diego said. "I never would have thought of it."

"Of course not. You are a man," she replied. "Here now, stuff this down the front of your shirt," she said, handing him the loaves. "If I put them down my chemise, they will fall through."

He smiled and winked at her and she blushed. He took the bread, put it carefully in his shirt, and handed the other loaves to his sisters. "You carry these. Now remember what I said about keeping your eyes closed, my sisters. I have never been more serious."

Maria picked up Luz. "Now turn your face into my neck," she ordered, "and close your eyes."

"Is this a game?" Luz asked.

"Yes, *querida*, a game. Now you must follow the rules. Like you did at the *acequia* when you were so brave."

With Diego in the lead, they entered the kitchen again. Maria clutched Luz tight against her, pushing her face farther into her hair. Diego walked swiftly down the hall, stumbling once over a body and nearly dropping Catarina. When she raised her head, he pushed her back against his shoulder.

Maria dogged his footsteps, covering Luz's eyes and nose with her free hand. Luz was crying soundlessly, her tears soaking into Maria's chemise, her shoulders shaking. Maria clung to her and stared straight ahead at Diego's back, noting how his blood had soaked through everything he wore until he was rust-colored.

Then they were in the Gutierrez chapel, staring at the destruction around them. "Did our chapel look like this, Diego?" Catarina asked in disbelief.

"Yes, it did, my sister." He sat down heavily next to Maria, weariness written on his features. Maria reached out to him, and he took her hand. "Maria, take the bread out of my shirt. Feed the girls." He let go of her hand and slid to the floor. With a few swipes he brushed aside the plaster shards from a ruined saint and laid his head down on the earthen floor. He was asleep before Maria had time to help him.

She knelt by Diego and pulled the bread from his shirt, pausing to put her hand on his heart. The rhythm was slow and regular, and she closed her eyes in relief. He seemed cooler, too, as if the fever was passing.

She stood up, brushing off her dress. "Come, girls, let us eat." Maria held out the blackened bread. "Bless us, Lord, and these Thy gifts," Maria murmured, making the sign of the cross over the black loaves. She tried to tear the bread into sections, but the crust was so tough and charred that it would not break. She looked at Diego, but he was lying on his knife, and she did not want to disturb him. Instead, she took the bread to the ruined altar and struck the loaf against the sharp corner.

The bread opened to reveal still-doughy centers. With no one alive to tend the ovens, the hot fires had gone out before the centers were cooked.

They ate silently, scooping out the uncooked dough, saving the hard shell for the last. Maria didn't think the girls would eat the crust, but they broke it into smaller pieces and sucked on them until they were soft enough to swallow.

When they finished, Catarina eyed the remaining loaves. Maria shook her head. "Let us save those for Diego."

Catarina nodded, even as her eyes lingered on the bread and she wiped her mouth with her nightgown sleeve. Maria put the remaining bread on the ground next to Diego, and with her hands swept a wide area by him clear of debris.

"Lie down now, my sisters," she said. "It will be a shorter day if you sleep."

Luz and Catarina curled up close to Diego. Luz pillowed

her head on her arm, then looked at Maria sitting by them on the bench. "Do you have a story?" she asked.

"But please, not about El Cid," begged Catarina.

"What? Have you had enough adventure?" Maria asked, sitting on the floor by Diego's head. "Ay, well, let us think." Leaning back against the bench, she closed her eyes and put her hand lightly on Diego's hair. He stirred but did not waken. "What about the little *pícaro* and the blind man?" she asked, then said, "No, no," hastily as she saw again the blind eyes of La Senora. When there was no comment from the sisters, she opened her eyes. Luz and Catarina were already asleep.

Maria sat on the floor of the Gutierrez chapel and looked around her. Daylight was creeping into the room. Everywhere she looked was ruin, unsoftened now by the gloom of early dawn. She thought of the Masferrer chapel and remembered the evening prayers, Diego leading them. How proud we all were, she thought, and see where it has led us.

Her fingers were still in Diego's hair. Absently she wound his black curls around her fingers. His hair was so black that it was almost blue in the morning light that filtered in through the small window. He stirred in his sleep and frowned. Maria saw his eyes moving behind his closed lids. And now he dreams, she thought, running her hand lightly over his eyes, covering them. When he was still again, she got up quietly and climbed out the patio window.

She stood on the patio for many minutes, trying to summon the courage to enter the hall of death again. The patio's small tiled fountain no longer ran, but a pool of water had collected in the blue basin. She washed her hands and face and drank deeply. After she smoothed down her chemise she walked into the hallway.

Flies buzzed and hummed around the festering bodies. The smell was so overwhelming that she turned back to the patio until her stomach was calm. Then she entered the hall again, crossing it quickly into one of the rooms where the door had been battered and smashed inward.

It was a family bedroom, stark in its simplicity like the rooms at Las Invernadas. The bedding was covered with blood and ripped to shreds, the altar splintered to kindling. It was the same in the next room she entered, and the next. The devastation was total. The Indians had left nothing in any of the rooms that could ever be used again by another, carting off whatever they coveted, destroying the rest.

The fury of madmen was everywhere as she wandered from room to room. The horrors of the past week had reached such a proportion that they were almost meaningless to her. Her fellow Spaniards lying like ruined dolls were not people anymore, but objects, not unlike the saints pulverized to dust in the chapel. It was all the same. Maria shuddered at her own callousness, and at the same time was grateful for it.

She finally came to a small bedroom at the back of the hacienda. It contained no dead body, but had been stripped and desecrated like the other rooms. With one difference. The bedding had been ripped, but not carried away or otherwise destroyed. They must have begun to tire, she thought to herself, or perhaps they were bored.

She pulled the torn sheet off the bed, folding it neatly into a small square. The disarray around her compelled her to fold the cloth carefully, precisely. The feather pillow was still intact, so she picked it up, putting her face to it for a moment.

Something about the room told her that it was a woman's place. She knelt by the bed and felt under it, smiling as her hand came in contact with a small basket. She pulled it out and looked inside, gasping with pleasure. It was a sewing basket, with needle, thread, and thimble. Erlinda always kept such a basket near her for late-night mending.

A careful search of the room revealed nothing else, so she let herself into the hall again and traveled the length of it to the kitchen, holding her breath, then breathing into the pillow.

In the kitchen the dried blood had stained and seasoned the food yanked from pantry shelves and strewn around. She picked her way among the bodies to the dry sink, found a wooden bowl only partly broken, and added it to her pile.

She forced herself to stay in the kitchen of death, watching out the window for an unendurable time until she was sure there was no one outside. She let herself out the door and set down her booty, spreading out the torn sheet. The Indians had ridden their dead masters' horses through the kitchen garden, but she managed to harvest two handfuls of crumpled beans and several tomatoes. She ate one on the spot, the juice dribbling down her chin.

By now the sun was high overhead. As she sat cross-legged

in the garden, she saw movement on the north road. Quickly she gathered up the small handful of food into the sheet and crawled toward the kitchen, pushing her bundle in front of her. Inside the kitchen, as she inched along the floor, her eyes were drawn to the feet of the corpses. She paused and sat up, looking more closely at the bodies.

Two of them were small girls. Swallowing several times, Maria gently pulled off their shoes, putting them on top of her sheet-covered pile. Luz and Catarina had been barefoot ever since she'd yanked them out of their beds at Las Invernadas.

She got to her feet and moved hurriedly out of the kitchen and down the hall again, forcing herself to look carefully at the bodies. She saw no clothing that was not torn or bloody, so she entered the patio and climbed back in the chapel window.

Diego sat there, waiting for her. "I told you not to leave the chapel, Maria," he said, his voice low and angry.

She said nothing.

"Don't you ever listen to anyone?" he asked, passing a hand across his eyes.

In answer Maria opened the bundle and extracted the wooden bowl. She climbed out the window again, filled the bowl from the tiled fountain, and carefully returned through the window again. "Here, drink this," she said, holding it out to Diego.

He did as she ordered, then leaned his head back against the bench, still exhausted. She got more water and set the lopsided bowl on the earthen floor.

"I found a needle and thread, Diego mio," she said as he watched her out of half-closed eyes. "I am going to sew up your arm."

He went visibly paler under his growth of beard, then sighed and held out his arm, resting it on the bench. "I suppose you are," he said. "Well, lead on, *capitana.*"

She knelt close to him and began to undo the knot on the soaked bandage. "Let me have your dagger," she said. He handed it to her and she cut through the knot.

"Gently," he whispered, "gently."

She unwrapped the bandage and gazed at the jagged cut. "I must clean this again," she said, dipping a square of the bed-sheet in the water. She swabbed his arm until all traces of the gypsum were gone, taking several trips to the patio for more water. When she was through, she pulled out the needle and thread, cut off a suitable length, and knotted one end. She looked at Diego and swallowed.

"I know, I know," he said, "you are going to tell me that this will hurt you more than me. Chiquita, I do not believe you."

She sighed. "I suppose you're right. Now hold still."

Taking several deep breaths, she began to sew up the wound, pausing after every stitch until Diego could control the tremors in his arm. She knew she was as white as he was, but she had to go on. She had to stop the bleeding. Several times he raised his other arm involuntarily to stop her, and she held his hand to her breast, squeezing his fingers with all her strength. Even in the coolness of the chapel, Diego was drenched with sweat. As she worked, sewing and wiping, she felt the sweat dripping down her back, too.

When she finished and bit off the thread, she sat with her head between her knees until the room stopped spinning. Then she fashioned a pad from the cleanest part of the sheet and made Diego hold it tight against his arm while she bound it with the long remaining strip of material, winding it around and around until his arm was covered from shoulder to elbow.

When she was through, Maria leaned back against the bench next to Diego and they sat together, staring at the crucifix that still hung behind the altar. The *Cristo* has been torn off, but still dangled at the foot of the cross. "Now what happens?" she whispered.

"We stay here until dark, then we walk to Santa Fe."

"Do you think you can?"

"I think I have to," he replied, sinking lower against the bench. "Lie down with me now."

She took the feather pillow and put it behind their heads, then turned sideways against him, and he laid his bandaged arm across her hip.

"Tell me a story, Maria," he said, his lips against her ear.

He was warm, but it wasn't the warmth of fever now. She huddled closer to him, relishing the comfort of his body. Her chemise was thin and she had been cold for so long.

"What story do you want to hear?" she asked as he kissed her ear.

"I like the story about the poor girl who marries the prince," he said, as he kissed her again.

"Who told you that one?"

"Catarina, I think. Maria . . . Maria?"

She was asleep.

Maria woke hours later. Diego's hand was covering her mouth. "Don't say anything," he whispered.

She opened her eyes and he took his hand away, grasping the dagger that was lying by her head.

"Indians," he whispered, "in the hacienda. They speak Tano, so they must be from Taos. Pray to God they will leave when they see there is nothing here."

"The girls?"

"Still sleeping."

She drew closer to Diego, feeling the rapid beating of his heart against her. "It isn't fair, you know," she whispered.

"What do you mean, *querida?*"

"I wanted to grow old with you. Would that not have been a fine thing?"

Diego was silent. He kissed her ear and sighed. They listened to the footsteps in the hall. No one entered the patio. There was deep silence, then much gagging and retching. After that, the footsteps hurried back to the kitchen again, and the hacienda was deathly silent once more.

After a long period of waiting, Diego sat up. He touched Maria's face with his fingertips. "We may grow old yet, *querida mia*. Do you think you could love an old man?"

"I would like to have the chance."

They sat together until the girls woke up. Maria took them to the patio where they washed their hands and faces in the remaining puddle of water. Back in the chapel she unplaited their braids and with her fingers, combed through their hair until it met her satisfaction, then rebraided their hair.

"There, you look better. Come see what I have for you." She handed them the slippers from the dead girls. Luz's fit snugly, but Catarina's were too large.

"Erlinda would say that I will grow," said Catarina, tugging at the rawhide thongs and tying them twice around her ankles. "I can keep them on."

In the deepening shadows of approaching evening, they ate the other loaves of bread and the few beans and tomatoes.

The four of them sat close to each other until night fell on the hacienda. When the shadows were dark across the chapel,

Diego got to his feet. He leaned against the bench for a brief moment, then straightened and reached for the bow and arrows that leaned against the wall. He slung the bow across his shoulder and handed the quiver of arrows to Maria. She gave him the dagger.

Diego turned to Catarina. "I do not think I can carry you this time, sister. Hang onto my belt and follow me. Maria, can you carry Luz?"

She picked up the child, who clung to her and put her face into Maria's neck again. Maria kissed her. They followed Diego and Catarina into the silent hall, picking their way through the bodies and debris. Catarina sobbed out loud, but she did not let go of her brother.

They hurried through the kitchen and out into the clean air. Diego wiped Catarina's face and held her close for a moment.

"Was it like that . . . at home?" she asked.

"It was. But we are still alive, Catarina. Mama wanted it that way, and we must fight to stay alive for her."

They left the shelter of the hacienda's walls and crossed the cornfield. "And now we will go to Santa Fe, my sisters," Diego said, holding tight to Catarina's hand.

Luz clapped her hands. "And will we stay with the Castellanos again?" she asked, dancing as Maria set her down.

Diego glanced at Maria, then back at his sister. "I pray we will, Luz. You pray, too."

They followed the river to the small stream that branched off toward Santa Fe. The mountains were dark in the moonlight and a small breeze played through the piñons. Maria shivered in the cold. Diego stopped and tried to take off his doublet.

"Here, Maria. I can take this off one side if you can help me with the other."

She pulled off his doublet and put it on. His homespun shirt was torn and rust-colored now from all the blood he had shed. It was the reddish-brown of the earth around them.

"I felt sure I would get another argument from you," he said.

"Not this time, *mi caballero muy elegante*," she replied. "I am too cold to argue."

286

They walked the remaining two leagues to Santa Fe, Maria carrying Luz, Catarina keeping up with her brother. The eastern rim of the elevation encircling Santa Fe was dotted with hundreds of campfires that looked like fireflies winking in a placid summer sky. Beyond the specks of light the sky was a dull glow. The *villa* of Santa Fe was on fire.

Masters of the Earth

•

*I*t *is as I feared,*" *Diego* said quietly. "Are we the only Spaniards alive in New Mexico?"

Maria's mouth was so dry she could not speak. The same glow she had seen from the grove of trees after the raid on the caravan now lighted the sky, only this time it was greater, and turned the night into early dawn.

"A week ago, I would have said nothing like this could happen," said Diego, "but now I do not know."

The glow deepened as they approached town. To avoid the Indians on the hills, they turned west and then south again, skirting the burning village and coming at it from Analco, the old Mexican Indian district that Maria had first seen so many months ago. They walked in the protective shelter of the cottonwoods as long as they could, then struck out across the cultivated fields, through the high corn. The chapel of San Miguel was a flaming ruin. As they came closer, the roof fell in with a roar, spraying sparks into the night sky.

Maria stood still in shocked amazement, letting Luz down to the ground. "Diego, is it all gone? All of it?" She turned her face into his chest and his fingers were heavy on her hair.

The dried blood on his shirt was scratchy against her face. She circled his waist with her arms, unwilling to move another step, more afraid now than she had been during the early-morning rampage at Las Invernadas. There was no belonging here. There was only death.

The four stood close together watching the flames of San Miguel, listening to the crackling of the fire in the church, breathing the smoky smell that had been in their nostrils for days. Suddenly Diego pushed Maria away and stalked some distance from them. He stood with his head cocked to one side, his weight on one leg in a gesture so reminiscent of Cristobal that Maria turned away.

"Listen!" he commanded.

They listened, hearing at first only the voracious flames that fed on neighboring huts, and the crashing of heavy timbers inside the church. Then she heard it, arquebus fire and the boom of a small cannon. It could only be one of the cannons that adorned the entrance to the governor's palace as a show-piece in better days.

Diego returned to the little group, leading them into the shelter of the cornfield again and out of the reflected glow of San Miguel. "Maria, we are not alone," he said, and his voice was full of enormous relief.

He looked toward the eastern elevation that surrounded the burning *villa*. "It appears that most of the Pueblos are camping north of the city. We have not seen anyone in Analco."

"Yes?" said Maria, waiting for him to continue. They were sitting in a cornfield, Indians were everywhere, dawn was coming, and they would be discovered when the sun rose, but still she relied on Diego to save them.

"As I see it, Maria, we have two choices."

She smiled again, feeling a sudden reassurance far out of proportion to their situation.

"We either leave Santa Fe now and strike out for the lower river kingdom around Ysleta, or we stay here and try to get into the governor's palace, never an easy task, as I recall, even under the best of conditions. But I fear that things are no better in Rio Abajo. Besides, I do not think any of us would get much beyond a league or two. We really have no choice."

So it was to be the governor's palace.

"But how?" Maria asked.

"I think the situation calls for one bold move. *Por Dios,* Maria, you had better do as I say this time! Let us get as close as we can to the palace while it is still dark. If the Indians have been at their mischief all night, they will tire with the dawn. You take the dagger, Maria, and put the quiver on my shoulder. Ah, this is well. And let us go now. Girls, be silent as mice, I beg you."

They followed the cornfield down to the ditch running by the side of the road, feeling the heat from San Miguel on their bodies as they walked, bare and exposed in the light of the flames. As they strode along, Diego reached behind him for an arrow and nocked it to the bowstring. Maria tightened her grip on his dagger.

When they reached the row of burned huts beyond San Miguel, Diego ducked inside the first intact doorway, pulling his sisters after him. Maria followed, stumbling over the charred doorframe. Diego crossed swiftly to the gaping window hole facing east and peered out. He stood there, silent and alert, for what seemed an interminable time. Then he turned away from the window, and with a finger to his lips, led the way out of the ruined adobe house. They sidled slowly along the outside wall of the ruin, toward the governor's palace.

The arquebus fire was louder now, but less frequent, just an occasional accent to the crackle of the fires all around them. For one sickening moment Maria feared that the garrison was being overwhelmed, the riflemen at their posts dying slowly one by one.

In the smoldering street before the plaza, two white-painted Pueblos in loincloths with scalps dangling from their waists stood carelessly at ease, gazing toward the plaza, hands on hips. In a sudden motion, Diego raised his bow to shoulder level, pulled back steadily on the bowstring, and sent an arrow deep into the back of one of them. The other whirled around, but Diego had already fitted another arrow to the bow and let it fly. The arrow penetrated the Pueblo's throat, the feathered end of the shaft protruding in front, a rapidly reddening decoration.

The girls flattened themselves against the side of a still-burning house while Diego motioned to Maria. "Here! Help me pull them into the shadows! We need their weapons."

She ran forward and grasped one of the dead bodies under the arms, tugging him toward the house where the girls hid. Luz shrieked in fright. Diego dropped his Indian and slapped her with the back of his hand. Luz drew further into the shadows, her hand to her face, her eyes wide with shock. Catarina grabbed her little sister around the waist and held her tight.

"See if he has a weapon," Diego hissed at Maria. She turned the Indian over and pulled a long knife from his scalp string. Her hand brushed against the bloody hair, but she did not hesitate.

"Hand it to me," Diego ordered. He stuck it in his belt and took out another arrow, wincing as he reached behind his shoulder with his bandaged arm. Maria looked at his arm anxiously, but there was no fresh blood on the bandage.

The arquebus fire dropped off, then stopped. They hastened around the last corner before the plaza and stood gaping at the sight before them.

The east end of the governor's palace was on fire and the smoke billowed across the plaza, enveloping it in a haze-like fog as if from a riverbank. Hundreds of Indians, stripped and painted for war, stood in the plaza, looking like the damned in one of the lower levels of hell. Diego crossed himself and muttered a Hail Mary, his voice a subdued whisper.

Many of the Indians sat on the ground. Some already slept, leaning against each other. Others were silent, watchful, their eyes on the burning palace, on the men and women inside, beating at the flames with Indian rugs. The multicolored weavings were a spot of brightness in the smoky, stinking haze.

She turned to speak to Diego, to plead with him to abandon the idea and take their chances in the desert, but he hushed her.

"We cannot turn back. It is too late," he said. "Now, this is what we will do." He looked into her eyes with a stirring intensity. His hands were bloody from the dead Indian, and he wiped them on his shirt, still holding her gaze. "Take the girls and walk along the rim of the plaza, keeping in the shadows. I am going the other way."

Maria tried to protest. "Be still!" Diego ordered. "Now listen to me for once, my love, and do as I say." He grabbed her shoulder and shook her. "Now. I will start shouting. When I do, you run straight for the gates. Do you understand?"

Tears streamed down Maria's face. He shook her again, his voice compelling. "I must have your word, Maria. The sky is light enough. Someone inside will see you. Wave your arms and yell as you approach the gates. Now, will you? Will you?" He shook her again.

"I cannot leave you, Diego."

He backed away and pulled her hands from his chest. "You have to," he said. Tears filled his eyes and he brushed them away. "Just remember me, *querida*. Now go."

He pushed her away from him and she stumbled back against Luz. Without another look at Diego, she turned, wiped her eyes on her chemise and took each girl by the hand, pulling them along the edge of the smoke-filled plaza.

The Indians stood as if made of stone, hands to their weapons, eyes on the burning palace. The smell of death rose from their bodies, each man wearing the scalp of his former master. Maria swallowed and hurried through the diminishing shadows with the children. She couldn't trust herself to look back for Diego, but she held Luz and Catarina in a death grip. The girls raced along beside her. Catarina's eyes were wide with terror, but Luz's face was vacant of all expression, as if she were somewhere else.

They were almost to the far side of the plaza when Maria was jerked around by a hand gripping her arm. Without a word, she let go of the girls and yanked the knife out of her waistband, cutting deep into the arm that held her. When the Indian let go in surprise, she plunged the knife into his heart, gagging at the putrefaction that rose from his scalp-decked body. The Indian grabbed her in death's reflex and pulled her to the ground on top of him. She jerked out the knife and plunged it in again and again, sobbing deep in her throat. The Indian went limp suddenly and bloody froth poured from his mouth.

Maria leaped to her feet, dropping the knife, and clutched Catarina's hand, her grip slippery. Luz had collapsed in a heap. Maria yanked her upright.

Then she heard Diego. With the ferocious cry of the *conquistadores*, he screamed "Santiago!" at the top of his lungs from the far side of the plaza.

The three of them pounded toward the burning governor's palace. The Indians had turned their attention to Diego. She saw him out of the corner of her eye, his back to a wall, shooting arrow after arrow.

They ran until they reached the smoldering portal. The wooden flooring was slippery with blood and burned in places. They fell once in a tangled heap, but they scrambled up and kept running toward the barred entrance gates.

"*Madre de Dios,* help us!" Maria screamed as they pounded the length of the walkway. Catarina and Luz cried, thin, piping wails of terror that Maria knew she would hear for the rest of her days. "Holy Mother, San Francisco, save us!" she shrieked.

As they ran faster, shouting and screaming, the gates slowly opened. Without another word, Maria shoved Catarina and Luz toward the outstretched arms and stopped. She whirled around to face the plaza. She could still see Diego, shooting with dreadful deliberation at the approaching Indians. His aim was excellent, and they moved slowly, cautiously toward him.

Maria started toward him, but someone seized the back of her chemise and yanked her toward the fortress gates again. She struggled to free herself, but other hands pulled her in and then pushed her to one side as the defenders of Santa Fe barged out through the gates with their own cry, "Santiago!"

When the smoke-blackened man let go of her, she leaped to her feet again and ran out the open gate, following the soldiers, compelled back into the plaza she had been so desperate to leave only minutes before.

The fighting swirled around her as she ran toward the last place she had seen Diego. The stench sickened her, the flash and roar of the arquebuses at close range deafened her, but she kept running, searching, her heart pounding, her mouth open as she gasped for breath.

And then it was over. Someone struck her from behind, and she dropped like a stone in the plaza.

She heard voices, Spanish voices, before she opened her eyes. Her exhausted mind turned the sounds over and over, but she was still afraid to open her eyes. Someone was stroking her cheek, running fingertips down her face. Only one person she knew had ever done that, and he was dead. She sobbed his name and the fingers stopped.

"Maria."

That was all. Her name. She opened her eyes and looked up into Diego Masferrer's dear face.

She closed her eyes quickly, then opened them again. He was still looking down at her, a slight smile on his face. Blood dribbled down the corner of his mouth, and she raised her hand to his lips. He ran his tongue over his teeth and winced.

"Diego." She patted his face, glorying in the familiarity of it.

"We were both too tough to kill, Maria *querida.*"

She reached up and put her arms around his neck. He winced again, and then gathered her close. "Maria, will you never listen to me?" he said into her shoulder.

She laughed and ran her hands over his broad back. "So we are not dead?"

She felt his laughter as she held him. "If you were dead, Maria, you would probably look better."

Maria let go of Diego and sat up, touching her face. Her left eye was swelling and her face felt strangely puffy.

"Between the two of us, *querida,*" said Diego, squatting back on his haunches, "I believe we have one good pair of eyes."

"For that, Senorita," began a familiar voice, "I must apologize."

Maria squinted into the sun. "Senor Castellano!" she exclaimed. "How good it is to see you!"

He knelt by her as she sat on the ground near the palace entrance. His face was black with smoke from the fire, and she almost didn't recognize him.

"Maria, you did not say how pleased you were to see me when I tried to stop you from going after Diego!"

"A thousand pardons," she said, putting her hand to her swollen face.

"I am afraid I had to strike you to stop you. It was not a thing I am proud of, Senorita, but you would not listen."

"Yes," murmured Diego, "that is something about her."

"Santos!" Castellano exclaimed, "you fought me like a tiger! But never mind. You two are alive." He struggled to control his emotions. "I never . . . we never . . . thought to see any of you ever again." Senor Castellano paused,

looking over his shoulder. "But here are two young ones I cannot hold back."

Luz and Catarina threw themselves at Maria and Diego. Maria clasped Luz in her arms, holding the child close.

"Maria," Luz whispered, "when you ran back out the gates, I tried to follow you, but they wouldn't let me."

"Oh, Luz," Maria whispered back, "we will not be parted again. Not for anything."

Diego leaned over and kissed Luz. "And will you forgive me for striking you, Luz?"

Silently she threw her arms around her brother.

Governor Otermin shouldered his way through the people that crowded around the fortress entrance. Like Senor Castellano, he was smoke-blackened. Gone were his fancy clothes, his elegant gold-handled cane. His shirt and breeches were in tatters, and he wore the look of one awake too long. He bowed slightly, a striking figure of authority even in his rags. "Accept my apologies and sympathy, Masferrer."

Diego held out his hand, and the governor grasped it in a firm grip. Then Otermin stepped back, looking at Maria and Diego's sisters. "At least you do not come to us empty-handed, Diego."

"I have nothing, sir," Diego replied. "Absolutely nothing."

"Ah. Here I see your sisters, and Maria Espinosa, the redoubtable Maria. Diego, she is formidable."

"They are not my possessions," snapped Diego. Maria put a hand on his arm but he ignored her. "I will never again have the . . . the audacity to think I can own anyone. We are together because we belong together, *por Dios*," he paused. "Sir."

Maria smiled at Diego and put her arm around his waist. The haunted look left his eyes. "You're a forward woman," he said to cover his embarrassment.

"And you, Masferrer," began the governor. "Well, I am pleased to note that this whole nightmare has not completely knocked out all your eccentricities. Such a dull colony this would be."

Maria looked around at the colony the governor spoke of. The plaza was crowded with people, refugees like themselves, women and children, dirty, hungry, and inexpressibly weary, their eyes vacant with exhaustion, or full of the terrors of the week they had survived. She pulled Luz and Catarina to her, thinking to shield them from the hopelessness around them, then loosened her grip on the girls as she realized that they were no better off.

Any area not occupied by the refugees was taken up with animals, whatever horses, sheep, goats, and cows the rancheros had managed to save.

"Like Noah's Ark, Maria," observed Luz.

"What? Oh, indeed. I think you must be right. *Ay de mi!* Could Noah have heard himself in such a racket!"

Luz tugged at Maria. "I am thirsty."

The governor turned from his own contemplation of the disorder around him, a look of perpetual wonder on his dirty face at such a bedraggled mob defacing his well-ordered patio. "Ah, water. The Indians have cut the *acequia* that flows into the plaza. We have no water." He looked at Diego. "To say that things are somewhat desperate is typical of the understatement of which only government officials are capable."

Diego laughed, and Otermin raised his eyebrows. "Masferrer, what makes you so cheerful?"

"Senor Excellency," he replied, "I am just pleased to be alive. Is there a priest around?"

"I would imagine. They have a resiliency that rivals your own. Try the chapel. I believe it is crammed with burning candles."

"And Excellency, is there any clothing around for Maria and my sisters?"

"Yes, an admirable point. Senor Castellano can direct you to the storehouse. Although if we leave Maria in her shift, she might be distracting enough to take the men's minds off water."

Diego did not laugh, even when Maria blushed and pulled his sisters in front of her. The governor looked from Maria to him. "I mean no offense, Masferrer, none at all. I was appealing to your evident humor, but I see that you do not laugh about Maria."

Diego bowed. "Oh, I do, Your Excellency, but you don't."

Otermin bowed in turn, and the two men went off to their separate tasks.

Maria looked around her again. The gates had been slammed shut again and bolted with a heavy cedar crosspiece. Black-faced boys and men watched at the rifle ports, silent, alert.

The governor walked among them, speaking to one, patting another.

Maria could hear nothing from the plaza. "Have the Indians left, Senor Castellano?" she asked.

"For now, perhaps, at least some of them. They carry away their wounded and dead, then return in a few hours, stronger than before. This has been their pattern for two or three days, maybe more. I cannot recall."

"We saw their campfires on the hills north."

"Yes. They have been there several days. It all begins to run together." Senor Castellano held his arm out for Maria. "Come with me now. I have someone who can help you and the girls."

Senora Castellano was sitting in a scrap of shade, a parasol at her feet, in an attitude of genteel repose, untouched by the activity around her. She rose when she saw Maria and held out her hand as if she were in her own *sala*. Then she clutched Maria in a strong embrace. "Maria," she said. "Words cannot express my feelings. Come, sit."

Maria sat next to La Senora Castellano. She smiled to see the Castellano sons and daughters around their mother. "How lucky you are, Senora," she said. "You have everyone here."

Senora Castellano regarded her children, then turned to Maria. "Yes, although I find myself counting them several times a day, as I did when they were younger. Maria, the tales we have heard! I cannot believe them."

"Believe them, Senora," said Maria wearily, "for they are true. We have seen things that will be with us forever."

"What of Senora Masferrer? Erlinda? and Cristobal?"

Maria shook her head and closed her eyes. Luz and Catarina leaned against her.

Senora Castellano reached out and put her hands on the children. "It would seem that you have acquired sisters, Maria," she said, motioning for her daughter to come forward with food.

"I have. Twice they have been given into my keeping, so I have sisters." Maria opened her eyes and said suddenly, "But what of *my* sister?"

Senora Castellano looked away. "La Viuda? A sad story, my dear. And have you not had enough of sad stories, Maria? La Viuda Guzman fled with the rest of us, she and her daughters, all of us just ahead of the Indians. Why did none of us think this would ever happen?" She stirred restlessly. "Well, when the Widow Guzman came through the gates, she remembered that she had left behind her strongbox, the one with the records of deeds and mortgages and loans. What can I say? She harangued the men to help her fetch it, and when no one would, she and her daughters returned for it. That was two days ago. We have not seen them since."

Maria bowed her head and sat in silence while La Senora handed her and the girls a trencher of dried meat and hardtack. She watched Luz and Catarina eat quickly, rapidly, then picked up a handful of meat. She ate.

"We are rationed heavily," said La Senora Castellano. "All of this is from the government storehouses. Here is a sip of wine. Only a sip, mind you. We have nothing more."

The wine was cheap and bitter, such as would be allotted to soldiers, but at least it was wet. Watching carefully, La Senora took the bottle back after it had gone around once. "Save the rest for Diego," she said.

Maria was silent, looking across the courtyard. The sun was hot and pitiless overhead, and she was grateful for the small shade. The townspeople had gotten the shady spots first, while the refugees who had managed to flee their haciendas with their lives alone sat and baked in the sun, staring with dull eyes at nothing. She got to her feet. "I must find Diego!" she told the Castellanos.

"Oh, sit, sit, child. He said he was only going to look for a priest."

But Maria would not sit. She backed away from Senora Castellano's restraining hand. "I must find him," she insisted. "Stay here, Luz and Catarina. I will be back. He is gone too long."

"Maria, it has been only a few minutes! Sit here and wait."

"You don't understand, Senora. I have to find him."

Her body ached and her eye was on fire, but she ran toward the chapel at the east end of the patio. Everywhere there were crying children and sun-burned women, just sitting in rags and tatters, staring.

The chapel was cool but crowded with refugees, women praying out loud, raising their hands to heaven, lamenting what had been lost, wailing for the dead, swaying back and forth, pulling at their hair. With a cry of relief, Maria saw Diego sitting on a bench toward the front of the church, talking to a brown-robed Franciscan. She ran forward and put her hands on Diego's shoulders. He jumped and grabbed her fingers, loosening his hold only when he looked over his shoulder and saw who it was.

"Ah, don't sneak up on me like that again," he said with a shaky laugh. "Sit down with me, *mi corazon*. This is Father Farfán. Father, Maria Espinosa de la Garza."

She came around the bench and sat beside Diego. He put her hand on his thigh in a gesture that made her think that he was not through with possessions just yet.

"I was hoping you would come," he said. "It is a curious thing. I feel so uneasy without you close by."

Maria nodded. "I was feeling the same thing."

Father Farfán leaned forward, looking at both of them. "We have seen that for the past week, especially with those who have come here from outlying areas, as you have. Whole families move about in groups. No one wants to be out of anyone's sight." He sighed and looked down at his hands. "They tell us, as you have told me, of the things they have witnessed, and I do not wonder at their reluctance to be separated." He looked at Maria. "Diego tells me you saw Father Pio."

"I did. Only do not ask me."

"I will not. There are worse fates than a martyr's cross. It would appear that some of us have been condemned to live and remember." He fingered the knotted cords at his waist. "But enough of that. It will be with us forever. Diego tells me that he wants to marry you. Now."

"I tried to talk him out of it last week."

"Ho, did you?" said Father Farfán with a smile. "You are a strange woman, indeed."

Diego spoke up. "She could not see how Diego Masferrer, hacienda owner and master of Indians, could ever survive the ignominy of marrying a *pobrecita*." He put his arm around Maria. "But a poor man is a different story, eh, Maria chiquita?"

She considered him seriously. "No, it isn't, Diego. I still should not. Someday you will have all this back again. Don't you think you might feel some regret that you did not marry into land and wealth?"

Diego considered the question, running his hand down Maria's bare shoulder. "No."

Maria sighed. "Well, perhaps we had better consider it then."

"I will give you no cause for regret, *querida mia.*" Diego smiled and squeezed her arm. "All that I have is yours. It may not look like much at the moment, but it is more than I could have given when I had everything, when I was master of the earth. You have my heart, my life, my body—for whatever it is worth these days."

"It is the same with me, Diego," Maria whispered. "All that I have."

Diego looked at the priest. "Do you see, Father? She agrees. Now, when can you marry us?"

"You know this is irregular. There should be banns for a month. . . ."

Diego interrupted. "We may not have even a day together, Father, and you talk of a month."

"I know, my son. Perhaps this once. This may be the last cheerful thing that ever happens in Santa Fe. This evening?"

"We will be here." Diego stood and pulled Maria to her feet. They leaned against each other, tired beyond words. *"Querida,* we are so decrepit!" he exclaimed, supporting her around the waist with his good arm. "At dusk?" he said to the priest.

"Yes. Go with God, my children."

They helped each other back across the courtyard. "Look at it this way, Maria," said Diego, talking loud to be heard above the cries of children and bawling of thirsty animals, "if the worst is behind us, we are more fortunate than most."

"You called me La Afortunada, did you not?"

"Indeed I did."

They rejoined the Castellanos in the shade. Diego shook his head when they offered him biscuits and jerky, but he took a sip of wine, recorking the bottle carefully.

Pulling Maria down beside him, they curled up together in the protection of each other's arms and slept, oblivious to the hard ground, the noise, the heat.

Maria woke up hours later. The sun was slanting across the courtyard and the dust was thick in the air. She was thirsty, but she said nothing. Luz and Catarina slept next to her, but

Diego was gone. She looked around quickly, and Senora Castellano came to her.

"He will be right back. My Reynaldo took him to the storehouses to try to find you a dress. And here, I have a brush and comb. Let us see what we can do."

Her hair was a hopeless tangle. "Should we cut it off and start over?" Maria suggested, only half in jest.

"No, no. This is still your best feature. Hold still now. This will take time."

Obediently, Maria sat cross-legged in front of Senora Castellano. She remembered the times when Erlinda had brushed her hair, carefully removing every snarl, talking in her gentle way about the Masferrers and their river kingdom. Tears rolled down her cheeks, and Senora Castellano looked at her in consternation.

"Do I pull too hard, Maria?"

"No. It is nothing," she replied. "I was just remembering."

"Perhaps it is better not to," La Senora replied, gently tugging the comb through Maria's hair. "Let us dwell on tomorrow, instead."

"Is that so much better?" Maria asked.

"There is no telling what tomorrow will bring, but at least there is some strength in numbers."

Neither woman said what she was thinking, how few were the soldiers, how many the Indians. Outside the gates, pawing through the still-smoldering *villa,* were more Indians than either of them had ever seen.

"Have we hope of rescue?" Maria asked finally.

"Governor Otermin seems to think that his lieutenant governor in the lower river kingdom of Rio Abajo will come to our aid, but who is to say that they are not worse off than we are?"

Maria began to feel the same uneasiness that had gnawed at her earlier when Diego was out of her sight. She stirred restlessly. "I really should find Diego, Senora."

La Senora put a firm hand on the girl's shoulder. "No. Now, listen to me. He will be right back."

Maria began to cry. The tears streamed down her face, and Senora Castellano stopped in surprise, her hands fluttering helplessly about Maria, uttering gentle crooning sounds. "Maria, Maria, do not do this. I know he will be right back. Look here at Luz and Catarina. They are not crying. Maria, please!" But Maria wiped her face on her dirty chemise and sobbed into the fabric, shaking off La Senora's hands. Finally, wiping her eyes, Maria looked up to see Diego with Senor Castellano, coming toward her from the government warehouses across the courtyard. Diego's expression was anxious, too, as if he had been gone past bearing from those he loved. He came to her quickly, wiping her eyes with the sleeve of his shirt. It was a new shirt, one of coarser fabric than Diego Masferrer had ever worn before.

He held her to him. *"Dios mio,* this is strange, Maria, but I cannot bear to be away from you."

Maria leaned her forehead against his chest. The rhythm of his heart steadied her.

"And see what I have for you, *mi corazon,* a dress." He pressed the brown bundle into her hands. "It is really quite ugly and much too large, but certainly more dignified than that scrap you are wearing. Here, take it."

She fingered the dress. The material was rough and heavy. "I think three of me will fit in this."

"Probably. Senor Castellano tells me that I should search around for a woman who is more of an armful. He cannot understand me when I insist that you will do." His eyes were laughing. "And you will do, Maria. I could even grow used to your black eye."

Maria kissed her fingers and touched Diego's eye. "You are no prize, either, Diego!"

"Pues bueno, perhaps we will have much to be joyful over in the coming days." He turned from Maria to his sisters, holding up the rest of the bundle he carried. "And look, *mis hermanas,* for you. One dress, two dresses. It is past the hour of nightgowns. Maria will help you. I must go again."

Maria put her hand on his arm, detaining him. She felt the blood rushing from her face again. Diego held his hand to her cheek. "No, Maria. I will not be long. The governor has asked the men to meet in the chapel. I suppose he is assigning the night's watches. Now change your clothes and let Senora Castellano finish your hair. You are only half done."

He left quickly again before Maria could object. Maria reached out for Luz and Catarina. "Let us dress. Senora, is there anyplace for some privacy?"

"Alas, no. Every room is taken, every corner used. My daughters and I will hold up blankets around you while you change."

Crouching down behind the blanket barricade, Maria helped the sisters out of their nightgowns, her heart turning over when she saw their thin bruised bodies.

When the girls were buttoned up the back, Maria pulled her chemise over her head and reached for the brown dress. Catarina touched her leg. "Oh, Maria, you have so many bruises! Look, Luz, *mira*."

"Hush, Catarina," said Luz surprisingly. "Diego would not like you teasing Maria. He told the governor so."

"Oh, sister," said Catarina, "he would tease her too, if he could see her."

Maria blushed and buttoned up the dress quickly, avoiding the glances the Castellano women exchanged with each other. Her face was on fire, and she put her hands to her cheeks.

"Well, he would!" insisted Catarina. "And what is so funny?" she demanded as the Castellanos began to giggle, in spite of their rigorous upbringing.

Maria hugged Catarina. "Never mind, my sister. I am sure you are right. I will let you know." She stood up and shook the dress down to her feet. The material hung on her, as Diego had predicted.

"How strange, Maria," said La Senora. "These clothes are sent from Mexico for the servants and soldiers' wives. Do they imagine we are so well-fed here?"

"Ay, Luz," said Maria as she gathered the brown serge in with her hands. "This is one time even Diego would have to admit that I cannot cut the cloak to fit the cloth!"

Senora Castellano dropped her end of the blanket and tore off a narrow strip from her light cloak hanging nearby. She wrapped the material several times around Maria's waist and tied it firmly in back. "This will do, until something better comes along. God alone knows when that will be. Sit now, and I will finish your hair."

Maria's hair was brushed, combed and carefully arranged on top of her head before the men returned from the chapel. The chill of night was in the air, and Maria heard Indians moving in great numbers in the plaza as they surrounded the governor's palace and the walled government houses. Luz and Catarina drew close to her and they sat together in silence.

The Indians hooted and beat against the adobe walls with their spears. The words sounded familiar. Maria looked at Senora Castellano. "What is it they say, my lady?"

"They have murdered Christ and his mother Maria. And soon they will start reciting the Mass. They do it every night." The woman leaned back, her hands clenched in her lap. "Do they hate us so much, Maria? Was what we did to them so wrong?"

Maria thought of her San Francisco lying broken in the bloody gypsum at Tesuque. "No, it was not wrong for us. But did anyone ever ask them?" she said, gesturing toward the outside wall.

She sat in silence, thinking of Cristobal. Then she saw Diego and the Castellanos leave the chapel and cross the courtyard, picking their way among the survivors, stopping here and there for a word, a touch. Diego spoke to several of the women, who covered their faces with their shawls at his words and rocked back and forth lamenting, adding his agony to their own. Diego's face was a mask of pain as he approached Maria. He sank down beside her.

Wordlessly she took his hand and held it to her. He leaned against her and closed his eyes.

"What did the governor speak of?" she asked.

"Nothing that will not keep, *querida*. Let me rest, then we will go find Father Farfán."

He put his head in her lap and was asleep in a moment. Maria settled herself against the cooling adobe wall. Her hands went to Diego's hair, and she began to twist his curls around her fingers. His hair was dull and matted with blood and dirt. She remembered how fastidious he was normally. But that was before.

Before. Would she always reckon time as *before* and *now*? She rested her hand lightly on Diego's head in the gesture of a blessing. Will we ever be the same again? And do we want to be?

The sound in the courtyard was deafening—animals restless and loud in their hunger and thirst, and children crying for food, water, comfort, their own beds, long since destroyed. Always there was the ceaseless wail of women mourning their losses. As one woman would stop her crying, exhausted, another would pick up the lament.

The Indians outside increased their dance of death, beating against the massive gates, lobbing stones over the wall. Children shrieked and cried in terror.

Diego opened his eyes and looked up at Maria. "We are at the gates of hell, Maria," he whispered, the strain showing on his face again. "Forgive me."

She held his face in her hands, brushing back the hair from his forehead and running her fingers over the deep wrinkle between his eyes. "Forgive you for what, my love?" she asked softly. "If all we have is this night, then it is more than I ever had before."

"Let us find Father Farfán, Maria."

She got to her feet and straightened her dress, patting down the too-large folds. She took Luz by one hand, Catarina by the other, and they crossed the noisy, dirty courtyard with the Castellanos, La Senora fretting aloud that it could not be a proper wedding party, and Senor Castellano smiling at some secret pleasure of his own.

"We amuse you?" asked Diego.

"You do," replied Don Reynaldo. "I think your father would be pleased, and I know that I am. Maria will always do her best to help you resist that strain of stuffiness in all Masferrers. And you can make it your life's calling to keep shoes on her feet and a dress on her back, something you have not done so well, heretofore."

Diego laughed. *"Bueno,* Senor! I notice that you did not tell me to expect much obedience."

Father Farfán was waiting for them at the chapel. Diego and the Castellanos went inside, but Maria hung back. Diego returned to her, all amusement gone from his face. "This is a serious thing we do, my heart. I do not wonder at your reluctance."

She stared back at him, but did not move.

"Can it be that you do not love me enough?" he asked, holding out his hand to her.

She shook her head, but did not touch him. "Not that, never that, Diego. It's just that. . . ." She stopped. "I am afraid."

"Of me?" he asked, coming closer.

"A little. And I—oh, this is silly! What must you think of me?" she said in embarrassment and frustration.

"You still wonder if you belong here," he said, his eyes gentle.

"Yes, I do. Are you sure, Diego?" she asked.

He nodded. "And do you know something, *querida?* When I was hiding in Emiliano's workshop—before you found me—all I wanted was to see your face again. I had not one other ambition. Everything I have ever worked for in my life all boiled down to that. You belong here with me."

"You're sure?" she repeated.

"Listen to me, my beloved. I do not pretend that I am a good man. You accused me once of cold-bloodedness and you were right. It is a curse I have, and I share it with my neighbors."

"Diego mio," she said, her fingers on his lips.

He kissed them, his eyes closed. "But change has been forced on me . . . on all of us. I would wander as a lost soul without you, Maria. Marry me."

She took his hand and walked with him into the chapel.

They were married in a hurried ceremony at the altar, Father Farfán's voice rising and falling in a steady, reassuring cadence as he united them. He interrupted the flow of words only long enough to ask Maria her full name and then to ask Diego if there was a ring.

Diego shook his head. "Not now. Later, perhaps."

The father continued, blessing their union, listening to their quiet responses. The chapel was still full of refugees crowding the benches, supplicating at the altar, crying and mourning. Maria heard arquebus fire outside the thick-walled church. She clung tighter to Diego's hand.

When the ceremony was over, Diego clasped the Franciscan's hand. "I wish that I could pay you, Father," he said, the words coming hard from him.

"Never mind, my son. This was the most pleasant task I have performed in days."

They stood at the chapel door with the Castellanos. "And now what will you do?" asked Father Farfán, fingering his rosary.

Diego shrugged. "I suppose I am on guard duty somewhere tonight. The Castellanos will show me, I am sure."

The Father shook his head. "No, that would not be right. Would you abandon your bride so soon?"

Diego blushed and looked at the priest. "I hardly think I have a choice, Father, in this crowded place."

"May I offer a solution?"

Diego grinned. "And are you a worker of miracles?"

The Father sighed and looked around him, the strain of the day showing on his face in a quick flash. "Only small miracles, my son. Very small ones. Come with me. And bid your friends goodnight, if you will."

Maria knelt and hugged Luz and Catarina. "Stay with the Castellanos, my young ones. I will be with you in the morning."

Luz kissed her, offering no protest, but Catarina clung to her hand. She stood on tiptoe and as Maria leaned forward, she whispered, "I am glad it is you, Maria."

"What do you mean?" Maria whispered back.

"I wondered whom Diego would marry. Luz and I . . . we were sure we would not like her."

Diego turned away to hide his smile, while Maria put her arms around the young girl. "Could you not trust your brother's judgment?" Maria asked, her eyes twinkling.

"Sometimes he is so serious!" said Catarina. "We were afraid he would marry someone serious. But he married you, Maria, and. . . ." She paused, then finished in a surge of feeling. "And you will tell us stories and laugh with us, and love us, too."

Maria hugged Catarina. "Always that, Catarina," she vowed, shutting her mind resolutely on the scarcity of their tomorrows, on the dangers that were their only absolute beyond each sunrise.

Luz came back to tug at her sister. "Come on, Catarina," she insisted, "Senora Castellano says they want to be with each other!"

Diego was unable to smother his laughter. "My sisters," he said as they joined the Castellanos, looking back for another wave and kiss of the hand from Maria.

"Yes, your sisters," she agreed, not looking him in the eye. "I love them."

"And now, you Masferrers," said Father Farfán, "come

with me. There is no reason for *everyone* to be miserable tonight."

He led them back into the chapel and through a side door by the altar. The passageway was filled with families bedding down for the night. Maria and Diego stepped carefully around sleeping forms and household goods. Father Farfán paused before a closed door and selected a large key from the bunch in his hand. He opened the door and Diego and Maria followed him in.

"It is only a cubbyhole," he apologized as he knelt to light a candle. "I use it for repairing vestments and for sitting and thinking, when I am tired of Santa Fe. And over here, I have something else."

They looked where he pointed. The priest unlocked a cabinet and drew out a stoppered pitcher of water.

"Holy Water," he said. "I remembered it was there this afternoon."

"Father, we could not!" said Diego, his eyes on the bottle.

"And did not David eat the showbread in the temple?" replied the priest, unstoppering the bottle and pouring a small amount of water into a copper basin. "Was his need so much greater than your own?"

Maria went to the priest. "Thank you, Father," she said as he handed her a towel and a bit of soap. "Someday..." she could not finish her sentence.

"Someday you will help others in need?" he finished for her. "There is no other payment. But you already know that. I bid you goodnight, my children, and wish you great joy in each other. And I had better lock you in. We have become a city of sleepwalkers."

As soon as Father Farfán let himself out and turned the key in the lock, Diego took Maria by the shoulders and pulled her to him. Her arms went around him and she clung to him in the silence of the small room. His lips were on her hair, her ears, her mouth and then in the hollow of her neck. She shivered and kissed him.

"You know something, Maria?" he said, his eyes closed.

She leaned her head on his chest, listening to his racing heart. Then he held her from him and began to undo the buttons on the front of her dress. She hooked her fingers in his belt, too shy to look at him.

When her dress was unbuttoned, she pulled away from Diego's embrace and went to the copper basin. She took a long drink, then pulled down her dress and began to wash.

After watching her in silence, Diego rummaged in the corner where the old vestments hung on pegs. He found a pallet and unrolled it on the floor. "Narrow," he commented. He sat down and took off Emiliano's moccasins, sighing. "I haven't had them off in days, Maria. I forgot I had toes."

She laughed and flicked some water from the basin at him. He smiled. "Don't waste it, chiquita. And save me some, will you? Although I think you are using it to better effect than I ever could. *Por dios,* you are thin, Maria."

"Is that a lover's language?" she teased, drying herself off.

"No, it is a husband's talk. You're all eyes and elbows. People will think I have not been treating you well."

"And have you?" she asked, pulling her dress up again over her shoulders.

"No," he said, sitting cross-legged on the pallet. "But you do not complain. I think you will make an excellent wife in the river kingdom. And now, it is my turn."

He got to his feet and took a long drink from the bottle of Holy Water.

"Stale. Maria, come scrub my back. Let that be your first official task as Maria Masferrer. *Dios,* I like the sound of that. My arm hurts and I cannot reach it."

She took the damp towel from him, and began scrubbing his back. When she finished, she put her arms around him, savoring the warmth of his bare skin on her body. She marveled at her own effrontery, then closed her eyes, thinking how short would be their time together. She began to cry, deep, gulping sobs. Diego turned quickly and pulled her against his chest.

"No, Maria! Don't even think about it. We have each other. No matter what happens we have tonight."

He picked her up and carried her to the pallet. As he took the pins out of her hair, it tumbled down, covering her shoulders. He sat back on his heels and looked at her. "Someday when I have the time, I am going to kiss every strand. But I haven't time right now, Maria."

She held out her arms to him and he came to her, pulling her down beside him on the narrow pallet. Even in his hurry he was gentle. He helped her out of her dress, running his hands over her ribs and laughing.

"Are you hungry, Maria?" he asked, his head on her breasts.

"Starving," she replied. "My stomach is rumbling. Cannot you hear it?"

"No, your heart is beating too loud, heart of my heart. But now, Maria chiquita, it is time you were a wife, my wife."

He kissed her, his fingers cradling her head from the hard pallet. There on the dirt floor behind the chapel he took her slowly, carefully and honestly. The fears that she could not get close enough to him were gone now. Maria accepted Diego willingly, joyfully as husband, lover and friend, her own earthly Trinity.

They lay together later, arms and legs entwined, Diego idly running his fingers across her stomach. "Maria, perhaps we are not as decrepit as we thought."

"Apparently not," she murmured, drowsy.

"Oh, love, do not go to sleep on me yet, not yet. I realize that what I have done is highly irregular. If things had been different, I would have come to your hacienda with a whole chest of beautiful clothing and a wedding dress." He paused and lifted her brown serge dress with one bare toe as she giggled. "And after the wedding you would have paraded around in the different dresses for the wedding guests. I could have puffed up my consequence at your display of my wealth."

She kissed him and his hands were gentle on her body. "Oh, Diego," she said, "how you run on." She twined her fingers in the hair on his chest and pulled it.

"Ay! I am awake!"

"Well then, tell me, husband. . . ." She paused. The word sounded so alien and yet so natural on her lips. "Husband, what of your meeting with the governor in the chapel? You never would say, and now I insist."

"The veriest shrew you are, Maria Masferrer."

Maria's hands slid to his waist and she rested her head on his chest. The sound of his heartbeat, slower now, was making her eyes close. "Tell me, husband."

"I like the way that sounds, wife. And am I a good husband?"

She kissed his chest. "You do not feed me, I have no clothes, but I cannot recall a time when I have been more content. But tell me, husband, what I ask."

He rubbed her arms and yawned. "His fearless Excellency would have us venture forth tomorrow for one last sortie. Those are his words. You know I do not talk like that. And so we shall."

He wrapped his arms around her bare shoulders. "We cannot stay here. The *acequia* is cut and food is running out. We will starve to death, one by one, until there is no one to resist. But Otermin seems to think that if we give them one final grand show, they will allow us to march out." His voice grew harsh as he continued. "And I'll be damned if I will stand by and watch you and my sisters starve to death!"

"Let me ask again," said Maria, inching closer to the warmth of her husband. "Do you mean that you are going to march out of here tomorrow and attack?"

"Yes. Mad, isn't it? I vow we all thought so, sitting there in the chapel, listening to our wise leader. But no one came up with anything better, so there you are."

She leaned her head on his arm and he kissed her. "Maria, Maria, skinny, beautiful Maria with the black eye," he said.

"At least I do not have any teeth gone."

"It is only one. I'll never miss it." He pulled her closer. "As I see it, wife, we have two choices at the moment. We can either go to sleep or make love."

"That's no choice," Maria replied, her fingers smoothing the tangle she had made of her husband's hair.

"Bravo, wife," he murmured, his mouth finding hers again.

Toward dawn Maria slept, an uneasy slumber filled with dreams. She and Diego's sisters were running slowly across the plaza, stumbling over the bodies of the Gutierrez family, while Cristobal, swollen to enormous size, chased them. With nightmare snail's crawl she reached the palace gates and banged on them until her knuckles bled, but the governor would only smile and wave. She banged harder.

Maria sat up, sweating and shivering at the same time. The room was still dark and cold. Diego was asleep, his hands relaxed. Still the banging continued. She shook Diego awake.

He woke up quickly, groping for his clothes. "It must be Father Farfán, Maria. Pull on your dress."

She slipped into her clothing as her husband pulled on his

breeches and shirt. He hurried to the door and leaned against it. "Father?" he asked in a soft voice.

The key turned in the lock, and the priest came in. "It is time, my children. The men are in the chapel for Mass. Father Asturiano is celebrating it this time, and I am hearing confession. It is your turn now, Diego. Maria, say goodbye and go back to Senora Castellano."

"No," she said.

"You cannot come with me, Maria," Diego said gently, "not this time." He enveloped her in a strong embrace, then pointed her toward the door. "I will see you and my sisters before I go."

She left the room without a backward glance. The passageway was still shrouded in gloom, so she stepped carefully, then opened the door to the chapel.

She stood in the doorway and counted the soldiers and landowners. Seventy-eight men. Seventy-eight against all those Indians. She stood rooted to the spot, finally beyond tears.

Some of the men slept, leaning against each other, while others sat staring into the distance, looking at the foreign territory that she and her loved ones had inhabited and would always carry with them. A few talked quietly among themselves, fathers and sons trying to say whatever it was fathers and sons would say at a moment like that. Their dirty, smoke-painted faces were serious, but she could see no fear, only a certain calmness that held more courage than brave words. They were desperate men, cornered men, men who would fight.

Diego came down the passageway behind her. He put his arm around her waist and walked her to the door of the chapel. She let him pull her along, her eyes going back to the men on the benches, then to her husband's face. He looked as they did, and she was glad.

He paused at the chapel door. Maria hugged him and made the sign of the cross on his forehead. "Go with God, my husband," she whispered.

"And you," he answered.

She patted his good arm and left the church swiftly, almost running. The courtyard was silent in the early dawn, the children exhausted by the terrors of the night. Smoke hung heavy and choking over the ground. Here and there younger children still slept, but the women were awake, staring without seeing.

She looked at the still mask of tragedy on each face, the calm acceptance of what the day would bring, and knew without consulting a mirror that she wore the same expression. Their sorrows were hers, finally. She had as much to lose as they. She watched the women of the upper colony and knew that she belonged in this hard place. The river kingdom in its death struggle had finally taken hold of her.

She walked across the silent, stinking plaza and sat down next to Senora Castellano. The woman pulled Maria close. "He is too old, my Reynaldo," said the woman, stroking Maria's hair. "And my sons too young."

Maria was silent, thinking of Diego and his love. They had their night. Now it was morning.

The men came out of the chapel. Governor Otermin stood at their head, a slender figure in his rags and dented helmet. Diego came toward her. He carried a sword, turning it over and over, testing the weight and heft of it.

Maria walked with him to the fortress gates. Other women joined their men. They were by nature a restrained and reticent people, unused to showing affection in public, but everywhere there were kisses and embraces, final words, last hurried instructions, as the colonists tried to express in a few seconds what they had waited a lifetime to say.

"Take care of my sisters," Diego said, then looked at the ground. "And if it should come to that, do not let yourselves be captured. If you should survive and I should not. . . ." He stopped, his voice full of unshed tears. *"Dios, querida, this is a cruel thing!"*

It was the closest he had come to a protest in all the days of their trial. He touched her cheek. "Then we will meet in Heaven, for we are in Purgatory now."

She hugged him to her, then forced herself to walk away.

"And I love you," he called after her. It was something no Spanish man ever said lightly, or even out loud. She turned and kissed her hand to him, amazed at her brazenness. They gazed at each other another moment, and then he was gone in the crowd around the gate.

Otermin stationed a guard at every third rifleport, then gave the signal for the gate to be opened. With a shout of "For God and Spain!" that roared from every throat, the remaining defenders rushed into the sleeping plaza, swords drawn, lances ready.

The noise of swiftly joined battle was deafening. The women in the fortress shrieked and ran back to their screaming children. Maria picked up her skirts and climbed the ladder to one of the vacant rifleports. She could see nothing but smoke from the arquebuses. At the next rifleport the guard fired, paused to reload, then fired again into the crowd of swirling Indian and New Mexican bodies. Maria reached for his arquebus. "If you can find another one," she shouted over the noise of the battle, "I can reload this one while you fire the other."

Without a word, he handed her the heavy firing piece and raised another one to the tripod. Awkwardly at first, she swabbed the barrel, rammed down another charge and ball, and handed the weapon back. The soldier, an elderly man, paused long enough to grin at her, his white teeth a contrast to his black face.

She stood at the rifleport all day. The August day was hot, but such a pall of smoke hung over Santa Fe that she could look directly at the dull copper ball that was the sun. The fighting spread through the *villa* as the remaining houses burned. Men returned to the gates bearing their wounded to be tended by women and priests. As soon as their wounds were bound, the men who could still walk hurried back to the fight.

Maria saw Diego once and called to him. He waved and blew her a kiss, then was gone again.

"Your husband?" It was the only thing the rifleman had said all day.

She nodded and took the hot gun he handed her, reloading it quickly and expertly, then giving it back. The muzzle was hot and her hands burned at the touch, but she did not stop. Her whole body ached, but she was bound up with Diego and his venture in the plaza. She leaned against the fortress wall and doggedly reloaded arquebuses. Other women joined her at other rifleports, and they all worked silently, swiftly, their faces filthy, their clothing sooty and burned in spots from the fire of the weapons.

In the middle of the afternoon, someone in the noisy courtyard gave a great shout. Maria whirled around quickly, fearful of Indians in their midst. Through the smoke and the haze, she saw water flowing in the *acequia* again. It was muddy and sluggish at first, but it was water. Soon young children came to the gun holes with drinks for everyone. Maria didn't wait for the sediment to sink to the bottom of the cup. She drank her portion in two swallows, spitting some of the water on her burning hands.

In late afternoon, Otermin's brave venture was over. One moment there was the noise of battle, then silence.

The quiet hummed in Maria's ears. The rifleman motioned for her to stop reloading. She rested the arquebus against the ledge and moved to the soldier for a glimpse out of his portal. She sucked in her breath at the sight, then turned away to lean against the wall, her eyes wide and staring.

The plaza was filled with bodies, running with blood. Maria sat down in a heap by the rifleport and put her head between her knees, clenching her fists and holding them tight against her body to keep her hands from shaking. I could walk from one side of the plaza to the other and never touch ground, she thought.

Her empty stomach churned and she put her hand to her mouth. The rifleman slumped down next to her and took her hand. They sat together, companions in misery, until the gates swung open.

Slowly, one by one, the soldiers and rancheros returned from their day's work. Maria let go of the rifleman's hand and crawled to the edge of the platform, too tired to stand. From her vantage point, she watched the men return.

Governor Otermin was carried in by two men. He was still alive, but he bled from several wounds. She didn't see a man coming through the gates who was not wounded. They were silent and grim as they had been in the chapel that morning. Most of the men barely cleared the gates before they collapsed against each other, their exhaustion complete.

Maria climbed down the ladder, her legs unsteady. The smell of blood and death in the plaza was overpowering, and she blinked back the tears she had been too busy to shed all day. Senora Castellano ran past to her husband, who sprawled on the ground, leaning against one of his young sons. Both were wounded, but they looked up when she put her arms around them, saying their names over and over in her own litany of devotion.

Maria rested by the wall close to the gate, watching the men straggle in. She looked for Diego, but could not find him among the soldiers limping in, dragging their weapons behind them. Some of the men dangled scalps from their belts, and one soldier carried an Indian's head, his fingers clenched in the long black hair. Maria shuddered and turned her face away as he passed, leaving a trail of dark blood.

"Where is Diego?" It was Catarina, tugging Luz after her.

Numbly, Maria walked back to their corner of the portal with her sisters. She accepted the bowl of water and scrap of towel from them and wiped the gunsmoke off her face and neck.

"Your hair is black like mine, Maria," said Luz, wrinkling her nose, "and you smell funny."

"It is just the gunpowder, chiquita," she said, digging the soot out of her ears.

Luz watched her, then put her hand to Maria's cheek. "Can we find Diego?" she asked.

"I will go look. You two stay here with the Castellanos and I . . . I will bring him back."

"But if he does not come?" Luz asked anxiously, searching Maria's face for reassurance.

"I will find him, Luz," said Maria. She hesitated and looked down at the familiar face turned up to hers. "But if . . . if I cannot find him, Luz, you have me. I will never leave you and Catarina."

"I know that," said Luz.

She kissed both girls and walked slowly toward the gate. More men had come in and were being led away by wives and children. Father Farfán rose from a wounded man he was tending and put his hand on her shoulder.

"He is not here?" the priest asked.

She shook her head. "I cannot see him. Oh, Father, do you think . . ."

"No," he interrupted firmly, "I do not. He will come."

She stood by the gate and looked out over the hazy plaza, thinking of her long watch along the Taos road that endless day before the massacre. The wait was long then, but nothing compared to this wait, this final wait.

Maria saw her husband just as the sun was going down. He and two other Spaniards were walking slowly, painfully, across the plaza, supporting each other. With a little cry of delight, she ran toward him, raising her skirt to keep the blood off the hem.

She stood before him in silence. He said nothing, but watched her, taking her into himself with his eyes as if she were water to drink, food to eat, a pillow to rest on. She touched his face and then his arm. He was not a dream. He had come back to her alive.

"Here, Maria, put your arm around this man."

She did as he said, hooking the fingers of her other hand possessively in Diego's belt.

"Here, here, woman!" he said, "I am not going anywhere!"

She could not trust herself to speak, or even to look at him. The four of them crossed the plaza and entered the governor's courtyard as the sun went down and night settled on the ruined *villa*.

The wounded men were quickly led away by their families. Diego took Maria in his arms and they stood close together by the gates. No words passed between them. She hugged her husband to her, knowing that there was nothing more in the world that she would ever need or want. It was enough to be with him.

After several long minutes of silence, she felt a lump against her back. Diego was carrying something that she had not noticed before, and it was digging into her. She tried to pull away from his embrace. "What is that?" she asked.

He didn't let go of her. Wincing, he brought his arm around in front of her. "Look what I have for you, my heart."

She took the small object from him and turned it over in her hands while she stood in the circle of his arms. It was her San Francisco. She stared at it, unbelieving.

The arms were both missing and someone had made a hole through the body and strung the figure on a rawhide thong. The image was still covered with pink gypsum, a memorial to the struggle of the brothers in the saintmaker's workshop. She ran her finger down the fold of San Francisco's robe, remembering again that wonderful afternoon when she had found the saint in the wood.

317

"Diego," she whispered, still unbelieving, "Diego mio, you didn't go back there!"

"No, no. Many of the Pueblos were wearing figures like this, or bits and pieces from the churches—vestments, sashes. I don't know why. For luck? For vengeance? I recognized our San Francisco, but I had to track that Indian almost to the hills to get it back for you."

He chuckled and drew her close again, the saint between them. "He didn't want to die anymore than I did, so we fought rather cautiously. Took a while."

"I can always clean it off and put on new arms," she said, closing her eyes as he kissed her ears, her neck.

"No," he said when he could speak. "Don't. Leave it the way it is. We will remember."

She nodded slowly. "And I will remember what Emiliano the saintmaker taught me."

"It is well. I believe that is what he intended."

With a grimace that stabbed at Maria's heart, Diego put his arm around her and started walking with her toward the Castellano's little corner. "Do you still have that needle and thread?" he asked suddenly.

Her eyes flew in alarm to his shoulder.

"No, not that. My pants are ripped. And it's my only pair." She patted his stomach and laughed.

"Ay, I am a wealthy man, Maria," he said. "I have a wife, a mother for my children, and my own saintmaker. But I do wish you could keep from ruining all the dresses I give you. Did you stay at that rifleport all day?"

"Of course," she said.

"'Of course,'" he echoed. "How could I have thought otherwise? I fear you will lead me in a merry dance, Senora Masferrer!"

After a quick meal of jerky and hardtack and a long, long drink from the *acequia,* Diego rested with his head in Maria's lap. His eyes were closed, but he was not asleep.

"Take a good look around, Maria," he said.

"What do you mean?" Maria asked, caressing her husband's face.

"After we rest for a couple of days, we are leaving. Walking south to try to find the rest of the colony at Ysleta, around the lower river."

"And then?"

"We will continue south. Perhaps to El Paso del Norte, the crossing."

"That is a long walk, Diego mio."

"You are equal to it, Maria La Formidable. Maria La Afortunada. Maria, Daughter of Fortune."

She kissed him. "And when we get to the crossing, what then?"

"We will start over again there. And perhaps when we are strong enough we will return to take this place back. If we want it."

"And do we?"

He smiled. "That may depend on what we have learned."

She looked toward the north where the Indian campfires still burned as brightly as ever. "Will they let us go?"

"Yes. After today, yes."

He closed his eyes and Maria leaned against the wall, cradling his head in her arms. "And Maria, one thing more," he said, long after she thought he was asleep.

"Qué es esto, my heart?" she asked.

He opened his eyes and looked at her shrewdly, a calculating expression on his face. "What if I had not come back?"

She considered his question and what the answer meant to him, to her. "I would have managed here, even without you," she said simply, pausing to let that sink in. "I probably would have remarried and raised your sisters."

"But you would have stayed with the colony," he persisted.

"Oh, yes. I belong here. And it has nothing to do with you."

Her words sounded hard, but he knew her as well as she knew herself now, and she was not surprised at his smile. It had nothing to do with him, although he was the dearest part of her life. It had to do with her only, and she could tell that he was glad.

He stirred and sat up, resting on his elbow. He kissed her, then rested his head in her lap again, content.

She was silent then, too, looking up at the Indian campfires. The smell of smoke and death would be in her nostrils for days, weeks to come. She knew she would wake up many nights, shivering with nightmares, but she knew that Diego would be lying beside her.

She looked down at him. His eyes closed even as she watched, and his neck and shoulders relaxed against her thighs. He sighed and slept.

Maria touched her finger to her lips and then to his cheek. He stirred but did not waken. She settled back against the wall, prepared to spend the night holding him in her arms.

It didn't matter to her that the cloth had been of Diego's making. She had cut the cloak, and it fit.

Epilogue

They left four days later, Diego and Maria Masferrer, Luz and Catarina, walking south to El Paso with the other defeated survivors of the vanquished colony of New Mexico. There were many deaths on the long, hot, and hungry journey to the crossing of the river more than two hundred miles away. They arrived at the northern crossing of the Rio Bravo and established the village of San Lorenzo, called in painful Spanish remembrance after the martyred saint on whose nameday the uprising had begun.

Not until thirteen years later, in 1693, were the colonists able to regain their lands in New Mexico. A man of thirty-two, Diego Masferrer and his oldest son Emiliano returned with the army of the conquering governor, Don Diego de Vargas.

Six months later, Maria followed with a month-old boy and four other sons and daughters. She left behind Luz and Catarina, Luz in a convent in Sonora and Catarina busy with husband and children of her own. Maria took with her the remembered skills of Emiliano the saintmaker.

She also took her San Francisco—a saint still armless and covered with fading gypsum, a reminder of other, darker days.

Maria Masferrer found many more saints in the woods by Tesuque and Las Invernadas. The holy ones had waited patiently in the wood for thirteen years. The saintmaker knew them when she saw them, and they, her.

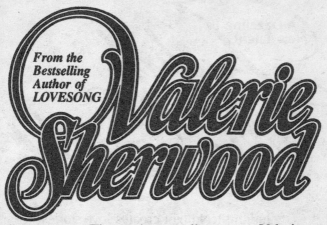

From the Bestselling Author of LOVESONG

Valerie Sherwood

The excitement lives on as Valerie Sherwood brings you a breathless love story in her new tantalizing trilogy. Sherwood first captured the hearts of millions with LOVESONG a sweeping tale of love and betrayal.

And the saga continues in WINDSONG as you are swept into exotic locations full of intrigue, danger, treachery and reckless desire.

_____ **LOVESONG** 49837/$3.95
_____ **WINDSONG** 49838/$3.95

COMING IN SEPTEMBER
NIGHTSONG